THE VIKING ON STAMFORD BRIDGE

A Heroic Saga

Brent Jordan

Satsu Press

"Cattle die, kindred die, every man is mortal, but the good name never dies of one who has done well."

--Havamal

"But there was one of the Norwegians who withstood the English folk, so that they could not pass over the bridge, nor complete the victory."

--Anglo-Saxon Chronicle, 1066 CE.

Trondheim Norway, Seventh day of Gormanudur, 1047 CE

"Fight hard. Die well. Leave a name worthy of song. This is the way to Valhöll, boy."

Gunnar Skullcrusher, grizzled veteran of more than two score wars and raids, sits before his longhouse on an oak log before a guttering fire. His magnificent battle-axe Skullseeker lies at rest across his lap.

Opposite the fire from the legendary berserker sits the boy, a smaller hand-axe in his lap in imitation of his grandfather. The boy, exceedingly large of frame and stoic of nature for his nine years, listens attentively to the old warrior's wisdom.

"The Valkyrie can not be fooled. They always know if you have done your best. They know where your heart lies. If you try to cheat the Valkyrie, they will see. They will pass over you when you die and leave you to be collected by Hel for her army of rabble."

The boy is rapt. Vivid dreams of heroes and the damned race through his imagination.

"Not every hero will win a seat in Valhöll. There are five hundred forty doors through which eight hundred warriors each shall pass. To earn your place you must live a worthy life and attain a notable death. A life and death which pleases the Aesir and satisfies the Norns. Yet you must resist that death with all your will and strength and skill. If you think to get to the afterlife early, allow your enemy to kill you without fighting your best, you will surely be doomed." Gunnar gazes into the fire for a long moment, lost in thought. The boy waits in silence for his grandfather to continue. Finally Gunnar's eyes clear and he shakes himself from his revery. "Now, sharpen your axe. And sharpen your skills while I am away, for this, I pray, shall be the war that shall send me to Valhöll."

The aged warrior runs a hone along the gleaming edge of Skullseeker. The boy does the same with his hand-axe. The waning fire shoots embers into the predawn sky.

When it is light enough to see, Gunnar stands from the fire to stretch his back. He goes to the paddock where his stallion, Grani, stomps and snorts in anticipation. Gunnar bridles and saddles the steed, then disappears into the longhouse.

The boy waits at the fire as the sun, hidden behind the dense morning brume, begins to define structures and trees from shadows: A longhouse of the old style stands in the clearing surrounded by a forest of ash, elm and oak. Birchwoods in vast stands, pale and ghostly, cover the jutting hills to the east. A shed and paddock for the horse, fenced yard for the goats where geese and chickens roam free, and a low sod outbuilding for the thrall. It is a fine farmstead built on the profits of raids and wars.

Dressed in full battle gear, Gunnar strides from the longhouse. His boar crested helm gleams in what little light the shrouded sun provides. A long iron-linked shirt falls to mid thigh. Skullseeker is carried in its frog beneath the colorful round shield strapped across the magnificent warrior's broad back. Finely woven woolen trousers are bound at the top of well worn, boar-hide boots.

Gunnar strides past the boy, takes Grani from his paddock, mounts the steed. He looks over the farmstead, and the boy, as if for the final time. Without another word, the legendary hero urges Grani away into the morning mists.

The boy stands, kicks snow and dirt onto the fire, and goes about his morning chores of feeding the stock and cleaning the paddocks.

* * *

Gunnar Skullcrusher rides Grani toward the docks on the fjord of Trondheim where more than thirty dragon prowed longships, sails stowed, await their turn to receive their crews. A bevy of men work on the docks loading ships with provisions for war. Hundreds of Norwegian warriors, toting arms and armor, mount the crafts as they are ushered to and away from their moorings. The warriors take their positions on rowing benches to propel the sleek ships to sea.

Gunnar rides to the edge of the docks, dismounts, hands Grani off to a waiting stable boy. He caresses the horse's thick neck, whispers in his ear, "No breeding the mares until my return." He speaks to the stableboy, "Care for him as if your life depends on it." Gunnar does not release Grani until the stable boy nervously nods his understanding.

The renowned berserker strides onto the docks. Warriors follow him with open stares. Even among the hardened Norsemen, this storied hero is revered.

Gunnar steps aboard a dreki. Warriors respectfully move to make room. They mutter greetings, and are honored when his eyes meet theirs. He makes his way forward. A nobleman at the prow relinquishes the position with a reverent bow of his head.

Gunnar Skullcrusher takes his rightful place beneath the carved dragon figurehead, looks upon the crew. "Are we to sail, or are we to wait for the Danes to die of old age?"

Warriors laugh, their spirits lifted by the presence of the hero. The longship is cast-off from the dock, rowed into the fjord toward the open ocean.

Gunnar doffs his helmet and mail shirt, stands at the prow like a second figurehead.

On the open sea, thirty and three longships bearing the army of King Magnus of Norway, sail southward along the coast. Their destination: Danmörk and war.

* * *

Pregnant clouds roll heavily across a darkened sky over an expansive plain which will soon be bathed in the blood of heroes.

A vast army of Danes forms up to the east. Their colorfully painted shields and fluttering war-banners stand out in bold contrast to their earthy woolen trousers and dull iron-linked shirts. Long-axes, spears and naked swords glint in what little sun finds its way through the leadened sky. The defenders of their homeland mill in eager anticipation of the battle to come.

On the west side of the plain, the army of King Magnus of Norway boldly face the Danes. Warriors sound upon their shields the din of war: strike swords and battle-axes against iron bosses to alert the gods of their coming.

Two great Norse armies to do battle. For what reason -- honor, treasure, sport... -- we may never know.

At the van of the Norwegian army, even before King Magnus himself, stands Gunnar Skullcrusher. The massive wild-eyed berserker grips his magnificent battle-axe Skull-seeker in one gnarled fist. The heroic figure brazenly faces the enemy, raises his voice to the heavens in prayer, "Odin! Take me first. I have fought countless battles in your name. Countless duels to honor you. I have no match on this field nor any other."

The Norwegians who amass behind are worked into a frenzy by the speech. They howl at the top of their voice, gnaw on shield rims and kick up the sod like wild beasts.

Gunnar shouts above the tumult, "Allfather, welcome me to Valhöll and I will fight at your side when the wolf breaks its fetters at Ragnarök."

Across the field, battle horns are sounded. The Dane army explodes into a sprint toward the invading Norwegians, their vicious battle cries rise above the pounding of boots upon the quaking earth.

Gunnar finishes his prayer even as the enemy descends upon him, "Send your wolves and your ravens, for the carrion will soon be plenty. And send your Valkyrie to carry me to your great hall."

The Danes are nearly upon the invaders.

Norwegian warriors strain to be at their enemy like rabid dogs on the leash.

Gunnar looks to Forni, the sage warrior/poet who stands at his side in his dark cloak and broad-brimmed hat, his magnificent rune-covered spear in hand. Gunnar nods.

Forni raises his spear overhead, turns to the army of King Magnus. "Odin! Tyr! Thor!" bellows Forni.

The Norwegians respond as one, "Fram, fram, Odinn-men, Tyrmenn, Thormenn!"

Forni turns to face the charging Dane army, picks his target, hurls his spear far over their heads. A standard bearer carrying the cross of the Christ in the rear ranks is speared and killed.

Gunnar follows Forni's spear into the fray, rushing headlong into the midst of the enemy, Skullseeker thirsting for blood.

The Norwegians follow their champion into battle without reserve.

And a battle it is! The two blood-mad armies clash in a resounding wave which sounds to the ends of the Nine Realms. Axes, swords, spears: hack, cleave, impale. Armor and flesh are rent and ruined. Blood and viscera, spilled to soak the earth to mud. Cries of elation! Cries of anguish!

Gunnar wields Skullseeker in the midst of it all, inflicting terrible damage upon the Danes. Blood-soaked, gore drenched, the great berserker soon stands amidst a host of enemy bodies which grows ever larger as brave warriors rush upon him, only to be laid asunder by his terrible weapon.

The battle wears on. Survivors of the initial clash of arms band together in loose knots to fight like numbers of the enemy.

Gunnar strides the battlefield alone. He searches out individuals and small groups of foes to challenge. "Fight me,"

Gunnar bellows across the lists.

A pair of Danes who have already bloodied their swords on more than a few invading Norwegians, accept Gunnar's challenge, advance.

Gunnar meets them with a vicious snarl and lightning quick blows of Skullseeker. The Danes block, parry, attack... yet are quickly overwhelmed. They fall to the skills and ferocity of the berserker.

Gunnar catches his breath, scans the field, finds the next grouping of the enemy, strides their direction. "Fight me!"

The set upon Danes look to the gore covered slayer of their countrymen, scatter to be away from him.

Gunnar curses, searches for yet another opponent when a spear careens off his helmet, ripping the finely crafted piece of armor from his head. He spins on the Dane spearman who takes up another of his three spears, throws. Gunnar snatches up a round shield from the battlefield, deflects the spear, charges the spearman. The spearman thrusts his final spear as the berserker closes with him. Gunnar allows the spear to slip past his belly as he raises the shield, punches the edge into the spearman's face, crushing his foeman's skull with a single strike.

On a small rise a short distance away, a massive Dane axeman swings his longaxe in huge looping strikes. The axe head is as broad and heavy as any two such weapons, the haft, nearly as long as a man is tall. Dead and dying Norwegians lie scattered about the magnificent warrior.

Gunnar heads his direction. The axeman sees his approach, awaits. Gunnar stops just outside the considerable reach of his longaxe. "Tell me your name so I might search for you in Valhöll," calls Gunnar.

The axeman glares upon his enemy with disdain. "I am Christian. I kill heathens in the name of the Almighty Lord Jesus Christ."

"I am Gunnar Skullcrusher, man of the Aesir, and I kill Christians for pleasure," is Gunnar's retort.

The two warriors clash. The axeman swings his weapon in a mighty loop, gaining fearsome momentum. Gunnar raises his shield. With a resounding crash, the shield is splintered with the impact. Gunnar discards the broken shield, attacks with Skullseeker in both hands. The axeman is well practiced and lightning quick reversing the path of his weapon. Gunnar is nearly decapitated, slips on a dead body, falls to his back. The Dane is on him in a flash! The blade of the long axe takes a piece of Gunnar's ear along with a swath of his scalp and hair as it skims past his head. But before the axeman can recover for another strike, Gunnar hooks the haft of the long axe with Skullseeker's beard. The axe heads are intertwined together. Christian and heathen engage in a tug-of-war with battle-axes. The Dane heaves with all his might to pull his axe free. At the same instant, Gunnar steps forward with the pull, draws his long knife, drives it through the Christian Dane's heart. The mighty axeman drops to his knees, dead, even before his mind can come to terms with the fact.

"Jesus... a waste of your magnificent valor," grumbles Gunnar, even as a half-dozen enemy with shields and axes raised, charge....

Gunnar battles -- kills in numbers even he would be hard pressed to recall -- until what is left of the day shows a battle-field without a single man left standing to face him.

Warriors of Norway and Danmörk litter the field. Here and there a wounded man groans in his death throes, crawls to desperately grasp his weapon to him before crossing to the next life. A vast murder of crows darken the sky, circle down to feast on the dead.

On the highest point of the field, perched on a stony out-cropping, Gunnar Skullcrusher sits with Skullseeker across his knees, the bloodied warrior and weapon finally at rest. The aged veteran is utterly exhausted, covered head to toe in the gore of battle, his hair and beard matted with blood and vis-cera. Gunnar looks to the sky, cries, "Odin!" then drops his chin to his chest, the venerable warrior too weary to even curse the gods.

The croaking of a pair of ravens, strangely distinct over the clamor of crows, causes Gunnar to raise his eyes to the battlefield. He blinks, wipes blood away to clear his vision, looks again.

Far across the field bathed in evening mist, Forni strides using his spear as a walking stave. Here and again he touches the rune-etched blade of his spear to a dead warrior. The warrior rises... is whisked away into the leadened sky by a flash of gold: A winged woman, it appears to Gunnar. But overwhelming fatigue following battle-madness has taken him. His eyes, stinging with blood, could surely deceive. Gunnar shudders in awed wonder. Then his head drops to his chest once again in grief. He barely has the strength to weep, "Odin...."

In the next breath, Forni is by his side. The Ancient One sits shoulder to shoulder with Gunnar, sharing the outcropping which overlooks the field of the dead.

Gunnar is aware of his presence, but does not raise his eyes when he asks, "Why do you forsake me? Have I not done enough? Have I not proven myself? Why do you not choose me?"

Forni's voice is as soothing to Gunnar as the counsel of a loving father, "It is said each man has his equal in battle. If he fights long enough, he will meet him."

Gunnar scoffs. Tears streak the dried blood on his cheeks. "I have searched every land for that man. I have fought as many battles as I have years in this world. Everyone I have ever known and loved now resides in the halls of Asgard. They feast and they sing..." Gunnar chokes back his tears.

"It is you they feast for. You they sing of," assures Forni.

Gunnar's frustration boils in him. "What must I do? Must I be old and bent, pissing my bed at night before you will take me? Already my bones creak and my vision blurs. My hands are bent and broken and can barely grip Skullseeker. I will be of no use to you before I am killed."

"In Asgard you are restored to your finest self, the very

best of your days. There is no pain, no grief. All your friends and your loves will greet you."

"Then take me now... Please," beseeches Gunnar.

"No," states Forni without malice.

Gunnar's body is racked with sobs of frustration.

Forni lays a hand on his shoulder. "I require one more task of you. You must be the one to walk from this battlefield so you will inspire generations of warriors to come. Already these days I collect fewer and fewer worthy of Valhöll. I fear in the future, it will be fewer yet."

Gunnar gathers himself, takes a breath, raises his chin. Charged with such a great duty, what choice has he? He looks off across the plain to hide his tears.

"Go to your home, see to the boy, set him on the path, and I shall prepare a great feast in your honor," says Forni as he stands to look down upon the grieving veteran. "Then, you can come to me."

Astonished by the offer, Gunnar looks up to Forni, but the Ancient One is gone.

The illustrious hero gathers himself, takes up his helmet, stands tall and commanding. He looks across the expanse of the dead, then turns his look to the clouded sky where a pair of ravens circle as if awaiting his decision. The great warrior issues a sigh... a smile of relief.

Gunnar Skullcrusher strides alone from the battlefield.

* * *

Night has fallen before Gunnar can see the thin trail of gray smoke rising from the smoke hole of his longhouse. His farmstead remains as he left it, the boy a conscientious and capable hand. He rides Grani to the stable, dismounts, removes the saddle and bridle, and allows the horse to roam the fenced yard.

He takes the tack into a small outbuilding, lights a candle. Within are farm tools, a hand cart, game sled, a coil of rope. Gunnar leaves the horse tack, takes the rope and returns to the yard.

He hauls a large splitting stump beneath the branches of the massive ash tree which dominates the farmstead, goes about building a small fire. The fire burns, shedding dancing light.

Gunnar stands on his toes on the splitting stump, loops the rope over a sturdy branch. At the end of the rope is a noose.

He sits on the stump, holds Skullseeker in his lap, runs a hone over the blade. The slow, steady rasping of stone on steel is peaceful, hypnotic.

The dim glow of the rising sun behind the morning overcast finds Gunnar still seated on the stump, polishing Skullseeker with an oiled cloth. He has fitted a new haft to the head in the night. The clean, fresh hardwood glows pale in the pre-dawn. New leather wrappings wound tight, shimmer with oil.

He looks up from his work to the east where the sky lightens with the coming dawn, as if judging the very worth of the day. Satisfied, he rises, heads to the longhouse.

"Outside," Gunnar commands as he enters to stand in the threshold of the home.

The boy wakes with a start, fumbles for the handaxe he sleeps with and is never without.

Gunnar turns and disappears from the longhouse as the boy scrambles from his bed to follow.

The storied warrior, dressed in full armor, carrying Skullseeker, leads the boy to the huge ash. He indicates a spot on the ground by the fire, facing the tree. "Sit."

The boy sits, back straight, legs folded before him, his axe across his lap.

A pair of ravens croak softly, perched high in the branches of the tree. The boy looks up to the carrion seekers, barely distinguishable in the dim glow of dawn.

Gunnar follows his eyes to the ravens, then returns them

to the boy to offer his final bit of advice, "Fight hard. Die well. Win your place in Odin's hall." The grizzled veteran of a lifetime of warring concentrates to ensure himself he is not leaving some measure of life advice unsaid. Satisfied he is not, he steps up on the splitting stump, places the noose around his thick neck. Gunnar Skullcrusher grips his treasured Skull-seeker for the final time.

The ravens stir, flutter, croak in their excitement.

Gunnar looks to Grani roaming the yard. He speaks to the boy, "Send the horse after me." He considers Skullseeker. "You can keep the axe."

The great warrior stands tall and formal, balanced on the stump. Clears his throat. Speaks in a loud, clear voice to the heavens, "Allfather, Odin, you have made no man my equal. None worthy to send me to your great hall. So I shall do it myself." He lowers his gaze to look into the eyes of the boy who sits facing him. "Cattle die, kindred die, every man is mortal. But I know one thing that never dies; the glory of the great dead." And with that, the legendary berserker Gunnar Skullcrusher kicks the stump from beneath his feet and is yanked to a halt inches above the ground as the hanging rope cuts deeply into his corded neck.

The ravens burst into flight on powerful wings, croaking announcement to the Aesir: The greatest of heroes is on his way to Valhöll.

※ ※ ※

It is nearing dusk of the third day following his grandfather's death before the boy can lay the body to rest. Days spent digging the grave in the stony soil of the highest peak on his grandfather's land. Transporting the body. Even with the use of the game sled, the task of hauling the heavy corpse to this spot proved nearly too much for the lad. Now the boy tugs the old man by his chainmail shirt, inch by inch, until he lies in repose in the shallow grave. The warrior's most valued possessions are placed in the grave with him: arm rings of silver and gold, a magnificent broadsword, shield, his ornate boar crested helm. What few coins the lad could find that had not been spent by the old man on mead and the company of women, go into the grave also. Exhausted, near failing, the boy piles stones upon his grandfather's body.

The sun is set many hours before the grave is properly covered. The boy trudges in the dark back to the longhouse.

There is no split wood for a fire, so the boy spends the cold night huddled beneath furs atop the straw mattress covering the plank bed that was his grandfather's. In the morning he sets out with his grandfather's wood axe to fell trees for firewood.

Though a sturdy lad, far larger than boys his age, the man-sized axe is heavy and unwieldy for the youth. He grips the axe at mid handle, uses short hacking strokes to take tiny bites from the trunk of the chosen tree. Yet after a day of labor, the tree falls. The boy sets about removing branches, portioning out the trunk.

Winter has come. The use of wood for the perpetual fires needed to maintain the warmth of the longhouse nearly outpaces the boy's ability to chop. Icy gales of the direful winter impede the lad's progress, send him staggering back to the longhouse after a long day's woodcutting with little to show for his efforts. Still, fire is life in this land, and the boy longs to live. He cuts wood all day, puts butchered sections of his grandfather's warhorse to the pot by night.

The boy eats well and grows quickly beneath his labors, so by first thaw the lad has grown to the stature of young men many years his senior.

When winter has finally passed and the ice in the fjord has splintered, warriors of Trondheim stir with restless energy and yearn to be off on adventures to distant lands to raid for wealth and glory.

The boy, determined never to go wanting for the

warmth of a fire ever again, busies himself felling trees and splitting wood to build his woodpile.

With his newfound size and strength he is able to wield the splitting axe well now, and is about his business one day when the blacksmith of Trondheim, a skilled artisan by the name of Ake, leads his ox-pulled cart along the road that passes the longhouse.

Ake considers the lad as he stands, sturdy and defiant, glaring back at the blacksmith. "This is the home of Gunnar Skullcrusher," says Ake, "are you his thrall?"

The boy has no reply but to re-grip his splitting axe, ready to fight.

Ake notes the boy's aggressive stance, remains at fair distance. "No, not his thrall. No thrall would be so impudent as to glare at a freeman in that way. His kin?"

The boy remains mute.

"I am Ake, the smith. Your master did not come by the shop this spring. I have come to see what weapons and armor he requires for this season of raids."

"He has all he needs in Valhöll," says the boy.

"The great Gunnar Skullcrusher has finally died? I would not have thought it possible. Who is here with you?"

The boy remains silent.

Ake steps forward. "Perhaps you should come with me, and...." A snarl and the axe brandished by the boy stops the smith. Ake looks around the farmstead. It is well maintained with goats, chickens and geese in the yard.

"At least allow me to cut you some firewood so you do not freeze to death," offers Ake.

"I can cut wood," says the boy.

Ake considers the lad, full of vigor and pride. "You can, can you?" He pulls a small coin from his purse, tosses it to the boy's feet. "Then cut wood for my forge. A cart load. If you do a good job, I will tell others." Ake turns his oxcart around to return to the city of Trondheim. "I will return in three days."

"I will have it ready in two," says the boy.

Ake grins, nods, sets out upon the road.

The boy looks at the coin at his feet, retrieves it, puts it in his purse and goes back to splitting wood.

* * *

Every half cycle of the moon or so, for many years following their first meeting, Ake would travel with his cart to the farmstead for split wood. The boy having grown to a man in that time, fit and strong from his labors, never failed the smith in his needs. Ake, for his part, kept his word and told the townspeople where they might buy split wood of all sort.

The man had become known simply as the woodcutter to the people of Trondheim, having no other name bestowed upon him.

Many of those who lived within the city relied upon him for firewood, as well as planks for longships, houses, tables and all manner of construction. No one could produce the quality or quantity the man could. He had become indispensable to families whose men died in the yearly wars and raids.

In the summer of the man's eighteenth year, Ake came to the farmstead for split wood for his forge, but he did not come alone. Riding on the oxcart were the smith's two daughters, Tora and Sassa, along with Tora's six-year-old son, Svend.

Tora, a renowned beauty whose husband had been killed while raiding, was coveted by every man who laid eyes upon her. Golden hair, features delicate and fair, she was courted by nobles from as far away as Iceland and Sweden.

Yet when the man gazed upon the daughters of the smith, Tora paled beside the resplendent beauty of her younger sister, Sassa. The moment he looked upon the girl of sixteen years, he was struck as if he were in the presence of the most fair of the Vanir: Freyja embodied in the daughter of a blacksmith. Sassa's skin and hair was soot smudged, as was the simple dress and apron she wore. Yet her eyes were the color of a stormy sea, and her bearing that of a goddess.

"Woodcutter," cheers Ake in greeting, "you have been busy. In Trondheim I have seen entire ships built with your split planks, and your woodpile grows large enough to warm the entire city through Fimbulwinter."

The man remains speechless, entranced by Sassa.

With his daughters sitting side by side, Ake makes the assumption the man is taken by Tora, as he fully expected he would be. He brought his widowed daughter to take stock of the man the people of the village spoke of as a giant -- or demigod -- for his incredible size and power of his physique.

And Tora is indeed taken. The man stands a head taller than any she has met, and is far more broad at the shoulder. Even his baggy linen shirt, sweat soaked through by his labors, can not hide the astounding muscularity developed by years of swinging an axe for his trade.

Tora eyes the man openly as Sassa sneaks furtive peeks from beneath soot-stained hair which obscures her face.

Tora's son, Svend, grows restless. His mother lowers him from the cart to run and play.

The day the man's grandfather hung himself, his elkhound bore a litter of pups. The dam was so grieved by her master's passing she killed each of her offspring as they emerged. All but one, a female, which the boy had rescued and nursed with his own hands to a full grown hound.

The she-hound is fine, fleet, and displays profound love for her master. Svend spots the dog where she lies by the splitting stump and trundles after her. The she-hound lopes away without humor from the rambunctious child as Svend relentlessly pursues.

"Take care, Svend, that hound may eat you for supper," calls Tora as she hikes up her skirt to be helped down from the cart by her father.

Sassa is left to climb from the cart herself. Yet before she can make the leap, the man is there, offering a hand.

Sassa knows not what to do. No man has ever taken notice of her while in the presence of her sister.

On her hesitation, the man lifts Sassa from the cart, his hands nearly encircling her waist. He sets her down as gently as the most delicate of treasures.

Sassa's breath is taken. Ake is perplexed. Tora's pride wounded. She gapes at her younger sister as if Sassa is to blame for stealing away the man's attention.

Ake attempts to salvage the situation with an introduction, "This is my daughter Tora. Her husband died in the raids."

The man's eyes travel to Tora -- her beauty, a thing of wonder -- then quickly return to Sassa as if drawn by some magical force.

Ake frowns. "Sassa, help him load the cart."

Sassa is quick to the wood pile to escape the intensity of the man's gaze. She is mystified as to why he studies her so, and with Tora merely an arms reach away. She gathers a bundle of split wood and would load it onto the cart, but the man steps in her path. He takes the split wood from the girl's arms.

"Sassa is stronger than she looks," assures Ake, "she helps in my forge. It is no trouble for her to load the wood."

"Until purchased, the wood belongs to me," says the man.

Ake rolls his eyes at the chivalry, yet is loath to begin an argument with the mountainous youth. He waves Sassa aside, allows the man to load the cart by himself.

The man carries great armloads of wood to the cart, stacks it carefully so the cart will carry a good deal more than was expected.

Svend returns to his mother to cry over the dog's unwillingness to subject itself to the child's version of play.

Yet Sassa finds great pleasure in the attention the she-hound lavishes upon her. Girl and hound frolic through the tall grass of the farmstead as the man loads the cart, his eyes rarely straying from his desire as he works.

Dejected, Tora sits on the cart with Svend, her back straight, her gaze averted from the man until the cart is filled.

Ake pays with a coin, takes the lead rope of the ox. "Sassa," he calls, "stop your play. There is work to be done." Sassa obediently hurries to the cart, but before she can climb on, the man sweeps her from her feet, lifts her to the seat as easily as he had lifted her down.

Sassa blushes. Tora fumes. Ake shakes his head, befuddled, as he leads the ox-cart on the path to Trondheim.

The man remains watching until the cart travels out of sight, then releases a huge shuddering breath. He strides to the longhouse. Leaving the door open for the light, he goes to his sleeping bench, pushes away the furs and straw mattress, pries up a board with his hand axe. Inside the bench is somewhat of a horde of valuables: his grandmother's belongings. He removes the items with care, lays them on the sleeping bench; a comb, mirror, ornate ivory hair pieces. A golden broach bearing the likeness of the goddess Freyja. A gold finger ring, and a splendid fox fur cloak.

Beneath it all is something nearly four-feet long wrapped in oil-cloth. The man leaves that where it lies.

He wraps the finger ring and broach in a piece of soft leather, places them into his purse. Drapes the cloak over a shoulder, takes up his splitting axe, and exits the longhouse.

The man begins down the path in the direction the ox-cart took moments before. His hound lopes along, leading the way.

❋ ❋ ❋

The sprawling city of Trondheim rests on the banks of the vast fjord. Modest homes of the modern style occupy small plots. Shops of craftsmen, artisans and merchants, along with livestock corrals filled with horses and sheep are intermingled with the homes.

It is dusk as the man strides through the empty streets, his hound by his side. Most of the shops close at sundown. Residents have taken to their homes to prepare the evening meal. The man continues until he finds Ake's blacksmith shop with a small house attached. He approaches, gathers himself, raps on the door of the home. "Am I welcome?" he calls, his voice seeming to him extraordinarily loud in the close confines of the city.

Inside the home, Ake, Tora, Sassa and Svend are preparing to eat when the greeting comes. They look to the door.

"Who is there?" calls Ake.

"Woodcutter."

The family looks to one another with varying degrees of surprise. Tora straightens her apron, checks that her hair is in place.

"You are welcome," calls Ake through the door.

The man must duck low to enter through the threshold. His hound follows him in. Everyone stares. He hangs the fox-fur cloak on a peg by the door, leans his axe against the wall.

"Sit. Share our supper with us," says Ake.

Sassa has washed the day's soot from her body and hair. She wears a clean but simple dress of sky blue and an apron of white linen. Her gild-red hair is down and freely flowing but for a pair of braids which keep it from her face. The man can not help himself. He stares at the achingly beautiful girl. Sassa casts her eyes downward, blushes at the open gaze of the man.

Tora quickly goes to a shelf to retrieve another place setting and cup. She sets them at the table, gestures for the man to take a seat. The man sits, rigid and self-conscious, having never been a guest in another's home before now. Tora pours his cup full of mead. She makes sure her hips brush ever so gently against him.

Sassa watches her sister flirt.

Ake raises his cup. "Skol."

They drink. The man nearly finishes his mead in a single quaff. Tora is quick to refill the cup.

Ake shoots a glance to Tora before returning his attention to the man. Already believing he knows the answer, he poses the question, "After all these years you have finally found a reason to visit our home. What brings you?"

"I would have your daughter as my wife," states the man.

Tora is taken, excited by the boldness of it.

Sassa looks to her sister, quivers.

Ake again looks to Tora, nods, content with the answer. "Let us take a meal first, then we shall discuss the prospect."

Tora and Sassa serve the meal. Svend is sat atop of a bag of straw on his bench so he might better reach his bowl to eat. When the women have served, they sit also. It is a stew of elk, freshly baked bread and small green apples. The man eats without reserve, now and again handing down bits of meat to his hound who sits quietly attentive beneath him at the table.

Throughout the meal, Ake eyes Tora. Tora eyes the man. The man gazes at Sassa. Sassa keeps her eyes down, only sneaking glances at the man when she will not be discovered. Svend gobbles his food then goes back to play.

Ake extols the virtues of Tora as they eat, "Calder Torsen was her husband. He owned herds of oxen and gained wealth and fame from raids."

"Father, must we speak of Calder?" says Tora.

Ake gestures with his head to the man. "He has a right to know the sort of man you have born a son to, and the type who seek your hand now." He speaks with pride to their guest, "Nobles, warriors... they have all come to call."

The man eats quietly without interrupting.

Ake cocks his head as if a matter has just occurred to him. "I have known you since you were barely older than Svend. I do not recall a time when you were not at your farmstead cutting wood. Do you not go to war or on the raids?"

The man hands a piece of meat down to his hound, drinks, sits up straight before he answers, "I do not."

Ake, feeling the pleasure of the mead, studies the man

with a half smile. "I have never met a man more built for war. Why do you not go?"

"Father...," Tora interjects, not wanting her prospective husband to find offense.

Ake waves a dismissing hand to his daughter, waits for the answer to his query.

The man looks to his dog. "Who would care for my hound?"

Ake scoffs, as if the man jests. "You deny riches and glory for a dog?"

The man rubs his dog's head, but remains silent.

Sassa's timid words can barely be heard when she says, "She is a fine hound."

The man locks eyes with Sassa. She does not look away.

"What did you say?" Ake asks his daughter.

Sassa holds the man's gaze, speaks louder, "She is a fine hound."

Ake does not understand the capricious mind of his youngest daughter. He shrugs, leans back on his bench, pats his belly. Tora fills cups with mead. The man sits straight and formally.

"Tora is a fine cook, is she not? She keeps a good household and can weave and spin as well as care for livestock," boasts Ake. He calls to Svend who plays at sword fighting in the corner of the room, "Come here, Svend." Svend approaches. Ake picks the child up, places him on his knee for display. "Tora has proven to bear strong, healthy children." Ake tousles the child's hair, sends him to his mother. "She has had many offers of marriage from men of standing. I have known you since you were a lad, so I will entertain your offer, however..."

The man, having heard enough of Tora, interrupts, "I have come for your other daughter."

Sassa's breath is taken, as is Tora's.

"Sassa? I do not understand," says Ake.

Tora's shock causes her to speak without prudence,

"Sassa is already sixteen and has yet to have a single offer of marriage."

"Tora, be still," chides Ake. He shakes his head, no. "I can not offer Sassa to you. I have no son, and Svend is not yet old enough, so Sassa serves me in my forge. Besides, I am afraid when you discover how the villagers speak of her you will hold me to blame."

"She plays at rune casting all day," blurts Tora. "The people say she is a völva. A practitioner of seidr."

"Tora!" Ake is furious with his outspoken daughter.

The man waits through this, and when Ake and Tora have nothing left to say, he repeats his desire, "Sassa."

Tora huffs and storms from the room.

Ake, certain there must be a mistake, seeks to redress the situation. "Tora has expressed a liking for you. I would take that into consideration when naming the bride price if you..."

"Name any price and I shall pay it," says the man, "for Sassa."

Sassa, her mind spinning, her breath taken, begins to rise to her full stature. She sits straight and proud under the gaze of her suitor.

Ake studies the man closely. It is clear he is steadfast, unyielding in his want.

"Free split wood for a year," ventures Ake.

"For life," says the man as he stands.

Ake looks from Sassa to the man. "I can see you are determined. Tomorrow I will begin the arrangements."

"I will not return to my home without her," states the man. Now he addresses Sassa directly, his voice softening with a moment of quivering doubt, "If she will have me."

"We can summon the völva tonight," Sassa quickly replies.

❋ ❋ ❋

On the steep cliffs overlooking the fjord of Trondheim, the man and Sassa stand before the völva, a seer and priestess of the Aesir. The moon is merely a sliver of itself, yet stars light the sky with clouds of silver brilliance.

Ake stands solemn. Tora does not look especially happy for her sister. Svend remains quietly at his mother's side, all to bear witness.

A bleating nanny goat is tied beside the völva. The völva takes the goat, ceremoniously waves a knife over the animal, simulating sacrifice, then passes the goat's tether to Sassa. Sassa passes the goat back to Ake, and Ake hands Sassa a broadsword. Sassa offers the sword to the man. The man accepts the sword, places his grandmother's finger ring on the tip and offers the ring to Sassa. The völva dips a sprig into a bowl of pig's blood, and making the sign of Thor's hammer -- one stroke down, one quick stroke from left to right -- splatters the couple and family with blood, consecrating the union. Sassa and the man are officially married.

The newly bonded couple look to one another with more than a bit of excited disbelief.

* * *

Husband and wife walk the road to the man's longhouse in the dark of night. The man carries his axe across his shoulders, the marriage sword in his belt.

Sassa wears the fox fur cloak the man brought, clasped with Freyja's broach. She leads the nanny goat. The hound travels ahead. They walk in silence, each consumed with their own thoughts of what the night has yet to offer.

As they come to the longhouse, the man opens the door, offers his hand. Sassa takes his hand, steps over the threshold. The man follows, closes the door behind.

Sassa stands just within the door of the darkened home, quivering as if cold.

The man sets his axe and wedding sword beside the door with the hunting spear. He takes the cloak from Sassa's shoulders, hangs it on a peg. Goes to the fire, stokes it to life and uses a brand to light candles about the room. He takes two cups from a shelf, fills them with mead from a pitcher, offers one to Sassa.

Sassa hasn't moved from the threshold. She stands unsure, timidly watching her husband. Her voice is small and soft when she asks, "Why?"

The man sets Sassa's cup on the table, sits, drinks from his own cup.

"My sister Tora could not stop speaking of you all the way home today. She told our father she wanted you for a husband and did not care about the bride price or if you were rich or poor. Tora is said to be the most beautiful woman in all of Norway. Why did you not choose her?"

The man looks to Sassa where she stands fearful, yet demanding of the answer.

"Who is Tora?" says the man.

Sassa can not help but smile. She steps forward until she is within the glow of the candle, stands like a bashful child.

The man rises from the table, approaches Sassa, stands very close. He takes in her beauty, her scent. "You are mistaken about your sister," he murmurs.

"I do not understand."

He speaks as if in a trance, "Your hair is this color because when you were born Freyja cried upon you tears of red-gold, for she knew she was no longer the most beautiful creature in the Nine Realms." The man gently lays a hand to touch her hair. Sassa instinctively leans into his touch. "I came for you this night because I feared if I waited one moment longer the Aesir would take notice of you and send their finest to claim you for their own." Sassa's breath shutters. He gently tilts her chin to look into her eyes. "I did not want to have to kill all the gods to have you for myself."

The room is lit by the dwindling fire and a single candle. Wife and husband stand facing one another by the sleeping benches covered in rich pelts. The man watches as Sassa unties her dress to allow it to slip from her shoulders to the floor. She stands before him -- perfect in figure and form -- pale skin glowing in the dim light. The man sheds his shirt and trousers, lifts Sassa with one sweeping motion onto the furs of the sleeping bench. He suspends himself over her as she lies looking up at him. She allows him between her legs, then her breath catches. The man stops. Sassa reaches down between his legs, startled. "No," she breathes.'

"No?"

Sassa's hand remains between their legs for a moment, her breath coming harder, faster… "Yes," she sighs. Painful, yet unable to stop herself, she arches into him.

The candle burns itself out. The only light that remains is the guttered embers of the cook fire glowing in the central hearth.

Sassa and the man lie side by side in the aftermath. He looks down upon her, stroking a bit of her hair, his voice barely above a whisper, "The Aesir have blessed me above all men."

Sassa smiles up at him. "You have wasted your life as a woodcutter," she says, then begins to giggle. The man is puzzled. Sassa does her best to stifle her giddy laughter. "You should have been a scald," she giggles as she rolls atop her husband to smother him with kisses.

In the morning, the man wakes on the bed alone. He looks across the room to the door where the gray light of dawn shows the coming day. Sassa kneels, carving runes around the door frame with a small knife. There are many runes, she has been at it a good while.

The man swings out of bed, pulls on his trousers, goes to Sassa. "Do you ask the Aesir for prosperity?"

She looks up to him from her work. "Asking the gods for more after they have given so much would be disrespectful. I am simply thanking the Aesir and the Norns for their blessings."

The man kneels behind Sassa, moves her hair aside to nibble on her neck. His hands roam her body. Sassa quivers with ecstasy beneath his touch, but when his hands drift between her legs, her body tightens.

"No," she sighs.

"No?"

Sassa looks up to her husband, embarrassment reddening her cheeks and breast. "I am still sore."

The man understands, removes his hand, turns her chin up to gently kiss her. He stands, pulls on a shirt and takes up his splitting axe, begins to exit.

Sassa watches him the whole while, but before he can step outside, she grabs his shirttail to stop him.

"Yes," she tells him.

He knows the woodcutting will wait.

❉ ❉ ❉

Trondheim has blossomed into a major trading center since the days of Gunnar Skullcrusher. No longer simply a launching point for wars and raids, trade ships come and go with goods and thralls from distant lands.

Jarl Hedin of Iceland, a tall, slender nobleman, his wealth displayed in a seal fur cloak, a fine sword and several gold and silver arm rings, travels through the town with his three nearly as impressively appointed noblemen companions. Here and again they stop to ask a merchant or villager for Ake the smith. They are given direction and find him in his forge with Svend.

Ake coughs and wheezes against the dense smoke of the forge as he hammers out white hot steel on his anvil. The past six years since giving his daughter Sassa to the woodcutter have taken a terrible toll on the smith. His hair has thinned to stringy wisps. His skin, turned sallow, hangs loose on his bones. The limp from his old wound is pronounced. He can hardly move from kiln to anvil without a stave to lean on.

The same six years have turned Svend into a stalwart lad of twelve. Grown fair of feature, he favors his mother. Svend works the bellows for his grandfather.

Jarl Hedin, trailed by his three companions, approaches, speaks without question, "You are Ake the smith."

Ake stops his work, faces the jarl, coughs. "I am."

"I am Jarl Hedin of Reykjavík. I have come seeking a wife among your people."

Svend and Ake look to one another.

"Noblemen and kings speak of your daughter. I would have a look for myself," says the jarl.

"Go fetch you mother," Ake tells Svend.

Svend hurries to the house.

"That is your daughter's son?" Jarl Hedin would know. Ake nods, yes. Jarl Hedin looks to his companions with satisfaction.

Svend finds his mother is at the loom, but she is not weaving. She sits slumped on her stool drinking ale as is her custom of late. She is more than a little drunk.

"Mother, there is a man asking of you," Svend announces.

"A man?"

"A nobleman from Iceland."

Tora sits up straighter and pulls the scarf from her hair.

Svend waits but his mother does not move from her stool. "Are you coming?"

"Go, tell him to wait. I will be out shortly."

Svend does as told. He runs from the house, returns to his grandfather's side, shrugs.

Ake and Jarl Hedin wait in awkward silence.

Tora changes her dress to one more becoming, places a comb in her hair. She examines herself in the polished plate of copper which serves as a mirror. Satisfied, she directs herself to her father's smithery. Tora saunters from the house with all the bravado, beauty and ale can provide.

Jarl Hedin and his men watch her come. Despite the nobleman's pride and annoyance at being made to wait, he is impressed. Even half-drunk and ill-kept, Tora is more beautiful than he imagined.

Ake notes the drunken swagger of his daughter. He sighs.

Tora pulls up before Jarl Hedin, looks him up and down affecting nonchalance. She looks to her father as if questioning why she was summoned.

Jarl Hedin speaks first, "Lady, I am Jarl Hedin of Reykjavík." He inclines his head in the manner of a bow.

"And?" queries Tora.

The nobles scoff at the impudence.

Ake cringes, pained. Coughs phlegm from his ruined lungs.

To his credit, Jarl Hedin maintains his composure. "And I have sailed with several of my ships to gather the finest livestock for breeding, the finest lumber for ship building, and the finest woman in all of Norway for my wife."

Tora's ale induced swagger is pronounced, yet her voice does not waver, "You list a wife along with livestock and lumber. You are wanting for more than a wife. You are wanting as a man."

"Tora! Mind your manner!" Ake barks, the exclamation causing him a long fit of wet coughing.

"You have been too long without a husband, woman," states Jarl Hedin, losing what little patience he possesses.

"My husband was a noble, a warrior, he spoke to me with respect. I expect no less from you."

"Your husband was a warrior. And your father was a landowner before his wound hobbled him and chained him to an anvil. I know your story already. Do you believe I would even be considering you if you were merely the daughter of a smith?"

"Even if I were a thrall, I would not have you," spits Tora.

Jarl Hedin scoffs. "You speak of who you once were as if

it holds sway. Now your husband is dead and your father has nothing but his pride."

Tora shoots a look to Ake.

"I am not asking your permission," says the jarl, "I have made my decision. You will be my wife, and you will be listed among my prize stock."

Ake, forging hammer in hand, takes a bold step forward. Jarl Hedin's men place their hands on the hilts of their swords. Ake's anger flushes his pale countenance. "You will not speak with my daughter in that fashion, no matter your station. Go find your wife elsewhere and leave this house in peace," demands Ake.

"I have not come all this way to be turned away by the daughter of a crippled smith," replies the jarl.

"You have been turned away," says Ake. "You are not welcome here."

"We shall see," rejoins Jarl Hedin, affecting a smile which contains no joy. The nobles turn from the smithery to take their leave. The jarl addresses Tora over his shoulder, "Begin packing your things, woman. I will return."

Tora enters the house, pours her cup full of ale. Ake follows her in with the support of Svend.

"Go, Svend. Leave me to speak with your mother," commands Ake.

Svend makes certain his grandfather is braced firmly against the dining table before he releases the old man and retreats from the house.

When Svend is gone, Ake speaks furiously to his daughter, "You reject suitors out of hand as if they are beneath you!"

"They are beneath me."

"You have been too long a widow. How is it fair to Svend to have no father to teach him the ways of a man?"

"He has you."

"I am dying. You know that as well as he."

"He has his uncle," says Tora

"Your own sister's husband. It is shameful you have

never given up hope of him as your own."

"I am the eldest. He should have been mine."

"He is not yours!" The outburst causes Ake a painful coughing fit.

Tora waits until her father can take a full breath before she continues, "Then a man like him."

Ake shakes his head sadly, softens his tone, his voice raspy and failing, "There is no man like him. You will wait forever."

"Then I will wait forever," declares Tora.

* * *

Trondheim's great hall stands on a rise surrounded by the city. A porch of heavy timber extends from the front of the hall, and a large courtyard for gatherings, announcements and festivals, lies between the looming structure and the docks of the fjord. The interior of the expansive hall is designed for feasts, and for housing visiting nobles during the raiding season. A long central hearth to maintain the hall's warmth and for roasting entire hogs and oxen. There are many benches and tables for sleeping and feasting.

Jarl Hedin and his men sit at a long table enjoying a meal and mead. Opposite them sits the hall owner, Carl Kolbrand, jarl of Trondheim. A half dozen of Kolbrand's þegns share the table and the meal.

Kolbrand, a jovial former warrior and raider grown wealthy and fat, finds himself without a care these days. As Trondheim flourishes, so does his household. Few are known to be as generous a host as the jarl.

"I have never been to Iceland," says Kolbrand. "They say it is a vast land where the hunting of sea-ivory can make a man wealthy as a king."

"It is true," replies Jarl Hedin, "though I myself am not a man of the sea. Horses are my main trade. I also breed oxen for their hides, and sheep for the finest wool."

Kolbrand gestures to the pile of skins and bales of wool Jarl Hedin has brought as gifts. "As your generous tributes have proven."

Jarl Hedin swigs mead, shrugs as if the valuable gifts are but a small token. "What Iceland lacks is breeding stock of another sort."

"Women," states Kolbrand, nodding in understanding.

"Women," Jarl Hedin confirms. "The finest in my homeland have already been claimed."

"So you travel to my city in search of a wife?"

"I have found one," states Jarl Hedin, "but she proves to be quite disagreeable."

"You find her disagreeable now, imagine what heartache she will bring after you make her your wife," says Kolbrand. His men-at-arms laugh along with their jarl.

Jarl Hedin, not accustomed to being the brunt of a jest, sets his jaw. "Any creature that eats can be tamed. The woman I speak of is the daughter of a smith, Tora Akesdóttir."

"Tora, yes. I sought her out myself after the death of her husband," admits Kolbrand.

"And she rejected you?" says Jarl Hedin. "I am surprised you would allow that slight to stand."

Kolbrand shrugs off the matter. "It is no slight. We are in good company, you and I, as Tora has rejected every offer from every sort of man."

"And you find this acceptable?"

"She is a free woman from a family of free men."

"In Iceland it is against our customs for a woman to remain unmarried when she should be bearing children for the sake of the community."

"It is so here, also, but..."

Jarl Hedin rudely interrupts his host, "Would you deny me the opportunity to call upon ancient custom and a nobleman's right to declare any unmarried free woman as his bride? It was once law," reminds Jarl Hedin.

Kolbrand is troubled by the request. He speaks with caution, "Long before our time, and never in this country that I am aware."

"But the law of our ancestors, nonetheless," presses Jarl Hedin.

Kolbrand dismisses the notion with a wave of his hand and a long drink from his mead cup. "Mine is a modern city. Ancient laws hold little sway. Find another more willing to be your wife. There are more women than men here, as the wars have taken many."

Jarl Hedin grows dark of mind and tongue, "Jarl Kolbrand, our kin were enemies once, a blood feud between them. Is this matter worth reigniting that feud?"

Kolbrand frowns. His men-at-arms sit straighter, legs coiled beneath them. Some slowly ease themselves from the benches to stand, their hands near the hilts of their swords. Jarl Hedin's men stand to match.

Jarl Hedin and Jarl Kolbrand maintain one another's hard stare until Kolbrand stands.

"Claim your bride then. But let the bride price be singularly impressive. And once back in Iceland, I suggest you do not return," warns Kolbrand.

Satisfied with the outcome despite the ultimatum, Jarl Hedin stands and strides from the great hall, his men close on his heels.

※ ※ ※

The man, wearing the modified yoke of an oxen, drags the trunk of a huge tree from the woods to his splitting station near the longhouse. The trunk has been stripped of branches, and hewn cleanly off toward the tip where it narrows. He shrugs out of the yoke and positions the trunk on blocks meant to keep it from rolling.

Sassa, seated on the bench outside the door of the

longhouse, mends a pair of boots while keeping one eye on their daughters: Kari, a timid yet exceptionally bright child of five, and her rambunctious sister, Nanna, nearly two years younger. The children play at stalking the chickens which scrounge the yard for seed. The girls are fair and happy with boundless energy and growing wit.

Sassa herself has grown even more radiant in the intervening six years, motherhood forming her fully from girl to woman. She wears her shimmering hair, uncovered, but braided to keep it from the ground.

Sassa watches her husband in his labors, admiring the way his legs and buttocks strain against trousers which only a few years ago were loose fitting. She makes a mental note to weave him a new pair, more fitting for his ever growing frame. The shirt still fits, though snugly against his arms and chest. She watches him peel the sweat-soaked garment from his torso, drape it over a low bush to dry. Enveloped in a young woman's daydreams of heroes, Sassa smiles an absent smile.

The man uses short sliding strokes of his axe to shed the bark from the long trunk until the shiny bare wood is clearly seen. He closely examines the lay of the grain, rotates the trunk until it lays just so in the restraining blocks. The man selects an iron wedge and hammer to begin taking planks from the log, when Svend runs onto the farmstead, red-faced and out of breath.

"Uncle, come quickly, my mother needs you," gasps Svend.

The man looks to Sassa who lays down the boots and stands. "Go. I will gather the girls and meet you there," says Sassa.

The man takes up his splitting axe, hurries after Svend on the road to Trondheim.

Sassa sighs, more annoyed than worried about what her sister might need from her husband this time.

* * *

In the town square lying between Trondheim's great hall and the docks, townspeople gather, lured by the commotion of a dispute. Jarl Kolbrand stands on the porch extending from the front of his great hall ready to preside over the conflict. Below him in the square, Jarl Hedin and his three companions stand facing Tora and Ake.

Ake grips a stave for support to stand as he continues his angry claim, "No deal has been struck. No arrangements made. Jarl Hedin makes claim to my daughter with no just cause."

Jarl Hedin remains calm with his rebuttal, for he already knows the outcome of the dispute, "I make claim as a nobleman and jarl."

Tora flings her response, "Your title means nothing to me."

"It means I may choose my wife from the karls of any land under the kings of Norway or Iceland, or any other land where our laws reign supreme."

Jarl Kolbrand attempts to remain in control of the contentious discourse. "What has he offered in compensation?"

"Horses and cattle...," Ake begins. He is interrupted by Tora's venomous cry.

"Horses and cattle!"

Ake tries to silence and calm his daughter to little avail.

"And silver. More than enough for five such brides," adds Jarl Hedin.

Tora spits at his feet in reply.

"She does not want to go with him, and I will not allow it," says Ake.

"Then you risk outlawry," states Jarl Hedin.

Ake and Tora look desperately to Jarl Kolbrand for favorable judgement.

Kolbrand is pained, yet unwilling to speak against the nobleman's claim for fear of repercussions and reigniting an ancient feud.

It seems the matter is settled when Svend and the man enter the square. They make their way through the gathered crowd toward Ake and Tora.

Jarl Kolbrand raises his voice to announce his final decision, "As I can find no authority to dispute Jarl Hedin's claim of ancient right, by law I must declare...

"Holmgang," the man interrupts in his rumbling voice which carries clearly over all gathered.

Everyone turns to look at the man who stands before Tora and Ake, his splitting axe held by his side.

Jarl Hedin is astounded by the size of the man. His retainers mill uneasily.

Kolbrand looks to the man to address him formally, though he knows him well enough,

"Who is it who calls for holmgang?"

"It is my uncle," shouts Svend.

The gathered villagers laugh at the interjection.

"He is husband to my youngest daughter and therefore kin," says Ake.

Jarl Hedin makes his voice heard, "He is not blood to this woman and has no concern in this matter."

Jarl Kolbrand, relieved that a remedy has presented itself, leaps at the opportunity. He proclaims, "Any man who feels he has been wronged or slighted may claim the right. Let holmgang decide this matter."

The crowd murmurs and mills, excited at the prospect of blood sport.

"Bring sailcloth and shields," calls Kolbrand. Several of the jarl's retainers hurry away from the porch at the command.

Jarl Hedin whispers to one of his companions, "Discover what there is to know about this giant."

So tasked, the nobleman moves into the milling crowd to question villagers.

The man stands waiting.

Svend holds his mother's hand tightly. Ake licks his lips in nervousness. Tora wets her lips in excitement as her eyes shift continually between the man and Jarl Hedin: two men to battle for her honor.

A sailcloth nine paces square is brought and laid on the ground. Three round shields are placed at the foot of Jarl Hedin, three at the foot of the man. The crowd grows all the more excited.

Jarl Hedin's man returns with news of his opponent, whispers the information in the jarl's ear, "The man you face is not a warrior. He is a simple farmer who has never been to war or on a raid. The villagers know him as the woodcutter as his trade is to provide planks for ships, and firewood for the winter season."

"Woodcutter," Jarl Hedin repeats thoughtfully. His confidence grows.

Another of his companions speaks to him, "And look, he bears no sword nor proper weapon, only that nub of a splitting axe."

"You are the best duelist of us all," says the third nobleman of Jarl Hedin's escort. "You shall easily defeat him, regardless of his size."

Jarl Hedin is bolstered by the information and the encouraging words of his fellows. He steps onto the sailcloth to take up one of the shields. Draws his fine pattern-welded sword from its sheath. Stands ready to do battle.

Sassa makes her way through the crowd to her family. She carries Nanna. Kari hurries along at her heels. Sassa takes in the situation at a glance and her breath shortens with distress.

Tora looks excitedly to Sassa. "He fights for me!"

Sassa scowls at her sister, but it is lost on Tora as her eyes again dart between the two combatants.

Ake lays a hand on Sassa's shoulder, but Sassa is not comforted.

With the holmgang battlefield prepared, Jarl Kolbrand makes the official pronouncement, "The law of holmgang has been invoked to determine if Jarl Hedin of Reykjavík Iceland may claim Tora Akesdóttir of Trondheim as his bride."

The surrounding villagers murmur and place wagers on the outcome. The sheer size and stature of the man is no doubt imposing, but the warrior who faces him is no less impressive with his fine weapon, confidence, and experience in battle. Speculation and coin flow through the crowd.

Jarl Kolbrand continues with the rules of the duel, "A blow that wounds so that either man can not continue settles the matter. A killing blow, and the matter is settled. Once settled, the matter may not be disputed, nor a feud over the result begun."

Jarl Hedin begins the duel by voicing the formal challenge, clear and commanding, "You are not a man's equal and not a man at heart!" He sounds two challenging strikes of sword on shield, advances toward the man.

The man, without taking up a shield, nor issuing the formal retort, advances in long, rapid strides across the sailcloth, his axe swaying at his side. Without slowing or breaking stride, the man swings his axe in a powerful arching overhead strike.

Jarl Hedin sees the strike coming and is well trained to raise his shield to catch it, knowing the axe will be deflected and he will have an open path to strike with his broadsword to the man's exposed body. Lacking armor, the counter will be deadly.

A resounding crash of axe on wood causes the entire gathering to recoil in shock. The man's axe shatters Jarl Hedin's shield, along with the arm holding it.

An agonized cry of pain is torn from Jarl Hedin as he staggers backward from the blow, his badly broken arm dangling. He drops to his knees, wavers near fainting.

An astounded gasp, then resounding silence issues from the villagers who bear witness.

Sassa blinks as if she disbelieves her eyes. Tora holds her breath, dumbfounded. Ake chuckles, and Svend is giddy with relief and joy.

The man looks down upon the defeated nobleman without emotion, then looks to the porch where Jarl Kolbrand stands in awed wonder.

"I would say the matter is settled," states Jarl Kolbrand with more than a bit of mirth in his voice.

The surrounding villagers come from their shock to shout their excitement and approval. They crowd tightly around the man to pat him on his back. All call in praise of the most impressive, if brief, duel they have ever seen or heard tell of.

Jarl Hedin is carried from the square by his three fellows who speak not a word.

* * *

The man walks the road to his farmstead with Kari perched upon his shoulders. Sassa carries Nanna.

Sassa, still very excited by her husband's impressive showing in the duel, speaks of it without cessation, "They will tell the tale for many years. You did not even take up a shield, yet bested a warrior, a nobleman... and with a single stroke of your axe!" Sassa's excitement turns dark. "The look on Tora's face... I know my sister. She wants you for her own. She always gets what she wants. She could have any man. Any man would fight for her. Now Tora has found a way to have you fight for her as well."

"Who is Tora?" replies the man.

Her husband's wry statement never fails to elicit a smile from Sassa.

The family continues to their home in high spirits.

* * *

In the four years that follow, the man's legend grows, not only from the holmgang duel he fought, but for the fact it was fought for the sister of his wife. It is rumored the man maintains two wives now, and they, sisters.

Tora, reveling in the talk and in her own fantasies, does little to dispel the rumor.

It is also said the man is Svend's true father. They cite as proof how the woodcutter cares for the lad now that the boy's grandfather has died. This rumor finds protest with Svend, yet they are weak denials as even Svend carries the invention deep in his heart.

* * *

First day of Tvímánuður, 1066 CE

The man is at peace as he cleaves foes conjured in his avid mind. His splitting-axe dully rings: the muted tolling of a bell calling the envisaged fallen through the death mists to Valhöll and to Helheim. His arms never tire. His shoulders never falter. His back never wilts. Legs splayed solid and unmoving as the roots of Yggdrasil. Each swing of the axe, a resounding death blow. If he smiled, he would smile now. If he sang, this would be the cause. If he were to be named, the name would evince this act.

Yet the enemies of his imagination are but a long-held dream. In reality, birch wood logs split one after the other and piled beyond vision in the heavy morning brume. Enough for a hundred homes. Enough for Fimbulwinter.

This, a secret diversion he has entertained from childhood: Turning his labor into glorious battle -- himself into a berserker from a line of berserker -- slaying foes unnumbered to his own renown and acclaim of the Aesir.

Frost-breath plumes from him in great billows as the sun rises to burn away the morning brume. His daughters seeing this imagine him to be the kin of dragons, descendent of the creatures from the stories their mother tells by the night fires. Kin of dragons, they call him. He does not deny it, not to his daughters, not to himself. For he himself cannot be certain.

The man is fated never to know his father: an enigmatic stranger who found warmth and welcome in his mother's bed while her husband was away at war. A titan of exceeding height and strength who spoke honeyed words to seduce and conquer. A comely wanderer with a gilded smile and a great steed with powerful flanks and flaxen mane. Three nights the stranger stayed, then was gone.

His mother's husband never returned from battle, and she herself perished with the bearing of him, as if his curse were to remain unknown and unnamed.

He knew his grandfather, knew him well. Raised to stalwart lad beneath his harsh, unyielding fist. A berserker of old, said to be spawned from the line of Odin's own bodyguard. A warrior of great renown who justified his appellation, Gunnar Skullcrusher, for the manner of use of his magnificent battle-axe to slay foemen numbered in the hundreds.

His grandmother, a Valkyrie they say. But it is only what they say.

The man has no name. His grandfather unwilling to bestow a name upon the creature who killed his only daughter in the birth of him, and no one else to name him.

Husband to his wife. Father to his daughters. Woodcutter to the villagers. This is the man.

And there his daughters: Kari and Nanna, harrying chickens and geese round and round the yard in merrymaking. With their gild-red hair fluttering free, they favor their mother. Nanna the younger by two years, passing her seventh summer. Bold and brash and demanding. Springing from the womb of such intrepid character. Winning her want by sheer force of indomitable will. Kari, their firstborn, so much the opposite of her sister in every manner, yet even more powerful for it. Able to bend her father's iron resolve with downcast eyes and a silent pout.

Each to themselves are a force. Together they are their mother.

Sassa, their mother; a divine beauty. The man tells Sassa her hair is the color of Freyja's tears because when she was born, Freyja wept for she knew she was no longer the most beautiful of creations. Sassa tells him not to repeat such things, as the goddess may take offense. But the man tells her again and again, and in secret she would have it this way, and no other.

Sassa balances on the short stool, her magnificent hair unbound and drawn across her lap to keep it from the muck. The sun-white skin of her slender arms taut and relax in practiced rhythm as she milks the nanny, heavy in udder, that suckles the spring kid. She watches her husband in his labors from this vantage, unabashed by her lust and love for the man.

The man swings his splitting-axe as the day brightens and warms. Sweat mats hair the color and texture of new corn silk that falls past his shoulders. His beard of a darker hue and with much red, shorn close around a set grin where his frost-breath condenses.

And with each mighty stroke of the axe his enemies are piled higher, and higher still.

❋ ❋ ❋

The squeak of greased iron and labored exclamations announce the arrival of Svend. At sixteen years, teetering on the brink of full manhood, Svend has grown to a stalwart youth yet to fully fill out his sturdy frame: A bit lean between joints, in the manner of a two-year-old racing stallion yet to realize its full potential.

Svend grudgingly hauls the two-wheeled cart piled to tipping with sectioned logs along the ruddy path, packed hard and worn deep through the forest loam toward the farmstead. The lad curses and grunts beneath his load as he arrives to his

uncle who never ceases his splitting. He shucks the heavy leather yoke from his neck, stands upright to stretch his back and
regain his full breath.

"Why do you not buy a horse uncle?" Svend would
know. Before the man can rejoin with the customary reply to
the oft-asked query, Svend repeats the well-worn line for him,
"Because I am cheaper than a horse. I know."

The man hides his grin by cleaving another log. The
wood splits cleanly with a satisfying crack.

Svend watches his uncle place yet another log on the
splitting block. "Do you never tire uncle?"

"I tire."

"Then why do you not stop?"

Another log is quartered and added to the pile before
the man replies, "Because there are more."

Svend shakes his head as if he truly does not understand,
sets about unloading the cart. Though he has yet to gain the
age to grant him a proper beard, the inability does not stop
Svend from trying. Fine patches of fiery red grow motley
across his winsome features. A curse of his family line; to be
beautiful beyond their station. There is more red than gold in
his hair he wears in the cropped style of the young warriors
and raiders of Trondheim. Long of leg and broad of shoulder,
a sturdy youth growing stronger season to season under the
labors imposed by his uncle.

Svend complains incessantly of being beset upon to divide and carry the trees felled by his uncle. But in truth, he
revels in the attention he is afforded by the folk of the village.
Kin to the man carries no shame, and many benefits. A dis-
cretionary respect is granted Svend and his mother, as none
would wish to face the man in a feud over honor of kindred.

Svend stacks wood as his uncle splits. He ponders how
to breach a despised subject without raising the ire of the man.
Though Svend's courage wanes in the face of his kinsman, his
enthusiasm for the gossip of the village causes him to speak
beyond prudence, "King Harald Hardrada is building an army,"

blurts Svend.

Hardrada. The man scoffs at the name. Was there another way to rule? Sigurdsson, the king's given name: A noble name passed down from the greatest of heroes. Hardrada, a surrogate title no doubt bestowed upon him by his enemies, or a disgruntled noble. Possibly the king himself chose the name, the man considers. How much easier to rule with a name that inspires anxiety and fear, rather than simply nobility?

Svend continues to speak of the coming war, pours out the remainder with a single breath, "He will sail to England as soon as he has gathered his army, for it is said Hardrada has a rightful claim to the English throne."

The man has heard the news also, but to this point it had meant little to him.

Svend speaks quickly as if to state his case before he is countered, "I am old enough now by a year. The king was younger than I when he fought alongside his brother for the crown of Norway, and just my own age when he became a captain of the Rus." Svend watches closely for his uncle's reaction. "I will be going with them," he concludes.

A deep grunt from the man as the axe-head lodges in a birch wood log without splitting it through. Knotty wood could be unpredictable.

At the sound, Sassa looks up from her milking. The ring of axe on wood was not right, nor the posture of her husband as he stands still as a runestone, her sister's son facing him, poised like a cautious bird ready to take flight.

Svend holds his breath, watches his uncle from behind as the man fills his lungs, the muscles clearly corded beneath his light shirt. Then, with a mighty heave, the man raises axe and log alike overhead -- welded together -- and brings them down with terrifying force on the splitting stump. The log shatters. The axe cleaves cleanly through to deeply embed itself in the stump.

The resounding echo thunders across the farmstead as if

Thor had laid Mjölnir to the skull of a giant.

Nanna and Kari stop in their play to anxiously stare at their father.

Sassa stands from the milking stool.

Svend remains silent, breathless. He licks his dry lips, summons his quavering voice, "I will gather more logs."

"This is enough for today," says the man.

Sassa still watches. The energy that radiates from her husband like heat from a kettle set boiling too long. "Svend," she calls.

Svend responds quickly, anxiously, "Yes, aunt Sassa?"

"Hurry home and tell your mother to come for supper tonight."

"She will not come again so soon. She says the heart bleeds in those who must beg at each meal for meat."

"It is not begging, she is my sister."

"But she says..."

The man turns on the lad with a look that quells Svend's voice. When he speaks it is barely above a whisper, but easily understood, "Do not make your aunt repeat herself."

Svend nods his understanding, calls to Sassa, "Thank you aunt Sassa. My mother and I will join you here before sundown." Svend returns his look to his uncle.

"Return straight away with your bow. I have a taste for boar tonight," says the man.

Greatly relieved, Svend does as told and runs the path home.

Sassa calls after him, "Tell her to not make me come and fetch you both. Supper will serve as payment for your work."

Svend raises a hand in acknowledgement as he disappears into the woods.

The man balances another log for splitting.

Sassa hitches up the hem of her thin rough-woven dress and strides through the barley grass cropped short by grazing goats toward her husband. The once sea-blue dress is faded and puckered in spots where mended, and mended again. The same dress serves as an undergarment in winter, a resting place for the newborn kids and chicks of spring, and her best wear to attend the midsummer festival.

The man watches her come and is awed to stillness. Her flowing hair a red-gold surrogate for the sun still only a dim glow beyond the morning overcast. An alfin smile on her full lips. High cheeks flush with a girlish blush at having her husband's eyes follow her so openly and with such intent.

Sassa reaches her husband, lets her skirts fall. She cranes her neck to look up at him from mid-chest height. The sight of her like this evokes the same reaction in him as the first time he laid eyes on her.

She picks up a splinter of shattered wood, tosses it onto the wood pile. "Now what could this poor piece of tree done to offend you so, I wonder?"

The man rocks his axe free from the splitting stump.

Sassa considers his mood. "Something Svend said upset you?" she guesses. "He is of that age. Everything he says is upsetting. You understand, you were once his age."

"And once had his dreams," admits the man.

"And?"

"And then I met you."

"And all your dreams came true," says Sassa with a coy lilt.

The man chuckles and is pulled from his funk. Sassa is pleased with her success. She takes her husband by the hand to lead him to the longhouse, her delicate hand completely eclipsed in his. She relishes the feel of his calloused hands, a bear's paws no more coarse and weathered. Hands which leave red trails across the milk-white skin of her back, her breasts, her thighs.... The trails fade, but the memories linger.

The man follows his wife without protest or reserve. He will deny her nothing.

Kari and Nanna watch them as they approach. Kari blushes, drops her eyes and quarters away as not to meet her parents' look. Nanna, the light of realization dawning on her open face, rushes to her father and shoves against his leg with all her might.

"But I'm hungry," Nanna protests.

Sassa giggles her laughter.

The man, one hand in his wife's, the other toting his axe, can do little but slow his gait and take care in his steps as not to topple the vexed child.

"We will eat soon enough," Sassa tells Nanna, trying to sound stern.

Nanna tugs and pulls at her father and summons her most demanding voice, "It's never soon... pappa...!"

The man stops. Now it is Sassa who tugs on him with all her might, to similar effect of the tiny child.

The man lays down his axe, scoops up his willful daughter in one arm. He holds her so they look to one another, nose to nose. The man furrows his own brow to match his daughter's. Down-turned lips display Nanna's displeasure.

"No," Sassa states plainly and clearly enough that the man sighs in mock surrender and pouts his own lips so Nana will know he is to be held blameless for her misery. He places Nanna's feet on the ground, yet the child clings to his arm and will not be dislodged.

"Nanna, stop!" demands Sassa through her poorly concealed mirth.

Nanna balls up a tiny fist and delivers her mightiest of blows to her father's arm in a gesture of both defiance and surrender. She stomps her foot, scowls up to her mother in challenge.

Sassa squats down to take Nanna by the shoulders, speaks in conciliatory earnest, "Stay out here and play with your sister, and you can have the center piece of the first fresh loaf when baked."

The child's mind visibly considers the bribe. She suddenly turns away, takes up a small stick from the yard and harangues the nearest goose into a honking fury.

Sassa stifles laughter and takes her husband by the hand

once again. She is surprised when he does not follow.

Kari sneaks peeks from beneath the silken hair that falls over her downcast eyes. The man kneels and makes the tiniest of gestures of his head toward his eldest. Kari eagerly rushes to her father, leaps to latch her arms around his neck. The man hoists her to look her in the eyes. He has to lift her extra high as her gaze refuses to meet his. When he succeeds, Kari smiles, takes her father's face in her delicate hands, kisses him repeatedly around his eyes and cheek.

Sassa waits her turn patiently. No point fighting battles where the outcome is in question.

Kari rests her forehead against her fathers for a silent moment between them. A moment only these two and no others could share or understand. The man gently lowers his daughter to the ground.

Kari chases after her sister. "Nanna stop," implores Kari, sounding much like her mother, "they won't lay eggs if you bother them too much."

"I don't like eggs," states Nanna.

"You do," rejoins Kari, "you are just being toilsome."

Sassa and the man look to one another, amused.

Sassa sighs, and with a coy smile releases her husband's hand. She strides into the longhouse without a word.

The man bends to retrieve his axe and nearly drops it again as he watches Sassa from behind. Her carriage borders on arrogance. The sway of her hair in perfect counterpoint to that of her hips. Her gait beckons, far more compelling than promising words and a tug on the hand.

* * *

The longhouse, built by the man's grandfather while he was at the peak of his wealth from profitable summer raids, stands towering and wide. Built of the old style, the once great lodge has over years of necessary upkeep, become more homey than grand. Thick windowless walls deny the cold. The steeply canted roof has been patched with sod so often its covering is now more lush barley than wood. The heavy plank door on oiled leather hinges fits well and keeps out the wind. It is a fine home.

The man enters to find Sassa with her back to him, stoking the fire in the long pit that dominates the center of the room. Sassa keeps the fire burning and the house warm year-long, as a woodcutter's home should be. A deep iron kettle hangs over the ember side of the pit, remaining always heated and ready for the evening meal.

The large open space of the longhouse is divided by low sections of stone walls: dairy, granary and stalls for the goats and fowl in winter. Sleeping benches parallel the fire pit and are covered in a variety of skins and furs: soft sheepskin for the girls. A plush long-haired horse skin where the man and Sassa lie. All well tanned and oiled to butter suppleness. The fragrance of winter-stabled animals has faded over the summer. Now the longhouse bears the heady aroma of wood smoke and savory boiled meat. Aromatic fodder stored in the loft. A horseshoe hangs on the heavy beam above the door for luck lest the beam fall and crush a guest. The door frame itself, skillfully carved with runes thanking the Aesir for their many blessings. A solid heavy plank table stands by the fire. Long benches for seating.

It is cozy and dark inside. The fire is low, no candles burn. The smoke-hole in the ceiling glows soft silver, admitting the light of the overcast day.

The man leans his splitting-axe near the door alongside the long shafted hunting spear. He greedily indulges in the vision of his wife.

As Sassa pokes at the embers with an iron rod, her dress falls from one shoulder. The man finds himself holding his breath. He knows she has unbound the laces. He yearns to go to her but is loath to disrupt this sublime vision. Sassa bends to lay down the stoking rod. The dress slips from her other shoulder. The man can resist no more. He crosses the room, takes his wife in his arms from behind, buries his face in the silky hair at the nape of her neck. She utters a gasp of shock and pleasure as his lips and teeth find the tender skin of her neck, shoulders.... His calloused hands brush lightly over her breasts, shedding the dress to gather around her waist. His hands follow the fall of the fabric and push it past her full hips to the floor, revealing her lavish form completely. He turns her to him. Her face flushes, her breath catches as he lifts her to set her on the table. She welcomes him between her legs, closes her legs around his waist as if to prevent his escape. Wife and husband rapt in desire. This moment, a most precious gift from the Aesir. He reaches for the tie on his trousers, but finds her hands already there. He allows her, her pleasure. His hands in her hair now. A firm grip avails her face and throat to his kisses. Her breath catches again at the onset as it always does. That initial moment having never grown commonplace. He slows to allow her to relax, take him in. She does. He doesn't slow again. He savors every sigh, gasp, subtle change in the tensing of her body, her face.

Her eyes flutter open to see him above her -- see into him, through him -- then they close again to maintain the image she would recall forever.

He is afraid to look away lest he wake from the resplendent dream.

She opens her eyes again to find him staring at her and she wants to cry, laugh, scream mindlessly....

A sliver of light from the doorway takes his gaze. He is startled from his rapture by the voice of his youngest.

"I'm hungry now," insists Nanna as she looks up to her coupled parents.

The lovers collapse in giddy frustration. They reluctantly separate, gather their clothes.

Sassa looks down on Nanna but cannot find it in herself to be stern. The proud, demanding child, always unapologetic in her wants.

The man looks to the open door where Kari hovers, bashful, peeking out from beneath fluttering lashes, adroitly manipulating her father's resolve. He goes to stand above her. Kari toes the floor, pulls anxiously at her shift as if steeling herself for a scolding, though she has never once been scolded by her father, not now, and never to be.

"I told her not to," says Kari.

Her father's grave look is unconvincing to the child and she hurries inside with a giggle to warm the heart of Hel herself.

The man takes up his axe from beside the door, the whetstone stored in the nook above, and with a final fatalistic look returned in kind by his wife, exits to hone his blade.

✻ ✻ ✻

Tora sits in a stupor staring at the weaving loom. The loom is not threaded and gathers dust. There is no fire in the fireplace. The cooking pot hanging above the cold ashes is empty. A bread baking pan lies unused on the hearth.

Svend emerges from his room with his longbow and a quiver of arrows. He stands, looks to his mother. "We are to go to aunt Sassa's for the evening meal," announces Svend.

Tora does not respond. It is unclear if she even heard.

"Mother..."

"We went only two days ago," says Tora without looking up.

"We have nothing to eat here," complains Svend, "not even an old loaf of bread. When I bring game home, you refuse to cook it."

"Do not trouble me Svend. I am tired."

"And have been so since grandfather died."

Tora reaches for her cup which sits on the bench beside her. The cup is empty. She replaces it.

Svend is pained, his voice pleading, "Mother, I have little skill for smithing, and there is no other trade for us here. We should go live with my uncle and aunt."

Tora sits up a little straighter, proud, but still will not make eye contact with her son. "I have prospects," she claims.

Svend's frustration nearly boils over, yet as a dutiful son, he remains circumspect. "Yes, mother. But still you must come to supper or aunt Sassa will scold me."

Tora absently nods her ascent.

Svend is relieved. "I am hunting with my uncle today. I will kill a boar, or maybe a stag, and it will be a great feast, you will see."

Tora smiles up at her son. She reaches to hold his arm for a moment before her hand limply falls to her lap.

Svend leaves his mother at the loom, staring at nothing.

* * *

The steady practiced scraping of stone on steel calls through the forest, beckons a pair of ravens who light on the uppermost branches of the giant ash to look down upon the man where he sits on his honing bench, working his worn splitting axe to a fine, fine edge. He wipes the forged head clean with an oiled cloth as the sun, racing ever faster across the sky from the pursuing wolf, sees fit to make an appearance. The dull metal of the axe glows in the warm light, more so from the freshly honed edge. The man tests the blade with his thumb, and acknowledges with pride a job well done. He strokes the long, smooth ash handle with the cloth before laying the axe across his knees to watch Svend approach.

Svend carries the yew-wood longbow and a quiver of straight, iron tipped arrows the man formed himself from the wood of a tree famous for such weapons. The draw of the bow proved too heavy for the youth at first attempts, but Svend's ever growing strength has become a match for the weapon's substantial resistance.

Svend stands before the man. "Where shall we hunt, uncle?"

The man simply shrugs, waits as he often does lately, prompting the lad to form his own mind.

Svend looks off into the forest, considering, then concludes, "A farmer from a glen to the east of here came to market with a cart filled with corn only days ago. He complained of a passel of hogs rooting in his fields." Svend turns his look to his uncle for approval. "He claimed they even overwhelmed his hounds. I doubt he would be offended if we hunt his land. He may even be grateful. We could offer him a portion of our kill."

The man nods, satisfied with his nephew's growing competence. He stands, clasps Svend's shoulder approvingly, turns to enter the house. Svend, tall and proud at the unspoken praise, follows.

Sassa offers the men a smile as she takes the baking pan from the coals. "The loaves are ready," she announces.

"I was promised the center piece," complains Nanna.

"You were promised the center piece if you played outside," reminds Sassa.

The man crosses to Sassa, takes her around the waist, kisses her deeply. He plucks a steaming loaf from the hot pan, tosses it to Svend. Takes a second loaf for himself. He begins to exit, then pauses where his daughters sit, bowls of steaming honey-sweetened porridge before them at the table. He tears his own loaf in half, scoops out the center portion with his fingers -- one for Kari, one for Nanna. The girls beam with pleasure.

Sassa sighs in mock exasperation.

The man does not turn to see his wife's disapproving look, he knows for certain it is there. He takes up his spear, axe and frog, strides out the door with Svend on his heels.

❋ ❋ ❋

It is not cold. The forest remains in full bloom in the waning days of summer. Only pin-drops of orange and yellow dotting the dense green foliage foretell the coming of winter.

Deep loam silences their step as Svend and the man trek toward their hunting ground. The man allows Svend to lead, though he knows the woods and the way well enough. The man carries his splitting-axe in the worn leather frog slung across his broad back. The long shank of his broad-tipped hunting spear rests on one shoulder. Each hunter is equipped with the hand axe and belt knife no man is ever without.

Ravens perched on the crown of the old-growth ash trees croak at their passing.

Svend carries his bow, arrow nocked, but with his constant chatter it would bewilder the man if they came across any game.

"The jarl will make the announcement at the Thing," Svend prattles. "Summer is near its end so the army will need to winter in England. The fjords will hold too much ice to return by the time we have won the war. I have never sailed on a longship. England is several days across open ocean. I'm not afraid though." Svend kicks at the moist leaves in frustration. "I wish we had a hound. With a hound we would have found game by now. The swine, or maybe an elk! When I return from the war with my riches, I will buy a whole pack of hunting dogs, one for you too uncle."

"I have had a hound," says the man.

"When?" queries Svend, "I do not remember."

The two stroll through the forest, the hunt forgotten for the moment as the man enjoys the filtered sunlight that sparkles through the leaves. Loses himself in reverie.

"You played with her when you were very young. She was with me before I met your aunt, when I was a child in the years following my grandfather's death. His bitch-hound was swollen with pups, and on the day my grandfather traveled to Valhöll, she gave birth to a litter of five. The creature was so afflicted with grief at her master's passing, she killed each of her own offspring as it came from her womb. All but the final one, a female which I snatched from her dam's jaws. I bound the bitch so she could kill no more, and nursed the pup on her mother's milk until it weaned, then on meat from my own plate.

"There was scant to eat in those days as I was but nine years old and could find no way to earn my own food but by splitting wood. Even then, I was too small and weak to cut more than a penny's worth in a full cycle of the moon.

"My she-hound grew strong and bold. We would hunt all manner of game. She even unearthed a bear once, but at my age I could find no way to kill it, so the bear was allowed to escape.

"She was long-legged and quick enough to cut the path from the way of a running stag. Bold enough to stand in the face of a team of wild boars until I could bring up my spear. She was the finest of hounds," the man concludes, "and I know she now waits in Asgard until we may hunt again." The man falls silent. His eyes travel to the dappled sun glittering through the leaves above.

Svend can not recall a single time his uncle waxed on so. As many words spoken at once as in all the years he has known him. But then he has never broached the subject of his hound before. Clearly a dear subject.

"I shall buy you another just as fine," boasts Svend.

"There are none as fine."

Without warning the man freezes in place, places a heavy hand on Svend's shoulder. Svend stops in mid-step, crouches, peers through the undergrowth in the direction his uncle gazes.

Now Svend hears it also: a low grunting and scraping of the earth by cloven hooves, only slightly beyond through the dense underbrush.

The man silently leads the way toward the sounds. His posture and gait resembles that of a huge wolf creeping upon its prey.

Svend eases forward in the shadow of his uncle, ready to draw and loose.

The forest becomes silent. Not a bird nor insect nor rustle of small creatures in the loam makes a sound.

Then a rustling of brush.... The man stands erect, exhales a sigh, continues less cautiously through the brush to an open spot where the damp earth has been turned as if readied for crops. He checks the remnants of mushrooms in the tattered earth.

"They were here," whispers Svend.

"Yes," murmurs the man, "apparently Odin has struck these hogs deaf."

A snorting, grumbling from the creatures just ahead causes both to resume their hunting posture. This time the man gestures for Svend to take the lead.

Svend readies his bow, stalks forward the way he has seen his uncle do, pausing to listen, heedful of the placement of each foot as to make no sound.

They travel into the wind and can smell the hogs now, wet and rank, their coarse hides thick with years of filth. A glimpse of movement just ahead. Bristles the color of the gnarled bark of a weathered oak. The hunters quicken their pace ducking beneath the low-slung branches, skirting dense patches of undergrowth with as little noise as they are able.

Abruptly, they come upon the sounder of sow and their young lolling about in the muck of a shallow wallow. The hogs snap to their feet, stand as statues, stare directly at Svend and the man with tiny black eyes. Their snouts snuff noisily at the air. Legs quiver, ready to bolt.

Svend in a single motion, raises his bow draws and looses. The muted twang of bowstring. The hiss, dull thud and sharp snort of breath from the creature as the arrow pierces the fore-quarter of the nearest sow.

At the sound, the hogs reel and flee, crashing through the underbrush with a clamor of squeals and grunts and the panicked scramble of sharp hooves.

Svend excitedly notches another arrow, but the man shakes his head, hands Svend his spear. Svend smiles broadly as he grips the spear. He understands this means his uncle is certain the first arrow found its mark. The spear is to finish the creature where it lies.

The hunters follow the trail of blood: deep red, arterial. Flecks of lighter color bubbled on the leaves, prove the arrow pierced a lung also. The sow has not run far. She lies hidden beneath a black currant heavy with berries. Her breath comes in wet labored snorts as blood fills her lungs.

Svend lies down his bow. He approaches the sow with care, spear at the ready.

The man stands back, admires the arrow placement. The lad has been practicing.

Svend presses the tangle of the bush aside, places the tip of the spear on the sow's throat, thrusts. The heavy blade glides through without resistance. Blood surges from the gaping wound. The creature convulses, then lays still. Svend lays down the spear, bends to drag the sow from beneath the bush by its hind legs. He smiles over his shoulder at his uncle, his eyes afire with the euphoria of the kill.

Suddenly the man comes alert, reaches for the axe on his back as he sprints for Svend.

Svend, startled and confused, recognizes the danger too late.

A gigantic boar charges through the underbrush in a maddened rush, it's head lowered, broad snout plowing through the wet loam. Twisted tusks protrude insanely from slathering jaws.

Svend scrambles for the spear but is too late as the monster is upon him.

The man clears his axe, barrels past Svend, his weapon already in a full pendulum swing. The mighty stroke rises up from the ground with fearsome strength born of desperation.

Man and beast come together with equal savage intent.

The axe meets the boar's neck a hair's-breadth before

tusks meet the man's groin.

The weight of the boar nearly doubles that of the man. The sturdy haft of the axe fractures in twain with a snap like a dry twig. In the same instant the man pivots to narrow his stance. Keen tusks tear through his trousers where his legs meet.

The momentum of the charge carries the beast through and on, past the man to crash snout-first with a prodigious spray of leaves and earth.

Svend scrambles for the spear, brandishes the weapon but remains where he stands.

The boar lies still, dead, the axe-head buried in the bones of its thick neck.

Svend turns to look wide-eyed at his uncle, who himself stands staring down upon the fallen creature in profound astonishment.

It is only then both notice the large rent in the man's trousers. He bleeds freely from a deep slash on his inner thigh.

The man returns Svend's disquieted look, then studies the ruined trousers growing heavy with his blood. He reaches inside the gaping hole to check for unseen damage... is relieved to find that Sassa may still be satisfied.

Despite the harrowing moment, Svend can not suppress his grin at watching his uncle confirm he is still intact as a man. "These beasts know nothing of honor in battle, would you say uncle?" smirks Svend.

The man shares in Svend's mirth, then turns his attention to the massive boar. With the haft sheared off at the shoulder, it requires several kicks to free the axe-head from the bones of the brute's neck. The man turns the blade for examination, frowns. The bit appears worse-for-wear, badly chipped.

"It seems the einherjar shall go hungry tonight," says Svend, "for surely that is Sæhrímnir you have killed." He kicks the beast with a boot. "That thing is too large to drag home."

"Then we shall make it smaller," says the man as he

draws his hand axe and sets to work parting out the creature's massive carcass.

* * *

The farmstead is a wealthy one: a newly built longhouse of the modern style flanked by two structures of nearly the same length to form a courtyard where several horses are pinned. On the expansive porch of the home, a dark skinned female thrall works at the butter churn with weary arms. A like-featured male thrall mucks filthy straw from the horses' enclosure.

The man and Svend have already trekked past a large herd of meaty oxen and through an expansive field of recently harvested corn by the time they arrive at the farmhouse. Svend drags a hind leg of the great boar, as large itself as a full grown sow. The man has the massive head and neck of the creature across his back. The long curling tusks wrapped in bits of the animal's own thick hide, serve as handles.

The thralls gape in horrified wonder at the two: A giant carrying the head of what could be naught but a mountain demon across his back. And an impressively built, yet relatively smaller man following with a portion of bloody meat, enough to feed a village, in tow. Both strangers are covered and dripping with gore.

Unable to bear the unnerving sight a moment longer, the female thrall leaps to her feet with a clattering of the overturned churning stool, rushes into the house, her strange tongue calling out in panic to her master. The male thrall stands resigned to whatever horrible fate approaches.

Onto the porch comes the lady of the house. She is well fed and unburdened by youth or comeliness. The lady wears a fine linen dress of shaded white. A scarf of the same material ties up her muddy yellow hair. She looks to the men with cautious reserve.

The man and Svend stop at a respectful distance.

"Are we welcome?" queries Svend.

"What is your name?" rejoins the lady.

"I am Svend Caldersen. This is my uncle."

"You are welcome," the lady states.

The man and Svend approach the porch toting their bounty.

The male thrall remains dumb as a post, muckrake in hand, jaw agape at the sight. The clean-limbed horses stir and snort uneasily. The female thrall timidly pokes her head from the dark interior of the longhouse as if wondering what manner of creature, these.

When they have reached the base of the porch where the lady stands, the man shrugs the boar's head from his back to let it fall with a heavy thud on the packed earth. The lady looks down on the grizzly offering as if it is a thing she can not fully identify.

"In reparations for hunting your land," states the man.

"And this," says Svend as he tugs the hind-leg alongside the severed head.

The lady gazes in astonishment at the remains, smiles queerly at the men. "Such gifts from strangers. Are you travelers? Will you take a meal?"

"We live only a few glens from here. We are expected home for supper," says Svend.

The lady looks to the man with no little wonder at his stature. Her eyes thoroughly take him in, then stop at the rent in his trousers where blood trickles even now. Her gaze lingers, then she shakes herself as if from a dream.

"And your name?" the lady would know of the man. "Who would my husband call upon, as a gift demands a gift."

Svend knows his uncle would deny any payment and answers quickly, "You may ask for the woodcutter. There are few who would not know him." Svend ignores the leaden sideways glance of his uncle.

"I doubt not," says the lady. Her eyes travel again to the

man's opened trousers. "You are wounded. A poultice for your leg?"

The man inclines his head in gratitude, but raises a hand in way of dismissal as he turns to leave. Svend follows.

The lady eagerly calls to stay them, "Mead for your journey home then."

The man stops abruptly, causing Svend to stumble into his back.

The lady turns to her female thrall cowering in the doorway, commands with a single word. The girl scurries inside only to quickly return with a weighty hammered pitcher and large drinking mugs. The lady takes the pitcher, fills the mugs with a fine golden mead, one for the man, one for Svend.

The man drains the mug in a single draft. The lady stands ready, refills his mug to overflowing.

"This appears only a small portion of meat from your kill," says the lady, "I bid you, take a game-sled and my thrall to bear the remainder to your home."

The man is in mid quaff when Svend answers for them both, "We would accept your generosity with great thanks."

The man chokes on a drop of mead. He looks down on his nephew with a frown, this time impossible for Svend to ignore.

"Come now," says the lady, "no man is so rich it truly pains him to be repaid."

The man assents to the wise words, looks to his empty mug, offers it to be refilled.

❊ ❊ ❊

The man is yoked to a loaned game-sled. A deep forward lean into the harness keeps the curved wood rails grinding onward at a steady pace over the worn earth of the narrow path. The giant boar's carcass overfills every side of the sled to drag on the ground. Sweat pours from the man's face and hair, soaks his shirt through until there is not a spot of dry cloth.

Svend and the dark-skinned thrall carry the sow between them lashed to a sapling cut to serve as a pole.

The lady's man-thrall has proved utterly useless in carrying even the sow alone, much less towing the sled. Though a grown man, he stands barely to Svend's shoulder, and is hardly half as stout as the youth.

Svend had many questions for the strange fellow at first; which land was he captured from, and how did he come to belong to the lady and her husband? If all the folk of his land were of such dark features, or if he had somehow been stained to his color? If there were any of his people who grew to the size and strength of a man?

The thrall claims he had been a man of wealth in his homeland. He had possessed land, goats, horses... groves of trees bearing figs and olives. He tells of vast orchards where the tree's branches sagged with clusters of sweet dates. He speaks of a land where the sun blazes warm even in the mid of winter.

Svend quickly grows weary of the man's ceaseless chatter. His high-pitched sing-song voice and butchery of their language grates on the boy's nerves until, annoyed, Svend queries, "What good is a thrall who can not labor, even to carry a yearling sow without help?"

The thrall misinterprets Svend's questioning as license to speak freely, "I can not alone bear such a load, it is true, but I was not bred as a pack animal. In my homeland I was an artisan of some note. And though here my arts are not desired, I can herd goats and draw milk from cattle and cure a horse of colic."

"As can any woman," grumbles Svend.

The thrall falls silent then, having learned well enough in his time with his Norse masters; 'A glib tongue that goes on chattering sings to its own harm.'

* * *

Sassa takes coin from the ship builder and bids him good journey as her husband, Svend, and the thrall emerge from the woods into the clearing of the farmstead.

The ship builder, seeing them also, urges his horse along, straining into the traces of the cart loaded with split planks the man had taken the day before from a straight-grained oak. He looks back over his shoulder often as he hurries away.

Sassa proudly holds up two tiny hammer-stamped pennies to show her husband as he approaches.

The man hauls the sled and boar carcass to where Sassa stands gaping with raised eyebrows and astounded amusement at the load he bears. He shrugs free of the harness, takes the pennies from Sassa to examine them: A pair of crudely stamped forgeries of Celtic coin with the likeness of a minor king of Ireland. The man frowns after the retreating ship builder as Sassa plucks the coins from his palm.

She is entranced with the massive carcass of the boar. "And what manner of whale is this that grows hair?" Her tone playful and mocking, "Tell me it is not for the cooking pot."

"It is a boar!" exclaims Svend, "A boar as large as an oxen when it was whole. Its tusks were as long as your arm, and it could have swallowed a hound with a single bite. We were hunting the thickest woods when I... when we came upon a drove of young sow..."

Sassa ignores the lad's rambling tale as she studies her husband.

The man is covered in blood of the battle, gore of the slaughter, and sweat-soaked through and through. He reaches for his wife.

Sassa repels him with straightened arms, a hurried step back, and a sharp proclamation, "You will be in the stream long before you are in my embrace."

Svend has not paused in his telling of the hunt, "...heard a crashing through the brush and I reached for the spear, but uncle..."

"Svend," interrupts Sassa, "a tale as wondrous as yours

should be told at table, and after a share of mead. You may be surprised how well a story grows with the proper nurturing." She looks down on the hulking carcass, cocks her head. "Though how much larger a tale than this in truth, I wonder.

"Now, the two of you finish with the butchering, fill my pot, send your strange little friend back to where he belongs, and for the sake of all that is good, scrub yourselves clean, clothes and all." With a sharp turn on her heel she is off.

Svend urges the thrall on toward the longhouse with the sow on the pole between them.

The man stands, watches Sassa until she disappears into their home, then sighs longingly and takes up the sled's harness once again.

❀ ❀ ❀

The aroma of boiling pork reaches Svend and the man as they bathe in the clear cold stream that cuts through the farmstead.

"We should have taken a meal at the farmer's home." Svend's complaints are nearly as loud as the grumbling of the man's stomach.

The men trudge from the stream and hastily dress in clothes still damp from washing, their hunger more demanding at the moment than their comfort. They gather their weapons and hurry to the longhouse.

Sassa has just settled the bread pan into the coals. The deep iron caldron which has been moved to hang over the hottest part of the fire, steams and bubbles. Onions and turnips balance atop the sections of sow, cut small to allow more in the generous pot. The heady aroma that fills the house sets the man's stomach to rumbling again.

Tora sits on the furs of the sleeping benches to braid Nanna's hair. Kari, in turn, practices her braids on a strand of Tora's hair. The women and girls look up to the men as they enter.

The man stows his weapons and goes to his wife. He allows her to stand from the fire before taking her in his arms, nuzzles his lips into her neck.

"Would you have your meal first, or..." Sassa allows her suggestive question to trail off.

"Have I a choice?" asks the man.

"No," says Sassa as she pushes herself from her husband's embrace. He allows it. A game they often play. The anticipation of what is delayed, second in pleasure only to the act itself.

"Sassa tells me the two of you traveled to Jötunheim to hunt boar this day," says Tora.

"Mother, such a beast you have never seen," says Svend, "and uncle, with a single blow of his axe, cleaved it nearly in two."

"And took a wound for it," says Sassa as she readies a poultice in her mixing stone. She grinds seeds and berries, pours a bit of liquid from a small vile made from a tip of antler, powder from another vile, a murmured chant in the old tongue, and the remedy is prepared.

Sassa gestures for her husband to take a seat on the sleeping bench. She kneels before him to apply the healing mixture to his leg through the rent in his damp trousers, rubs the smooth poultice onto the wound much longer than necessary as she looks up to her husband with her playful grin from between his legs. He reaches for her but she scampers away before he can pull her to him. "The bread!" she exclaims as she hurries to take the iron baking pan from the coals.

The bread is blackened on the bottom, but the butter sweet, and the boiled pork is tender and savory with onions and turnips. The mead, divine, at the peak of ferment. The family feasts to Svend's telling of the day's adventure.

Sassa and Tora playfully interject their own outlandish exaggerations when Svend's tale strays too far from sooth. Kari and Nanna giggle with the laughter of the others.

The man eats unrestrained, plenty for all this night. His appetite, legendary on the worst of days, tonight, beyond reckoning, fueled by the long day and welcome company.

When all have eaten their fill, the mead has worked its blissful magic, and the girls doze on lambskins by the waning fire, Sassa smiles to her sister and broaches a heard rumor, "You have had a proposal of marriage."

"Tolaf Sorrensson," announces Tora without enthusiasm.

Svend, well into his cups, speaks with thinly veiled derision and the hubris of his age, "He is a merchant."

"And your uncle a woodcutter," reminds Sassa.

"Yes, but the greatest woodcutter there has ever been," counters Svend.

Tora remains patient with the subject, a delicate one with her son. "Tolaf Sorrensson is a fine man. He owns land and his own trading fleet."

"Three boats is not a fleet, mother," grumbles Svend, tipping his already empty cup to his lips. He frowns at the empty mug, looks to his uncle. "He trades in furs and wax and other things he does not even produce himself."

"He is a respected man," says Tora with little conviction.

Svend reaches for the mead pitcher. Sassa pulls it from his reach.

Svend smirks and raises his chin with pride. "Father was a respected man. He was a warrior. He went raiding and took what he wanted from the same cities Tolaf Sorrensson makes trade with."

"And it killed him," blurts Tora, her cheeks flush with passion.

Svend scoffs, "It is better to be a dead warrior than a live merchant."

Tora lowers her eyes, covers her mouth with a quavering hand as if to prevent unwelcome words from taking flight.

The silence Svend has brought to the house gives him

pause.

All look to the man for the final word on the subject.

"'It is better to be blind than to burn on a pyre. There is nothing the dead can do,'" says the man, reciting the well known and respected maxim.

"The dead can not provide," adds Tora.

Svend is too young and too drunk for circumspection. "I will win fame and wealth and be an important man. And you, mother, you will want for nothing."

Tora has lost her energy for the fight as she pleads with her son, "The raids have taken every man in our family. If they take you too, what becomes of me?"

"I'm not going to die," scoffs Svend.

His mother cringes at the words.

"Are you so different than the gods who breathed life into you, Svend?" Sassa would know. "Even the gods die."

Svend shrugs off the notion with a wave of his empty cup. "Then I will die when I am old and gray and have had many adventures and won much wealth." Svend raises his chin to the man. "Like his grandfather. And I will leave a great hoard of treasure for my kin."

There is little profit arguing with the certainty of youth. The listeners fall silent.

A fatalistic grin twists the man's lips. He stands from the table, lays a hand on his nephew's shoulder. "It is good to be young and know our own fate," he says. He goes to the door to take up his broken hafted axe and whetstone. The man takes his place at the fire to hone the chip from the blade. He taps the head from the bit of haft, tosses the wood onto the fire. Examines the bit with a frown. A great deal of steel will need to be removed to give the blade its shape again.

Svend's mood grows dark with drink and the mocking tone of his uncle. He looks to Sassa. "Tell me my fate aunt Sassa. Divine from the runes if what I claim is not true."

"I will not," states Sassa. "'Let no man his fate before him see, and he will remain free from sorrow.'" She looks to her sister, fallen to melancholy from the turn of the discussion, lays a consoling hand on Tora's trembling hand. "Take a brand from the fire to guide your way home," offers Sassa.

Thus dismissed, Svend and Tora take their leave of the troubled house.

* * *

Sassa straddles her husband, facing him on his lap on the bench where he had been steadily honing. A deep notch remains in the bit, taken by the giant boar's spine. The notch will not be honed out. The ruined axe head lays on the floor now as the man's hands are occupied with Sassa's generous hips which undulate ever so gently. She holds in her palm the pennies with which the ship builder had purchased planks, turning them to catch the muted light of the single burning candle.

The man has little interest in the coins. His singular concern, the warmth and pressure of Sassa where her body meets his. The flowing motion of her hips. The soft curve of her breasts beneath the light dress worn thin through the years. Breasts rising and falling gently with each breath, and in such close proximity.

"He offered a single coin for the loaded cart," tells Sassa, "but I have not your eye for measure and I guessed that he would try and cheat me so I demanded two. Are they worth a lot?"

"A great fortune," murmurs the man.

Sassa is astounded, then notes the man is neither looking at, nor referring to the coins. She uses a firm hand to tilt his chin upward. "The coins," she says.

"They are false," he replies as he returns his attention to the smooth beauty of her glowing skin.

Sassa pouts, feeling foolish, disappointed at the revelation. Her hips cease to move.

"You received twice the amount I would have demanded, false or not," says the man.

Sassa's eyes come alight. "Truly? Enough for a new axe?"

"There are things we are more in need of."

Sassa drops the pennies on the table. The sound they make is thin, tinny.

"A new dress, perhaps," says the man as he runs his fingers softly along the lines of the frock, savoring the flow as it takes on the shape of his wife.

Sassa relishes the gentle touch of the hands that could be so brutal.

"But what use have I of a dress?" breathes Sassa, her voice growing husky with passion, "The days are still long and the house warm." She eases the garment from her shoulders allowing it to pool around her waist. His hands continue to flow, on bare skin now.

"I would leave you bare as the Valkyrie," murmurs the man into her ear, "but husbands would cease to love their wives, and wives would grow bitter with jealousy."

"And what concern have we with the men and women of this world?"

"None. I have but one concern."

Her mining for compliments never fails as if the man guards his tongue like a treasure horde, pouring forth riches only when compelled. His words valued as much as his embrace which she falls into now with abandon.

❊ ❊ ❊

The crispness of the morning air hints at the coming of winter as Sassa and the man trek the quarter-day to the city of Trondheim. Nanna balances on her father's shoulders. Kari hurries alongside her mother, envious of her young sister who is carried as if on a fabled steed, yearning for the days when she was not too old for such things.

The road to Trondheim is well traveled, and the family

is passed now and again by groups in horse drawn carts who offer friendly exchanges and good tidings. The travelers speak of news and rumors. Of gossip, new and old.

As the road crests a low rise, the sprawling city of Trondheim lies below. The expansive fjord is dotted with longboats -- well-nigh two-hundred in number -- anchored, with war banners of the various clans fluttering on their masts. Norway's King Hardrada's banner is prominent amongst them.

It is to be a war after all, the man knows, for a raiding fleet of such number would empty the coffers of a hundred kingdoms. Neither the man nor Sassa have seen so many ships before in their lives. They marvel at the vast number as the family continues to the city.

The city is packed to overflowing with warriors, merchants and families come to hear the announcement.

Men-at-arms of magnificent stature group together, drink mead from curved horns, call out compliments to passing women. The women receive the compliments with smiles and friendly jibes in return. Some stop to playfully flirt with the randy warriors, and receive outlandish promises of vast wealth for their attentions. Children run unchecked through the crush of humanity.

Sassa's eyes are wide with gleeful wonder. She keeps Kari and Nanna close. The man clears a path for his family through the morass.

A vendor at a small cart sells bits of honeycomb. The man stops and buys two small pieces for his daughters. They continue on.

They stop by the home of Tora and Svend. The smithery stands cold and abandoned. A single goose and two starved chickens wander the yard without hope of finding a morsel on the scavenged earth, and to what end without a gander or cock? The roof of the house sags unevenly and will collect crushing snow if not repaired before winter. The door fits poorly on dry, cracked leather hinges, worthless for shutting out the cold. Sassa and the man look to one another, silently sharing the knowledge that the house, and those in it, will require exceptional good fortune to survive another winter.

Sassa knocks on the door, calls inside for her sister. There is no answer. She looks without hope to the swarming mass of villagers and visitors. "We will never find them in this."

The man gazes above the heads of the crowd. He spots an argument brewing between two noblemen. A crowd forms around them in a circle to watch the coming fight. The man gestures. Sassa follows his gaze. Neither are surprised to find Tora is the cause of the dispute.

Tora, at the fore of the circle of onlookers, is filled with eager anticipation for the outcome of the fight.

The two noblemen shed their weapons, circle one another hurling insults back and forth.

"What use have you of a woman in any case? You are half mare yourself," says one.

"I am sorry to have interrupted your conversation with the lady as I mistook you for her mother," says the other.

Suddenly the two combatants rush one another, clash, grapple. They go to the ground fighting. The crowd cheers and jeers with excitement.

Sassa presses through the crowd to Tora. "This is your doing?" accuses Sassa.

Tora smiles innocently. "I was only speaking with one, then the other... suddenly they found fault with one another."

Sassa rolls her eyes, pulls Tora away by the arm. They disappear into the crowd with the man, Kari and Nanna.

When the grappling noblemen notice Tora has left, they lose interest in their quarrel, help each other to their feet, look foolishly to where Tora has disappeared. The crowd wanders away, searching for other amusement.

The man leads his family through the milling crowd. Sassa must raise her voice to be heard, "Where is Svend?"

"He was here a moment ago," says Tora. "Have you ever

seen such excitement? Jarls and noblemen from as far as Uppsala have come. They say the king himself will arrive soon."

"I never knew there were so many people in all of Norway," says Sassa with wonder.

The man presses through the crowded streets with his family in tow. Sassa and Tora chatter and gossip in a steady discursive flow close sisters can maintain endlessly. They speak with eager anticipation of the day to come.

Tora wears a comb in her hair and her most becoming dress. She will attract the attentions of the host of petty jarls and self-important merchants that populate the town for the announcement. It worries her not that the visiting suitors will tend more toward sweet lies, vast promises and a single night of clumsy, sweaty coupling, than true prospects.

Sassa wears her hair free and flowing but for a pair of thin braids from her temples to the base of her neck to keep her splendid locks from her face. Dressed in her faded blue dress she wears unbelted and without pinafore or undergarment, she draws more than her share of admiring looks. It would matter little if she were dressed in rags and wore a hay sack to cover her hair, advances from all manner of men will be plenty. Sassa neither encourages nor shuns the overtures. Any man's folly -- karl to king -- at vying for her attention remains mere amusement for her. For in the end, man must be compared to man, and there is no comparison to hers.

The man takes secret pleasure in the attentions his wife draws from the highest of noble to the lowest of thrall. The unconscious swagger it inspires in Sassa's bearing makes her all the more beautiful for the lust she inspires. He has never heard a single tale of the goddess Freyja -- the most beautiful of the Vanir -- subduing her own beauty for any reason: a beauty coveted by man, god and giant in equal measure. He likewise can find no reason for Sassa to subdue her own beauty. The comparison of his wife to the goddess is a just one to the man's mind, and he would challenge any man, giant or god to dispute it.

The sun makes an early appearance, burning through the overcast, warming the day. The family enjoys Frey's blessing as they travel through the tangle of streets and alleyways that make up Trondheim.

Merchants of every sort line the avenues to hawk their wares from beneath temporary tented stalls butted up against small homes and out-buildings. Vendors call to passing men in proclamations of the finest, the sharpest, the sturdiest of battle items. Theirs and theirs alone will bring good fortune in war.

Goods for women, children and others not going to war are even more plentiful. Hammered silver and gold arm rings and necklaces guaranteed to win the lasting love and fidelity of any white-armed woman while her husband is away. Exotic trinkets from lands unnamed. Thralls also from those lands: strange cowering folk with dark eyes that never rise to meet their prospective masters are on display, their worth exaggerated to embarrassing heights.

Sassa and Tora keep tight their grip on Nanna and Kari as they press through the throng, following the man who cleaves a path like the prow of a heavy longship cutting through unformed ice.

The clamor of twenty-thousand voices calling one above the other is deafening. The rank smell of so many closely packed together, dizzyingly odious. It is as if Loki the prankster had called for all dozen of the yearly festivals to be held at once, then left the revelers, each to their own antithetical purpose.

Sassa can not suppress her giddy smile at the sheer force of capricious energy that envelops them. She has never dreamed of a gathering such as this. People laugh and sing their intoxicated pleasure. Annoyed parents chide children. Fights erupt at random, causing great masses to gather around to shout encouragement to the combatants, and place wagers on the outcome.

The man overlooks it all, as he stands a head above the

tallest of warriors. A vendor's wares arrest his attention. He guides his family to the stand.

When Sassa sights where they are headed, she hurries ahead as if drawn by an incantation. Exquisite bolts of fabric in mounds of vibrant color, the weaving tight and fine. Silk, wool, linens... materials she can only guess at, transported from lands faraway and unknown to her. She is hesitant to touch the exotic cloths as if frightened they may turn to smoke under her caress.

The man stands over her, witness to the pleasure of his wife, knowing he has chosen well.

Tora and the girls rummage about the fabrics, each new color taking their attention from the last.

Sassa is mesmerized by a bolt of lavish material the color of deep violet fading to sun-drenched blue. She allows her fingers to lightly graze its silky surface with the caress of a lover.

The textile merchant patters on about the origin of the fabric: from far south and east where dyes made from only the most rare and precious of berries and flowers are used.

A noblewoman of high status, her wealth prominently displayed in the silver, glass and gold which adorns her neck and arms, takes interest in the bolt Sassa covets.

The man drifts casually yet insistently between the noblewoman and Sassa, leaving his wife in sole possession of bolt both women would have.

Sassa has seen cloth as fine as this only once. It was during the Thing, years ago, when a lady of the king's family sat presiding beside her husband, a high-born noble of the Rus. The lady had sat upright on her stool, dignified and elegant in her trappings. Sassa had marveled at how the breath-light material of her dress clung to the curvature of the ladies breasts, hips, legs. Sassa had never seen the likes of such fabric before, and not again until now.

Sassa suddenly comes to herself, hastily replaces the bolt where she had found it, steps back from the table.

The noblewoman immediately reaches for the cloth, but the man gathers it up before she can claim it for her own.

The merchant tingles with the prospect of two parties bidding for his wares until the man digs into the leather purse that hangs at his hip and produces a single thin coin.

"That is meant for a new axe," states Sassa firmly.

The man wedges the coin into a crevice between the wooden planks of the table and bends the coin toward, then away. The silver coin snaps in twain. He places half the penny in his purse, looks to the merchant to finalize the purchase.

The merchant licks his lips nervously. His eyes dart to the noblewoman, then to the man, then the half penny still wedged in the table. More than a fair price for two such bolts on any other day, but far less than he had hoped with the village filled to overflowing with foreign wealth.

The man looks down upon the merchant, his eyes narrowed, unblinking. The merchant drops his eyes to the half-pen, tugs it from the table, nods his assent.

The noblewoman huffs her displeasure.

Sassa buries her face into her husband's shirt, tugs at it in delight to vent her excitement.

The man would have paid double... a thousand times the amount for such a reaction.

Sassa looks up to her husband, her eyes brimming, lips trembling with a smile. He presses the fabric into her arms, places a hand on her back to usher her away into the throng.

The cloth merchant breathes a sigh of relief as the giant gains distance from his stall.

"Let me carry it," insists Nanna.

"With your sister," says Sassa. She can not take her eyes from the luxurious fabric. "It will make a beautiful dress, dresses for all of us, and you Tora. Gowns!"

Tora looks longingly at the fabric and jealously at the man. She makes her best attempt at a happy smile.

An eager murmur ripples outward through the crowd as the sea of humanity flows toward the town meeting place for the announcement.

The meeting place is a wide-open courtyard not far from the docks, headed by the towering great hall, circled by stables and storage buildings. It is already packed beyond capacity with those come to hear the announcement.

On the elevated porch which extends from the hall, Jarl Carr Kolbrand of Trondheim presides. A host of noblemen of high standing take their places on the porch and wait for the crowd to settle so their voices might be heard.

Jarl Kolbrand drums on the heavy wood planks of the porch with the end of a stout stave designed for the purpose. The crowd begins to quiet. Time and success have aged the jarl, as it will any man. He has taken on the look of a once-mighty warrior who has become wealthy and gone to seed. His belly strains against his belt. Though thinning to reveal pink scalp beneath, his hair is worn long and recedes well past the crown of his head.

At Jarl Kolbrand's shoulder stands Eystein Orri, captain of the king's army and betroth to King Hardrada's youngest daughter, Maria. While still shy of his thirtieth year, Eystein has already gained reputation as a warrior of great strategy and cunning. Tall, well muscled, in his prime of life. A magnificent sword slung at his hip and a confident half-smile which extends to his eyes. It would come to be known that wisp of smile rarely leaves the captain, not in the thick of battle, not in his sleep. King Hardrada recognized Eystein's potential from an early age and has groomed him accordingly. Eystein Orri will enter the line of succession to the throne upon his marriage to Maria, only behind the king's own sons. He is well spoken and keen of mind. A handsome man of winning ways, it is said he has a matchless eye for quality in horses and men.

When the dense rumble of those assembled can be

shouted over, Jarl Kolbrand begins his address, "Neighbors, friends... many of you know me. I am Carr Kolbrand, jarl of Trondheim and I welcome you, welcome you all from near and far."

The crowd responds with drunken fervor. Many of the men have not been free of their cups since the day before.

The jarl continues when he can be heard again. He gestures to the great hall behind him, "My hall is warm and well appointed. When you travel you are welcome to a seat at my tables."

A few confirming cheers rise from the crowd.

"I will state what seems to be obvious. King Hardrada, our mighty ruler, is gathering an army."

Competing chants of various loosely banded squads of warriors from across Norway drown out Jarl Kolbrand. The jarl pounds on the boards with his sounding staff. The chants fade, cease, allowing Kolbrand to continue, "The king of England has died without an heir. King Hardrada lays legal claim to the crown."

A lone voice rises from the crowd, "Of England?"

"Lay down your mead horn for a moment and clear your ears," Jarl Kolbrand gibes, "Yes, England! He is already king of Norway!"

The crowd erupts in cries of laughter and jeers. The jarl allows the moment to play with an entertained smile creasing his features.

Eystein Orri remains stoic, impossible to determine if it is amusement or disdain he expresses with his vague smile. He scans the crowd with a practiced eye. Many warriors stand out in the morass -- a predator of men recognizes like -- but his eyes are arrested when they land on the man.

Though a full head above the tallest in the crowd, two tiny heads rise even above his. The red-gold of their hair flames in the sun. Daughters, no doubt, Eystein believes, hoisted on their father's shoulders for better vantage of the happenings. At first sight Eystein Orri reckons the man to be standing on a box or riser of some sort, but the constant ebb and flow of the crowd proves the man stands on nothing but the soles of his boots. Powerfully built and broad of shoulder as one of the Aesir.

Eystein leans to one of Jarl Kolbrand's retainers who share the porch with them, a man whose name he has already forgotten. "That man," Eystein queries without taking his eyes from the giant, "the one in the back who appears to be mounted. What is his name?"

The retainer needs no clarification. The one of whom they speak stands as a man among children. "He is the woodcutter," states the retainer.

"His name," demands Eystein once again.

"He bears no name other than that."

Woodcutter. The mystery of it leaves Eystein intrigued.

Jarl Kolbrand's talent lies in his ability to inspire a mob. His voice rises clearly above the murmuring din, "Every man who accompanies the king as a warrior of his army will be granted a plot of English land and English thralls to work it."

The voice of the crowd begins to rise. The jarl's energy rises to match.

"There is goodly rain and little snow in England. The rivers never ice over. The soil is black, the women, ripe, and the treasures... Every man shall be rich!"

The warriors within the crowd erupt with fervor, crush toward the porch to be the first to sign on for the voyage.

Jarl Kolbrand continues to shout though few can hear now for the clamor, "Every man who would gain riches, take up your weapons and ready yourself at the fjord the day after the morrow when we sail for our new kingdom!"

Eystein Orri watches, bewildered, as the man turns his back, and with the frenzied crowd parting for him like a giant stone in a raging river, plows his way in opposition to the surging mass.

❄ ❄ ❄

On the edge of the city, clear of the hysteria of the mob, the family stops to gather themselves.

"We have surely lost Svend to the war," weeps Tora.

Sassa is there to comfort her sister. "It is still two days until they sail. He will have to come home before then. We will talk sense into him. You will see." Cradling Tora's head on her shoulder, Sassa looks up to her husband without conviction.

The man had recognized Svend as one of the first to reach the stand where the jarl and his men were taking war recruits. No need to reveal this to Tora. Her plaintive sobs for the duration of their long walk home would not do.

The girls sleep soundly carried in their father's arms for the trek home. Sassa carries the bolt of fine fabric like a third child. Tora carries only her grief.

They no sooner reach the farmstead when Tora insists on returning to the city. Sassa offers her sister a bed for the night, but Tora, afraid Svend might return to find her not there, and leave again, insists on returning to her own home.

Ravenous with hunger for the excitement of the day, the girls wake before their father can put them to their beds. Nanna demands to be fed. Kari's wants go unannounced, her soft timid voice rarely heard for such matters. Instead, she pouts quietly in her manner to make her desire known.

Sassa stokes the fire to life and places the pot filled with last-nights stew over the renewed flames to boil.

The man exits but returns shortly with a great arm-load of split wood for Sassa to avail herself.

Before steam rises from the cooking pot, Nanna is asleep again, and Kari teeters where she sits on the sleeping bench, her eyelids drooping heavily.

The man sits at the table fitting his axe-head with a hew haft. A greatly futile task as the axe is all but useless, the notch in the ruined bit beyond repair. But even a damaged axe is better than no axe at all.

An extravagance using the half-pen to purchase such

fine and expensive material for his wife, but daydreams of
how Sassa will look in a dress made from it erases all remorse.

The remaining half-pen for a new axe head, a full penny
for fodder and stores for the coming winter, and they will
again be left with little. But they have had little before, and
little has always proved to be more than enough.

The house has warmed and filled with the aroma of
wood smoke, savory meat and boiling onions. Sassa places
yesterday's cold loaves on the table along with a pitcher of
buttermilk, and is about to announce supper prepared when
there is a solid thumping on the door.

The man stands from the table, his axe in hand, held to
his side. Kari comes fully awake with a start. The man and
Sassa look to one another. Visitors here, nearly unheard of...
and after nightfall.

"Am I welcome?" the call from outside the door is issued
in a substantial voice comfortable with the request.

"What is your name," rejoins Sassa.

"I am Eystein Orri of Ringerike."

Sassa looks to her husband, disconcerted. The man nods
his assent.

"You are welcome," says Sassa.

The one who enters their home is even more impressive
and well appointed than he appeared at the gathering. The
king's captain wears a fine linen shirt the color of a stormy sea
draped loosely over his solid frame, and well fitting trousers
made of soft kid skin. His boots are of a heavier leather but
equally as fine. The pommel and cross guard of the sword on
his hip are cast in silver, and he wears many silver arm rings
of various design. He stands in the threshold, examining every
dark corner of the home before entering further.

"There are no enemies awaiting you here," assures Sassa.

Eystein Orri's smile increases for a heartbeat, then fades
to its protective standard. He carefully closes the door behind
himself. "'Rash is the man who relies on his good luck in a hall
not his own,'" recites the visitor.

Eystein commands himself not to stare at the man, but a person of such impressive stature he has never seen. Even King Hardrada himself, though well-nigh as tall, has not the thickness of shoulder and arm as the man. Eystein relents to take in the giant from boots to eyes, which he holds, but not without a slight craning of his own neck.

The man allows the visitor to look up to him a moment longer, then retakes his seat, easily cradling his axe across his thighs. He gestures with a nod for the visitor to sit also.

Eystein chooses a seat at the table quartered away from the man, out of arm's reach, and allows himself a more leisurely examination of the home: Common enough, but of exceptional craftsmanship of the old style. Exceedingly well maintained. Runes skillfully carved around the door frame, inside and out.

The beautiful child who shoots bashful looks at him from beneath flaming red locks is near his youngest son's age. The other, younger still, sleeps sprawled on top of the bedding for the cozy warmth of the home.

"Supper is prepared," announces Sassa to include the visitor.

"I took an early meal before traveling here," states Eystein, "but in truth, I was able to follow the wonderful aroma of your cooking pot from a glen away."

"A small bowl then," says Sassa as she places a large wood trencher heaped with savory pork stew before her husband. She pours each man's cup full of mead, places the pitcher between them. Kari brings a bowl of soft butter from the home's dairy.

Nanna sleeps, tiny snoring noises coming from the child with each deep breath.

Sassa serves Eystein next then Kari then herself. She sets a full bowl and a bit of bread aside perchance Nanna should wake. When everyone is served and seated, they begin.

Despite his claim to having already eaten, Eystein shows an appetite to rival the man's. He eats a whole loaf, a second large bowl of stew, and gives thanks for each of many refills of his cup. He sits erect at the table, chews each mouthful thoroughly and only speaks to compliment Sassa on the quality of the meal.

The man speaks not at all.

When the pot has been emptied and the last of the stew has been mopped from bowls with the final loaf of bread, Sassa fills cups with mead once again.

Eystein looks to the man with his queer half-smile as if the world were designed to amuse him. "To whom do I give thanks for this generous hospitality?"

Sassa and Kari clear the table of empty bowls and spoons.

"I am Sassa, Kari and Nanna are our daughters. This is my husband."

A curious response thinks Eystein. "Are you an outlaw to hide your name?"

"I have none," states the man.

"You asked in the village before traveling here," says Sassa without question.

"I did," says Eystein.

"And what did you hear?"

Eystein struggles to not become annoyed with the woman and the seeming insolence. "That your husband has no name."

Sassa shrugs to end the discussion.

Eystein persists, "What do you call him?"

"Husband."

"And to kin?"

"He has none to claim," says Sassa.

Eystein allows his bravado to override his habit of circumspection, his mocking tone directed to the man, "Then perhaps you sprang forth by the hand of God, fashioned of clay. Or of the old gods, perhaps, carved by Odin himself from the wood of an ash. Life breathed into you by his brothers."

The man remains stoically fixed on the nobleman.

Sassa smiles as she speaks with conspiratorial sincerity to their visitor, "You must try harder if you wish for a rise from him. 'The wise man has his way of dealing with those who taunt him at table: He smiles through the meal, not seeming to hear the twaddle talked by his foes.'"

Eystein is incensed. Simple folk, lowly karls do not speak with men of standing in such a manner. He sits more erect, his legs coiled beneath him ready to spring to his feet if his next words draw a violent response, "I do not speak twaddle, and I have not come here as a foe, but if you wish to make it so..."

"Would you care for his tale?" interrupts Sassa with a gentle lilt and a warm smile.

The man's posture does not change, nor does the fix of his gaze. His hands never leave the haft of his axe.

"Does he not speak for himself?" Eystein's voice rings with annoyance. The coy game has gone on long enough.

"When need be," answers Sassa.

"Then speak now for there is need! I am Eystein Orri, captain to the king's army, and I will be answered!"

Violence is near. The men coiled, strain to be at one another.

Sassa circles behind Eystein, runs a delicate hand across his shoulders from one to the other. It is a long journey and the woman takes her time. "A man is master at home. He does his own bidding," Sassa reminds their visitor. "And most men would prefer my voice to his, in any case."

The glare maintained between the men is broken as the adroit touch of the woman of such singular beauty takes precedence over all other thought. Eystein's eyes are taken by Sassa as she rounds him to assume a seat on her husband's side of the table. Not the most steadfast of men could have done differently.

Sassa drinks from her husband's cup and begins, "In a land far to the north where the sun lingers endlessly in summer and hides away at length in winter, a man and a woman made their home. He was a farmer and warrior, who each season would travel on raids to far away lands, and return with riches to make their home a prosperous and comfortable one. She, the daughter of a great warrior, the greatest of his time. Tall and fair, with the spirit of her father and the beauty of a Valkyrie. Vanadis, her name." Sassa pauses in her telling as Nanna wakes, sleepy-eyed, grumpy and crying for her supper.

The man stands and places a hand on Sassa's shoulder to keep her seated as he takes his youngest her cup of buttermilk and bowl of stew.

Eystein's anger is halved as his curiosity is piqued. A man who rises to care for his daughter when a stranger sits at their table: A revealing insight to character, one which will make his task here ever so much more difficult, if achieved at all.

Kari brings a bit of bread to Nanna as an excuse to curl up in her father's lap. Nanna is silent with her supper as Sassa continues her telling of her husband's tale.

"One fair summer day while the woman's husband was away with the raids, a stranger came to their home. He was mounted on a giant stallion with a golden mane, and his ready smile shone as gold also. He was tall as a god, and knew well how to speak honeyed words, so when he asked if he were welcome, the woman was eager to have him stay." Sassa sips mead from her husband's cup, looks to her listener with wide eyes and a cloying smile. "And stay he did -- for three days and three nights -- then was gone."

Eystein is entranced by the telling: the rich words and the lips that speak them.

Sassa continues with melodramatic sorrow, "The lady Vanadis' husband never returned from the raids." Her eyes and voice light with dramatic uplift. "But it came to be that she was with child!" Sassa drops her eyes behind her long lashes, fully aware of the beguiling effect she is having on her listener.

And it is true. Eystein is mesmerized.

"Sadly, the lady perished with the bearing of the magnificent infant: a boy who came forth from her womb in silence," tells Sassa. "The babe was suckled by the women of the village until weaned. Then on that day, the boy's grandfather -- the father of his mother -- came to collect him.

"Upon first meeting, the great warrior looked down upon the weanling and spoke these very words to him; 'You have killed my beautiful daughter, my only living kin left in this world, and you will surely die before we reach our destination.' And with that he gathered up the child, placed him in a basket, and carried him away."

Sassa seeks inspiration from the mead cup once again and leans toward her listener as she continues, "Yet the boy did not die that day, nor the next, and they landed here in the forest of Trondheim where the great warrior made his home.

"Each morning the grandfather would wake the boy with a rough hand and the harsh words, 'You shall not live through this day.' Yet each day, not only did the child live, but he thrived, growing ever larger and stronger.

"There were few visitors to the home as the grandfather's temperament did not lend itself to friendship. But for a half-mad Christian thrall, the frequent calls upon the legendary warrior by many of the village women were the boy's only company, and they only welcomed for a night of boisterous rutting, then in the morn were sent scurrying back to their husbands.

"Not few were the holmgang duels the boy witnessed between his grandfather and jealous husbands. But his grandfather was peerless in battle and he fell each of his challengers with crushing blows of his venerable battle-axe... Skull-seeker."

Eystein is startled from his trance by the title of the storied weapon. He shoots an astonished look to the man. Could it be true? Eystein's mind swirls.

The man reclines on an elbow to cradle his daughters as they sleep at his side, a soft humming from him to lull the children.

Sassa continues, "When the boy was not yet knee-high to his grandfather, a hand-axe was placed in his tiny fist -- as large to the boy as a long-axe to a grown man -- and he was set to work cutting bark and kindling for the winter fires.

"The boy took to the task with a fervor that should have filled his grandfather with wondrous pride. Yet the hard man's only words to the lad were the same, and the same every day.

"In the night when the grandfather was deep into his cups, and the boy hid in the shadows to be out of mind and out of reach of the strap, the aged warrior would sing tales of battles and of the gods. In that way the boy came to know of Odin, Freyja, Tyr, Thor and all the Aesir. He learned of the giants and their never ending battles with the gods. Of Loki and his hateful children; the serpent, the wolf, and Hel. He came to know of the craftsmen dwarves and magical elves. Of Asgard and Helheim and of all manner of being of the Nine Realms. Never were these tales intended for the boy, but for the old warrior's glory alone.

"Each summer when the ice broke in the fjord, the boy's grandfather would lead the raids to lands so distant they have yet to be named. Each winter he would return with the riches that expanded his holdings until he held sole possession of the vast forest that surrounds us now."

Sassa whets her tongue and a rivulet of mead runs from her lips, down her chin to drip and disappear beyond her dress between her breasts.

Eystein follows the honeywine's golden trail with breathless, rapt attention. When he regains control of his faculty, he remembers himself, risks a glance to the man.

The man stares at Eystein without emotion, holds his eyes until the nobleman shakes himself free of the stoic gaze, returns his attention to Sassa and the story she tells.

Sassa blesses her husband with a coy smile that encompasses eyes as well as lips, the mead working its magic to remove what little modesty she possesses from her bearing.

"The boy grew fast and strong, and first hefted his grandfather's splitting axe when he was but seven years of age. The lad was equal in size to boys traveling to their first Thing when he was eight. Still the grandfather refused to show pride nor utter words other than the bitter ones already offered."

Sassa looks to her husband who tends to Nanna and Kari, covering them with soft furs where they sleep on their bench. She continues with melancholy, "When the boy was nine, his grandfather, the renowned berserk warrior, Gunnar Skull-crusher, having grown weary of slaughtering mortals, offered himself up to Odin. He rides the benches of Valhöll to this day, awaiting Ragnarök when he will lead the Allfather's einher-jar against the giants and the rabble army of Hel and her sire, Loki."

Awed and intrigued as the truth of the man's lineage comes upon him, Eystein leans forward in rapt fascination.

"Yet the boy's story does not end there," Sassa continues, "He buried his grandfather in a ship-mound on the highest crest on the land, and began working his trade as a woodcutter."

Sassa's eyes sparkle with a playful light as she blushes at her husband who watches her now. She continues with a seductive lilt, her gaze never leaving his. "When the man was fully grown, as grown as any man has ever grown, he met a maiden. She was the most fair and alluring maiden he had ever, or will ever lay eyes or hands upon. Their love was deep and true for one another at first meeting, and in their love they had two most beautiful daughters." Sassa directs the closing of her tale to their visitor, "And happily they lived for all time."

The smile on Eystein's face is of genuine pleasure as he raises his cup in salute to Sassa. "Your father's name would not be Bragi, would it?"

Sassa blushes anew at the high praise for her telling and rises on slightly unsteady legs for the prodigious amount of mead required to properly recite such a saga. She carries the remaining dining bowls from the table to the washing tub, plops down on the stool to clean them.

Anger and notions of violence are forgotten as Eystein raises his cup to the man. "Skol, grandson of Gunnarr Skullcrusher... Son of Rig," he says, looking closely for reaction in the man.

Sassa looks from Eystein to her husband. Will he at last accept an honorable name given?

The man rises from his daughter's sleeping bench to resume his seat at the table. He raises his cup to Eystein. "Skol."

Hearing no protest from the man, Eystein states, "I shall dub you Rigsen, for there seems little doubt to who your true father is."

The man considers the notion and name, but not for the first time. He nods his assent, drinks.

Eystein waits until the man has raised his cup to his lips before he speaks again, "In any case, it is better than my calling you husband."

A bit of mead coughed from the man's nose brings joyous laughter from both Sassa and Eystein. The man eyes them both with a sham scowl as he brushes mead from his shirtfront.

"I will be honored to afford you a prominent position on my own longship when we sail for England," says Eystein.

Sassa's look flicks suddenly to their visitor, hardens there.

"I am not going to England," says the man.

Eystein is taken by surprise, yet undaunted. He knows he must have this man in his guard, if not for his lineage that will surely bolster the fighting men, then for his physical stature which will doubtless strike fear in the heart of the bravest of foes. "You must have guessed the reason for my visit," says Eystein, "As fine as the meal was, and as glorious the saga told, I have come for a warrior."

"I am no warrior."

"You are no woodcutter. Your destiny lies far beyond this forest. Your lineage demands it."

"Do you demand it?" challenges Sassa.

"I have been a warrior since my fourteenth year," says Eystein, "I have commanded great armies, and command one now. I have traveled widely and know what spirit governs the men I meet. And this I know; forcing a man to war makes a poor warrior." Eystein notes the carved symbols around the door's frame. "You are versed in runes?"

Sassa speaks a warning, "I know how to cut them, read them, stain them, prove them, call them, and score them. And I know how to send them." She adds menace to her voice as she repeats, "I know how to send them."

"Cast them for me now," says Eystein ignoring the thinly veiled threat, "tell me how the battle will go. It may ease your mind about your husband going to war."

Sassa considers Eystein for a moment longer, then moves across the room to a carved wood box near the sleeping benches. Inside is a leather bag which she retrieves. She returns to the table. Sassa chants an incantation under her breath in a language the men are not privy to, then abruptly upends the bag. Thumb-sized chips of wood carved with rune symbols spill onto the table.

Both men watch as Sassa hovers over the runes to divine what they have to tell.

"What do you see?" asks Eystein.

Sassa looks up solemnly from her divination. "I see the raven at rest."

"A good sign!" declares Eystein, his smile broadening, "No carrion for ravens."

"Or they have eaten their fill," says Sassa.

A flighty wave of Eystein's hand dismisses the notion. A heavy gilded crucifix on a leather thong falls from his shirt with the gesture.

"You are Christian," states Sassa with a frown of puzzlement, "the runes hold no sway with you."

Eystein self-consciously tucks the crucifix back into his shirt. "I am bound to King Hardrada. The king has taken the new god, so his captain and son-in-law-to-be must take him also," says Eystein with no little lament. "An afterlife walking hand in hand with the Christ for eternity like a helpless child...." He shakes his head sadly. "A lifetime of glorious warring gone to waste." He suddenly looks up to the man, his eyes alight with mead-stoked fire. "But you I envy! To fight, feast and spend the ages until Ragnarök with the Valkyrie at hand. That is an afterlife!" Eystein's grin is restored as he concludes, "Only if your fate is to die in battle, of course."

Sassa stands abruptly. Her bearing radiates with barely contained fury. "We are gratified you enjoyed the meal and the story. Take care not to lose the road on your way home."

Eystein slumps heavily. He is flustered but not yet defeated, and unwilling to quit in his aim. "I have heard of your grandfather," he tells the man, "his saga is told in every great hall across Norway. Further, no doubt, across the entire world. Gunnarr Skullcrusher. His name given for his favoring the butt end of his axe over the bit. It is fabled that he developed the killing habit, for the blade of his battle-axe, Skullseeker, was so finely engraved that he was loathe to see it damaged against the iron shirts and helms of his enemies." Eystein's passion is piqued. "May I see his weapon?"

"Buried with him," says the man. "Gone with him to Valhöll.

"Of course," says Eystein. "May I ask, why did you not take his name? Your grandfather's?"

"It was not offered."

"Then Rig."

"That name is of no use," proclaims Sassa.

"To a woodcutter," amends the man in a voice so low as to be mistaken for the wind.

"Then any name to be known by," says Eystein.

"Is this a man you would forget or mistake for another, name or no?" asks Sassa.

Eystein relents, changes tack, gestures widely. "This land, this fine home, won by your grandfather with wealth from the raids. Yours now by chance of birth. Come to England with me and win your own fortune. You will become wealthy, more wealthy even than your grandfather."

The man looks to Sassa and his daughters. "I have won wealth enough."

"Indeed," concedes Eystein, "but what of your family? When your daughters are of age and men come to court, what sort of suitor will they be? As beautiful as the girls will no doubt be, the daughter of a woodcutter brings one sort, the daughter of a man of wealth, another."

"So you have come for the benefit of our daughters?" says Sassa as she takes position at her husband's shoulder.

"I have come for my own benefit. It would be a fool of a captain who did not seek out the largest and strongest when searching for warriors."

"You are searching in the wrong home," states Sassa more firmly than is prudent, "and your words have become offensive."

"Does the offense come from lies? Is there a thing I have said that is untrue?"

"An unbridled truth is often more offensive than a lie," reminds Sassa.

Eystein sighs heavily, places both hands flat on the table in surrender. "Truth or not, I have spoken poorly. Too many years spent in my own hall. It seems I have forgotten the wisdom in the saying; 'He starts to stink who outstays his welcome in a hall that is not his own.'" Eystein stands. "I will ask only once more. Is there nothing I can offer to persuade you to join me?"

The man remains silent.

Eystein's wonted smile returns. "Then I thank you for welcoming me into your fine home." He turns and moves to the door. Before he leaves he removes a heavy silver torque from his wrist, hangs it on the door latch. "For your hospitality," he says, then is gone into the night.

❊ ❊ ❊

It is late. Sassa sits at the table turning Eystein's gift over and over in her hands, transfixed by the weight and beauty and immense worth of the fine arm ring. "A new axe. A gander and billy for Tora. Cows, oxen... how many?" she wonders. "An outbuilding to keep the stock in the winter. And given freely as price for yesterday's supper."

The day's mead finished, the man sits opposite Sassa making idle circles with his finger in the spilled residual on the table before him.

Sassa drops the torque onto the table. It lands with a satisfying thud for its weight. "It is a bribe," she says, the excitement and wonder gone from her voice, "a bribe to entice you away to war."

"It does not entice," says the man.

"No. You have never had a lust for gold and silver. I have never asked, but...." Sassa catches herself, clenches her lips tightly.

"Ask what you will," offers her husband.

She chooses her words with care, "You have never gone to war nor to raid. Yet I watch you by day and by night. Every stroke of your axe is another enemy cleaved. Every sled of logs to split, a treasure horde carried home. You war in your heart by day and in your dreams by night, yet you have never gone."

"To go to war means to leave you, to leave Kari and Nanna. It is my second greatest fear."

Sassa scoffs, reaches to hold her husband's hand across the table. "You have no fears. There is not one thing in this world that scares you."

"Not of this world," says the man, "yet I know a fear greater than any man has ever known. Greater than any man can bear."

Sassa considers her husband queerly, as if being toyed with. Her quizzical smile fades as she comes to realize her husband tells the truth. But how could it be? The man she knows so intimately, so completely. Every secret of his being revealed to her years ago. Words unnecessary to convey the want of his soul. The heaviness of her heart puts a tremor in her whispered voice, "What could trouble you so, my love?"

The man remains focused on the dissipating circle of moisture on the table for a long moment before he gazes up into his wife's welling eyes. "You will spend your afterlife in Freja's hall, Sessrumnir."

Sassa does not understand the course of his words, answers with tentative caution, "Freyja and I have that kinship, yes."

"Freyja has no use for a woodcutter," states the man.

In the moment of realization, tears burst from Sassa's eyes. She bolts from her seat to round the table, take her husband's face in both hands. "No, no...," she murmurs desperately through her sobs.

The man quiets Sassa with gentle fingers to her lips. "Freyja has first choice of fallen warriors. If I die of illness or of age in my bed..."

"No, no, no...," breathes Sassa over and over, clutching at his hands to cling to them with all her might.

"This life, for all the pleasures and love I have been granted, is but the blink of an eye to time in the afterlife," he concludes.

Sassa clenches her eyes tightly, unable to open them to the truth. Her knuckles grow white in her grip on her husband. The verity of his statement rends her soul.

"An eternity without you is my only fear," says the man.

❋ ❋ ❋

It is deep into the night before Sassa, wrapped in her husband's arms, finally cries herself to sleep.

The man sleeps not at all.

❋ ❋ ❋

The sun has only just freed the eastern mountains from the shadows of night when Tora bursts through their door, her eyes wild and red, cheeks streaked with tears through caked dust. "Svend has gone!" she blurts, "He must have come in the night and gathered his things as I slept. His bow and his heavy cloak... he is gone!"

The man and Sassa sit up in their bed. Sassa blinks the sleep from her eyes and tries to quiet Nanna who wakes crying at the startling intrusion.

The man pulls on his trousers. "I will go retrieve him."

"Will you fetter him to a stone?" asks Sassa. "He will only run away again."

"Just until the war fleet has departed," pleads Tora, grasping for hope, "Please!"

Sassa quiets Nanna as she speaks with her sister, "He will find a merchant ship then. If a man is determined to go to war, he will find a way."

"But he is only a boy. My son!" Tora stands in the door-way in her night clothes, her tangled hair fallen around her quaking shoulders like a woman whose wits have been stolen along with her most precious of possessions.

"Gather yourself sister and sit, and for the sake of good quiet your voice," Sassa grumbles, her mood still foul with pity for herself, "it is too early in the day for hysterics."

Tora does as told. Her voice is a harsh whisper as she asks the man, "Is it true? Will he go despite... everything?"

"It is true."

"Then go with him!" hisses Tora, "Go and fight beside him. Shield him from harm. Then return him to me!"

Sassa glares at her sister.

The man's eyes drop to the floor. "I am bound to my own family."

"Is Svend not your family?" Tora's voice is on the rise, hysterical panic creeping its way back into her appeal, "You are more a father to him than any man. And I? Am I not the sister of your wife? We are your family, also."

"Tora," pleads Sassa, "think of what you ask."

"I ask only that my son lives!" Svend's mother chokes on her grief and will not be consoled.

* * *

It is far past milking time and the nanny bleats incessantly for relief before Sassa is able to calm Tora enough so she can go about her chores.

The man broods in a darkened corner of the longhouse. His thoughts are his own and kept to himself.

Nanna and Kari enter with a basket of the day's eggs.

"I tried to milk the nanny but she kicked the bucket over," says Kari.

"It is all right Kari, I will help you later," Sassa tells her daughter as she strokes her sister's hair where they sit at the table.

Tora turns a spoon endlessly through a bowl of cold porridge. She suddenly looks up as if just now aware of her surroundings. "I should make bread! Kari, Nanna, help me make bread!" She stands, begins the task as if nothing out of the ordinary has happened.

Sassa looks to where her husband sits at the far end of the room. He watches Tora also, with the same concern for her wavering mind.

Sassa finds herself with an unexpected sense of calm and resolve despite the grim decision she has come to since Tora's arrival with news of Svend. Her only hesitation now is in declaring that decision aloud to her husband, for she knows once stated, it can not be taken back.

Not knowing her present state of mind, the man is puzzled at the strange bearing of his wife: erect of posture and sure of step. A wisp of a smile, beautiful in its simplicity yet terrible in its portent.

Sassa rises, goes to her husband, straddles his lap as is

her wont. She looks deeply into his eyes, holds them with her gaze as if for the final time. Her lips move but she finds no voice and must brace herself before she speaks, "Freyja is afforded first choice of fallen warriors for her hall. The goddess chooses men not only of great valor, but of great worth." She steadies herself with a deep breath before she can finish, "If you fall, be certain your death catches her attention."

The man pauses to assure himself he has fully understood, then pulls his wife to him in loving embrace. Sassa clenches her husband tightly to her breast. They hold one another without words until Tora declares the morning meal ready.

The man is ravenous, his appetite seemingly insatiable. Sassa teases that his craving for her sister's food is much greater than for her own. Kari and Nanna laugh along with their mother and push the remainders of their own meals before their father to watch it be devoured.

When there is nothing left to eat, the man stands from the table with great vigor and pats his belly with both hands for the amusement of his daughters. He goes to his craft tools which hang above the stalls, returns to the sleeping benches with a straight bar.

As the women and children watch in astonishment, the man shoves aside the bedding, pries up a plank of the bench. He reaches in and withdraws a cloth wrapped item as long as his leg to the hip. The man carefully lays it aside, replaces the plank of the bench, then carries the item outside into the warming day.

Nanna and Kari rush to the bench to check if there are any more hidden treasures waiting to be discovered.

Tora looks to Sassa in question. Sassa does not know what was hidden. She has never been privy to such a secret. She stands, takes up a soft sheepskin from the store awaiting winter, and follows her husband outside.

The man sits on the bench on the porch of the longhouse to pull the oiled cloth from Skullseeker, his grandfather's battle-axe. His hands move in a strangely delicate manner as if uncovering a gosling from its shell.

The deeply oiled handle is of cream colored ash that startles the man. He remembers the haft having been stained nearly black by blood and the sweat of his grandfather's hand. Then he recalls his grandfather fashioning a new handle each time after returning from the raids or that year's war. He would choose the perfect grain from a core of seasoned wood, fashion it to curve just so, perfect to his hand in balance and circumference. He would oil the weapon -- iron, wood and leather -- every day for a week, every week for a month, every month for a year until the following season when it was called upon again to draw blood. The man, as a boy, did the same for a year after his grandfather's passing, then had laid Skullseeker to rest.

Iron wrapped shoulder, winding front and back in the form of the world serpent. Cured ox-hide wrapped belly and throat wound taught then shrunk to crushing by boiling water. Runes lay carved in the haft beneath the wrapping -- powerful staves -- names of the Aesir his grandfather gave thanks to for the gift of combat. Tyr named twice. The heel, leather wrapped also, abruptly widening so a grip on the handle would never be lost. The haft protrudes from the eye and is capped with iron, this in the form of a ravenous wolf's head. Eddies and currents of the pattern-welded blade shine dully in the sun's morning glow where it lightens the sky from behind the thinning overcast. The bit shines brighter yet, honed to the sharpness of a sheering razor. The cheeks are carved with a flowing knotted pattern with no beginning nor end. Huginn and Muninn take flight endlessly within the swirling flow of etched iron. Unlike a typical battle-axe, the butt protrudes two-fingers width, adding heft to a strike and to act as a warhammer.

The man caresses the majestic weapon from heel to eye with an unsoiled bit of the cloth. Skullseeker glows with terrible radiance.

He stands to brandish the weapon in his practiced hands. The swirling ocean of the pattern welds catch the light like the sun on a disturbed tidal pool. Subtle ripples reflect across his face. Perfect balance, yet much lighter and faster in his hand than in his memories. But then his memories are that of a child, not of the man he has become.

"It is magnificent," says Sassa as she approaches with the sheepskin, "a true hero's weapon. But the fleet does not sail until tomorrow. Today you are mine."

The man takes his wife's hand, leads her through the sparse woods to the sparkling creek which cuts the land.

They lay the sheepskin upon a soft bed of leaves beneath a tall elm which dips its roots into the clear stream. This, a favorite spot of theirs when they were young to make love and speak of their future together. The sweet aroma of decomposing leaves, the soft tinkling of the stream just as it was so many years before.

The great battle-axe of his grandfather is set aside. The man takes Sassa in his arms, gently lays her down.

They love, dappled in sun filtered through fluttering leaves of the grand elm. The day is clear, warm and still. It is long before the shadows of the forest to the west reach over the swain couple and the first chill of the coming night touches their sweat-moistened skin.

Sassa lies with her head pressed to her husband's chest, a sun-white leg draped over his as is her custom in the aftermath. She listens to his heart as it gradually slows from climax. Feels the calluses on his hand catch gently in her damp hair as he strokes her tresses of golden amber in a soft, calming rhythm. Her hand traces the line of muscles across his chest and belly, his thigh... until she feels him stir again with coming passion.

Enough love for the moment. There are things she must know. Sassa withdraws her hand to place over his heart so she can feel as well as hear his pulsing life.

"Do you believe the Valkyrie are as beautiful as they

say? queries Sassa, her voice trembling against his chest.

"Yes."

"I fear if you reach the afterlife before me you will fall in love with one and forget about me."

Without hesitation the man easily turns Sassa onto her back. She gasps with the suddenness of it. He crushes on top of her, the intensity in his eyes, startling. "Freyja herself could bind me with spells and chains and I would break the fetters to be with you, now and always," the man tells his wife.

Sassa has swore an oath to herself not to cry this day, yet she cries now. Her husband kisses her tears away, drinks them in greedily. Suddenly she begins to giggle and can not stop, her entire body heaves with giddy wracking spasms of laughter. The man looks upon her in question. Sassa speaks through her choking, sobbing laughter, "You have wasted your life as a woodcutter. With honey-dripping words such as those, you should have been a scald."

He levels a sham frown upon her. She makes an effort to push him away but the effort is wasted as he will not be moved. He forces himself between her legs. She playfully struggles against him.

"No," she demands, but he only snuggles his hips deeper. "No, no, no...," she repeats, affecting sternness, "I must return home to prepare supper." The gambit may have worked but for the sudden gasp she emits at feeling his readiness.

"No?"

"Yes," she commands, pulling him closer.

❊ ❊ ❊

The lovers, barely aware when night overcame them, make their way home through the black of the forest -- Sassa with the sheepskin cloaked around her shoulders, the man bearing Skullseeker in his fist as if it has always been there -- both comfortable and content in the silence they share.

Tora has made super and the children have already eaten by the time they arrive home. Sassa and the man devour the remainder of the meal with well-earned appetite.

After, the man sits on the girl's bed to remind them of his never ending love for them both in low whispers as if the truth is a conspiracy between them. It pleases him to accept their embraces and kisses for as long as they will. Nanna puts an end to her goodbye's long before Kari who is content to rest in her father's arms as he gently rocks, her forehead resting against his in their singular bond. He holds his daughter until she nods with sleep, then lays her to bed.

Sassa watches from her seat at the fire. She smiles in gratitude at the generous blessings of the Norns, for who could have fared better in fate than she?

The man packs his travel bag with shirt, trousers, hone. A handful of jerked boar for the walk to Trondheim.

Sassa watches her husband prepare for the journey.

Tora watches her sister.

When there is nothing remaining to be done or said, the man kisses Sassa, kisses her once again, then goes to their bed to sleep. He lays atop the furs, shirtless and bootless, and in a matter of moments is soundly asleep.

Sassa wonders at her husband's ability to so easily sleep at such times, and so much better it seems for his course having been fixed.

The women pass the night in their own counsel at the fire, quietly speaking of all matters but husbands, sons and wars.

In the false dawn of the following day the man wakes as if gently summoned by a familiar voice. He dresses, ties up his boots, goes to the fire where the women remain as if the long night passed in a trice. He lays a consoling hand upon Tora's shoulder. She holds it to her for a moment before releasing him to his wife.

The man leans to kiss Sassa's neck, cheek, ear.... He whispers to her words that raise a melancholy smile on her lips.

The man kisses those smiling lips, gathers his travel bag, takes up Skullseeker from behind the door, and is gone.

* * *

Harold Godwinson, newly crowned king of the whole of England, finds himself faced with yet another difficult decision in a year of difficult decisions. The crown bestowed upon him by the witan following King Edward's death is contested by no less than three would-be usurpers. It seems all decisions in the foreseen future will be difficult ones.

Fair of hair and tall amongst his own people, Harold Godwinson strikes a handsome image. He wears no beard, but his mustache is full and curled in the current style of the court. He sits erect, burdened in layers of royal trappings, robes and head-piece. This inconvenience so that the earls and nobles gathered will not forget that though newly crowned and contested from every side, the fact remains: he is king.

The heat and closeness of the room over which he presides has Harold sweating profusely in his ornate trappings. The unseemly annoyance of it sets him in a foul mood. The bickering nobles wear at his nerves further and lend an uncomfortable tightness to his neck and shoulders. He slumps with the desire that he were anywhere but here at this moment.

The witan, for all their professed breeding and wisdom, prove to be of little use in the current dilemma: William, Duke of Normandy, is staging a vast army across the channel to the south, and threatens to cross into England with the changing of the wind. Tostig Godwinson, the king's own deposed brother, has formed an alliance with King Hardrada of Norway to attack from the north. If that were not troublesome enough, a host of petty kings and earls from within his own country swarm like flies to pester and annoy while he is occupied with the two genuine threats to his kingdom.

Nobles, earls and strategists of the witan, not unlike swarming flies themselves, crowd his strategy room. The air in the room is close and depleted. The stone-work walls seem to swell even closer for the rank wet heat of agitated body and breath as nobles vie to have their voice heard above the others.

The heavy iron reinforced table in the center of the crowded room holds a huge map of the kingdom skillfully illuminated on parchment, laid flat and secured by heavy pewter discs at the corners bearing the late King Edward the Confessor's seal. An annoyance to King Godwinson, having not yet the opportunity to mint his own likeness to seal. The image of his predecessor staring up at him, judging him, mocking him in his turmoil.

The single voice Harold would hear is that of Gyrth, his younger brother, earl of East Anglia and captain of the standing army of Dane huscarls: the professional soldiers hired to defend the English isle. Gyrth, the most studied and prudent of the Godwinson clan, has proven his knowledge of martial skills many times without fail. Harold is confident Gyrth has already worked out a stratagem for the coming wars, but his brother has yet to take part in the chaos of the discussions.

Gyrth reclines peacefully on a stool in the back of the room wearing a bemused smile that riles with impudence -- by design it seems to Harold. Now as king he would have Gyrth's advice. King Godwinson calls for quiet. The room falls to a begrudging silence. "Gyrth, your thoughts," bids Harold.

Gyrth reluctantly heaves himself to his feet as if the king's order is a great burden. He is a slightly built Englishman of thirty-six years who maintains the dress, hair style and much of the manner of the Dane huscarls he commands and reveres. Gyrth is attired in a loose fitting tunic that falls to mid-thigh, soft leather boots and worn linen trousers. His beard, trimmed close to his chin, displays best his features that would otherwise run to common. He is armed with a substantial sheathed seax worn horizontal on his wide leather belt in the manner of the huscarls. Though arms are strictly forbidden at such gatherings, it is doubtful Gyrth is without the weapon even in the midst of coupling.

"Face Hardrada first," states Gyrth. "If he sails on the brink of winter he does not plan a return voyage. The man without a plan of retreat will be the more determined of the two."

Osmont Rice, bishop of Hastings, esteemed member of the witan, is quick to counter, "As learned a soldier as your brother and captain is, King Harold, I believe he overestimates the threat of Hardrada. Though it is easily understood and as easily forgiven."

"And what am I to be understood and forgiven for?" queries Gyrth in an easy taunting manner.

"Your overly familiar relations with the Dane huscarls is widely known," says the bishop, "and a Northman is a Northman."

Gyrth's voice is calm though booming in the stone-walled room. His tone holds caution, "I am English by birth and by right. Born to a family devoted to Christ our Lord and baptized by your own master and predecessor, Bishop Rice. And as to the Danes which make up our standing army, they are baptized and as Christian as yourself."

Bishop Rice snorts at the ludicrous statement. "The Danes raided this land as sure as the Norwegians. Their forefathers were heathen sea rovers."

"And your forefathers heathens of Saxony," rejoins Gyrth. Before the angered bishop can retort, Gyrth adds, "And two-hundred ships bearing an army of Norsemen, Christian or heathen, would be difficult to overestimate."

"Yet if Hardrada lands to the north as we have seen

invaders of their country commonly do," says Earl Herley, a ranking member of the witan, "Mercia, Northumbria, York... all with men-at-arms and the ability to summon fyrd in defense, stand in their path."

"And once removed from their ships and on foot, the Norsemen are less troublesome than the ten-thousand mounted soldiers Duke William will likely summon," adds Earl Mundford of Surrey.

"Might your opinion be influenced by the fact your earldom lies in William's path?" mocks Gyrth.

Earl Mundford stirs with resentment yet remains silent in the face of the king's brother.

"It is also my opinion," declares Bishop Rice, "and that opinion is blessedly influenced by a power higher than all the great minds of this room, including your own, Earl Gyrth."

Gyrth's grin is restored as he returns to his seat to assume the posture of a man enjoying an idle day on the sunny banks of a stream. "God planned your war strategy then," Gyrth nods thoughtfully. "Will He take up a spear as well?"

Bishop Rice is outraged, as are many of the nobles in the room who would not have one, even the king's brother, speak so freely against other nobles and so openly blasphemous.

"It would do you well to recall that your brother is king, and you by extension are earl by the want and declaration of the witan," warns Bishop Rice.

"And could be as easily stripped?" adds Gyrth. "I would have you recall that my brother is indeed king, by your word, and the family Godwinson holds a goodly number of earldoms throughout England."

There is a rumbling through the nobles at the bald-faced threat.

"Enough," barks King Godwinson.

Gyrth bows his head to cover his grin, raises his hands in way of surrender to calm and quiet the commotion he has enkindled. "I have given my advice as directed, and will fight to the north or to the south as directed."

Harold wishes for more from his brother, void of the naysaying of overly cautious nobles more concerned with their own wealth and welfare than the welfare of the country. He also wishes he had a great deal more time to make his decision, but fears appearing irresolute in the face of the gathered nobles. "Send scouts north to warn of Hardrada and Tostig," says Harold. "My army will remain in Pevensey to face Duke William if he dares the channel crossing."

The decision made, Gyrth, agile and quick of foot, takes his leave.

* * *

Gyrth is greeted with smiles and courtesy as he makes his way to the kitchen of the fortress. He is a nobleman very popular among the commoners of the household. His reputation is that of being slow to anger and light of hand.

Orm Hungry Beard -- as the Englishman has been dubbed by the troops of Dane huscarls he is assigned to -- sits atop the food preparation table in the center of the kitchen, forcing the bevy of cooks and serving women to give him wide berth as they scurry to prepare a feast for the visiting nobles. A thin, twisted wire of a creature with close set eyes and sporadic hair growth on top of his scabbed and narrow skull, Orm much resembles a starving rat afflicted with the mange more so than a man. His unruly beard is matted with bits of food, new and old, fresh and fetid, as to take on the appearance of a crow's nest formed from eclectic bits of refuse and carrion. For his appetite, it would seem Orm would be much larger than the narrow rail of a frame he possesses. Evidently the fellow has an esurient worm inside that is as ravenous in appetite as Orm himself. An Englishman born and bred, Orm gained position with the professional soldiers of the Dane huscarls by way of his cunning tongue and eagerness to do what other professional soldiers would find objectionable and against their conscience and honor. Orm, unburdened by neither conscience nor honor, is the one, necessary in time of war, who finds solutions to untenable problems. He does so with the perverted glee of a sadistic child who searches out newborn kittens to bag and drown in a river. His very nature, others find repulsive. But rather than curb his inclinations, Orm fosters and sharpens them for his own amusement and gain.

Orm sits on his perch picking at seeping scabs on his arms and face as he snatches morsels from passing trays. He is partial to breads and sweets but feigns a lunge toward nearly every item for the harried reaction amongst the serving staff his antics provoke.

The kitchen staff look to Gyrth with relief as he enters to collect his troublesome lieutenant.

Orm nabs a pitcher of wine to carry with him as he follows Gyrth from the kitchen. As much of the wine winds up in his matted beard as in his gullet.

"It is south," says Gyrth.

"As I claimed," replies Orm, a spray of wine and rank odor following his words through graying teeth haphazardly set in rotting gums.

Gyrth grimaces. Worse than being wrong in his own battle predictions is Orm being right in his.

Gyrth detests his lieutenant. Orm is a man, no man would call friend. An ugly, hate-filled creature lacking any semblance of pride or honor. But war is an ugly creature itself. Pride and honor in war are things for sagas, not the field. Wars are fought to be won. Men like Orm are required to do the things a man of worth will not do if victory is to be had.

Gyrth leaves Orm to pass word to the huscarls of the king's decision, then turns his mount to his home in Oxfordshire to bathe the stench of his recent encounters from him. Once again he must set matters right in his household, for each time to war is possibly the final time.

The journey to his home requires the better part of two

days, ridden at an easy pace. When Gyrth arrives with his personal guard he is not off his horse more than a few minutes before he is in his bedchamber availing himself of one of the many serving girls who maintain his household. The act is more for relief than pleasure, and when Gyrth finishes he tugs up his trousers from around his ankles, stretches his back and heaves a deep sigh.

Gyrth is only mildly surprised to find his mother Gytha in the open doorway of his bedchamber, a perpetually sour look creasing her countenance. Gyrth restores the girl's dress to cover her bare rump, gives her a pat on the behind and an order in way of dismissal, "Run and draw me a bath."

The girl hurries from the chamber skirting Gytha with a quick duck through the doorway.

Gytha enters the bedchamber as her son laces up his trousers. She pours two goblets of wine from a pitcher. "If you would marry, you would not need to avail yourself of your servants."

"I avail myself of my servants so I will not feel the need to marry," Gyrth counters.

Gytha offers Gyrth a cup of wine. "You need an heir."

Gyrth accepts the cup, exits the room. Gytha follows.

The home is rich and well appointed: broad hallways, spacious rooms, tapestries and ornate trappings of all sort.

"I must have a bastard or two around here someplace," Gyrth murmurs.

The doorway to a small chapel stands open. Gyrth would pass, but Gytha stays him with a grip on his sleeve. Gyrth sighs dramatically and allows his mother to pull him into the chapel.

The room is long and narrow. Benches in rows face a Christian altar at the head of the room. Gytha drags her son to the altar, encourages him to kneel. She bows her head, begins to pray as Gyrth dips his chin, mumbles a few terse words, stands and strides from the room before his mother can stop him. Gytha quickly finishes her prayer to hurry after her son.

"Gyrth, it is unseemly for a man of your age to remain unmarried," harps Gytha.

"What good is a wife and heir to me?"

"You are the strongest and smartest of your brothers. You should be king, and your heir, king succeeding you."

Gyrth stops to speak in earnest with his mother, "Mother, I am fourth born. I will never be closer to the throne than captain of the huscarls." He finishes the wine in his cup, places it on a nearby table, continues on in an attempt to escape the discussion.

Gytha stays on his heels. "The captain of the huscarls could take the throne whenever he pleases."

Gyrth turns on his mother, his voice a low hiss, "Mother, that is treason. Your own son, my elder brother Harold is king. He will one day make a fine king and he will do so with my assistance and loyalty... and yours."

Gyrth continues to the bathing room. Gytha doggedly follows.

The young girl from Gyrth's bedchamber, along with two more servants of similar age, fill a tub with steaming water from buckets carried from the kitchen. Gyrth sits on a bench to pull off his boots. His eyes rest on one of the slightly framed girls.

Gytha does not curtail her speech for the presence of servants, "There are too many who oppose your brother to believe he will have a long reign."

"Mother..."

"I have already petitioned the witan to name you as successor if Harold falls in battle or to illness."

Gyrth stands, steps out of his trousers. The serving girls avert their eyes and begin to exit. He holds the one he was eying by the arm. "You, stay," orders Gyrth. The girl stands passively with her gaze on the floor.

Gyrth declines to cover himself as he speaks with his mother, "If Harold falls in battle, do you imagine I will not fall alongside him?"

"I have prayed with the bishop. He promises me it will not be so."

"Well, that is a relief," says Gyrth as he pulls the dress from the young girl.

Gytha is exasperated with her son. "Gyrth, for the sake of good!"

Gyrth helps the young girl into the tub while shooting a mocking smile to his mother. "I need an heir to my future throne."

Gytha throws up her arms in frustration and turns from the room.

* * *

It requires less than half the time for the man to travel to the city of Trondheim than when he made the journey with his family. His stride matches that of any long-limbed horse, and the road beneath his feet can barely be felt for his fevered exhilaration.

The head of Skullseeker cradled in the frog across his back remains covered in cloth as not to draw unneeded attention. His hunting spear and wedding sword he left behind for Sassa's defense. A working knife and hand axe on his belt, a single change of clothes in a woven bag slung over one shoulder, is all he carries with him.

The din of uncounted thousands of voices born along with the smoke from hundreds of cook fires rumbles on the wind coming off the fjord to reach the man even before he crests the hills overlooking Trondheim. The clamor of iron, boots, hooves, baying of hounds, bleating of sheep, goats, snorting and stomping of horses, the bellowing of cows and oxen, all blend to quake the earth in a mighty storm of confusion.

The man enters the city, wades into the throng to make his way to the docks. Even with his vantage above the heads of the masses, he sees no one he recognizes. With suddenness it occurs to him he may be unable to find, much less protect his nephew in the milling sea of humanity, and they have yet to be immersed in the disorientation of battle.

The newly realized concern spurs the man on, roughly forcing his way past any who are slow to yield. Occasionally an angry shouted challenge follows the man but he pays no heed and the offended individual is quickly lost in the closing tide of bodies behind him.

A picket line of the king's personal bodyguard denies access to the docks where King Hardrada and his advisors plan for their departure. Each guard a berserker, fully armored in a boar-crested helm, glistering iron shirt and colorful shield painted in the king's colors. Along with axes and swords, each is armed with a broad-headed war-spear, its blade the length of a man's forearm. Together they form an impenetrable wall.

The man approaches only to be stopped at spear point.

"Remove yourself from the docks," demands the guard. "You will be told when to board your ship."

The man peers over the heads of the guards to see Eystein Orri consulting with the king himself.

Eystein's gaze is in constant movement as he speaks with the king, scanning the crowd beyond, be it for threats, or simply a life-long martial habit is impossible to say. His eyes stop when they fall on the man.

The man watches as Eystein speaks to the king. The king turns to look his way.

Eystein approaches, ushers the man past the line of guards onto the docks. "Son of Rig!" Eystein nearly shouts in joyful greeting, "You have changed your mind. I am glad. I will make a place on my own longship for you."

"If I am to sail with you, I will need two places," says the man, "I have only come to watch over my nephew."

Eystein nods his understanding but hides a deeper concern at the news. No man lives long in battle if his own interests are placed behind another's.

The way is lead to King Harald Hardrada.

The man is astounded at the king's size. Never before has he stood at full height and looked another in the eye.

Hardrada: a giant of a man with a full beard and gilded locks. Broad of shoulder, narrow of waist, long of leg -- an imposing, regal figure to be sure. More imposing yet are the king's eyes -- intense -- set above high, sharp cheeks, and alight with fierce intelligence and a smoldering fury that never extinguishes.

The king gazes back at the man in like wonder.

Hardrada is dressed in fine but simple battle clothes for wear beneath tunic and mail. But for his extraordinary size and magnificent bearing, he could be just another nobleman warrior.

"King Harald," announces Eystein, "this is the man I told you of. This is Rigsen."

The king studies the man closely. "I believed myself to be the greatest in stature in all of Norway, but now I wonder if the legends of my prominence are exaggerated."

"There are others as large as you," Eystein tells the king with a mocking grin, "but none with the imprudence to not bend their knee or bow their head in your presence."

The king and the man hold one another's eyes for a moment. Hardrada nods with satisfaction, smiles. "Men lacking such prudence are the only ones to be held in esteem in these times." The king roughly clasps the man on the shoulder before he is taken away on other business.

The man and Eystein watch the king go. "He likes you," declares Eystein.

The man takes his leave with the promise to return when he finds Svend, and goes on the hunt for his nephew: A hopeless endeavor it seems at first, but soon the man recognizes men tend to gather with their like in packs.

Old veterans of a lifetime of campaigns with their worn, notched armor and weapons, rest easily in the lee-side of buildings, sip mead from curved horns and recount oft-told tales of glorious days gone.

Imposing warriors in their prime gather in smaller groups of four and five, lean on tall spears, their shields, iron shirts and polished helms bound ready for carry, stacked close to hand. Swords, axes and long knives hang heavily on their belts. Their roaming gaze critically appraise their country-men for potential allies and liabilities in battle. They speak of past and future battles, of treasure and fame yet to be won.

War profiteers in the guise of merchants slink amongst the men-at-arms, trafficking in battle wares and forming alliances for trade of plunder. Their ever-shifting eyes shoot from one of their kind to another, like starving rats wary of others competing for carrion.

Stalwart youths -- virgins to battle -- bond in tight groups to speak in overly confident voices of the coming war. Overheard stories of veterans are repeated as if they themselves had lived the event. Among these young men is where Svend is found. He is not hard to discover. Svend's brash voice carries above the others as he tells his vision of how he and his new-found friends will conquer the Saxons with little need of assistance from the rest of the army.

Svend is alerted to his uncle's presence as the swaggering lads surrounding him fall silent and fix their stares as if Thor himself approaches.

Svend turns to see his uncle standing over him bearing a grim expression. The lad, still into his cups from the night before, is emboldened rather than put to caution by his uncle's presence. "This is my uncle," Svend announces, "grandson to Gunnar Skullcrusher, the greatest warrior to ever take to battle."

The lads are awed by the man, his lineage, and Svend's relation to him.

The man looks over the gathering -- each young face keen for recognition -- before returning to Svend. He rolls his neck as if relieving a troublesome knot there, turns from his nephew, moves away. Svend, much of his hubris lost, follows.

After a short distance the man turns to address his nephew. He sees Svend carries only his cloak and a sword in a cracked and weathered scabbard. "Where is your bow?" the man would know.

"I was able to trade it for this sword," says Svend, excitement filling his voice. He offers the sword to his uncle as proof.

The man takes the sword, turns it in his hand, eyes the weapon critically. The blade is rusted in spots which have been hastily scraped over to hide the fact from undiscerning eyes. A hairline splits the patterned iron near the hilt, and the leather wrapping on the handle is loose and rotting. The man frowns at the weapon, then at Svend. "And you, grandson of a smith." He shakes his head in disappointment. "Who made this trade with you?"

"A veteran of many battles," says Svend, "Halfdan the Bold. He says a bow is the weapon of a coward. He says to fight from a distance is no way to win fame in battle. A sword is the weapon of heroes. This one is called Belly Opener and it can cut through iron shirts without pause."

"And where might I find this generous fellow, Halfdan?" Queries the man, his voice little above a growling whisper.

* * *

Halfdan the Bold makes trade with a young warrior: a shield for a broad-bladed spear. Halfdan is a well-fed, powerfully built warrior in his prime. His umber hair is worn short, his beard is full and long, braided and bound in leather and beads. Halfdan strikes an impressive figure in his shining mail shirt and intricately pommeled sword at his side.

An array of weapons, shields and armor lie on a hand cart under the watchful eye of Halfdan's crony, a tall, thin man with narrow shoulders and a long ill-kept beard. The hair atop his head is shorn close and is split by a jagged white scar traversing from crown to brow. An impressive indentation remains in his skull from whatever manner of weapon was laid there to form such a defacement.

The man places a hand on Svend's chest to pause him as they approach. He continues to Halfdan and his crony to search through the pile of weapons.

Halfdan eyes the man critically. A giant of a man, but obviously a common farmer. He wears no arm ring, armor nor weapon but for the large cloth wrapped axe crossing his back. A rusty wood-splitter whose head has been honed to a nub no doubt, thinks Halfdan. A profitable man to sell weapons to.

"I have no single mail shirt to fit you," says Halfdan, "but perhaps two woven together. And no helm so large as to rest on your head, but what of a shield? Every man to war could find use of a shield."

The man ignores the pitch, finds Svend's bow and quiver amongst the litter of inferior weapons. He takes up the bow, stands fully erect to face Halfdan.

Halfdan scoffs involuntarily, astonished, as the man is even larger than he first appeared hunched over the weapons the way he was. He quickly recovers his composure, offers the man a conciliatory smile. "That bow may be of too light a pull for you."

The man simply stands with the weapon, holds Halfdan's eyes.

Halfdan shrugs. "Have you silver or do you wish to trade? What is that you carry on your back?"

The man reaches behind him to where Svend nervously waits, takes the sword the trader had given Svend for his bow, offers the sword to Halfdan.

Halfdan does not recognize Svend nor the weapon, it appears, for he takes the sword and purses his lips in thoughtful consideration. He unsheathes the weapon, shakes his head dolefully. "This sword has been ill cared for," says Halfdan with regret. "The blade is notched beyond honing. And there is rust, see?" He offers the blade up for examination. "And here, a hairline. This sword is not to be trusted. That bow you have chosen is a fine weapon, worth many times this sword."

Svend strains forward, his hand axe drawn and gripped tightly in his fist. "You have just made that same trade with me last night!"

The man stops Svend with an arm across his path as he notes the crony standing watch over the weapons has drawn his long-knife, stands ready to fight.

Halfdan now recognizes Svend. He looks from the boy to the man. "You are kin?"

"He is my uncle. And by your own admission you have cheated me!"

"Tell the lad to mind his tongue," warns Halfdan, "I will not be labeled a cheat. Take your sword, leave the bow and be gone." He thrusts the sword toward the man.

The man stands unmoving. He does not reach for the sword, nor does he replace the bow.

The crony with the long knife licks his flaking lips, looks to Halfdan for counsel.

Halfdan sets his jaw, fixes the man with his best battle gaze. His hand moves to the hilt of his sword. This no idle threat or boast, but a declaration.

Without looking away from either of the two facing him, the man passes the bow and a quiver of arrows to Svend, forces him to take a step back. Svend accepts the weapon, retreats under the pressure of his uncle while maintaining his scowl at Halfdan.

The man waits without change in his expression or demeanor. Whether weapons are drawn or remain sheathed makes little difference to him.

The moment draws on too long. No course of action is settled on. Without the man brandishing a weapon, Halfdan and his crony remain frozen in indecision.

The moment past, the man turns and ushers Svend away into the milling crowd.

Svend quakes in anger and adrenaline, and is emboldened by both. "If you have come to take me home, I will not go.

I can not gain fame and riches as a farmer or as a hand on a trading ship as my mother would have."

The man keeps close watch on those passing the opposite direction in the crowd. It is their eyes that will alert him to danger from behind.

"My mother does not understand these things," grumbles Svend, "but she will understand when I return with my bag overflowing with treasure. People of Trondheim will speak of her as the mother of a great warrior. I will gain fame and land and riches..." Svend's bold speech falters as his stomach knots and grumbles with hunger. "Uncle, have you brought anything to eat? They will not feed us as part of the army until we board the ships. I have not eaten since yesterday and have nothing to trade worth even a bowl of porridge."

The man pulls Svend into an alcove between two livestock pens, hands his travel bag to his nephew. Svend eagerly unties the bag to dig inside. To the man's surprise his nephew comes out with a loaf of bread. The famished lad devours the loaf in great mouthfuls as the man peers into the bag. Sassa has filled it with loaves of bread, apples and dried meat. The man takes a sliver of jerked boar the size of his hand, holds it in his teeth as he re-ties the bag. He guides Svend toward the docks.

As they approach the docks there is a disturbance behind them. The king's guard stands at the ready as several of the village guard approach with Halfdan and his crony.

"There, those two!" shouts Halfdan, pointing to the man and Svend, "Those are the thieves."

The man eases Svend behind him as he turns to face Halfdan backed by the village guard. Uncle and nephew are pressed with the king's guard behind, the village guard before.

"We are no thieves," shouts Svend, "I was cheated!"

The captain of the village guard steps forward but is careful to remain out of arm's reach of the man. "We will have the bow," he demands.

Svend begins to hand over the weapon when the man stays him with a slight gesture.

Svend regains some of his courage. "The bow is mine. He was returned what was given for it. We are even."

"This sword is corroded and failing," says Halfdan. "I agreed to no trade. We are far from even."

"And arrows," says Halfdan's crony, "they took more arrows than were given."

The village guard ready their shields and weapons, await a decision to be made by their captain.

Resolving trade disputes is beyond the purview of the captain of the village guard, but the demand to relinquish the bow has already been issued and it would not stand for a denial. The captain of the guard looks up at the giant before him, thankful the man does not wear armor nor carry a shield or unsheathed weapon, but it grants him only a very small measure of relief. What the captain truly hopes is for a nobleman far above his position to take the decision what to do from him.

The man stands resolute.

Svend steels himself, eases his hand toward the axe wedged in his belt.

Halfdan and his crony subtly drift to the side to gain advantage of a flank attack upon the man and Svend in the coming fight.

A great crowd of onlookers has gathered. Experienced eyes see no hope for the lad and his uncle.

Silence in anticipation of bloodshed resounds.

"A dispute easy enough to resolve," says Eystein Orri, his voice booming as he approaches across the docks. The king's guard part to allow him to pass. Eystein looks to Svend. "You say the bow is yours?"

"My uncle formed it with his own hands," says Svend, "and here, my name in runes carved by my aunt."

Eystein looks to Halfdan. "And you say it belongs to you."

"Fairly traded for," says Halfdan.

Eystein's dampened smile declares he understands the

claims. He makes his proclamation, "Being that all the claimants in the case are warriors in the king's army, we will allow might to determine right." Eystein commands a retainer at his shoulder, "Bring sailcloth and a single shield each. Holmgang will settle this matter."

The onlookers press close, murmur excitedly.

Halfdan grins in sadistic pleasure as he fixes his gaze upon Svend.

Svend's breath shutters. He nervously licks his lips which have become suddenly dry, but holds Halfdan's gaze with all the courage he possesses.

The man rolls his neck. He has set his mind. He will not allow Svend to fight the seasoned warrior. He will cut Halfdan down himself. The act would be his last in this world, the man knows. To defy the rules of holmgang will end his arrest, trial and death. And Svend's also, for he knows well enough the lad will not stand by without taking his part in a fight. But what choice has he? To return home to tell Tora that he stood by and watched her son slaughtered over a trade dispute?

Eystein's half-smile never leaves him as he studies the man, seeming to know his thoughts.

A square sailcloth is brought. Onlookers are pressed back to make space as the cloth, nine paces in square, is stretched out on the ground.

Warriors who have seen many duels fought place their feet on the edges of the cloth to secure it in place. They hold their shields at the ready as not to be injured by an errant swing of a sword, and to force the combatants back onto the island of sailcloth if need be. Two shields of the king's guard are laid at opposing ends of the cloth for the combatants.

"One shield each as we are pressed for time," announces Eystein, "the tide is soon shifting and we must be on our way."

Halfdan, victor in many such duels -- as his business and demeanor lends itself to dispute -- confidently draws his sword and takes up the shield on his side of the square.

Svend does not hesitate, but steps onto the battleground with a stiff stride to take up the other shield. He must wipe the palm of his hand on his trousers before he can take a sure grip on his hand axe.

Halfdan's smile grows ever larger as he faces the trembling youth.

The onlookers pass coin and silver between themselves: wagers placed on how long the youth will survive against the impressive looking warrior that is Halfdan.

The man eases the leather strap of his frog higher on his shoulder for quick removal of Skullseeker.

"Hold!" Eystein shouts to command the attention of those gathered. He looks curiously to Halfdan. "You say this lad wrested the bow from your hands?"

"His uncle took it," blurts Halfdan's crony.

Halfdan cringes at the unwelcome edification.

"Then the boy stole nothing," says Eystein. "Your complaint is not with the boy, but with his uncle."

Eystein looks to the man.

The man steps onto the sailcloth.

The smile drops from Halfdan's face.

Odds are quickly amended. Coin changes hands through the crowd in renewed wagering.

"I am not afraid to fight him," declares Svend.

"You have proven as much," says Eystein as he lays a hand on Svend's shoulder, "but this is not your fight." He pulls Svend from the square.

Eystein draws his own sword, offers it to the man. It is an immaculate weapon of patterned-welded iron, solid silver cross guard and pommel with gold and jewel inlays. An engagement gift from King Hardrada, it is the finest sword any bearing witness have ever seen.

"Would you borrow my sword," asks Eystein, "or will you use whatever manner of weapon it is you carry so closely to you?"

The man easily draws Skullseeker from his back, pulls the shroud from it. The legendary weapon is displayed in all its terrible brilliance.

The surrounding crowd presses closer. An astonished muttering passes through them as they lay eyes on the saga-inspiring weapon of Gunnar Skullcrusher.

Deep concern usurps the fury in Halfdan's eyes. A duel with a boy, turned to a fight with a very large but simple farmer, has turned to something more... much more.

Eystein is entranced with the glorious weapon. "It seems your grandfather wields a different weapon on Odin's field after all." Eystein returns his sword to its scabbard, takes the shield from Svend, offers it to the man.

The man takes up the offered shield of solid alder planks reinforced with heavy iron straps, fittings and rim. It has a heavy domed iron boss in the center and is painted vibrantly in the king's colors. He holds it, a foreign, awkward thing in his hand.

Halfdan notes his opponent's unwieldy carry of the shield and his confidence is bolstered once again. Giant or no, the man knows not how to make proper use of a shield, and iron bites all flesh equally.

"You're not the like of a man and not a man in your chest!" Halfdan bellows the official challenge, then sounds two heavy strikes with sword on shield in way of commencing the duel.

The man raises shield and axe to mirror Halfdan's challenge, but with the first strike of Skullseeker on shield, the heavy planking is shattered with a thunderous clap. Wood is splintered, iron straps are bent, torn free from seasoned timber.

The onlookers gasp, fall silent. Not one of them has ever been witness to such: a shield in hand shattered with what seemed nothing more than a single solid rap from the man.

The man casts the ruined shield aside. He stands, Skullseeker extending from one massive arm to sway lightly brushing the surface of the sailcloth.

All await Halfdan's advance, yet it seems the combatant

has forgotten his purpose as he stares at the broken, discarded shield.

Halfdan clears his throat, and with a strong voice that belies his wavering heart, speaks, "As it has been stated by Jarl Eystein Orri, we are, each of us, members of our king's army. I would not be so selfish as to diminish its fighting number by even one, as we will need every man of us to fight in the coming war." Halfdan must clear his throat again before he continues, "I declare no right nor wrong in this dispute and am willing to step from this isle of justice and take up arms with all my countrymen to battle against the Saxons of England.

There is a long silence among those gathered that causes Halfdan to shift uneasily in his stance as he awaits the man's response.

Eystein examines the broken shield with no little astonishment. He steps forward to address the man, "Does this settle the matter in your mind, or would you have further retribution?"

In way of answer the man returns Skullseeker to its frog, yet does not step from the sailcloth.

All eyes shift to Halfdan. Halfdan lays down his shield, turns heel and standing as tall as he might, retreats through the throng. Onlookers quickly clear a path for the shamed warrior.

No coward is Halfdan, he has killed many in war and in single combat. Yet as with all who would bully, sure advantage must be secured before risk of life or limb. No profit can be won by the dead.

Seemingly gratified by the outcome, Eystein Orri, captain of the king's army, shouts above the growing din of the crowd assembled, "Men, gather to your ship leaders and prepare to sail. There are lands to be won, riches to be hoarded and Saxons to be slaughtered!"

The vast army roars its blood frenzy to alert the Valkyrie: War is coming.

* * *

Gyrth rides at the right shoulder of King Harold Godwinson. The king, a warrior of note himself, bristles at such convention -- by his younger brother nonetheless -- but Gyrth, as captain and king's protector, maintains his rightful position and will not be put from it. They ride at an easy gait saving horse and rider for battle, if there is to be one at the end of their journey.

Three-thousand professional soldiers of the Dane huscarls ride in formation behind. The huscarls -- a well trained, well equipped standing army of Dane warriors -- established in England by King Cnut and maintained by his successors. Though sworn to the Christ, more than a few Mjölnir amulets can be found dangling alongside wooden crosses on leather thongs hung from sturdy necks. All but a few wear their hair and beards in the fashion of their Dane forbearers. Generations of bodyguards to kings are the huscarls, and proud to be.

Their circuitous route south to the channel takes the English army through the major townships between London and Pevensey, the most likely landing spot for Duke William perchance he makes good on his threat to cross the channel from Normandy. In each township they acquire fyrd: the civilian militia conscripted to war in time of need.

The elite huscarls look with disdain upon the peasant soldiers. Their clumsy wielding of weapons and ill-fitting, poorly cared-for armor irks the professional soldiers. As does the rank smell of their boiling vegetables in camp, their incessant complaining of being taken from their homes, gripes of the unseasonably warm weather and seemingly every other condition and burden of the march.

The peasants of the fyrd scowl in return at the proud Danes: oppressors who hold no skills other than wielding an axe and shield. Can these hired men till the land or produce a field of potatoes and onions or maintain a flock of sheep? No, but they can eat, and they do without reserve each time they march to war. They think nothing of commandeering a farmer's meager stores, slaughtering their stock and bedding their wives and daughters with or without consent. Defenders of their country... little better than an invading army. At least invaders do not require farmers to fight in the forefront to be slaughtered in the first wave of attack.

The English high-born nobles that ride with the king frown upon both huscarls and fyrd. Huscarls: invading Northmen whose service has been secured with English gold. Foreign mercenaries, their fealty proven, yet men forever alien to this land. Tolerated for their prowess in battle, sparing the English nobles who in their stead would be expected to lead the way to war.

And the fyrd: low-born commoners little better than slaves, and less useful as their freeborn status gives them the belief they are free to determine their own fates, even against the wishes of those of higher standing. A stew-pot of inferior breeding and ignorance. Yet their masses necessary to stop the flight of arrows and spears, and to entangle the hooves of an enemy's cavalry.

This, the army of England: nobles, huscarls and fyrd. Bound together in war yet without camaraderie or affinity.

The Godwinson's, Harold and Gyrth, being brothers and having battled many times together, speak at ease without the formality of king to earl as they ride shoulder to shoulder through the countryside. They bear no little discomfort as the scorching sun makes each regret having donned mail and helm for the journey. The tension of the coming battle does not lend itself to long silences where worst outcomes can be imagined. Questions asked and reassurance given fill the space between king and captain.

"How many men will we bring to battle?" Harold puts to his brother, though he knows the number as well as Gyrth.

"Nigh three-thousand huscarls between our own and

those of the nobles who fight with us. The census claims as many as twenty thousand fyrd, though if we acquire half as many I will be satisfied," answers Gyrth.

"None are more cunning than farmers and tradesmen when it comes time for evading war or taxes," scoffs Harold.

"It is a difficult thing for a farmer to leave his home to fight a war he has no interest in," counters Gyrth.

"Any man should fight more eagerly for his own home, for king and country, than for any other cause."

"True, but his home remains his home regardless of king. And taxes are a burden regardless who levies them." Gyrth regards Harold from the corner of his eye. "Might there be a matter other than this war burdening your mind?" Gyrth's voice holds a gentle goad, "I would not have this toilsome attack on your throne distract you from larger plans."

Harold can not hold back a chuckle. His younger brother has been sharp of tongue and iron of nerve from boyhood. The man who can make merry in the face of death is a good man with which to go to war.

"Will it be enough?" wonders Harold, "the number we will put to field."

"Well," says Gyrth with high spirits as he turns his mount toward the rear of the column, "I know of only one way to know for certain!"

Gyrth rides past the long cavalcade of Dane huscarls, each offering him a nod or raised hand in salute.

Following the formation of mounted huscarls are the peasant soldiers of the fyrd, on foot, coughing and squinting against choking dust stirred up by the hooves of three-thousand horses.

Gyrth gives words of encouragement to those who will meet his eyes. Most in the fyrd keep their chins tucked to their bony chests as they shuffle along as if on a doomed procession to Hell. Even the cattle and sheep herded along to the rear of the column to be butchered as food during the campaign step more lively, thinks Gyrth.

Though he speaks in their defense to his brother and other nobles, Gyrth has never fully understood the commoners reluctance to war. War: A childhood dream of his from first memory, realized at fourteen years, and with good fortune continued to his dying day.

Every male child from the moment he can stand will eagerly take up a stick as a weapon and make play of defending his kinfolk against the trolls and dragons and armies that are ever present in his fertile mind. As he ages his dreams are hardly diminished, but grow even more grandiose as he recognizes heroes of war as men to be emulated, their deeds and standing to be coveted.

No boy nor man may know what lies in the dreams of a female child. Perhaps visions of a hero who takes up weapons against trolls and dragons and armies.

God loves a warrior, Gyrth knows. Nearly every story told by the poets at banquet begin and end with great warriors fighting for a cause where God tips the scales in the favor of the righteous, even stopping the sun in the sky if need be to give his chosen more time to slay the enemy. What higher calling could there be than to war in the name of God?

Gyrth passes the smith wagons heavily burdened with anvil and iron for the repair of weapons and armor, and his thoughts of war and glory grow dark with concern. Less than half a score smiths in all. He urges his mount on at a quicker pace.

Orm is found with the support train pulling up the rear of the column that stretches nigh on a full league behind the king. He harangues the driver and ancient cook of a cart which carries ready-boiled porridge for reheating in camp. Orm forces the old man to fetch him great ladle-fulls of the thick, gray stuff to slurp down while riding alongside. The lieutenant is covered from beard to groin with greasy dripping porridge as the pitching of the cart and swaying gait of his horse does not lend itself to proper eating.

Gyrth stays his ever-present urge to slay the repellent

creature as he reins up to address his lieutenant, "Might you save some for camp... and the rest of your fellows?"

"Not to worry," says Orm, "after the first skirmish there will be more food than mouths to feed judging by the state of our fine army."

The conscripted farmers within earshot are unsettled by Orm's assessment. Gyrth knows there will be a general mood of doom through the ranks by nightfall.

"I saw only a few smiths," says Gyrth.

"The townships are getting better at hiding their craftsmen... and their women," answers Orm.

"Eight smiths to mend armor and weapons for an army of fifteen thousand will not do. Take a squad of huscarls, backtrack to each village and round up all with hammer and forge."

"Done," says Orm as he reigns his horse tightly about and spurs it on to select his detail from the rearguard.

Done. Far too eager was Orm to take up the task. Gyrth is certain he does not want to know by what means his lieutenant will uncover more smiths from villages already stripped of nearly every man between fifteen and fifty. But smiths they need and smiths they shall have, by whatever means.

✳ ✳ ✳

A tiny village of fewer than fifty residents lies off the old Roman highway. Small herds of hornless cattle and sheep, patches of tilled soil to grow vegetables, tiny shanties with thatch roofs and mud and dung walls. Villages like this dot the English countryside, springing from nothing. Most disappear as quickly.

Townspeople -- women, old men and small children -- go about their business of scratching a living from the wilderness. A few scrawny teen-age boys, filthy and ragged, lead horses from their hiding places in the woods now that the army has passed. Boys and horses alike, hidden to prevent their being conscripted into the king's army. The town in whole is caught unawares as Orm and his recruiters ride into their midst. The townspeople stare guiltily at the king's men.

"So you had horses after all," smirks Orm. "What else have you hidden from us?" Orm raises his chin at the teen-age boys. "And where were you striplings when we were recruiting? The lot of you appear old enough for war, as squires at least."

The largest of the boys, barely fifteen, stands tall to speak to Orm, "You have taken nearly every man of the village. The women will starve if someone is not left to help with the harvest."

Orm is unmoved by the plea. He gestures to his recruiters who quickly dismount to take charge of the villager's horses and teens. Orm looks over the motley group without much hope. "Have you any smiths?"

The townspeople glare at Orm, keep their lips pressed tightly together.

A crooked, scrawny lad by the name of Crompton speaks up, "Our smith hides in the fodder stores, there." He gestures with a bony finger to an outbuilding.

The other teens and townspeople shoot hard looks at the traitor.

Orm considers the lad. Crompton's narrow skull sprouts a shock of mangy hair. Rotting teeth are set askew in his slack maw. A haphazard patch of beard here and there on sunken cheeks prove he is older than the other boys, yet smaller and less fit.

Orm grins, rides to the outbuilding, calls to Crompton, "Come here boy." Orm indicates a pitchfork leaning on the wall of the shack. "Take that and bring the smith out."

Crompton hesitates only an instant before he takes up the pitchfork and enters the rickety building. There is the brief sound of a struggle from within. Crompton's high pitched voice can be heard; "Out, get out!"

A moment later, a hunched old blacksmith comes stumbling from the shack at the point of Crompton's prodding pitchfork. The blacksmith stands hangdog before Orm.

Orm grins, impressed. "What is your name, boy?"

"Crompton."

"Crompton," Orm repeats with a scoff. "Fitting. You have just earned yourself a proper meal. You seem a lad I might find use for."

The townspeople glare at the vile youth with unveiled hate.

Crompton quivers with excitement.

* * *

The harbormaster skillfully untangles the mass of longships from the docks of Trondheim. Men lean to oars to clear the shelter of the fjord and gain the wind. With shields hung and oars shipped, the great fleet of King Harold Hardrada sails the favorable tide to the open ocean.

The man and Svend occupy benches very near the bow on Eystein Orri's own ship which leads the armada, set even before Hardrada's own.

Behind, scattered to the horizon across the endless sea, longships with their tall serpent prows, colorfully dyed sails bowed and straining, fly over the swell like primordial winged beasts of legend. The ships are filled rail to rail with rowdy warriors eager for battle, their bawdy songs echoing over Aegir's daughters.

Broad, sturdy supply ships follow at their best clip. Heavily burdened, they ride low in the water with the necessities of war.

Svend huddles in his winter coat against the soaking spindrift of the sea. He does his best to maintain a bearing of being an experienced hand, and not a lad on his first voyage.

The man, eschewing even a shirt against the pelting spray, sets his gaze on the horizon before them. He has never been on the open ocean. The vastness of it awes and exhilarates him.

The crew of warriors crowding Eystein's ship are an impressive lot; magnificent, tall and sturdy. Each proudly displays the wealth of successful raids in their arm rings, pendants, weaponry and armor. Rich and well-oiled leather jerkins adorned with iron and brass ringlets stretch across broad chests, muscled frames. Stoic faces to the wind, their long braided and beaded hair trails them like the plumage of a cock in flight.

The euphoria of coming battle emanates from the younger warriors as they taunt and gibe one another in good spirits, claiming knowledge of their companions foundering in combat with men, and inadequacies in conquest of women.

Reserved elder statesmen of countless raids and wars lounge on benches, interject now and again in the young warrior's banter when they are offered ripe opportunity, their energies better spent on schemes of how the new-won wealth of the coming expedition might further their already elevated station.

Young and old alike, each in a phase of his prime, be it physically, or in skill and cunning. Men of noble birth, handchosen by Eystein himself, are good company to one another on this adventure.

Eystein reclines by the helmsman to overlook his crew. Familiar faces all, each having sailed and fought at his side in numerous wars and raids. Each time to war, a few newer members, proven, groomed and eager to replace those fallen in battle, or grown too old and too wealthy to maintain a taste for war.

Svend wonders at the joyful banter of men speeding to their prospective deaths. He is awed by the vast wealth carelessly displayed and recklessly wagered on trifles such as the fall of a dice or the throw of a knife, and is overwhelmed by it all. Only in fanciful tales has he heard of such a gathering of noble warriors. Even then, the tales no match for the group he now finds himself part of.

The veterans in turn wonder at the man and Svend, and their role amongst them. The two appear as simple karls, out of place among the grouping of warriors of high birth and noble lineage. No man voices the question aloud as they are aware each among them has been selected by the captain himself, and each for a very specific purpose. They trust that if that purpose is only known to Eystein Orri for now, it will become apparent to all in time.

There is one who seems to Svend more out of place among these high-born warriors than even himself and his uncle: a cloaked figure whose face is obscured by a broad-brimmed hat pulled low against the wind. He sits in a comfortable, elevated position with his back to the mast, a large crate covered in sackcloth at his feet. Low muttered croaking comes now and again from within the crate. It seems to Svend the cloaked man is very old, ancient perhaps, though there is nothing in his robust and upright carriage to give evidence to it. Simply an impression, like a primordial tree, bold and strong, thriving against the millennia -- its roots taking hold when the world was young -- yet with untold years yet to prosper. Svend does not remember the cloaked figure boarding the ship, nor the first moment he noticed his presence, yet there he sits as if he has always been.

Svend reaches to gain the attention of his uncle and asks, "Uncle, who is the one in the cloak?"

Tarbin, a burly figure more bear than man, stands from his nearby bench to wade his way with surprising dexterity across the pitching deck, through the tangle of bodies, to take a seat facing the benches where Svend and the man are posted. A massive bearskin is thrown across Tarbin's thick shoulders in lieu of a shirt, the shaggy cape even heavier now for the sea it holds. His smile is broad beneath a thick beard which sprouts from chin, neck, shoulders and chest alike. His teeth are straight, his nose crooked, his voice as deep and resounding as a waterfall carrying the snow melt of Harpa.

"That, lad, is Forni," says Tarbin. "I do not remember a time he has not sailed to war with a king's fleet, and always on the lead ship."

"What is in the crate?"

"Why, ravens of course."

"Ravens? For what purpose?"

Tarbin does not try to hide the bewilderment in his sparkling eyes. "Have you never sailed before?"

"Not past the fishing banks, and never outside of sight of land."

The notion amuses Tarbin. "Then you have never sailed. What is your name, lad and how did you come to gain passage on this warship of all ships?"

"I am Svend Caldersen. I am here with my uncle." Svend shifts his gaze to the man who remains silent beside him.

"Your uncle!" roars Tarbin, "The one our captain borrowed from Jötunheim for this war? The giant called Rigsen is your kin?"

"We are from the glens in the mountains of Trondheim and I do not know him by that name," says Svend.

Tarbin chuckles without taking offense. "With the blessing of the Norns... and a little help from the scalds, perhaps one day you shall." He reclines against the ship's rail, laces his hands behind his head, props his feet up on the bench to make his declaration; "I am Tarbin Bjornsen, sprung from the unholy mating of a berserk and a bear, and I had lost count of my adventures by the time I was your age. I have won and lost fortunes that could ransom kings. Women from every tribe on this earth, I have left with child. I have killed every sort of man and creature who walks, crawls, swims or flies in this world, and even now the einherjar of Valhöll prepare a feast in my name and eagerly await my arrival."

Testy from lack of sleep, too much mead gone sour in his belly, ill from the sway of the ship, and emboldened by his uncle at his shoulder, Svend speaks without prudence, "I believe you boast."

Tarbin lolls his head back on his thick neck and laughs until his face reddens and spittle hangs from his beard. "I do!" booms Tarbin, "I boast greater than any man or god short of Thor!" He leans to confide to Svend, "But that does not mean it is not true."

Tarbin's dauntless cheer is infectious. Soon other warriors join the grouping around Svend and the man to share stories and good-natured gibes.

Eystein maintains his position beside the helmsman and takes a turn manning the star-board himself, holding the course true. The captain shares in the elevated mood of his men but not in their banter. He maintains the comportment of a leader, yet one who would ask nothing of a man he would not undertake himself.

Neither does the man join in the telling of past exploits, and none seek to draw any from him. He maintains his gaze on the distant horizon with the greatest of awe far into the evening, past the sinking of the sun and coming of the stars.

Warriors eat their rations of bread and dried meat, and long for the cracking of a mead keg which never comes. As the stars warm the night sky in a broad silver band, men slowly part from their groupings and drift to their benches to sleep.

Svend, swearing too much excitement for sleep only a short while ago, now snores beneath his sodden cloak. His sleep-sounds join the others as the ship falls to silence but for the creaking of timber, snapping of sail and the rush of the waves beneath the keel.

Only the helmsman and navigator maintain the vigil, their eyes on the stars that traverse the endless sky above.

Even Eystein rests seated at his place in the stern, his chin to his chest, yet never losing his noble bearing even in sleep.

The man sleeps little, his mind alive with the mystery of how they will ever find land again. But then there are many mysteries of Midgard that go unexplained. How their way is determined across the whale-road, just one more.

A matter of even greater curiosity to the man is their captain. Eystein Orri, a Christian by his own admission, yet seemingly every warrior in his company bound in allegiance to the Aesir. From his experience with Christians the man knows them to hold little love, and less tolerance for those who refuse their god.

As if his thoughts were voiced aloud, the one called Forni, beneath his cloak the color of night, speaks from his place at the mast, "Your captain may claim the Christ god to appease his king, but he will not by choice sail with Christians. A Christian clings to life above all else -- above honor and loyalty and dignity -- and knows nothing of a glorious death and the afterlife it brings."

"Why then," asks the man, "does the captain, the king himself, claim such a god?"

"Gold can make a fool of any man," says Forni, his voice clear though the man can hardly make him out in the dark. "A wealthy man's wisdom wanes with his waxing pride, he sinks from sense to conceit." A raven's croak from the crate causes Forni to whisper to the bird in a voice that does not carry. When the raven is silent once again he continues to lecture the man; "The young god is a greedy god. He gathers to him gold and wealth beyond reason. Beyond what is needed for a thousand lifetimes, even the lifetimes of a god. Once he has won wealth enough, a man should not crave for more: What he saves for friends, foes may take. Hopes are often liars." Forni seems to heave with a sigh, his voice nearly fails him, "Gold is the falsest of friends."

"Then what use this war if not for riches? And why is its call so compelling to men who already have enough?"

"It shall all be made clear to you soon. Sleep now and seek your truths in the light of day."

The man would know more but Forni has retreated to his own being -- be it sleep or a thing far deeper -- and will answer no more this night.

His mind spins with dizzying query: Why do the fantasies of war from his youth, from his earliest memories, still come to him? Why have those fantasies never abated though he has won more than war can give: the love of a good woman and a family.

When the man is honest with himself he admits his longing for an afterlife in the great halls of Asgard is only part of his terrible hunger to be victorious in heroic battle. Even without the eternal reward, there is an overwhelming yearning to fight and to kill that has been with him always, and always would be. Death at once paramount and trivial: Only the chosen will reach Asgard, yet every man dies. How a man lives his life and the manner of his death, the defining difference.

What foremost troubles the man's mind and keeps sleep from him is his sworn oath to protect Svend. A promise coaxed from him by a distraught mother. An oath given with the best of intent, yet with no honest way of being realized. How does one protect a man in war?

Of oaths, the man feels Forni has great knowledge. He would put to him how once given, could such a promise be fulfilled.

Before he can query, Forni's voice once again comes through the dark, "The fool lies awake at night to worry. A weary man when morning comes, he finds all as bad as before."

Disconcerted, the man ponders how it is Forni seemingly knows his inner musings better than he knows them himself. Then not another thought comes to him until he wakes in the morning.

❈ ❈ ❈

In the morning the sea is at rest. There is sun, and a favorable wind fills their sails. Open ocean to the horizon in every direction.

Men stir, relieve themselves over the side of the longship. They dig for bread and dried meat in the food sacks.

The man comes awake, hardly aware he had slept, though well rested and eager for the day. More eager yet for the feel of solid land beneath his feet. He looks to the cloaked figure, the last image he remembers before nothingness overtook him.

Forni still sits, back to the mast, as if no time has passed. His ravens croak anxiously from beneath the sackcloth covered crate at his feet.

Svend grumbles himself awake, blinks the sleep from his eyes, crawls to the rail of the heeling ship to vomit over the side.

Tarbin grins knowingly at the seasick lad, catches the man's eye, tosses a loaf. The man tears the loaf in half, waits for Svend to rejoin him, offers him his share of bread.

Svend holds a hand to reject the offering. "It will not stay in my stomach," he belches.

"Nonsense," says Tarbin, "you show good sea legs already. A meal will turn them to iron. Eat."

Svend takes the bread, forces himself to swallow a small bite. Joyful that it does not make an immediate return, he slumps on the bench to worry at the bread with growing hunger.

"When I took my first voyage," boasts Tarbin, "the seas were high as three masts, giant whales were turned asunder in the swell, and..."

"And your breakfast was coming out of you from both ends," says Ull: beardless, tall, long limbed, and as comely a man as to be found. Flowing hair of sun-bleached gold and features carved of alabaster by ancient Romans, it seems.

Tarbin grumbles curses directed toward Ull's animal-coupling parents.

Ull persists in his roiling of Tarbin, "Your tales grow as old and weathered as Hyndla in her cave. Have you no new lies to add to your fables?"

Tarbin raises his chin to the man and Svend to confide, "Ull is brought on these journeys in the case there are no women to be had and we must make due with this smooth one."

"Come and take your kiss from my smooth cheeks whenever you dare," says Ull with a smile, "and we will see if you return to your bench with your manhood intact."

Tarbin grumpily waves a hand in dismissal, tears huge mouthfuls from his loaf to be swallowed without chewing.

Svend finishes his half-loaf, searches a food sack for more. "I should have a sword," gripes Svend to his uncle, "or at least a proper axe. You at least have your battle-axe."

The man is at a loss as the problem of returning Svend to his mother alive, grows.

Ull notes the worry in the man, looks to the longbow in Svend's belongings. "The bow is your weapon," says Ull, "as is mine." Ull produces a gleaming longbow magnificently wound with silver and oiled horse hide. He strings the bow and offers the fine yew-wood weapon to Svend.

Svend examines the weapon with astonishment. "Look uncle, have you ever seen such a bow?"

The man runs a hand over the finely polished wood, nods his profound appreciation.

Svend attempts to draw the longbow but the pull is far too heavy.

"A bow must be matched to its user. May I examine yours?" requests Ull.

Svend offers his bow to Ull who strings and studies the weapon with an educated eye. "Fine workmanship of quality wood. A sturdy weapon," claims Ull as he tests the pull, "and perfectly suited to the warrior who wields it. You will drive shafts through countless Saxons, no doubt."

Svend reconsiders his bow and beams with pride at the archer's assessment.

"Any fool can hack away at another with a sword," concludes Ull, "but few can kill properly with a weapon of skill."

"How does one do it properly?" asks Svend.

Ull settles in to address the boy in earnest, "A skilled

archer does not simply hurl his shafts into the masses, blindly loosing and hoping for the best. He chooses his victim in the chaos of battle. While death swirls around him he is blind to all but his target. He finds a clean kill, be it below the shield in the arteries of the groin, or above the shield through the throat or the eye opening of the helm."

"You can place an arrow through an eye?" Svend is astonished.

"Of course," says Ull, "and you shall too, with a little training. I shall teach you when we reach land."

Svend is excited at the prospect.

There is gratitude in the man's eyes as he steals a look to Ull.

The ship suddenly grows silent of men's banter. All eyes turn to Forni as he draws the sackcloth from his slatted crate to reveal two of the largest ravens the man has ever seen. The birds croak and stir with eager anticipation. Their glossy feathers shine as polished onyx. Jet eyes twitch and blink against the light.

It is only now, when Forni looks up from under his broad-brimmed hat in the light of day, the man sees he has but a single eye, the other torn from its socket, by what manner or purpose the man can only guess. The socket beneath a drooping lid, naught but a concave mass of scar healed and sealed many years in the past. Wanton fury in that single eye that blazes at the warriors gathered about him. Forni: scarred, silver bearded and haired, regal and fierce. Much older a man than might be expected on such a venture, yet younger and more war-fit than would be determined by his majestic bearing alone.

Forni leans, whispers to the birds as a loving father to his children, then lifts the lid from the crate. The ravens quickly hop to the edge, croaking excitedly, then leap into the air, their powerful wings driving them high above and beyond the longship in an instant. Quickly they are black dots on the horizon, then they are gone.

"Why did he release the birds?" wonders Svend.

"If they return," says Tarbin, "we are still more than a raven's flight from land. If they do not, we will see land before the day is out."

The man eats his bread without hunger and hopes in earnest the ravens do not return.

* * *

Sassa casts the runes once again, a set look of determination on her features as she wills the outcome to change. There is no change: The runes read as before.

Tora waits in the threshold of Sassa's home watching her sister's frustration and anxiety build. "Perhaps you ask the wrong questions," ventures Tora.

"The fate of my husband... and your son are the only questions," says Sassa, her eyes never leaving the bits of sapling root carved with the magic symbols.

"What do they tell you?"

"Svend is bound for a long and fruitful life," admits Sassa.

"And your husband?"

"Everlasting fame and glory."

Tora enters, encouraged by the news and bewildered by Sassa's gloomy concern. "This is wonderful, is it not?"

"There is only one sure way for a man to gain everlasting glory and fame in war," says Sassa as she prepares to cast the staves yet again.

Tora comes to her side to stay her hand. "Sassa," Tora begins in a soft, earnest voice, "I will tell you a thing I have sworn never to say aloud. You are my younger sister. Your husband, by all rights, should have been mine."

Sassa is hardly shocked by the admission. Her sister had made her desire for the man plain since their first meeting. Still, Tora had never voiced her desire aloud. Sassa contemplates her sister's confession and is puzzled. "Why do you tell me this?"

"Even after you were wed, had I the chance, I would have made him my own. It is shameful, yet true. But your husband is not like other men. His eyes have never strayed from you, not to me, nor any other woman. Yours is unlike any man I have ever seen or heard tell of. He is stronger and more determined than even the heroes of the sagas. If you told me he is a god, I would believe. Therefore I do not believe he can be killed."

"Even gods can be killed."

Tora shakes her head in dismissal. "I know he shall return to your arms. It matters not what the runes or Norns or even the Aesir have to say. Your love will hold you again."

Sassa turns away and does not tell her sister the runes have assured her of that, also. But what was not told, was if it would be in this life, or the next.

* * *

The day wears on as leagues are left behind in the wake of the longships. Forni's ravens do not return. On the haze of the horizon before them, the man can make out the dream of land rising from the sea.

The mood of the ship is elevated. Young warriors make ready iron shirts and helms, keep weapons at hand. Older warriors maintain their lax posture. More than enough time to prepare themselves before landing.

A few score more than two hundred longships carrying warriors and supplies, formerly stretched out over several leagues on the sea, gather more tightly upon approach of the beach. A friendly landing they are assured -- this, a Norse outpost secured from the Scots, and ruled by a minor Norwegian king -- but only a fool relies on good luck when approaching a land not his own.

Svend readies his bow, stands nervously at the prow beneath the carved serpent's head to watch the island gain definition through the haze.

"Take care not to loose on these Zetlanders," says Ull, "they may well deserve a shaft through their treacherous hearts, but they are allies in this current cause."

"This is not England?" asks Svend.

"No, not England," chuckles Ull. "We have sojourns yet to make."

"To acquire Saxon fodder," adds Tarbin.

"Then why do you prepare to fight?" wonders Svend.

Forni speaks from his place at the mast, "A man should not walk unarmed, but always have his weapons to hand. Especially in these times."

Svend is made nervous at the pronouncement.

Tarbin, struggling into his iron shirt, speaks to calm the lad, "Don't mind Forni, lad. The old man sees gloom and doom wherever he travels."

Forni stands from his bench to loom over Tarbin, speaks with an ironic grin,. "From shriveled skin, from scraggy things -- that hand among the hides, and move amid the guts -- clear words often come," Forni makes his way back to the helm to confer with Eystein.

"A clear word!" scoffs Tarbin, "A thing Forni has never spoken. I can not decide if he is a sage or a madman."

"The Ancient One is not wrong," declares Tyrulf. "It is always better to carry an unused sword, than to have need of a sword and fail have it at hand." Tyrulf's speech is uttered through a clenched jaw which failed to heal properly after a break. His hair and beard is shorn close to deny purchase by an enemy, and he wears his leather, iron ringed jerkin fitted skin tight for the same purpose. As Ull appears carved from fine stone to perfection, Tyrulf -- in feature and physique -- appears of unformed granite that only the most choice among mortal women, or a Valkyrie, could truly appreciate. His manner is that of a warrior, only. No other trade would be fitting. Each and every fear and doubt he possesses is transformed into a forward step and the desire to cross arms in test against others of his ilk: This is a warrior.

A contingent of several hundred native Scot men-at-arms await the armada's landing on the gentle slope of a gravel beach bordered by steep rocky cliffs. The Scots are small of stature and an eclectic mix. Some bear full mail armor and helms in the style of the Norsemen. Others are barely clothed, wearing only coarse woven wool shirts of horse-piss yellow. More than a few are clad in nothing but bits of unnamed animal skin which still bear the creature's shaggy fur. All in all they are a fierce and wild looking lot armed with spears, long dirks and strangely formed axes with spikes protruding from the butt and eye. Their small round bucklers bear narrow spikes from the bosses as well. Much of their skin and faces appear painted or tattooed, vibrant blue being the prominent color.

At the fore of the Scot army, a grouping of two-score Norsemen, armed and armored, await. They stand tall above the native Zetlanders. The odd grouping appears as if Norse soldiers have brought their illegitimate children to war.

By now, even the older warriors aboard Eystein's longship have donned their mail shirts and helms. All maintain swords, spears and shields at hand.

Sails lowered, half the warriors of each ship in the fleet lean to oars, the remaining half stand forward with shields ready.

Without shields to bear, the man and Svend pull on oars, their eyes rearward on the vast armada. Svend steals looks over his shoulder to the strange army on the shore.

Tyrulf, cloaked in the pelts of wolves, makes his way to the bow. Forsaking a shield, but brandishing broadsword and axe, the grizzled veteran climbs to the high place on the curved dragon-necked prow. The others allow him to take the position without protest as though it is his birthright. Tyrulf stands his station, tall and menacing as a second figurehead.

"Ship oars and brace yourselves," Eystein commands.

The long oars are quickly drawn into the ship. Every hand grips rigging or wood. Abruptly, the longship grinds to a listing halt in the fine, wave-tumbled gravel of the beach.

Tyrulf uses the forward momentum of the ship to launch himself from the dragon's neck to the shallow waters of the shore. He trudges forth toward the waiting army without pause.

As if Tyrulf their signal, men from the longship eagerly leap from the rails to follow.

A hundred longships grind to a halt up and down the shoreline. Battle-ready warriors flood the beach like a rogue wave.

Svend quickly takes up his bow, leaps into the shallow water to follow the army up the beach before his uncle can lay hand to stop him.

The man vaults over the side of the longship to join the great Norwegian army on the island of Zetland. He is startled to find his legs unsure on the solid land as if they had forgotten in two days what a lifetime had taught them.

Svend mills with others from their ship as Eystein Orri joins King Hardrada and his personal guard. King and captain stride up the beach to be greeted by the local petty-king, Fell the Dark.

King Fell, a Norseman bearing an oddly swarthy complexion beneath a stringy, umber beard, inclines his head steeply on a long neck to look up to King Hardrada as he approaches to make greeting. The petty-king, though not exceptional in size, stands a full head over the Scots of his army.

The Scots themselves, though barely able to be seen over a Norseman's shoulder, bear the fierce, menacing demeanor of hardened, confident warriors. Many Scot eyes are drawn to the man where he stands in the midst of Eystein's crew. The slight Zetlanders bristle as if the man's extraordinary size is of personal affront to them.

Following a brief formal greeting, Fell the Dark guides

the joined armies of Norsemen and Scots off the beach and up the rocky coast to the fort. They trek across the rolling countryside in a long line confined to a narrow path. Huge rock formations spring like islands from the sea of tall grasses that bow and flutter in the persistent wind. The man is astonished that the island bears nary a tree worthy of the name. The trees that do cling to the rocky hills are bowed, twisted and dwarfed by the ever-gusting current of air that sweeps off the ocean without reprieve. Crab-apple growing close to the ground are worried by great herds of shaggy sheep which roam unattended.

They march on toward a citadel which lies in the distance on the highest peak of the low hills. The line of four thousand men, half Hardrada's army, strung out for nearly half a league.

The other half of the army remains to guard the ships. Those men openly grumble at their lot. At the fort there will be a feast: fresh meat, hot loaves, drink, sport... women for rent or for the taking. The army's own supply ships will provide food and drink for those left behind, but the honor of accompanying the king and captain is a thing every warrior longs for.

Being of the captain's crew, the man and Svend march near the front of the column, with only King Hardrada and his berserk bodyguard to their fore.

When they arrive at the citadel the man is amazed at the looming stonework structure. Never has he seen stone piled so high or so tightly mortised. In the vast plain surrounding the fort, small stone thatched-roofed huts dot the land. Cook pits smolder before each hut. The smell of charred mutton clouds the air.

The king and his personal guard are admitted into the citadel along with Eystein and several nobles of high rank.

The men of Eystein's crew gather around the cook pit of the hut closest to the fortress gates. Another crew of Norwegians contests the spot but are quickly on their way as even among the Norsemen, the men of Eystein's personal guard are the most brutal and notorious of warriors.

The man wonders where the wood for the fires comes from as he has yet to see a tree taller than one of the tiny Scots who inhabit the forsaken island.

The gates to the fortress open and scrawny thralls draped in muddy rags drag two-wheeled carts heavily burdened with kegs of ale out to the waiting army. The first carts do not make it far before they are commandeered by the nearest to the gates. The ale which does make it past the gauntlet is quickly overtaken by the next closest and so on until even the warriors attending the furthest hut and cook pit have their share. Keg lids are staved by hand axes. Men eagerly dip their cups.

The man carries no cup, but plows his way to the cart, hoists an unopened keg to his shoulder and makes his way back to a flat rock half the size of a longship, blanketed in deep, soft moss, to sit and drink.

When the bread is baked, the men attack the loaves with good-natured wolfish greed. The first batch of bread is gone before Svend can fight his way to the fire. The lad broods over his ale cup as a fresh batch is put to the coals.

Forni approaches the man where he sits overlooking the ravenous battle for food and drink. From beneath his worn cloak, Forni draws a large steaming loaf and an empty cup.

No small wonder the man has for how the Ancient One might have procured a loaf from the esurient young warriors. He takes the cup from Forni, dips it in the keg, offers it back dripping with rich ale. Forni tears the loaf in two, offers half to the man. The two figures sit side by side overlooking the vast army.

"With half a loaf and an empty cup I have found myself a friend," says Forni.

"Are you are a king?" asks the man.

"I sire kings."

"And you possess a name and wealth."

"A greater name and more wealth than a man could put to use."

"Then why do you sail to war?" the man would know.

"To incite," answers Forni without hesitation. He looks up at the man beside him from beneath the brim of his hat. "To ensure there will be no talk of peace or reconciliation."

The man drinks from Forni's cup which rests between them, ponders the sage's proclamation in silence. He has no understanding of such things.

"Why do you believe man was created?" Forni puts to the man. Before the man can respond, Forni answers his own question, "To serve the gods in war. Odin and Vili and Vé slaughtered the giant and formed the earth and the sky. And of all the great and wondrous beings of the Nine Realms, only the men of Midgard do they call upon for aid in Ragnarök. Not giants nor elves nor dwarves... only man. The brothers carved and breathed life and sense into man for a single purpose: to forge in war the einherjar who will fight and defend the All-father when the wolf breaks its fetters and comes to devour him."

"To what end?" says the man, "Odin sees the future as it will be. He knows he will not prevail."

"What sort of creature does not fight his demise with all his power, even when fate has ordained him to fail? To be made meal of by the hateful wolf? Who would not raise an army to fight such a fate?" Forni has not eaten his bread but drinks deeply of the ale passed between the two. He tells the man, "Gods created mankind in their own image and likeness out of necessity. It is for gods and men to live and to die. But man nor god truly die until their name is uttered for the final time. This is why Odin has so many names, roams so far and spawns so many children. It is so he will live on past his death in the sagas and in the minds and hearts of his kindred: those of likeness and image."

The man considers this for a long moment, his eyes un-focused, ale cup forgotten in his hand. "And if a man has no name?" he mutters.

"Then he builds one through deed!" states Forni, his voice rising boldly. "Great deeds will be sung of for all time, even past Ragnarök. Cattle die, kindred die, every man is mortal, but the good name never dies of one who has done well."

"This I have heard before," admits the man.

"And shall again," assures Forni.

"To fight well and to die," says the man, mulling the notion.

"And to leave his good name to be sung, inspiring generations to follow," amends Forni. "Men must speak of men's deeds. What happens may not be hidden."

"And what of women? What is their purpose in it all?"

Forni tilts his head up to look at the man with his single eye, now aflame with lust. "Women! To inspire it all of course! Who but a woman could put kings to one another's throats for nothing but a bit of land of which there is far more than enough?" Forni laughs and his eye sparkles with mischief. "Do not query too much of women, my friend, for even the gods are puzzled at their whims. Spun on a wheel were women's hearts, in their breasts was implanted caprice."

Forni takes the ale cup from the man, drains it, then raises his voice to Svend who carves a rib from a roast sheep which has been drawn from the pit, "Boy, bring a hind-quarter of that mutton for your uncle and an old man, and we will see if we can entice my ravens back to service with the promise of a feast!"

❊ ❊ ❊

After the meal, men sated and yearning for distraction build up fires to shed light in the failing day. More kegs of ale are brought and opened. Two squat, shaggy ponies are led forth and harnessed to a post in the center of a rock-ringed circle to fight.

Tensions run high between the Scot warriors and their Norwegian allies with vile insults and gestures being less concealed with each cup of ale emptied.

A small band of women thralls is brought to dance and to be enjoyed, but before any man can lay hand on the first of them Scot and Norse swords are drawn. Blood is shed. Jarls of King Hardrada's army rush from the citadel to quell the petty battles and herd their men back to the ships before any more damage can be done.

The way to the ships is dark as mist covers the moon and stars, gusting low over the rocky hillocks of the island. Norwegian warriors, still fueled by bloodshed and ale, recite the events of the night with bellowing laughter and insults toward their host as they stagger their way down the narrow rocky path to the coast.

The man has lost Svend in the dark, but hears Forni's mirth-filled voice close at hand.

"Less good than belief would have it is ale for the sons of men," scoffs Forni, a mere shadow in the mist. "The more he drinks the less he knows, becomes a befuddled fool."

The man listens to the roar of pointless threats and ill wishes directed at their Scot allies from the crapulent Norsemen who travel with him, and he fully understands Forni's wisdom.

In the morning two men who did not survive their injuries from the night before are laid to rest. Longship-shaped mounds bordered by rocks form the death beds. In the distance, pyres sending a half-dozen Scots to the afterlife billow black smoke into a gray sky. Men mill around the grounded ships, grumble sourly of aching skulls and missed opportunities with slave-women.

The man stands over Svend as he rests on his knees in the gentle tide lapping the shore to rinse the taste of his up-slung supper from his mouth with sea-water.

Forni passes carrying his crate to board the ship. His ravens have returned but no man could say when or why. The old sage speaks to the lad in passing, "Best is the banquet one looks back on after and remembers all that happened."

Forni's mocking tone riles Svend, but the boy keeps his lips pressed tight. A mouthful of curses go unvoiced.

In the days following, the army is not allowed to leave the beach. Men mill and gripe, vent their pent-up aggression in grappling matches and games of battle-skills. Even so, the outlet is not enough and each man is yearning to kill by the time the call to board the ships is finally sounded. Warriors scramble to their longships, shove with all their might to free the vessels from the shore and be on their way.

The man puts effort to the task with little enthusiasm. Not so far a walk to England, he thinks.

The Norwegians mounted on their longships, sailing freely on the open ocean, turn the bows south, their armada increased by a score and seven warships filled with Scot warriors.

* * *

Gyrth, as captain of the king's army, is less concerned at present with the potential of a Norman invasion than he is with the king's mood.

The army of huscarls and fyrd had marched well and reached the channel days before. Now, with the wind to their backs, they camp on the shore and gaze across the water to await the ships bearing the army of Duke William of Normandy.

King Harold Godwinson stands today, like the day before and the day before that, on the sloping knoll which gives vantage to the channel.

Gyrth approaches his brother from behind. "Will it all you like, but even a king can not change the tides," says Gyrth.

"William can not sail against the wind."

"True."

"Yet our army must still eat... and be paid."

"True."

Harold turns on Gyrth, his face reddening with frustration. "If that shall be the extent of your counsel, I may be better served with another captain and counselor."

Gyrth can not suppress his grin. "True," he says.

Harold fumes.

Brothers grown close seldom have pity for the miseries of their sibling.

Gyrth takes his brother by the shoulder to lead him a short distance from his retainers so they might speak in confidence. "Harold, you are a great warrior of as many battles as I, and you know as well as I, the kings mood is his army's mood. If you show impatience, they will show impatience."

"They already show impatience. But for the huscarls my army is made up of farmers, herders, tradesmen.... They may do their duty, but in their hearts they wish only to return to their families and beds."

"What are your thoughts?" Gyrth would know.

"My coffers run low. I will keep the fyrd five days more. By then if the wind has not changed I must send them to their homes."

The brothers stand shoulder to shoulder in silence overlooking the channel.

King Harold sighs away his anger. "And your thoughts?"

"My thoughts run the same direction as they have for many days now," says Gyrth, "I am grateful I am not the king."

* * *

A mere days journey south and the fleet of King Hardrada once again takes to shore. This landing at an island of an archipelago on the northern coast of Scotland. There are no docks and little beach so the vast majority of ships of the armada drop anchor to slow their drift and remain bobbing and swaying in the choppy waters off the coast.

The man is glad to find his legs do not betray him this time as he wades ashore. Neither is he saddened when it is announced that the portion of the army that has come ashore is to remain with the ships until Hardrada can confer with the king of the Scots, Malcolm III.

King Malcolm, a man of noble appearance nearing his fortieth year, stands on a rise overlooking the landing. He is dressed in layers of finery of red and gold, and is flanked by no less than a hundred heavily armed and armored soldiers who carry tall spears and long shields of the English style, each bearing the Scottish king's Standing Lion crest.

The Norsemen lounge in what little shade the beached ships provide, watch King Hardrada, Eystein Orri and a small troop of nobles and axe-men stride up the cart path to the Scot king.

Standing face to face, King Malcolm appears as a half-grown child in the presence of Hardrada. The burly Norsemen guffaw at the sight.

"We ask aid from a dwarf," gibes Tarbin.

"A dwarf could at least provide weapons of magic. All we will receive from this king are more half-men," says Ull.

"I lack a shield," says Svend. "These people are not much larger. Perhaps I could bind one of their soldiers to my arm and use him as my shield."

The men burst into a fresh fit of laughter. Svend is slapped on the back by many hands in appreciation of his wit. The lad beams with pride at the praise.

Forni speaks gently. All who surround him quiet to listen. "I have seen the smallest of dogs fight to victory against the largest. The outcome is not always determined by the size of the man, nor the size of the army. If it were, no man nor army need ever fight, simply stand back to back to measure height, or count numbers of soldiers."

The men fall silent, shamed by their arrogance. They nod and mutter their agreement to the sage words, each claiming that he has been witness to such a thing, and that size and numbers are no way to determine victory in battle.

A grin can be seen beneath the brim of Forni's hat as he pushes himself to his feet, speaks gayly, "Words from the lips of the old and learned seem to carry prodigious weight, do they not?" Forni moves to where the man sits, his back against the ship's hull, places a weathered hand upon his shoulder. "In truth, when skill and will are of equal measure, I will choose the larger man in a fight every time." Forni chuckles as he continues away.

Tarbin shakes his head in dazed wonder. "Forni keeps me dizzy with his mocking of us for heeding his words."

"But Tarbin my friend," says Ull, "you must remain dizzy at all times, for I have never known a man more easily mocked."

The men burst into laughter once again.

The man watches Forni disappear into the gathered Norsemen as he wonders at the old warrior's words. Directed to him, no doubt, but in honor or disparagement, yet to be seen.

Having completed their formal greetings, King Malcom gazes out to sea, takes in the depth and breadth of Hardrada's fleet. "When I was informed you were coming with two hundred warships I told the emissary to his face that it was a lie. I would not have imagined so many ships in your entire kingdom."

"Well over two-hundred," brags Hardrada, "and more than a few privateers no doubt. It is my hope we will leave with even more... filled with your own warriors."

"Come, we will discuss the matter over a feast and an open keg," says King Malcom as he leads the way from the beach.

Hardrada speaks to the captain of his bodyguard, a brute called Tor, "Follow with the tribute."

Tor returns to Hardrada's longship, calls for a cart to be handed down. Several crates and sacks of silver, gold, coins and trinkets are carried from the longship, loaded onto the cart. Tor's eyes search the men of Eystein's crew, land on the man. "You, the big one, take hold of this cart and follow me," commands Tor.

The man takes up the cart's handles to follow Tor along the path away from the beach.

The kings, Hardrada and Malcom, approach the Scot king's fortress. A stone and wood picket wall surrounds the compound where a tall stonework castle looms over the land. Large gates are swung open to allow the kings to enter.

King Malcom turns to Hardrada. "Lambs will be roasted and ale brought to your men."

"These are the king's private men," says Eystein. "They come inside with us."

"Not into my fortress," states King Malcom. "You and the others will be cared for out here."

"That is acceptable," says Hardrada, affecting nonchalance.

Eystein turns Hardrada away from King Malcom with a hand on his arm. They speak in the Norwegian language so the Scots will not understand. "I will not allow you to go into his stronghold without me," states Eystein.

"You will not allow it?" scoffs Hardrada.

"No sire, I will not."

"King Malcom is to take charge of my wife and daughters until our return. We are far past the time for doubts."

"I am your captain and have earned the right to be present during negotiations. And why bother to maintain a bodyguard if they are to be locked outside the gates of a fortress not your own?"

Hardrada smiles and grips Eystein's shoulder. "This is why you are my captain. Not even my own mother ever worried so much about my wellbeing." Hardrada looks to his bodyguard, speaks under his breath to Eystein, "No more than a dozen. I would rather be slaughtered than appear fearful of these sheep-loving vermin."

Hardrada turns to King Malcom, smiles, speaks in the language of the Scots. "Only a handful of men to accompany me... to maintain appearances."

"Of course," King Malcom concedes.

The man pulls up the treasure cart, sets the handles down. Two Scot guardsmen take up a handle each, pull on the cart. Yet the cart, heavily burdened as it is, does not budge. Eystein gestures with his head for the man to bring the cart inside. The man takes the handles from the Scot guards and easily pulls the treasure cart into the compound.

The guards begin to close the heavy gates when Tor places a hand on each gate to hold them open. His proclamation is directed to the Scot army in general; "Any harm comes to my king and they will rename this island, Torsheim, after me, Tor of Alfheimer, the man who killed you all."

Scot warriors bristle. Though the language is not understood, the meaning is clear enough.

The gates are closed and barred against Tor and the bulk of Hardrada's berserkers, who remain outside the citadel.

King Malcom sits at the head of the banquet table. Hardrada, Eystein and their dozen chosen berserkers sit along one side of the table. Scot warriors fill the other side. Each side favors the other with their hardest war gaze.

To the right hand of King Malcolm sit the sit the brothers Paul and Erlend Thorfinnsson, jarls of Orkney and sons to Thorfinn Sigurdsson; a friend to King Hardrada before his death a year earlier. The brothers take great interest in the negotiations.

The man, seated at the far end of the table, eats without thought or concern for the battle of intimidation which goes on between the warriors. If there is a fight, he will fight. If there is peace, he will fill his belly, which he does now in quantity that would give even Thor pause.

When, nothing but the remainders of the great feast worried down to bones and scraps lays on the table before them, the kings begin their negotiations. Ale cups are filled and emptied as points of contention are raised and settled.

King Malcom's latest claim causes Hardrada to shake his head and state, "Tostig has no right to promise my land away."

"It is not yet your land," reminds King Malcom.

"Soon, it will be."

"Perhaps... with my help."

"I shall win England with or without your help," states Hardrada.

King Malcom rocks back in his seat, raises his arms in arrogant question, "Then why do you waste your time coming here?"

Hardrada looks to Eystein who wears his standard mildly amused expression. Eystein produces a gold coin in his palm, spins it on the table before him like a child's toy.

Hardrada smiles. "The land I will not give. I will pay you handsomely in silver and gold for the use of your army.

"Tostig promised my borders would be stretched past Northumbria for my aid in this war," complains King Malcom.

"It is not Tostig's land to give any more than it is mine, yet you take his promise for a section of it?"

"A few leagues of land. What is that paltry amount to a king such as yourself?"

"Every league is paid for with the blood of my people," says Hardrada.

"Yet you ask my people to shed their blood for less," counters King Malcom.

A berserker murmurs to his fellows in the language of the Norwegians, "A Scotsman's life is worth less than a Norwegians'."

A round of chuckles from the berserkers causes the Scot guards to ease their hands to the hilts of their swords.

The man glances up from the feast, determines the threat negligible, cracks the thigh bone of a mutton to get at the marrow.

The loud snapping of bone draws the attention of everyone at the table. The man sucks at the marrow, heedless of their looks.

It troubles the Scots that the Norwegian giant remains unconcerned with the mood of the room or the prospect of a fight, continuing his feasting though all others had finished long before when the negotiations began.

Hardrada notes the befuddled looks of his potential allies at the antics of the man, chuckles. He rocks back on his bench, studies King Malcom. "How many ships and men do you say you are able to provide?" asks Hardrada.

King Malcom looks down, clears his throat.

Eystein slaps the spinning coin flat on the table. "Thirty ships. Two thousand men... at best," he states.

"Fine warriors, all," protests King Malcom.

"Indeed," agrees Hardrada, "every ship, every man a treasure to me in my cause, King Malcom, and I thank you graciously for them." Hardrada looks to Eystein with a good-humored grin, leans toward King Malcom enthusiastically. "If you have no use of silver and gold and insist on land, here is my proposal. I will grant you all the land your entire army can plow in a full week's time."

King Malcom does the calculations in his mind, frowns. "How much silver and gold?"

Eystein's smile broadens as he bounces the gold coin off the table to land in King Malcom's lap.

Hardrada laughs and clasps the Scot king's shoulder to seal the deal. He stands to take his leave, but King Malcolm stays him with an amendment.

"The brothers Thorfinnsson have shown a keen interest in aiding you in your cause. You were close with their father," says King Malcolm.

"I was," agrees Hardrada betraying nothing of his anger at the Scot king's hedging.

"They will accompany you as my representatives with their own earldom's complement of ships and soldiers."

Hardrada looks to the brothers with a fatherly nod and smile, then turns his look to Eystein.

"A score of ships. Less than a thousand men between them," says Eystein in the Norwegian language.

Hardrada's glower is set upon King Malcolm. "The sons of Thorfinn the Mighty are more than I could have hoped for from you, King Malcolm," says Hardrada in a flat tone which carries no gratitude.

King Malcolm adjusts himself uneasily in his seat beneath the glare of the Norwegian king until Hardrada suddenly slams his palms flat on the table, jostling every cup. Hardrada's voice booms with hearty cheer, "I accept!"

Berserkers rise from the table affecting indifference, yet take care to not reveal their backs to their newly formed allies. King Hardrada and Eystein rise also to take their leave.

The man continues to pick through the scraps of the feast until Eystein's long stare causes him to press himself to his feet. He stretches, the full measure of him astounding. The man takes a cup from before a Scot guard, drains it in a single quaff, stifles a belch, then strides from the room. Every eye follows him.

Once outside the fortress gates, Hardrada and his berserkers join their fellows to begin the short trek back to the ships.

Eystein walks beside the man. "I pray the end of our negotiations to gain an army did not disrupt your meal," says Eystein.

"I have no taste for Scot food," says the man. "I was only seeking to be polite." The man's long stride leaves Eystein behind.

Eystein remains puzzled as to if the fear the man instilled in their allies was intentional, or truly happenstance.

❈ ❈ ❈

Enlarged by thirteen Scot warships, Hardrada's force sails south with the final tide before dawn. By the time the moon has won his race and the sun has begun hers, the coast of England can be seen to the starboard.

Longships skim the waves with the favorable wind. Banners of the tribes of Northmen flutter and snap from the masts, pointing the direction to war. The ships sail in tight formation, each within sight of the others, all within sight of the coast. In full view, the English will know of their coming, but little to be done. Nine-thousand warriors under the banner of King Hardrada will descend upon England within the day. The decisive battle for the crown will be fought before the fall of winter.

The Norwegians emanate excitement, though banter becomes less and less the further south they sail. War-faces are set to even the most jovial of their number. Tarbin's swagger has become nearly theatrical. Ull's stoic visage seems carved of stone. Eystein's set smile, a fearful thing in the best of times, would now cause an enemy's knees to weaken. Even Svend has few questions and little to say. The time for talk is past. Near is the time for war.

The man suffers no change in demeanor: Change unnecessary for one born to this. He looks to the south, the ship's constant motion no longer a bother. Worries of Svend, Sassa, his daughters... a distant mist in his mind. Everything a man could do for his family has been done.

Battle by necessity is a selfish endeavor. In the end one looks to himself and to no others. Conquering another man of like mind is every man's first true love and true purpose. Family, friends, oaths and gods must follow. To fight well and to die. To leave a name to be sung. Rise to fight again for the Allfather on the plains of Vigrid -- all that is expected of man from his maker.

With these thoughts in his mind, and his face turned to the island of England for no one to see, wondrous delight overtakes the man.

* * *

The wind has not changed. Duke William's crossing from Normandy is no longer impending.

Gyrth never ceases to be amazed at how much more quickly a villager can gather up his belongings to begin his march home, away from war, than when summoned to it.

A general excitement envelops the fyrd at the announcement they have been released from duty, yet with the warning they may be called upon again shortly to defend king and country. The citizen militia makes their retreat from the shores of the channel, dragging their kits behind them in their haste.

No word yet from the scouts sent to the northern earldoms of Yorkshire and Northumbria to watch for Hardrada and Tostig. What once seemed an imminent war on two fronts has become a game of waiting.

The combined armies of Mercia, York and Northumbria are trusted by the king's advisors to repel any invaders, yet a thimble could hold the amount of trust Gyrth has for the guidance of the king's advisors. He wishes to know of any advance upon the country long before London herself is found under siege. Gyrth remains unconvinced that Tostig has given up his quest to wrest England from their brother Harold's grasp. Nor has he discarded the rumors of Tostig's pairing with Hardrada of Norway. It seems likely to Gyrth, knowing Tostig as he does, he has not heard the last of his ambitious brother.

Gyrth watches the last of the fyrd trot away north on the old Roman highway. He goes to Harold's tent.

The king's men are already packing away goods for travel. Gyrth finds his brother being attended to by a monk who prays along with the king for the wind to never cease to blow from the north, and to keep the Duke of Normandy's fleet grounded on their own side of the channel.

Gyrth patiently awaits the amen's, then queries the king, "So, it is back to London with us?"

"Unless you can discover a way to hasten this war," says Harold. "I have been assured Duke William will postpone any attack for a year or more."

"And Hardrada?"

"More than enough men between Mercia and Northumbria to turn him back, if indeed he comes at all," says Harold with utter confidence.

Gyrth has had his fill of his advice going unheeded. He keeps his teeth together and turns from the king's tent to his own encampment to see it struck for the return home.

Scouts with fleet horses are posted along the coast to remain on watch, as the wind must change one day. But when?

❊ ❊ ❊

Chickens, goats and geese taken in trade for split wood roam the farmstead in plenty. The woodpile is diminished only by half, though villagers come daily now to purchase firewood for the coming winter. Night has fallen and the longhouse stands quiet and dark but for light from inside which seeps out around the door.

Sassa, Tora, Kari and Nanna prepare the evening meal when there is a knock on the door. Sassa looks to Tora, startled.

From outside the door the standard request is called in a gruff voice, "Am I welcome?"

"What is your name?" calls Sassa in reply.

"I am Bard of Vestfold."

The women again look to one another, the name unknown to them.

"You are not welcome," calls Tora. "There is nothing for you here."

Outside the door, Bard, a large man dressed in filthy rags, stands in the dark listening close at the door. He calls again, "I am a traveler in need of rest and a meal."

Sassa silently takes up the hunting spear from near the door. Only silence from outside. She raises her voice, "There are chickens in the yard. You are welcome to one. Take it and go."

"It is against custom to deny a weary traveler," calls Bard. "Might I speak with your men?"

Tora takes a step toward the door. Her voice quivers, "They are hunting game. They are overdue and will be back soon."

Sassa sees the door latch begin to rise. She quickly lowers the bar in place to secure it.

Suddenly the door is struck violently, rattles on its sturdy hinges as if their unwelcome visitor has put his shoulder to it. The women leap back away from the door in fear.

"Woman, open the door!" commands Bard.

Sassa backs away, the hunting spear held defensively before her. There is a long moment of silence. The women and children wait breathlessly.

Bard's voice again comes to them, this time with restraint, "You misunderstand. I was only looking for warmth and a meal. I will go."

Long moments of silence follow as the women maintain their vigil.

Outside the longhouse, Bard backs away then turns to two more men who wait only a few paces away in the dark. Bard whispers to his fellows, "Kill three chickens. We will camp in the forest, wait the night through. In the morning they will come out."

The youngest of the three, a wiry youth named Waller, whispers, "What of their men?"

"There are no men here. They are all at war," says the third of their company, a squat, stout man known as Ransu.

The three move quietly away into the dark.

Tora goes to the sleeping benches with the children to comfort and quiet them. Sassa stands guard at the door with the spear.

"Has he gone?" whispers Tora.

"We sleep with sword and spear tonight," replies Sassa.

The night is long. Sassa and Tora sleep little. Every creak of the wind or stirring of an animal from outside sets the women on edge. Sassa has armed Tora with the sword their father had given her husband as a wedding gift. Tora clutches it through the night.

When morning finally arrives, the cock calls and the goats bleat for their milking, Sassa and Tora gather themselves to venture outside.

The overcast glows with the rising sun. Frost breath plumes from the women as they cautiously emerge from the longhouse, weapons at the ready. There is no one in sight. Nothing in the yard is disturbed. The goats and foul stir anxiously for their feeding.

Sassa and Tora remain cautious.

"One does chores while the other stands guard," announces Sassa.

"What of Kari and Nanna?" Tora would know.

"Today they remain inside," says Sassa. She hands Tora the spear and goes about her work.

The livestock is fed and the nanny's milked without disturbance or interruption. Satisfied last night's visitor has truly gone, Sassa sets about making a breakfast of porridge and honey for her daughters, as Tora collects the eggs from the chicken roost. Nanna sits on her stool at the table, swinging her legs in eager anticipation of her breakfast. Kari helps her mother by placing the bread pan into the coals.

Tora enters with a basket of only a few eggs. "The chickens did not lay this morning for their being disturbed last night."

"Are there many missing?" Sassa would know.

"A few, but I think..."

Suddenly Tora is viciously tackled from behind by Bard as he charges into the longhouse followed by his fellows, Waller and Ransu. Tora and Bard tumble to the floor in a heap.

Sassa lunges for the spear which rests against the table, manages to grip it, but Waller and Ransu are on her before the weapon can be brought to bear.

Kari snatches Nanna from her seat, drags her to the far side of the room where the girls huddle in breathless terror.

Sassa screams in fury, struggles, strikes, claws at the men who hold her. The men rain heavy blows on her with clenched fists, battering her face and body.

"Get the spear!" Waller shouts. Ransu pries it from Sassa's grip.

Sassa fights like a ferocious animal caught in a trap. Ransu drops the spear, strikes Sassa viciously about the head and face with heavy fisted blows. Her lip splits, her nose is bloodied, yet she continues to fight.

Bard has landed on top of Tora on the floor, holds her by the arms, forces himself between her legs. He can not untie his belt for her struggling so he releases her arms to grip her around the throat with a strangling grip. Tora gasps for breath. Her struggles become less and less as she begins to fade from consciousness. Bard's cruel scowl is inches from Tora's face. "You should have let us in last night," he hisses. "We would have been more gentle."

Waller and Ransu struggle Sassa to the table, stretch her over it face down. Waller tries to untie his trousers but Sassa's struggles make it impossible to release her for even an instant without losing control of her.

"Hold her still!" Waller shouts to Ransu.

Ransu draws a rusted broadsword from his belt, hammers the butt end into the back of Sassa's head.

Stars burst before her eyes. The world spins. Sound is dim, far away. Sassa slumps unmoving on the table.

Waller grips Sassa by the back of the neck with one hand, unties his belt. The belt and weapons fall to the floor. He fumbles with the ties on his trousers.

Kari and Nanna cower in the dark corner, too frightened to even weep.

Bard struggles with Tora. "Help me with this one," he calls. Ransu goes to Bard. "Hold her arms," Bard commands.

THE VIKING ON STAMFORD BRIDGE

Ransu sets his sword down, grips Tora by the wrists. Bard rises to his knees to shuck his weapon's belt.

Waller, leaning heavily on Sassa's neck from behind, works his trousers down...

Kari sneaks from her place in the shadows, takes the bread pan from the coals by its long handle and rams the hot iron as hard as she is able into the crease of Waller's exposed buttocks.

Waller howls in pain, thrashes, dances frantically to be away from the searing iron. He flails, knocks the bread pan from Kari's hands, advances on the girl with killer intent.

Ransu calls from where he holds Tora, "Do not kill her. I like them that age."

Waller ignores Ransu's plea, reaches to strangle the life from the girl.

Sassa pushes herself from the table, dazed. Her face swollen and bleeding. There is a cut on the back of her head from the butt of Ransu's sword which pours blood, and her eyes still show the glassy effects of the blow. She takes up the mead pitcher that had toppled from the table, rushes Waller from behind just as he reaches Kari. Sassa smashes the pitcher into the back of Waller's head with all her might. Waller, trousers still around his ankles, goes down in a heap.

Ransu releases Tora, leaps to his feet, rushes Sassa but Sassa is quicker. She snatches up the spear from where it was dropped, turns it on the charging wretch. Ransu runs headlong onto the spear and is impaled through and through. He sits heavily on the floor staring stupidly at the spear shaft which protrudes from his belly.

Bard pushes himself to his feet, draws up his trousers, hastily ties them.

Sassa attempts to pull the spear from Ransu, but the dying man grips the shaft with the last of his strength. She can not pull it free.

Bard draws a knife from his weapons belt on the floor, advances on Sassa.

BRENT JORDAN

Sassa's eyes dart around the room, desperately searching for anything that might serve as a weapon, but Bard is already upon her...

Suddenly, Bard seizes in a violent convulsion as Tora runs him through from behind with his own sword. He drops like a sack of grain as his spine is severed.

Tora stands holding the sword, her eyes wide in shock.

Waller, recovering from the blow of the pitcher to his head, staggers to his feet, stands on unsure legs to get his bearings.

Sassa grips the spear shaft protruding from Ransu, stands on his chest, yanks the weapon free. She turns the spear on Waller who backs away, his hands raised in pleading surrender. Sassa and Tora advance upon Waller, weapons leveled, no mercy to be found in either woman. Sassa thrusts with her spear. The blade is buried into Waller's groin. He screams in pain, grabs at the spear but only catches blade as Sassa yanks it from him. Waller's hand is severed nigh in two. Tora cleaves at the would-be rapist with the sword. Sassa thrusts the spear again and again, long after Waller lies dead and butchered on the floor.

The remainder of the day is consumed with the task of hanging three decapitated corpses by their heels from the giant ash tree which towers above the longhouse. The heads of the three men rest on tall stakes before each body. A wood plank scored with runes in the blood of the dead men hangs by a nail on the tree. Only those few versed in runes would know what the sign reads, but Sassa does not mind. She carved the message for her own pleasure: 'Outlaws welcome to take your place on the tree.'

* * *

The fleet of longships flying the banner of King Hardrada continues south. The warmth of air and sea continues to rise. Men shed their shirts and cloaks, go bare chested looking for relief from the heat. To pass the time and drain tension from their coiled bodies and minds, they oil mail and leather, rewrap hilts, check rivets on shield bosses for the hundredth time.

The man makes no such preparations. Lacking armor and shield, and confident Skullseeker is fully prepared for battle, he reclines with an open stores sack to make a meal of dried herring and apples.

He looks across the short distance to King Hardrada's longship where two young women stand at the helm, their fine dresses billowing.

Eystein moves among the men offering casual banter and compliments on their weaponry. He notes the man gazing at the girls on Hardrada's ship. "Hardrada's daughters," explains Eystein, "Ingegerd and my betrothed, Maria."

"Why would a man bring his daughters to war?"

"England is to be their new home. He does not trust their passage with any escort but himself. Before we take to land they will be returned to Scotland to await our victory. Harald has no great love for the Scot king and would leave them in his care as little time as possible."

The man frowns his disapproval, bites the head from a dried herring. "I do not understand it."

"I share your feelings and would not put them at such risk myself. But they are willful women and demanded that they not sail all this way and not be allowed to lay eyes on England. I believe their father indulges them far too much."

"That I do understand," says the man. "It is difficult to deny a daughter her want."

"Aye, but your daughters are young still and easier to mold to your will."

The man chokes on his herring at the assumption. "If that is so, you might tell them," says the man, brushing chewed herring from his chest. "And even if it were, one day they will be of that age. I do not know if even the gods can help me then."

Eystein chuckles and smiles broadly. He clasps the man on his shoulder in empathy as he moves on to check on others.

Svend leans over the ships gunwale to take the cooling sea-spray over his exposed skin when he suddenly points and shouts, "Ships! There! Ahead!"

Warriors raise their eyes from their battle preparations to look.

A grouping of a dozen ships of English make appear on the horizon near the mouth of a wide estuary. They seem to be anchored, unmoving.

"The English have sent their fleet to fight us!" exclaims Svend.

The veterans turn back to their work.

"You have sharp eyes," says Ull, "but see, they fly the banner of Tostig Godwinson."

"Tostig," Tarbin spits the name, "a traitor to his own brother, and we are to trust him?"

"We need not trust him far," says Ull, "it would appear he provides only eleven or twelve ships, and fair to say less than six-hundred fighters."

"And them, Flemings," growls Tyrulf, "hardly worth dulling a blade on."

"Then what need do we have of them?" asks Svend, his frustration apparent, "And are we to ever reach England?"

"We have reached it my young friend," says Ull, "the war only awaits our landing. As to Tostig, when King Hardrada takes the throne the former king's brother at his side will lend an air of legitimacy."

"My bull's ass has more legitimacy," scoffs Tarbin. "The wretch was ousted from his own earldom, denied the support of his brothers and now turns on them. A useless lot, the English."

Forni speaks in low tones from beneath his wide-brimmed hat, "Oaths broken, brother set against brother and the world at war. All signs of Ragnarök."

"Signs of Ragnarök appear to you from everywhere, old

man," grumbles Tarbin. "If it is so, where is Firmbulwinter? I would welcome its coming. It is as though Surt has laid his sword to this infernal land."

"You might leave your furs in the ship for the return trip home," says Ull, "and not wear them like a preening cock if the heat is a concern."

"A fine one to speak of preening cocks," replies Tarbin, "I have watched you spend half a day combing your locks. And it is high-time you grew a beard. I have no desire to fight beside a man with smoother cheeks and more beautiful than my wife."

"If comparison in beauty to your wife is your standard for companionship, I am afraid you will fight alone," says Ull.

"He speaks the truth concerning my wife," admits Tarbin to the group in general. "She is an unsightly creature. But the woman bears me many children, no matter how uncomely they be. And besides, it is not so hard to leave home to raid and war when your wife is no pleasure to look at."

Surrounding warriors laugh heartily.

The man alone finds no joy in the levity. The talk of family has brought Sassa to mind as nearly any subject does a dozen times a day.

Resolve in the face of strife can be difficult to maintain when reminded of the comforts and pleasures of home.

❈ ❈ ❈

Sassa finishes helping the farm woman load her horse drawn cart with split wood. She accepts a token payment without dickering. With nary a healthy grown man left in all of Trondheim, and winter quickly approaching, Sassa knows the women of the village will be in dire need of firewood. She has no desire to impose any more toll on her neighbors than has already been extracted by the war.

The corpses still hang in the tree. The severed heads staked before them grow more motley by the day. Ravens and crows gather in the great ash to strip flesh from the dead men and dig at their offal for their meals.

The farm woman sees Sassa in a whole new light than she and her friends had on previous visits to the farmstead. Sassa: too thin, too conscious of her beauty. Sharing a husband with her own sister, they would say. Now, Sassa: killer of outlaws. Not a woman to be spoken poorly of.

Thanking Sassa for the wood, the farm woman urges the swayback nag to lean into the traces. The cart creaks its way along the path toward town.

Following the incident with the outlaws, Tora gathered her things to join Sassa and the girls in their home. Safety in numbers, Sassa tells her, and no point in maintaining two homes through the winter. Sisters are good company to one another in times such as these.

Sassa has taken careful stock of their stores and knows them to be excessive. The brined and smoked boar will be feasted on for a year. Butter, buttermilk, cheese, skyr, pickled apples, onions... all in plenty. The arm ring Eystein Orri left will be hacked into a half-dozen pieces, each worth a year's grain, fish, bread and porridge.

Sassa knows she and her daughters have been left wanting for nothing -- nothing but husband and father.

Kari has fashioned a shield and sword from old planks of lumber. She practices her sword-fighting daily on the poles holding the heads of the outlaws. In her vivid imagination, she kills the men over and over again.

In other times Sassa might discourage such play, but not now... Now it seems an appropriate game for a daughter whose father is gone at war.

✻ ✻ ✻

Tostig Godwinson, King Harold Godwinson's wayward brother, a bit too narrow of face and frame to be named handsome, stands on the deck of his Flemish warship watching the approach of Hardrada's vast fleet. Dressed in English finery, Tostig's hunched carriage and many nervous habits are unbecoming of a nobleman. The ship -- and the dozen more which accompany it -- are filled with Fleming mercenaries: Tostig's hired army.

Joric, captain of the Fleming mercenaries, is a stout warrior in his prime who wears impressive armor and a proud demeanor. He stands at Tostig's shoulder, eyes the oncoming fleet of King Hardrada which stretches beyond sight on the calm sea.

"Lord Tostig, we should put you ashore until we are confident of King Hardrada's commitment to your cause," says Joric.

Tostig smirks, his lip twitches with his response, "His only commitment is to himself. My cause is mere convenience to him."

"I do not understand why you risk life and treasure to support his quest to be king."

"Hardrada's ambition is never ending. After becoming king of England he will move on to Normandy, or continue his ambition to rule the Danes. In his absence, I will remain."

Joric nods his understanding of the cunning nobleman's plan. "A native born Saxon who sits on the throne would hold more sway over the English people than a foreign born king."

"There are still a goodly number of nobles who share sentiments with me," claims Tostig.

"Will they provide warriors to this fight?"

"They will not. They will wait for the outcome between Hardrada and my brother, Harold."

"And if Hardrada wins?"

"The nobles will back me with the witan, and the throne will by rights be mine."

"By rights and by sword are often two different matters," reminds Joric.

"It is my hope your countrymen will see the benefits of

having me as king over Hardrada."

Joric inclines his head. "That is the very reason we have joined you in your cause, Lord Tostig."

❋ ❋ ❋

King Hardrada's armada is beached for miles along the coast bordering the estuary of the river Ouse. The army has set camp for the night. Fires roast entire beef and swine. Kegs of mead are opened and Norsemen fill their drinking cups and horns frequently. The mood is elevated with song and laughter from warriors filled with excitement for the adventure.

Tostig Godwinson sits erect and formal on a stool at King Hardrada's fire. Joric along with several serious minded Fleming mercenaries flank Tostig, fully armed and armored as bodyguards to their retainer.

Across the fire from Tostig, King Hardrada dips his ornate drinking horn in an open keg of mead, drinks heartily. He is surrounded by his lax troop of berserkers mingled with the men of Eystein's crew. All are well on their way to being drunk. The man and Svend share a place near the fire, join in the exuberant mood of the army.

Hardrada is in the midst of a story to amuse his listeners; "...Finally, the young lady acquiesced to my honeyed words and we found ourselves on the fur rugs of the throne room itself."

The warriors surrounding the fire lean forward, entertained.

Hardrada drinks from his horn before he continues, "Now, had I been aware she was the second wife of the Rus king, or had I known the king would be returning so soon, I might have made a more hasty withdrawal. Alas, as it stood, I was caught in mid thrust of my naked... sword."

The Norsemen howl their laughter. Tostig and his Flemings, understanding little of the language, remain erect and stoic.

Hardrada continues, "The Rus king was short of humor for his bride being attended to so thoroughly, and the fool of a cuckold took offense. After slaughtering half of the king's private guard, I embarked on my travels southward to the empire of the Byzantine where I became captain of the Varangian guard."

Tyrulf shouts to the king, "After pulling up your trousers, I hope!"

Norsemen bay their laughter, fall drunkenly from their seats.

King Hardrada laughs with them. "Aye, but that is a saga for another time."

Howling protests from the entertained warriors cause Hardrada to raise his hands for silence. "Enough tales for one night. Feast and drink the night through. Our host and I must make plans for the morrow. Plans to slaughter Saxons, gain riches and win the crown of England!"

Warriors cheer, chant, howl their excitement in such a ruckus one could imagine the war already won.

Hardrada gestures for Eystein to follow. The two of them approach Tostig. Tostig stands, leads the way to his tent.

Candles burn, lighting the expansive interior of the shelter. A table in the center holds a map of the English isle. Two attendant guards stand by the entrance. Tostig, Hardrada and Eystein enter to study the map.

"You are acquainted with our language, Tostig. Do my stories bore you?" jibes Hardrada.

"Not at all, Sire. I am afraid the task of wresting the crown from my brother weighs more heavily on my mind than it does yours."

Hardrada quotes a well loved maxim of the Allfather; "'It befits a man to be merry and glad until the day of his death.'"

"My brother Gyrth has a saying much the same," says Tostig.

"Your brother knows of Odin?" queries Eystein.

"Gyrth knows of seemingly everything," says Tostig. "As a child he read and studied until the priests swore he would go blind. He is now captain of Harold's army."

"An educated man, and a warrior," muses Hardrada. "It will be an honor to kill such a fascinating man."

Tostig is pained at the thought. "King Hardrada, I have joined you to engage in war against my brothers, but must we speak of it in those terms?"

"Do you know of other terms?" asks Eystein. "Death is part of life. Killing is part of war."

Tostig remains silent.

Hardrada grips the distraught nobleman's shoulder with one massive hand. "There is no shame in showing love for your brothers, Tostig, even in war. Yet remember, your lot has been cast. You have sworn loyalty to me, and I to you. Our cause is linked."

"I have sworn an oath and I shall stand by it," says Tostig.

Satisfied, Hardrada stands over the map of England. "Come, show me the way to London. If we kill enough Saxons on our journey, your brothers may understand the futility of standing against me and be spared yet."

❖ ❖ ❖

Sails stowed, each man pulls on an oar driving the longships up England's river Ouse. The sleek ships race as if unburdened by the opposing current, driven by Norse warriors eager for war and plunder. Lookouts perched high on bare masts of each ship scan the banks for settlements worthy of attack.

English fishermen and farmers abandon their villages, scurry away with only their lives before the fleet which blankets the river miles inland to the estuary. Lagging ships of the armada pull ashore to clear the small villages of anything of worth, while the bulk of Hardrada's army sails inland without pause.

"There! Ahead! Smoke!" the alert shouted by lookouts of several ships.

Every man's eye looks to the sky ahead where above the trees rises a prodigious amount of pale smoke from what could only be a large town's cook fires. The men lean to oars with vigor. The longships skate onward.

The foremost of the ships come alongside the rising smoke and are driven into the marshes of the shallows banking the river.

Tyrulf again is the first to launch himself from the ship's rail into the shallows. Eschewing a shield, the lone vanguard slogs ashore with sword in one hand, axe in the other. A mass of Norsemen quickly follow bearing weapons. Most remain unburdened by helms, mail or shields as they anticipate an easy fight and are unwilling to occupy hands that will be needed to secure their share of plunder.

Svend grips his bow and a quiver of arrows, leaps from the ship. The man follows closely, Skullseeker firmly strapped across his bare back. They trail their countrymen who sprint en masse up the wooded slope to the city of Cliffland.

Terrified screams can be heard through the woods even before the man and Svend break from the forest onto the open plain. A large sprawling city with scant defenses lies ahead. The horrific screams rise from there. Already, burning homes and buildings join the cook fires in billowing black smoke into the mid-day sky.

Svend's bow is ready with a notched arrow, but the lad can find no target to loose on.

Dead and dying English men, women and children litter the streets like so much chaff after the harvest. An English merchant, gutted and left to die, mews in mind-torn agony as he sits splay-legged before his shop, gathering his spilled entrails to him from the blood-muddied street. Englishwomen, speared, impaled immobile to tables, scream mindlessly and cling desperately to life as they are raped. Wailing children clutch at dead and dying parents to await the sword. Other tiny bodies are trampled to unrecognizable pulp beneath the boots of the crush of invaders.

The man gapes at it all, his mind unwilling to grasp the reality of what his eyes are witness to. He is jarred in his stance as an endless flow of raiders from trailing ships swarm into the city to take their share of the slaughter and pillage.

Gasping sounds of one drowning cause the man to turn. One of the few armed city guards slumps, pinned to the turf wall of a small home by his own spear thrust through his lung. The guard weeps and blubbers through foaming blood an incoherent bit of prayer to his god, pleading for life or death.

Svend trembles as he watches his uncle approach the guard and with a short snap of Skullseeker, take the Englishman's head from his body. The man and Svend stare down on the glassy-eyed head lolling in the dirt, then turn to the city.

The man travels the streets putting an end to the wounded and suffering. There seems no end to them yet he keeps at his work, silencing agonized cries and pleas to a deaf and blind god.

Svend follows but does not take part in the slaughter, the despoiling of the city, nor his uncle's work. He watches the plunder as arm-loads of items, some valuable, some common, are carried from shops and homes to be piled in the street. Commandeered carts, sacks, bedding... anything to be filled and carried, are used to tote the goods away.

Halfdan the Bold has gathered a half-dozen young men to him; this, their first experience at war. The band rushes from home to home, shop to shop, killing everything that lives. Dogs, chickens, goats, hogs, children, women and men, butchered without discrimination. The gang is consumed in the glee of uncontested slaughter and kill for sport.

Halfdan keeps an eye out for wealth when he finally finds what he is looking for. "There! The Christ church!" Halfdan calls to his band. He leads the way at a run to a large building with huge ornately carved doors and a tall crucifix standing at the peak of the roofline.

Inside the church a harried priest stands between altar and apse trying urgently to silence the thirty-some parishioners who crowd the nave -- on their knees, wailing -- praying to be saved.

Three young monks, terror creasing their faces, shush the weeping men, women and children.

The priest calls over the clamor of his flock, "Quiet, quiet. You are safe here, but for the sake of good, be quiet."

Suddenly, the doors are rammed inward. Halfdan and his band of young raiders burst in, weapons at the ready.

The parishioners shriek anew, scurry to the feet of the priest.

Halfdan takes in the riches of the church at a glance; gold crucifix, candelabras, bowls, chalices, silk trappings....

The priest screams at the intruders, his voice carrying above the panicked cries of his flock, "Out! Out heathen devils. This is the house of the Lord!"

Halfdan, familiar enough with the language of the Saxons, retorts, "Heathen? I am as Christian as you!" He displays from around his neck a thong with a large variety of gold and silver crucifixes won in previous raids.

Halfdan snatches a spear from one of his band, hurls it with all his strength at the priest. A young monk leaps in front of the cast and is killed, sparing the priest.

The raiders, wasting no more time, descend upon the huddled parishioners with swords and axes. A horrific slaughter ensues. The young Norwegians hack away at the huddled bodies with no aim or purpose but to kill.

Halfdan hefts a large, heavy gold crucifix from a table with greedy awe.

❧ ❧ ❧

The man and Svend have made their way through the city

to the church. They stand outside listening as the screams of those dying inside slowly fade, then cease.

Halfdan emerges from the church dragging the flailing, sobbing priest by an ankle. He still grips the heavy gold crucifix in one hand. Halfdan glares at the man, raises his voice above the cries of the dying, "You are too late woodcutter, this god's wealth is mine!"

Halfdan's band emerge from the church to dump their armloads of loot into a pile at their commander's feet, then rush back into the church for more.

The priest flops and flails on the ground, chatters in a language none understand.

Halfdan breaks his stare-down with the man, turns his attention to the priest. He straddles the Christ-monk, raises the crucifix, brings it down on the simpering wight's head. Again and again Halfdan strikes with the gilded cross. The priest's skull splinters. The cleric stops his blubbering. The body seizes tightly, like a spider touched by a flame, then slowly releases to lie still. Gore splattered, heaving for breath, Halfdan glares insanely at the man. His half-dozen chosen emerge from the church to stand, backing their leader.

The man would advance then, put an end to their feud -- nothing lost in this world without one such as Halfdan in it -- but Svend, seeing the intent in his uncle and the numbers against them, grips the man by his belt to drag him away deeper into the city.

The man and Svend travel the empty streets deep within Cliffland. Smoke from innumerable fires wafts like the dense fog of the underworld. It's quiet here, the sounds of slaughter, distant.

Suddenly four Saxon villagers -- three men, and a woman carrying an infant to her breast -- burst into the street from between homes. They freeze to stare at the man and Svend like surprised deer.

Svend raises his bow to shoot.

The men turn and run, leaving the woman with the infant limping after them, frantic to catch up. The group of villagers disappear into the smoke.

Svend lowers his bow, perplexed. "They will not fight. They do not even raise a sword against us, yet they beg for life even as they lie dying. I do not understand."

"There is nothing I wish to understand about this place," states the man.

They continue down the eerily quiet street through the murk of drifting smoke when a soft whimpering coming from a goat stable arrests their attention.

It is gloomy inside the shack, but the man can clearly see a boy in his teens lying slaughtered amongst the dead goats in the muck and straw. Quiet, pained sobs draw the man and Svend deeper into the gloom.

Huddled in the furthest corner, a young mother sits like a rag doll in an expanding pool of her own blood. Her face is ghostly white, and it is only by force of will she is still alive. As the two approach the dying woman, she repeats the same word over and over without energy or hope; "Please...."

The man, already crouched double for the low roof, kneels to examine the woman more closely. Nothing to be done for her.

A child's soft whimpering comes from beneath a pile of straw. The man brushes aside the straw to reveal two young girls near the age of his own daughters, cowering and crying in terror.

"Are they hurt?" asks Svend. His voice carries a soft tremble.

The young mother lacks the strength to move. She sags limply. "Please. Please do not kill them."

The man commands her language well enough. "They will not live without you," he says.

"Please..."

Svend looks outside to the approaching fires. "Uncle, the fire is getting close."

The man looks again to the two young girls.

"Do not let them die. Please," their mother begs with the last of her voice.

"They will be slaves. That is worse," says the man.

The young mother would beseech again, but all that comes from her lips is blood and a weak coughing.

The man holsters Skullseeker in its frog across his back, reaches for the girls, carries them from the shack.

Svend and the man rush in their attempt to escape the city, dodging through the narrow streets as fire rages all around them. They shelter the two young girls with their bodies as embers and flaming bits of thatch rain down. The foul smoke that envelops them is dense, choking and can not be seen through for more than a few feet in any direction.

Finally they emerge at the far side of Cliffland into an open pasture where cattle gather to stare stupidly at the flames and smoke.

The men's clothes and skin are burned in a hundred places from embers, yet they are alive and suck in great lungfuls of clean air to restore themselves.

The girls, frightened and covered in soot, cough smoke from their lungs, but they have stopped crying.

Svend looks upon the children with pity. "Uncle... can we just let them go? There are probably more of their people hiding in the woods, or..."

"They will die," states the man.

"Maybe they won't. You speak their language. Tell them they are free to go."

The man speaks to the children without hope, "Go. Run away."

The girls only stand, shiver, hold themselves in shock. Both look blankly at the man.

The man looks to the sky, blackened by innumerable crows which circle and call. The carrion birds float down through the smoke to feed upon the dead.

Packs of wild dogs lured by the smell of blood dart in and out of the city, braving the smoke and flames to have at the feast of dead Clifflanders inside.

A pack of half-starved curs approach closely, lured by the mewing of the children. Svend swipes his bow and shouts at the dogs. They dodge away, but continue to pace and circle.

With nothing more to be done, the man and Svend head back to the ships. The young girls follow.

Fires rage until there is nothing left to burn. The city of Cliffland is razed to ash, and the wind takes that. In a year, there will be little here to prove these people had ever lived at all.

* * *

As the sun declines, the Norwegians set up camp just inside the tree-line of the woods bordering the river. They cut down saplings, bind them together to create protective barricades. Guards are posted.

The army celebrates the ease of the victory. They feast on cattle and hogs taken from Cliffland, drink mead and boast loudly of their part in the day's adventure. Some wash away proof of the massacre from their bodies and clothes in the shallows of the river. Others leave the fetid remains matting their hair and cloaking their skin and clothes in proud display.

The man and Svend enter the camp of Eystein's crew with the two girls. The crew shouts their greetings.

"Svend, we thought you and your uncle had lost your way," calls Ull.

"I told him you had stayed behind to sift through the ash for a final piece of gold for that fine mother of yours," says Tarbin.

"We took no gold," says Svend.

"What is that you have with you?" queries Eystein, considering the two young girls. "Too young for thralls, don't you think?"

"Too young to be killed in war," says the man.

The warriors fall silent.

"Death in war knows nothing of age," says Eystein. "Var, take them to the thrall ships for return to Norway." Eystein's retainer ushers the girls away. The captain amends with a look to the man, "Make sure they are fed."

Eystein, not content with the doldrums fallen over his men, attempts to brighten the mood. "Rigsen, I was told you bloodied your axe on a hundred English, but took no bounty. And Svend, how did you fare? You appear unscathed."

"There was no one to fight," answers Svend.

"Your first battle," says Eystein with a dismissive wave of his hand, "you will learn to be quicker. Not to worry. No man goes without a share. We fight together, we profit together. That is war."

"War is for profit then," says the man.

"War without profit is simply slaughter," reminds Eystein.

"This is not war," replies the man as he strides from the gathering toward the ships beached in the shallow marshes of the river.

Svend begins to follow his uncle when Ull calls to him, "Svend, leave your uncle to himself for the night. Come join us. Eat, drink. It will restore you."

Svend remains standing in indecision, looking after his uncle.

Eystein moves in beside him, drapes an arm across his shoulders. "Not to worry. A night's rest and a good meal and your uncle will be back to his usual garrulous self," assures the captain.

Svend looks to Eystein, bewildered.

Eystein laughs at his own wit and the gullibility of the lad. The other warriors laugh along with their captain. Svend blushes. He takes an offered cup of mead and a seat at the fire.

Eystein's smile fades as he looks the direction the man took. It is the fault of the sagas, he knows, that men in their first experience misunderstand the true nature of war. The sagas claim war to be glorious combat -- man against man, may the best prevail -- and at its best that is the grandest yet the smallest part of it. Sagas hint at only an inkling of the whole. They tell nothing of the soul-piercing cries of agony, fear, lament. The reek of emptied bowels and bladders. The churning of blood and gore into blackened mud. Of deep wounds, even in victory, which cripple and never heal. Of the fires -- the noisome fires stripping human flesh from bone -- a constant in all war.

For a nation to be conquered the will of the people must be destroyed, not simply their bodies and homes. Great warriors meeting in noble combat will never accomplish that end. It only serves to build pride in one's own, and embolden men to take up arms to gain the glory of which the sagas tell.

Perhaps that is why the war of saga is reserved for Valhöll: For if war on earth was as magnificent as in Asgard, what man would have use of gods?

* * *

Cargo ships, designed for the purpose, are loaded with plunder. Those already filled, turn downriver to make the journey back to Norway.

The man sits on his bench aboard Eystein's longship and watches the smoke of the razed city dwindle, then disappear into the shadow of night. He cleans Skullseeker with water from a bucket dipped in the slow moving river, hones the blade again to a fine edge. Cleaned and honed, the man follows the carved knotted pattern on his battle-axe with an oiled cloth, caressing the head as if soothing a disquieted lover.

Forni sits with his back against the mast. His ravens returned to him bloated from the feast and now squat croaking contentedly in their crate. The man could not swear that Forni had moved at all since the landing.

He considers himself and finds he is caked with dried

blood and viscera. He uses the remainder of the water in the bucket with which he cleaned Skullseeker to clean himself.

On shore, cook fires are built up. Iron pots boil and steam with the evening meal. Soon savory smells eclipse even the rank odor of death.

The man's eyes follow the swirling pattern etched on the head of Skullseeker until he is dizzy with entrancement of it. When he finally raises his eyes, he finds Forni steadily staring at him from beneath his hat.

"Is this the way to Sessrumnir and Valhöll then?" asks the man, his voice tired and sullen.

Forni regards the man with his single eye. "You name Sessrumnir over Valhöll."

"Freyja has first choice of the fallen, does she not?"

Forni grins and his eye sparkles. "If you know a better way to keep peace in a household…" His mirth leaves him. His eye darkens. "No, this is not the way. The Valkyrie were absent from the field. Nothing to be gained by Freyja or Odin on this day. The Aesir are in need of warriors, not butchers."

"How then? How will I join my wife when she is called to Freyja's hall?"

"It is yet to be told if you shall," says Forni. "The greatness of a warrior can only be judged by the greatness of his opponent."

The man is troubled by the revelations of the day. How will he find an enemy great enough to gain notoriety amongst these merchants and farmers who piss themselves in terror at his approach? Milksops who cower and plead for life without even the nerve to take up an axe or knife in their own defense or the defense of their wives and children. Where is the honor and glory to be found in their slaughter?

And if no glory, how to gain a seat in the halls of Asgard?

❊ ❊ ❊

The great Norwegian army sleeps on the banks of the river Ouse, sentries posted, weapons close at hand, but there is no counter attack by the English. No one comes to avenge the massacre of Cliffland.

Before the sun presses the dark from the sky, the longships are again on the river, driven upstream by powerful Norsemen lusting for wealth.

Tostig Godwinson rides on King Hardrada's ship near the fore of the armada. He knows the land well and guides the invading army to villages and towns otherwise bypassed. Inhabitants flee in panic before the marauders like a flock of doves before a hawk.

Tostig is a toad of a man, made to appear even more reptilian in the presence of the long-limbed, broad shouldered Hardrada. He wears English armor and bears an English forged sword, but even the Norsemen within his earshot are not shy to quip that Hardrada will wear the English crown long before Tostig's armor is tested or he clears sword from scabbard.

Hamlets, villages and small undefended cities are sacked without resistance. English too slow or too dim to flee are put to death along with every manner of livestock, work animal, fowl and dog. Every creature that can not fly or flee, dies. Everything that can burn is burnt. What can not be killed or burnt, is crushed and scattered. All things of worth, stolen. The devastation wrought by Harald Hardrada's army is absolute.

The man watches all this from his place at the bow of the ship. He does not go ashore again, nor does he allow Svend to go.

Eystein announces the man and Svend are to be ship guards along with a small rotating troop of warriors who grumble and complain of being relegated to such duty.

When the crew of Eystein's ship return from a raid, they give looks to the man but none speak disparagingly. Each warrior seasoned enough to know it is not cowardice that has settled upon him. Simply not all were born to this.

If every man born were fit for the halls of Asgard, the benches of Valhöll would have been filled millennia ago. Five-hundred-forty doors in the great hall through which eight-hundred warriors each shall pass. Of all the warriors the world has ever known, only the elite of those -- the select few -- may join the Aesir in the fight at Ragnarök. If any man could be declared a hero, every man would, and the value of a seat in the great halls would be naught. This and no other, the way it is and must be.

Where the Ouse grows narrow and the forest thick, the hiss of half a hundred arrows suddenly assails the lead ships from the port side. The man covers Svend, hunkers over him behind the shields hung to the rail. All the warriors aboard the longships do the same as arrow shafts thump hollowly, striking the heavy shields and ship planks.

The instant the initial volley subsides, Ull and archers from other ships fire a barrage of arrows back into the forested banks of the river. Svend frees his bow from where it is stowed, joins in returning arrow fire until Eystein calls a halt to it.

The sounds of a scurrying retreat from the banks, flashes of colored cloth and glinting armor prove the assailing barrage was not conjured from thin air.

The Norwegians rise cautiously from behind shields to peer into the forest, but there is nothing more to be seen.

King Hardrada stands the prow of his ship holding a shield feathered with several arrows.

Eystein calls to Hardrada, "Shall we pursue?"

"No. Tostig claims the city of York is not far. This is merely their fond welcome," returns Hardrada.

A murmur of laughter from the warriors within earshot.

"On to York then," bellows Eystein as he plucks an Saxon arrow from the plank near his feet, holds it high, "so we might return these fine gifts to their owners."

There is more roaring laughter as the army leans to oars, the ships doubling speed toward battle.

The man pulls steady and strong, eager now that they

have found a willing enemy to oppose them.

Svend shoots anxious looks over his shoulder to the woods which encroach on the smoothly flowing river, but there is no further harassment of the ships.

The fleet makes use of the marshes and low banks at Riccall where the grassland slopes gently to the Ouse, to take to shore. Warriors struggle into mail shirts, fit helmets over arming caps, secure weapons and debark the longships.

A grand energy has overtaken the army entire. Each man assists others in their preparations, their eyes alight in eager anticipation of the battle to come.

The man and Svend, grateful to be lacking armor or shields in the oppressive heat, take to shore. Their spirits are elevated with the jovial mood of their war mates.

Forni releases his ravens, sets the crate aside. From beneath the ship's benches he produces a magnificent spear, the blade near the length of a man's forearm and artfully etched with runes. The shaft also bears runes, carved and stained with care in the fine, polished ash wood. Forni dawns neither mail nor helm nor shield. He vaults from the longship, spear in hand, to join Hardrada's army. With the coiled spring of vitality and strength in his step, Forni appears old no more: A man-at-arms in his prime, fervent for battle and glory.

King Hardrada takes to shore surrounded by Eystein, Tostig and several other leaders to plot their advance.

Tostig squats, uses an arrow to etch a map in the sandy bank. "Yorkshire is no more than three leagues north. A series of small forts along this route. No doubt Edwin and Morcar have been drawn out by news of our coming and will use these outposts to counter and rally. We will be harried all the way to the city," predicts Tostig.

King Hardrada studies the sand-map. "There is a river through York."

"Yes, here," says Tostig as he sketches a serpentine line in the sand, "and marshlands, here, that flood with the tide."

King Hardrada looks north as he mulls over the plan of

attack, "The tides on this river are impressive."

"Aye, their distributaries grow shallow," adds Eystein.

"With proper timing..."

"Agreed," says Eystein. "Shall we take a meal, or march?"

"March," announces the king without hesitation. "This heat wearies the men more than hunger."

Battle horns are sounded. Commanders rally their men to follow King Hardrada and Eystein Orri who lead the march to York.

* * *

Kari, armed with her shield of old plank and her stick sword, charges forward screaming her battle cry to duel with a stake with an outlaw's head impaled atop. The child strikes relentlessly at the stake with her sword. Startled crows burst into flight, disturbed from their feeding on the outlaw corpses hanging from the ash tree.

Nanna hurls rocks at a head on another stake.

Though only nine, Kari fights well. She defends imaginary strikes from her opponent; attacks with vicious swings of her branch-sword. She is tireless, only stopping when she sees Jarl Kolbrand and his nephew Frode, attended by two retainers, riding their horses at a walk toward the farmstead.

Nanna drops her rocks and runs to the longhouse.

Kari stands her ground.

Jarl Kolbrand and his men stop their horses when they come to the hanging outlaws.

"So it is true," Jarl Kolbrand says. He looks down from his horse to Kari. "Who killed these men, child?"

"I helped," Kari boasts.

"Where is your father?"

"At war."

"Your mother, then."

Sassa comes toward them, her natural swinging gate reduced to painful limping steps. Tora and Nanna follow closely. Sassa's face is still badly bruised from the fight. Frode is instantly taken with Sassa despite her battered appearance.

Sassa smiles her warmest smile through swollen lips. "Jarl Kolbrand, you are welcome."

"This is the woodcutter's home, is it not?" queries Kolbrand.

"It is. I am Sassa, his wife."

Frode has not taken his eyes from Sassa.

Kolbrand dismounts. His men follow suit.

"There seem to be dead men decorating your tree," says Kolbrand.

"Indeed," agrees Sassa.

"How did they get there?" the jarl would know.

"They entered my home without welcome. I thought the tree a fitting place for them."

A retainer looks closely at the remains of a head on a stake. "Outlaws," he confirms.

"You did this yourself?" asks Kolbrand, doubt tinging his voice.

"My sister Tora and I," states Sassa.

"And me," amends Kari.

Sassa smiles upon her daughter and passes a loving hand over her hair.

Kolbrand looks more than a little dubious at the story.

"Uncle Carr, these women have obviously been in a fight. Might we take them at their word?" offers Frode.

Sassa looks to Frode. He stands straighter, taller. Sassa returns her attention to Jarl Kolbrand. "I have fresh stew in the pot. Would you care for the story over a meal and mead?" she offers.

"This is a tale I would love to hear," admits Kolbrand. "There is enough for all of us?"

"More than enough. I am still accustomed to cooking for my husband," says Sassa. She gathers up Kari and Nanna and heads for the longhouse.

Jarl Kolbrand and his retainers follow.

Tora falls in beside the jarl, addresses him with comfortable familiarity using his given name, "Carr, it is good to see you."

"You as well, Tora."

Tora gently touches the fine cloak Kolbrand wears. She smiles. "You have fared well since we last met."

"I have become older and fatter."

"Wiser and more prosperous," suggests Tora.

Kolbrand smiles. "You do not make life easy on a married man, Tora Gunnersen."

"On any man," Tora corrects. She loops her arm through his as they walk together to the longhouse.

Laughter and mead flow as Sassa and Tora host Jarl Kolbrand, Frode and their two retainers.

Tora ladles another helping of stew onto Kolbrand's plate. He tries to wave her off. "No more. You have filled me to the brim," he protests.

Tora sits across the jarl's lap. She takes up a spoonful of stew from his plate to feed it to him. "Here, I will help," she giggles. Kolbrand opens wide. Tora gets some of the stew in his mouth, the remainder, down his chin and shirt.

Sassa, her daughters and the men laugh heartily.

Tora wipes the jarl's chin with a hand, sucks stew from her fingers. Kolbrand is mesmerized. Tora playfully raises her eyebrows at him, reaches for his mead cup. She tips the cup to his lips.

"I feel you are trying to bribe me away from making an inquiry as to how those men in your tree came to be there," says the jarl.

"Is it working?" asks Tora.

"Yes!" Kolbrand blurts with a laugh.

Laughter is bellowed from the men.

Sassa stands from the table to clear the plates to the washing tub. "I stand by what I have told you," she states curtly.

Kolbrand waves a hand in dismissal. "There will be no inquiry. In fact, I may call upon you to deal with all outlaws in my city from now on."

Frode watches Sassa at the wash tub. He rises to join her. "Those men deserve to hang from that tree for nothing more than defacing your singular beauty," says Frode.

Sassa smiles, continues her work washing dishes.

Emboldened by her response, he ventures further, "King Hardrada's army will no doubt winter in England. Your husband will be away for the whole of the season. You might find use of a man..." Frode is stopped by Sassa's cautioning look. He is careful with the next; "... to protect your household, your daughters and sister."

Sassa grins at the circumspect conclusion.

"I would be honored to serve as your champion until the return of your husband," announces Frode.

"The three hanging in my tree found me capable enough," says Sassa.

Frode gently touches Sassa's bruised cheek. "At what cost?"

Sassa sighs, knows too well what is coming next.

"Surely your husband would not begrudge you protection... and the warmth of companionship while he is so far away," concludes Frode.

"You are bold," says Sassa.

"Fortune favors the bold," answers Frode.

"I wonder if you would be so bold if my husband were here."

"I am no coward," says Frode in protest, "I would fight and risk death for you."

Sassa stops washing dishes, wipes her hands on her apron. She favors Frode with a sad smile. "I do not want you to die for me. I want you to live in peace. And I want you to allow me and mine to do the same."

As the men take their leave, Tora stands aside with Frode as he prepares his horse. They speak in low tones so the others do not hear.

"She will not take to me," says Frode.

"Nonsense," whispers Tora, "it is just a woman's way. She must protest to keep her virtue intact."

Frode shakes his head, unsure.

Tora presses, "You want her, do you not?"

"Yes, but..."

"Then maintain your resolve and we shall both have what we want," whispers Tora. "Her husband will be away for the better part of a year. Before his return, you and she will be long gone to your home in Uppsala."

"Will he not come for her?"

"I will ensure he does not."

"You have designs on your sister's husband?"

"He should be mine," hisses Tora. "I am eldest. He fought a duel for me."

Frode considers the conspiracy, shakes his head, mounts his horse. "Find another to help you fulfill your schemes," says Frode as he reigns his horse tightly around, spurs it in the direction of Trondheim.

Tora, left standing alone, covers her frustration with a smile and nod to Jarl Kolbrand who watches, intrigued at the secret conversation between her and his nephew.

Sassa also watches her sister, apprehensive at what designs Tora might have for the kin to the jarl.

❊ ❊ ❊

The gentle land falls away beneath them as the army advances through the shire of York. They travel unmolested, pausing only to set torch to hamlets and farmhouses along the way. The army eats dried meat, fruit and bread on the march. Each man speaks little, his voice low, keeping counsel with only the warrior to his left or right. Svend travels beside Ull who has gathered other archers to him.

The man has been selected to march at the fore of the army. When he ventures looks behind to his nephew, Svend's eyes remain always upon him.

The army does not hurry. Whatever preparations the English have, they have made already. They pass battlements, yet despite Tostig's grim prediction, the fortifications are abandoned.

Saxons scurry away at their approach like rats fleeing from the light of an opened door.

Tostig has been sent to command his Fleming mercenaries, combined with the Scots and Zetlanders on the army's left flank. King Hardrada appears relieved to be rid of the English lord.

The banners of the vast army flutter over the plain, each troop proudly flying the standard of their region, yet all following the Landwaster banner of King Hardrada.

A finely embroidered black raven on white background is Landwaster. The totem held high on a tall staff by a proud warrior always at Hardrada's heel. It is said the three daughters of Ragnar Lodbrok wove the banner during a single midday's time. Legend states if the army following that banner were to win a battle, there was to be seen in the center of the signum, a raven gaily flapping its wings. But if they were to be defeated, the raven dropped motionless. And this always proved true. Further it was known though the banner could bring victory to the army who followed it, it would bring sure death to the one who carried it. And this also always proved true.

Though a token of his own death, it is a great honor to be chosen to bear Landwaster. The warrior who carries the banner at the fore of the great Norwegian army does so with exceeding pride and a bold step.

Ever before the advancing army, a Saxon scout lightly armored on a fine steed watches their advance. Never closer than twice the distance of a bow shot, the Saxon rides ahead as if a herald to announce their coming.

The man travels at the apex of the army where King Hardrada himself has placed him. Skullseeker, the great battle-axe of his ancestor, rests across his bare shoulders. Lacking mail, he sees no purpose of a shirt. A lifetime of swinging an axe and hauling felled trees has muscled the man to a startling degree. Even the professional warriors of Eystein's guard -- hugely powerful men -- have never seen such thews. The man's torso glistens with sweat that drains from him in a never-ending stream. His hair and beard drip with it. Sweat stings his eyes, soaks into his trousers. The scorching heat of the day causes the man to wonder if they had sailed too far and landed in Muspelheim. The promise of winning land in this country seems a cruel irony.

King Hardrada travels with his berserk bodyguard mingled with the warriors of Eystein's ship. Even they follow on the heels of the man.

Hardrada's chosen: Berserkers of renowned lineage. Huge, fierce men with giant axes and heavy plank shields. Helms crested with boars, wolves and serpents formed of gold. Fierce eyes look out from beneath the embellished iron. Their hair and thick beards are decorated with beads, leather and the claws and fangs of all manner of beasts they have killed.

They curse their mail shirts that cook them in the infernal sun. As berserker, they long to shed the armor and go naked into battle -- even before the shield wall -- as did their fathers and grandfathers before them. But King Hardrada, having conceded enough to surround himself with heathens such as his guard, insists they at least fight clothed, wearing armor like proper Christians. The berserk chafe, grumble and are keen to take their frustrations out in battle.

The man now clearly understands why, though not a seasoned warrior, he has been chosen for the honor of being presented at the head of the army. The sheer size and ferocity displayed by the lead hundred warriors will give pause to any sane Englishman. And he, along with the king, stand nearly a head taller than even the massive berserkers surrounding them. Head and shoulders larger than the largest Saxon that will face them. To a forward scout of the Saxons it will appear Jötunheim had opened to release an army of giants upon their land.

The effect of intimidation and fear on the outcome of a fight can not be overstated.

The man suspects a secondary reason for his placement at the forefront of the invading army. He will be the prime target in the initial attack: A fine trophy for any brave Saxon archer or spearman. It will be his lot to draw attention and fire away from the king. The knowledge implants a mirthless grin firmly upon his features. What finer way to establish a name in legend than to be the paramount target of the enemy? Now, only to not be killed by the first arrow... and to make the most of the opportunity given him.

At Fulford on the outskirts of York where a sparse wood meets an open plain, Hardrada calls a halt to the march. Warriors doff helms, take knees, drink greedily from water flasks. Wool, leather and iron, ill suited to the climate.

On the far side of the open plain nearly a half-mile across, the combined armies of Yorkshire and Northumbria make camp. A broad shallow river which feeds the Ouse cuts the plain between armies. An overgrown marsh borders the field to the east.

"So they are not going to force us to march all the way to London after all," says Eystein.

"They have chosen their field well," says Hardrada. "I have no desire to slog through the river to get at them, and the marsh will work against us if we are flanked."

"Have Tostig earn his title of jarl, if he is to have it," says Eystein. "He and his Flemings to our flank, along with the Scots. Let us take their army head on when the river wanes."

The king is content with the plan. "Give the command," says Hardrada, "and rest the men. There is still time before the tide ebbs."

Eystein speaks to a runner who shadows him. The young messenger sprints away to relay the orders.

As the orders ripple through the army, men set down their shields and sit in the dry grass to drink empty their water flasks.

The man remains standing, looking through the breeze-blown foliage of the willows to the far bank of the river where the expansive Saxon army is camped. Pickets and fortifications have been erected. Thousands of spearheads reflect the sun which rides high in the mercilessly unclouded sky.

Svend plops into the grass, mops the sweat from his face with the tail of his shirt. "Why would anyone make a home in this land? It is as though we are traveling through a smithing forge."

Tarbin shucks his mail and the sweat-drenched shirt beneath before he makes claim, "I have been to lands where the sun heats iron until the mail burns patterns into your skin."

"Fortunately for you," goads Ull, "you wear another fur beneath your shirt."

Tarbin lies back in the grass, runs a hand over the thick matted hair of his chest and stomach. "One day, if you are truly blessed, you may be graced with such manly covering also."

Ull dismisses Tarbin as he looks to the man who stands as a carved statue gazing across the river at the army of Saxons. "Does he never rest?"

Svend regards his uncle. "I have seen him stand waiting for a stag to cross a trail from dawn until dusk, so still and unmoving even I would forget where he stood."

"You might tell your uncle the English are not going anywhere," says Tarbin as he yawns and stretches lazily in the grass. "I have seen this many times. When the tide of the river wanes the motherless dogs will send simpering emissaries to negotiate with King Hardrada. They will offer Danegeld, the king will counter for more. Larger offers will be made. The king will accept. In the end, their army will be spared and we

194

will be made to take the long path around their city to London."

"They will not fight?" asks Svend, astounded at the notion.

"Not unless forced to do so," confirms Ull.

"But this is their land and their army is far larger than ours."

"Larger in what way?" scoffs Tarbin.

"Well... in numbers," says Svend, puzzled at having to state such an obvious fact to a veteran warrior.

"Numbers will not always tell the outcome of a battle," says Ull. "Pit a dozen lambs against a single wolf and tell me of the outcome."

"A silver arm ring wagered that we have marched all this way to listen to wealthy men barter for more wealth," says Tarbin with a gaping yawn. "I do not believe they will fight."

"They will fight," says Forni as he passes. He uses his long-hafted spear as a walking stave as he strides to where the man stands at the edge of the field.

Tarbin sighs, sits upright and begins pulling on his shirt and mail.

"How can he be sure?" Asks Svend.

"This you can put your trust in," sighs Tarbin, "if the old man says they will fight, they will fight."

Forni approaches the man, stands at his shoulder propped on his spear as a third leg. Both men gaze across the river. They stand like that for a very long time, unmoving as the trees, silent as the still grass.

The man speaks so only Forni can hear, "Are they worthy?"

"As an enemy to grant you a seat in the halls of Asgard? Any man who takes up arms and fights bravely is a worthy enemy."

The man quietly studies the answer.

Forni peers up at the man from beneath the brim of his hat. His eye has taken on a twinkling spark of concealed knowledge, his lips a grin of barely repressed mirth. "You worry that it will not be enough."

"Every man in this army has done more. A hundred times more," says the man.

"And you feel this makes them more deserving than you."

The man remains silent, watches the English army mill in their preparations on the far bank.

Forni shrugs. "It is true, there are many here who could claim a seat in Valhöll. And some will. But there are others, great warriors that they are, the Valkyrie will pass over." Forni's speech grows in intensity and urgency until it is a fervent plea, "If a warrior fights only because he is conscripted to a king, or for wealth, or because he knows no other way to make a life for his family. If his heart is not with the battle, fighting only for the sake of battle, would he not be less worthy than a man who fights from pure desire? For the love of the battle itself? Because he understands that to battle is his true purpose and path to Asgard?"

The revelation is of no solace to the man, for he fights for neither wealth nor desire of battle, and states as much to Forni.

"But for love!" exclaims Forni, his bearing alight with fevered intoxication for the subject, "Better still! What greater purpose could there be?"

"I can not speak to such things," says the man as his eyes break from the Saxons to travel the length of Forni's spear. Scored and stained runes cover the shaft from butt to head. "My wife Sassa knows of runes, but she would not tell me what she read of my destiny. She would only say…"

"That no man may know his future, so let him sleep in peace," Forni recites the well known maxim.

The man looks to Forni, once again astonished at his seeming knowledge of his innermost thoughts, but the Ancient One's face is hidden by the brim of his sagging hat. Possibly the curse of the aged, imagines the man: knowing the thoughts of men after a long life of bearing them.

"Your Sassa is a learned wife," says Forni, "a fine woman worthy of a great hero."

"I would be a hero worthy of her," says the man.

"Then be that hero!"

There is a stirring amongst the Saxon's as a contingent rides across the waning river to approach Hardrada's army. The Norwegians stir and stand to watch the proceedings. Saxon negotiators halt a good distance from their enemy.

Hardrada, Eystein and several jarls stride forward to meet the defenders of Yorkshire. The Landwaster banner ripples above them -- the raven taking flight. It seems even the Saxons understand the portent.

The grouping of Norwegian and Saxon nobles speak out of earshot of either army. Hardrada, in the forefront, stands nearly at eye-level with the mounted emissaries.

The man and Forni stand shoulder to shoulder to watch the proceedings.

"Would a hero have war?" asks Forni.

"I would."

"Then you shall."

Forni turns to face the Norwegian army gathered behind, raises his spear high above his head.

Hardrada's berserkers, seeing and understanding this, excitedly take up their war chant: "Fram! Fram! Odinmenn, Tyrmenn Thormenn! -- Forward! Forward! Men of Odin, men of Tyr, men of Thor!" -- They thump resounding rhythm with sword and axe on shields in time with the chant.

Troops of Norsemen sworn to the Christ take up their opposing chant: "Fram! Fram! Kristmenn, krossmenn, kongsmenn! -- Forward! Forward! Men of Christ, men of the cross, men of the king!"

Throughout Hardrada's army, competing chants are bellowed in earnest, each in their convivial attempt to drown the other out.

The rising din causes the horses of the Saxon emissaries

to step nervously, and their riders to look back to their own army with rising anxiety.

Eystein, resigned to the augury of his fellow Norsemen worked into such a frenzy, turns to face the mass of chanting warriors. In doing so, he places his hand on the hilt of his sheathed sword.

Hardrada does not turn, but chuckles, shakes his head, sighs heavily, accepting the inevitable.

Satisfied with the uprising, Forni turns to the Saxon line, strides forward gaining momentum until at a lope -- his spear in his fist, his arm coiled like a striking adder -- hurls his weapon. The missile sails faster than a diving eagle over the impossible distance to impale the lead Saxon emissary through the chest, the force driving him from his startled horse.

A moment of shock freezes the company of Saxon negotiators, and that moment is their undoing. Hardrada, Eystein and the jarls draw swords, hack to pieces Saxon horse and rider alike.

Competing chants turn to a unified roaring cheer: Nine-thousand voices rise in elation.

An alarmed cry of discord rises from the Saxon army across the waning river, followed by a volley of arrows which sail into the sky like a flock of startled sparrows.

Forni is already striding back past the man toward the horde of Norsemen who bellow their battle cries as they surge forward in a great wave of iron and fury.

❉ ❉ ❉

The man finds himself in a dead sprint toward the enemy before he truly understands his actions. Skullseeker gripped in his fist, his long strides propel him toward the line of Saxons who trudge through the shallows of the river to meet him. The man's heart thunders in his chest. He barely feels the plain racing beneath his feet, and is only vaguely aware of the flood of his countrymen trailing on his heels, their clamor muted in his ears as if from a great distance. Hissing arrows cloud the sky in both directions, yet the man neither hesitates nor alters the direct line of his charge, trusting the Norns in this, his moment.

In an instant, the man and the foremost Saxons close, abruptly clash. All thoughts are gone as he puts his shoulder to the lead Saxon's shield. The soldier bearing it is hurled backward through the air by the crushing impact. The man is aware of spears thrusting, swords slashing at him. He does not know if he is cut or if he is killed. His body fights on, though his mind spins in disarray. Skullseeker is swung with furious strokes to left and right, hewing bones and flesh in sunder. All within reach is cleaved. The impacts seem less than the resistance of a sturdy birch log to the man, yet Saxons fall around him. Huge rents in armor, in torsos. Severed limbs. Blood. Blood! Blood in vast amounts covers all. The man's eyes sting with it, his vision consumed. His mouth is filled with its metallic taste. The grip on Skullseeker becomes tenuous with its slime. The ground beneath his boots turns to blackened mud, reeking and slick.

It is then, in the midst of that all-enveloping blood, the chaos in his mind evaporates. The world slows and quiets. In this moment he has never seen so clearly nor heard so sharply. Never felt as quick and strong and tireless. Pure euphoria grips the man as he is witness to all; every spear thrust, sword strike, shield split.... Every agony-filled face of those who fall beneath his attack.

The pungent odor of spilled bladder, bowels, viscera assails but does not deter. Nor do the cries of fury, cries of agony, cries of terror, of mercy, of sworn vengeance... all unheeded in the rapture of the fray.

He presses forward, crushing, killing, treading upon the dead and dying in his advance. Soon there are none to engage as the Saxons fall away from him like smoke before a gale wind.

The man stands in the midst of carnage of his own creation, heaving hot air into his taxed lungs. He bears witness to the battle surrounding him.

Mounted Saxons charge upon the shield-wall formation of a band of Hardrada's army, trample Norwegians beneath the hooves of their terror-blinded steeds.

Hardrada's berserkers form together with long spears, descend upon the horsemen, baying and howling their fury. Charging horses are impaled, tumble to the earth with high-pitched screams that carry over the din of battle. The sound of the dying creatures somehow far more nerve-shattering than even the death-shriek of men.

Spear hafts are splintered, buried deep in thick necks and chests of terrified animals, their wide eyes showing white as they roll crazed in their sockets. Horse and rider and berserker alike are sprawled in thrashing heaps. Frantic hooves flail, kill as surely as any sword as the beasts are set upon by berserkers with great axes, hacking away at their skulls and straining necks until they lie still.

Fallen riders who are still able to stand, stagger to their feet dazed and broken from their fall and are hacked to pieces in the manner of their steeds.

The man snorts blood from his nostrils in a red mist, wipes blood from his eyes with an equally bloody arm. He watches warriors of his own army fight with animalistic fury. Tight shield formations drive back the Saxons, scattering them to be singled out and cut down.

Battle desire again rises in the man. Discontent to simply bear witness, he treads over the fallen toward the nearest grouping of Saxons where they have gathered tightly behind their elongated shields, their wavering swords held in an anemic defense toward him, more talisman than weapon.

The man's unbroken stride quickens to bring him to close with the band of enemy soldiers. The crushing ring of axe on shield sounds again. The death-screams of men so assaulted, muted, meaningless, as his own exultant pulse thunders in his ears.

Urgent commands are shouted by captains on both sides of the conflict. But the man heeds no command save his own: Wherever an enemy soldier stands, he aims his blows.

Uncounted Saxons fall to Skullseeker and do not rise.

Soon, battle cries and shouts of fury fade. Only the sounds of steel on steel, steel on shield, steel on flesh. Grunts of exertion, of over-taxed breathing. The wailing cries of the mortally wounded carry over the battlefield.

The once dense fighting is scattered to pockets of individuals hacking away at one another with mindless violence born of desperation.

The man fights his way across the river, up the far bank, deep into the field on the opposite side where the enemy encampment lies in ruins. Yet he could not say how he got there. Following the fight where it flows is his only inclination and sole direction.

The day wears toward evening. Saxon warriors retreat from the battlefield pursued by ravenous, fleet-footed Scots.

Those who can not or will not run, gather in tight groups. Their shields and swords hang loosely in their numb grips. The man seeks them out.

Blood drenched and gore slathered, the man strides the battlefield like a primeval war god from an unremembered past, born for naught but bloodletting and slaughter. An entity neither giving nor accepting quarter. Mercy, a concept wholly spurned.

Despairing Saxon warriors are compelled to take up arms against the man though they know full well what the result will be. Impotent thrusts at the giant carried on prayers of good fortune, prayers to land any sort of blow that will stay their execution. But in the face of the man, good fortune does not exist. Prayers to a gentle and loving god go unanswered.

The man slays until there are none left to slay, then once again surveys the battlefield surrounding him.

The dead and dying lie across the field as cobblestones on a highway. Bodies of Saxon and Norwegian alike fill the river and marsh forming a causeway across the shallow water. In the distance, the rout of the Saxon army continues into the marsh but the man does not join. Norsemen surround what remains of the Saxons, cut them down like so much ripe barley. Cries of hopeless frustration rise as English soldiers mired in the bog are taken at the leisure of Norse archers.

Already Hardrada's warriors roam the battlefield to assist their wounded folk, gather broken weapons and armor for resmithing.

Halfdan scavenges the battlefield, hurrying from one body to the next. Pries arm-rings from dead Norsemen, empties the purses of the Saxons. He gathers coin and trinkets from the dead, adds them to his own kit bag. Halfdan looks up from his ignoble work to find the man staring at him from across a sea of bodies, but only pauses as long as it takes to taunt, "You will make me rich, woodcutter!" Halfdan, hurls an emptied Saxon purse the direction of the man.

The man denies his first impulse, goes in search of Svend.

Svend is found drawing arrows from the bodies of the dead and dispatching mortally wounded Saxons with his hand axe. He gives comfort and water to a maimed countryman until other of his folk come to carry him away.

When Svend sees the man he hurries to him, gushes, "Uncle, how did you fare? I saw you charge their army, then the press of the fight closed around me and I had no time for anything but my bow. Men have been approaching me with praise of your feats. Are they true?"

"I fought," answers the man.

Svend allows the answer to stand for the moment. Now is no time for recounting the battle as the wounded need be gathered and carted back to the ships, and Hardrada's army to be reformed for the march on York.

* * *

It is not far to the city of York, yet even before the freshly bloodied army can lay siege, emissaries emerge from the gates to offer surrender.

The Norsemen would still have plunder, but Tostig entreats King Hardrada to spare the city, as he wishes to make it his own after Hardrada takes the English crown.

The king acquiesces. The city is spared with the promise of hostages to be exchanged in the days following: One hundred men and women of good birth from families of high standing will be given up to King Hardrada as guarantee York will not join in any counterattack nor attempt to bar its gates against its new ruler. In return, the king promises the city shall remain whole, and the hostages will be treated no worse than any other thrall.

Hardrada's army retreats to the battleground at Fulford to care for their dead and to plan the coming campaign.

* * *

Laying eyes upon the battlefield again, this time from a distance, the man is astounded by the carnage. The sky is black with carrion birds beyond counting. The raucous fowl circle and drift down to take part of the abundant feast. Quarrelsome dogs, their bellies already distended and full to bursting, gorge on the corpses.

Dog and fowl alike shy away from the intruders as Norwegians take to the field to retrieve their dead. But it is not until Svend looses an arrow to send a cur yelping to its death do the creatures fully yield to man.

King Hardrada travels the field with a Christian bishop at his heels. The king slowly passes the gathered dead where they are lined in formal rows like soldiers in formation. Weapons and meager personal belongings rest on their still chests. He pauses on occasion to kneel, touch a familiar face, whisper consoling words for the souls to carry to the afterlife.

The bishop in his long robes and pointed hat, bears a somber manner. He holds a gilded crucifix aloft, waves it over the dead as he recites orisons in Latin.

Many Norse warriors bow their heads in solemn acknowledgement of the Christian ritual. Yet many others glare at the bishop with flat looks of contempt and rebuke.

Hardrada, though claiming his kingdom of Norway Christian in whole, refuses to admonish the dissenting warriors for their sacrilege. To his mind, a man who faces death in battle under his banner may embrace any belief and love any god befitting him. A man fights without reserve when assured of the afterlife of his own choosing.

Forges of the smiths smolder. The ring of hammer on anvil carries long and sharp over the still land as weapons and armor are mended. Pilfered gold and silver are melted and formed into ingots for their journey back to the homes of those who risked or realized their death in this foreign land.

A troop of Norwegians, farmers and fishermen by trade, are directed to the forest to gather wood for the funeral pyres. The man joins them without command or invite as he would have something familiar to occupy his hands and mind in the midst of all this bloodshed -- death on this scale, a thing unknown to him.

His companions, suspicious of a man of such standing, take to the woods without banter. Their destination; a large stand of diseased, dying trees which cover a swath of ground risen from the moor. Axes are barely needed to break apart the dry timber. The troop sets about loading wood-sleds with fuel.

The man fixes himself upon trees yet unrotted, knowing they will burn longer and hotter, necessary to transform flesh to ash. The borrowed wood axe is small and light in his hands after the day wielding Skullcrusher, but it bites well and the trees fall with little resistance.

His fevered mind soothes at the wonted task as the muscles in his shoulders and back -- tight as bowstrings from the travail of battle -- soon soften to perform in steady rhythm.

The men of the detail watch in wonder at the ease which the man works -- a strange rhythmic dance performed by a master -- yet they remain wary of the silent giant. He is the most imposing warrior any has ever seen, and one of the captain's ship, no less. A professional fighting man no doubt, judging by his stature and the ornate battle-axe he carries across his back: a treasure worth a fleet of fishing boats, or a vast herd of cattle. A man chosen to take the forefront in battle, yet lacking armor; surely a berserker of legendary birth: A thing more fabled creature than man. They direct no query nor banter toward him as they know they have naught in common with such a brute. The man is best left to himself.

As the day wears to dusk and the man consumes himself fully in his labors of felling one tree after another -- and has apparently not lured this troop into the woods for slaughter -- the others eventually ease their minds and tongues, and as men will do, speak of themselves.

Audun, a squat man of Salt Fjord who wears his beard trimmed close to conceal the graying, speaks wistfully, "The jarls of my town raided this land for many years. Each time I longed to stay. The winters here are short and wheat grows tall. The earth, though rocky, never freezes, and fruit bearing trees of many sort thrive here. I will bring my family, build a longhouse here on this very spot, and grow fat off this land."

"For the grazing alone," says a man called Hackett for the unfortunate shape of his nose, "I would claim my land and herd oxen, I think. I own a bull the likes of which you have never seen. This tall at the shoulder," indicates Hackett, holding his hand in measure, "and as big around as this one's wife," he says, gesturing with his chin to a fellow. "Bellower, I named him, after the legend."

"It is fine land for oxen," agrees Olin, a stout man of many good meals, "and goats and horses... any beast who would fill their bellies with these rich grains which grow without tending. I have never seen such ripe fields. I am told there are no wolves here, and their bears are hardly larger than our dogs. This is a fine land."

"You can have the land," says Fiske, a fisherman whose eyes remain permanently squinted as if shielding salt spray even now. "There are no walrus to hunt, no seals, and fish in these warm waters would be cooked before they were laid to fire. It is a cursed land and I long to be home."

"You gripe without cease," says Olin, "yet you are here of your own will."

"With the riches won I will buy my own fleet to sail to the ice and take sea-ivory until my ships threaten to flounder under the weight," claims Fiske.

"I have love of the sea as well," avows Audun, "but the cold and damp makes my old bones ache. I think it is time I farmed and understood why farmers grow so fat and lazy, like this one." Audun playfully shoves Olin in jest.

Olin pats his prodigious belly. "Envious of my success with herds, I see. Not to worry Audun, I will teach you how to farm. You may never grow as fat as me, but at least you will not starve."

The fellows laugh and jabber as the man works dividing the felled trees. They drag the resulting logs to their wood sleds and pile them high.

❊ ❊ ❊

Great fires are built. The dead of Hardrada's army are sent to their makers on vast plumes of rank smoke.

The Saxons are left to the crows and dogs.

Entire herds of English cattle are slaughtered to be roasted in long cook pits, and the men of the North draw up every keg of mead and ale they can muster to feast in celebration. A crushing victory, and Yorkshire only the first of England's city-states to fall.

Halfdan attempts to endear himself to King Hardrada by presenting him with a sack of gold and silver stripped from the dead. Buys himself a seat at the king's fire along with nobles of many prestigious households, including Eystein Orri and his ship's crew.

Already drunk though the feast has just begun, Halfdan's roistering boasts of his feats in battle quickly weary the revelers, yet none challenge him. The king's table is a place for circumspection of speech; 'It is, and shall be, a shameful thing when guest quarrels with guest.'

Only Forni speaks ill of the besotted fool, and that under his breath so only the man, who sits at his shoulder, can hear, "Wise is he not who is never silent, mouthing meaningless words: A glib tongue that goes on chattering sings to its own harm."

The man fully understands the words, and Forni's purpose for speaking them, yet remains stoic. He knows this is not his place nor his time to take action. For now, he remains a guest at the king's fire.

Eystein's face darkens with Halfdan's endless chatter as the garrulous fool guzzles mead and makes immodest claims.

"These Saxons are of little use as warriors," boasts Halfdan. "They piss themselves at my approach and fall as sheep before my sword."

"They fought well enough," says Eystein in a pointed manner. "Sheep flee before the wolf. There are many thousand Saxons who shall never leave the field that prove they are far from sheep. And our own funeral pyres cloud the sky."

Halfdan stews at the censure, yet is not so deep into his cups as to mistake the captain's words as mere debate. He fills his mouth with meat, falls to brooding silence, to the relief of all. Halfdan's eyes dart from warrior to warrior searching for camaraderie, but those rebuked seldom find solace. None will meet Halfdan's look but for the man whose gaze openly wonders at one so lacking in prudence, even at the table of a king. In the absence of sympathy, Halfdan falls to fuming resentment at the unflinching open disdain he finds in the look.

Eystein Orri raises his voice, "If we are to have tales of the day, I put to King Harald that he be the teller of them. His skill as a skald rivals that of Bragi himself! Or so is boasted," he adds with a grin directed toward the king.

Harald Hardrada, a man who prides himself on his storied ability to create and embellish sagas, smiles broadly at the invitation from his captain. He draughts deeply of his mead horn, stands to speak.

"Early in the day we accepted the arrow-laced invite of the enemy. We debarked from our longships to march on the Saxon army through such heat as to send a sun-loving adder slithering for his hole," Hardrada begins in his deep, commanding voice.

The men quiet, settle in to drink and be entertained.

"We came upon the Saxons, vast in number and well armed and armored, guarded behind fortifications years in the making. Their nobles were mounted on fine English steeds, their flanks quivering in readiness for battle."

"Fine English steeds," bellows Tarbin, holding his knife aloft, impaled on which is a large hunk of roasted horse flesh.

Those seated at the king's fire send up a cheer in agreement.

Hardrada chuckles, raises his horn to acknowledge the embellishment, then continues, "The Saxons chose the field well: an impassible marsh to their flank, a swollen river to their fore, and open ground all the way to their own high-walled city of York for their retreat. Their failing," confides Hardrada, "was they are not men of the sea and have little knowledge of the tides. They did not account for the ebb of the river that was to be their protector. When the river grew shallow and their noblemen crossed to offer silver and beg our mercy, I knew; if their horses could cross, so could our army."

The men nod and agree with one another that their king is indeed a fine strategist.

"I was in the midst of securing a generous Danegeld payment to spare their lives when the negotiations came to a rather curt halt, I would say, as Forni's never-failing spear claimed the final word." Hardrada pointedly raises his mead horn to Forni.

Forni gives the king an acknowledging tilt of his broad-brimmed hat.

Hardrada scoffs with amused pleasure. "It was a magnificent cast, I concede, from such distance and with such accuracy even the finest bowman would find it difficult to match.

"Your own captain, Eystein, ungrateful retainer that he is," says Hardrada with a grin, "tried his utmost to best me to the first kill -- behind Forni's that is -- but my sword was quicker and at least three..." he clears his throat and amends, "five of their silver-tongued earls fell to my blade."

"Piercing their breasts after they are already dead of my blows does not count," shouts Eystein jovially.

Hardrada and the men laugh. The king again amends, "Perhaps it was more even than I recall," says Hardrada waving his hand in a dismissive flourish, "for we were in the heat of it. Either way, the battle had begun!"

The listeners roar their excitement at the turn of the story.

The king's voice rises in urgency to match the tale's action, "Saxon arrows flew at us as hail, but none found their mark."

"Then what is this I wear in my wolf-joint?" shouts Tyrulf, holding his bloodied, bandaged arm aloft as proof.

Hardrada makes the revision, "Few found their mark... and only in those without the sense to move out of their way."

Tyrulf shrugs concurrence. There is hearty laughter around the fire. "Good sense," says Tyrulf, "a thing I have never been held to blame for."

"How did you manage to take an arrow there?" is called out.

"I thought to catch it on my shield," replies Tyrulf.

"But you carried no shield," says Svend.

"Aaah," says Tyrulf as if a truth dawning upon him, "now I see the flaw in my plan."

A burst of roaring laughter rolls across the joyous camp. Svend is shouldered playfully for his gullibility.

Even the man chuckles beneath his grin, gratified by the acceptance Svend enjoys among the hardened warriors of this class.

When Hardrada can subdue his own laughter, he continues, "Then, just as I would rally the army to me, a giant charges past! At first I thought it to be a herd of wild bulls, but nay, a single man! Bare-chested and bearing a great battle-axe -- a weapon wielded by man, but forged for the gods."

Many admiring looks are laid upon the man. Only Halfdan scowls with displeasure, his enemy gaining such prominence in the king's tale.

Hardrada's voice quickens and rises as his saga builds momentum, "This bold warrior crushed through the Saxon line, cleaving soldiers by the dozen with each one-handed stroke of his mighty weapon. Hurling them from him with his free hand to lie crushed on the field!"

Several hands reach to slap the man on the back and grip his shoulder in recognition of the honor of such distinction in the saga.

Halfdan spits into the fire, belches loudly and drains his cup.

"As a berserker of legend the giant fought. It was only by quickness of foot I myself was able to engage in battle before this warrior," says Hardrada, gesturing with his mead horn to the man, "finished their army entire. Fortunately for the remainder of us, the Saxon's brought a large troop, ample enough for all to wet their blades in English blood."

A roar of joyous sound rises from the listeners. Mead

horns are raised and emptied.

Hardrada shouts for the finish of his story to be heard above the riotous din, "In the end, we crushed the Saxons and tread upon their bodies. So fearsome our army that the city of York fell to us from sheer fright."

The listeners are heartened by the finely told tale.

But Halfdan stands to call to the king, "Wonderfully recounted, King Harald! For certain to be recited by scalds for all time.

"But tell us. This great giant of a warrior you speak of, what tribute does he offer? Having slain half the Saxon army by himself, as you skillfully tell, the treasures he must have claimed and honored you with could no doubt fill a horde." Halfdan addresses the man, "Is that so?"

The warriors fall silent at the challenge. All follow Halfdan's eyes to the man. Even King Hardrada and Eystein await the man's rebuttal to the barb.

The man cradles Skullseeker across his knees but does not stand nor look up from the fire. His voice rings clear through the camp, "Some earn a place at the king's table. Others simply buy a seat."

Halfdan grips the hilt of his sword, takes an angry step toward the man, but halts and does not draw the blade as the man looks up into his eyes from where he sits opposite the fire.

A profound silence has settled over the gathering. The crackling and hissing of the fire, the only sound.

"If you were a true warrior and not simply a lowly field hand, you would understand," hisses Halfdan, "the enemy you see to your front is not the only threat on a battlefield."

The man calmly stands.

Those seated between the two ease away from the fire, giving way.

Halfdan clenches his bared teeth, grips the hilt of his weapon, his knuckles white. The blade, half-drawn, reflects the firelight in cold mimicry.

Yet the man does not advance, nor does he have anything further to say. He simply turns his back to his enemy, sits, offers his mead cup for filling.

Halfdan hesitates, glaring at the back of the man. All eyes remain on the enraged warrior.

Suddenly Halfdan turns, shoves his way from the gathering.

A roar of astounded cheers and laughter from those with a seat at the king's fire pursue Halfdan into the dark.

And the celebration rages long into the night.

* * *

Jarvis needed not witness the outcome of the battle before he reigned his mount southward and rode with great haste to London.

Further scouts of King Godwinson's army remain in York, but it is Jarvis' duty to inform the king as to the level of success of earls Edwin and Morcar in halting the Norse invasion. Success. The word relieved of all meaning as the young Saxon scout sat his mount and bore witness to such slaughter of his countrymen as to leave the battlefield littered with their bones for a thousand years to come. Even at his young age, Jarvis has no little experience in battle. He has fought in many skirmishes in defense of King Godwinson against the united earls and petty kings who contest the new king's right to the throne, but never had he imagined such a battle as was brought by the giant's of the North. Their king stood as tall as a man mounted on a war-horse. His warriors nigh as large, and powerfully built as horses themselves. Marching at the fore of their army, an enormous creature, resembling a man only larger. Half naked and formed as though wearing a Roman breastplate. Each single stride of the giant covering two of a mortal man. Each stroke of his great axe tearing a swath through the Saxons as broad as the Roman road he now rides. The Northmen came in numbers beyond counting, chanting gleeful songs as if headed to a joyful celebration, not to war.

Jarvis watched as the joint armies of Edwin and Morcar, ten-thousand in number, crashed against the shield wall of the Norwegians like waves against the cliffs, and to as much effect. The sheer ferocity of the invaders, a fearful thing to witness. Their unwillingness to take a single step in retreat: an act fit for story and legend, not for true war. How are such men to be fought?

These and more are the dire thoughts of the brave Saxon scout as he runs his horse flat-out along the highway, south to London.

* * *

The first of the treasure ships returns to Trondheim. The entire village and surrounding farmsteads turn out to the port to marvel at the riches won in England. Many strong men are required to unburden the ship's holds of crates and sacks of fine English goods: silver plates, bowls, finger rings and delicate chains of pure gold. Fine gems of every color torn from the necks of English nobility. Dresses and tunics of rich silk, and much more.

Sassa makes the day-trip to Trondheim to query the ship's crew of news of her husband. No one can tell her of her husband or how he fares, only that Hardrada's army crushes village after village with scant contestation from the English. The news is of little relief to Sassa. A single spear or sword strike or errant arrow… a hundred ways to die in battle, won or lost, she knows.

The runes have little to say of her husband's fate either, only that he stands alone. Stands alone, but in victory or defeat? As a sole survivor, or the last killed? Stands alone is no divination. He has always stood alone.

The frustration of the riddle threatens to drive Sassa mad. She stops divining and begins casting: Runespells to protect. Runespells to dull blades so they will not cut. Runespells to return husband and father to his loves.

Each day Kari and Nanna ask of their father. Each day Sassa tells them he comes to them at night in their sleep, to cradle them, to comfort them. But these are her own dreams, they hold little comfort for her daughters.

Kari sleeps too often now. Sassa knows it is her invention that is the cause. She returns from selling split-wood or tending the livestock to find Nanna playing in the yard alone, Kari inside the house curled in her bed beneath her sheepskin, sleeping, or pretending to sleep so her father will come.

Sometimes though, when the house is quiet and still, he is there with her. In the smell of his cloak, the hollow in their bed. In that twilight between sleep and wake, he is there. That glorious instant of divine rapture before truth crashes upon her and pain returns, he is there.

❋ ❋ ❋

"Return with the bulk of the army to the ships," says Hardrada, "and take this infernal armor with you. I roast like a lamb on a spit in this heat." The king kicks at his mail shirt which lays at his feet alongside his shield.

"You are staying?" asks Eystein.

"I conferred with Tostig. Hostages will be delivered at a place called Stamford Bridge three days hence."

"I should stay and accept the hostages. You return with the army to the ships," says Eystein.

"Eystein, I trust you with my army, but I only trust Tostig Godwinson with myself. If he conspires against me with his brother I would like to be the one to split him from groin to throat."

"You doubt Tostig's loyalty."

"Of course I doubt him," laughs Hardrada. "A man without loyalty to his own family has loyalty to no one."

"I would leave my own ships crew with you," says Eystein.

"And I would have them. No captain can choose men more sagely than yourself." Hardrada stands to stretch his back. His head brushes the tent erected to shade him. "My guard and your chosen warriors with me," says Hardrada, "and a thousand more should suffice."

"And if the Saxons plan an ambush in place of a hostage exchange?"

"If only they were so bold. I have agreed on Stamford Bridge for its open fields and deep river. A single bridge spans the river. No place for an ambush. But if one is planned, a thousand men could hold the bank against a like force until you can bring up the army."

"And following the exchange?"

King Hardrada shrugs at the simplicity of it. "We march to London."

Before the day has reached its midpoint, Eystein leads the bulk of the army to join with the men guarding the ships at Riccall, while Hardrada marches with his thousand and one-hundred chosen to Stamford Bridge.

✳ ✳ ✳

The man marches with his ship's company, Svend at his side. It is not far to Stamford Bridge, three hours walk, and the troop travels unhurried. Blessedly free of their mail and helms, and bearing very few shields, the heat of the day is less a burden on men weary from battle, followed by a night-long victory celebration.

Several Norwegian noblemen make the journey mounted on English horses procured in from Fulford and York. Hardrada strides at the fore of his troop, no common horse so large as to bear the king without his boots dragging the ground.

It is now the warriors take stock of injuries they took no notice of in the midst of battle, nor following while in their cups during the victory feast. They note broken bones, smashed fingers. A multitude of cuts, some far more than superficial, beginning to fester in the heat. Many limp, cringe with each step, grumble of the reward the next Saxon they encounter will suffer for their discomfort.

Halfdan who wishes to have returned to the ships with his treasure, marches with the company. His purchase of a place at the king's table for the victory feast has also bought him a spot with the thousand-man brigade chosen to accept treasure and hostages at Stamford Bridge. Halfdan curses his poor fortune. A waste of wealth, he laments, buying the king's favor if this is to be the result: part of a group destined to sleep in a pasture of reeking cattle, and no opportunity to secure further riches from the simple Scots who know little of dice or other games of chance he excels at. This group he travels with, the foremost of Hardrada's army, will suffer no fleecing at dice nor any other game. Their minds set only to battle, feast, and drink. Though what riches could be had with a few female captives among this lot, wonders Halfdan. Lucre to be won yet from these lusty fellows. But he has no captives, nor thralls to rent. The thought only serves to further agitate his already foul mood.

* * *

Jarvis rides his horse to lather and exchanges it for a fresh mount twice in a single day. He stops only for water and a mouthful of bread, then is on again to London.

News of the Norwegian invasion travels on the scouts heels like a wildfire driven by strong winds, so by the time he made his report to the king, the country north of London is deep in panic.

City scouts tell of the rider's approach several minutes

before exhausted horse and rider reign up before Gyrth and Harold Godwinson. Having been alerted to the scout's coming, the king and his brother stand in the inner courtyard of the king's stronghold within the city where the huscarls are barracked. Jarvis dismounts and staggers, his boots touching ground for the first time in half a day. His throat is dry, his voice cracks at his first failed attempt at words.

"Water," commands Gyrth.

Jarvis accepts an offered skin, drinks, then blurts out the news in a single breath, "The Norwegians have reached Fulford. Morcar and Edwin of Northumbria combined forces and still they fell in less than a day."

"And the city? Does the city of York yet stand?" queries the king.

"I know not, Sire. I was ordered to report the moment I was certain of the battle."

"And you are confident of the outcome," presses Gyrth.

"Edwin and Morcar fled the battlefield for the city, yet nary a soldier of their army followed. They were cut down to a man. The few who attempted flight were sunk in the bog and floundered helpless as the enemy feathered them with arrows and impaled them with spears where they lie. Others were drown in their attempt to swim the river."

Huscarls have gathered to listen to the scouts tale. An angry murmur flows through the professional soldiers.

"And you stood safe on a hill and watched?" says one.

"I longed to join the battle," protests Jarvis, "but I had been commanded to watch and to ride, that is all."

"You did well," says Gyrth. He commands those around him in general, "Care for his horse and give this man wine and food, for he will soon be given the chance to avenge his countrymen, as will you all."

The men quickly disperse to spread the news through the barracks.

Gyrth trails his brother through the stockade to a planning room to form their new strategy.

King Godwinson paces in frustration before the table which holds a large map of his country. "If Yorkshire and Northumbria have fallen, there is little to prevent Hardrada's march on London."

"London is still nigh a week's march from York," says Gyrth, "and York is well fortified. It could withstand a determined siege which would delay Hardrada longer still."

"I would not have the heart of my country under attack. The city of York may be under siege even now. If we march within the day we might collect the fyrd along the way and catch Hardrada between the city walls and our army."

"And what of Duke William?" Gyrth would know. "If we go north we will be a week's march further from the channel if he crosses."

"The man taunts us," complains Harold, "staging his crossing up and down the coast, but has yet to sail. And the wind may hold for many days yet."

"And it may shift in one."

The king paces as he thinks on the problem, then turns to his brother with the answer, "With all haste to York to crush Hardrada, then return to face William. And God be with us and grant us His blessings and good fortune."

Gyrth has left pickets along the channel to warn of William of Normandy's coming. Now he sends forerunners on horseback to villages and townships across the island to command the farmers and tradesmen of the fyrd to take up their weapons and join their army on the road to York.

Gyrth calls his man Orm to him for orders. His lieutenant's slovenly and insolent manner is offensive to him, yet he needs Orm's skills now more than ever. When his lieutenant arrives as bid, his stench water's Gyrth's eyes. Gyrth tries to speak without inhaling, "I would have you trail the main force on the march with a dozen men of your choosing."

"To chew on dust and wade through animal dung?" gripes Orm.

"To ensure there are no stragglers or desertions," replies

Gyrth. "We will need every man in this war."

"Then you believe the threat of Tostig and Hardrada is dire."

"I believe we will require great fortune and God's will... along with every man with a spear this land can provide if we are to save my brother's crown."

The huscarls assembled and the fyrd rallied, the army of England sets upon the Roman road built nearly a thousand years before for this exact purpose; to speed troops to war.

* * *

The huge open plain at Stamford Bridge is cut through by the river Derwent, wide and swift moving. Its banks are over-grown by reeds, cascading willows and tall grasses buzzing with flying insects and singing with frogs. Cattle freely roam the fields, growing fat upon the lush grasses. A single wooden bridge, large and broad enough for two horse-drawn carts to pass one another, arched in the style of the Roman's, joins the east bank with the west.

When the men of Hardrada's brigade reach the Derwent, many shed their sweat-soaked shirts, run splashing into the shallows of the river to seek relief from the heat of the scorch-ing sun.

King Hardrada orders camp to be made on the east side of the river, and posts a troop of a hundred sentries to the west.

The man sets himself to gathering firewood for the cook pits when Tyrulf seeks him out.

"How is your spear arm?" asks Tyrulf of the man, "Mine is yet unfit." Tyrulf's right wrist and hand is heavily bandaged from the English arrow which pierced it. He carries three broad-bladed spears in his left hand.

The man hands off the woodcutting axe he carries to an-other fellow and follows Tyrulf who leads a party of a score of spear-wielding hunters across the bridge.

The large herd of cattle which graze the west bank move as one to keep their distance from the men. The cattle are domesticated, but nonetheless wary of the smell of blood, each Northman's battle clothes still stiff with gore from the previous day's fight.

The hunters move slowly, giving wide birth to the herd as they form a half-circle, pressing the mass of cattle to the river's edge, then they strike. Hurled spears are sunk deep into the ribs of the grunting creatures as they mill stupidly, each attempting to force their way to the center of the herd, away from the edges where the hunters fell one after another. Their dying shrieks set off a chain reaction of mad bellowing from the frightened bovine. More than twenty bulls and cows are killed to be butchered where they lie. Men hurry across the bridge to tote huge sections of beef back to their cook fires.

Soon the heady aroma of roasting meat envelops the camp. The sun retreats behind the hills to the west. At last, the day blessedly cools.

The man and Svend eat at Hardrada's fire, drink mead, and enjoy the camaraderie of men bonded in combat.

For fun and sport, King Hardrada and the captain of his berserk bodyguard, Tor, compete in an axe throwing contest: A tree, as big around as two men, their target. Their audience wagers huge amounts of wealth on the friendly match.

Tor throws. The axe imbeds in the tree near dead-center.

Those watching roar their approval. Silver and gold is transferred from the losers piles to the winners.

Hardrada throws. His axe imbeds alongside Tor's. Men howl their laughter and loot is transferred back to its original owners.

Tarbin stands on unsteady legs, his usual swagger pronounced by the copious amounts of mead he has consumed. "I have won and lost a king's ransom on this contest already. There will be no victor until the sun rises at this rate." He staggers to the tree, hangs an impressive silver arm ring on a broken branch which protrudes like a spike from the trunk. "The closest to the ring. Best of three axes," Tarbin announces.

Tarbin has not retreated a step from the target when Hardrada throws, narrowly missing Tarbin's head. The warrior's instincts save him as he hurls himself flat on the ground.

The men roar laughter at Tarbin who grumpily makes it to his feet and staggers back to his seat at the fire.

The thrown axe is embedded in the tree, far from the arm ring.

"That counts as your first throw," says Tor.

"Take advantage of your king, will you?" says Hardrada. "I must remember to never sleep with my back to you."

The men are well entertained by the contest. They quickly place bets on the next throw.

Tor playfully shoulders Hardrada aside to take his first throw. It lands very close to the arm ring. Hardrada takes his second throw. It lands even closer than Tor's. Tor throws... closer yet. Hardrada throws. The axe nearly touches the arm ring.

The audience is fully aroused now. Cheers and taunts to Tor to affect his aim are deafening.

Tor takes careful aim, throws at the same instant several men shout to distract him. The axe clanks off the steel head of Hardrada's axe, falls to the ground.

A great roar goes up from the drunken warriors.

Tor curses, turns to Hardrada. "I nearly had you this time."

"Nearly so," says Hardrada as the two embrace.

"Is there anyone else?" shouts Hardrada to the camp in general.

Halfdan, forever lurking on the outskirts of the noble grouping, calls to be heard, "I wager my share of today's bounty that no one here can match the king's ability with an axe."

The warriors grow silent as not to encourage Halfdan in his pandering, nor to lose any more wealth to the skills of their king.

"My uncle can best the king," announces Svend.

Every eye turns to Svend, then to the man who sits by his side.

Halfdan sneers, "The stripling speaks out of turn."

"I speak the truth," says Svend.

"My day's share against yours then," says Halfdan.

Everyone looks to the man.

"Will you have the contest?" asks Hardrada.

The man remains silent.

"Then the lad forfeits. His share is mine," says Halfdan.

"Not yet," says Ull. The archer recruits Tarbin and Tyrulf to help hoist the man reluctantly to his feet. The surrounding warriors cheer him on. The axes are retrieved.

The man stands beside Hardrada. The king offers him three axes, then stands aside, gestures for the man to take the first throws at the arm ring on the tree.

The man considers the target for a moment, tucks the axes in his belt, draws Skullseeker from his back.

Everyone watches the man as he goes to the fire roasting an entire bull, grips the bull by a horn and lops its head from the carcass with his battle-axe.

The man totes the bull's head to the tree and impales it on the broken branch which protrudes like a spike from the tree's trunk. He returns to Hardrada.

"Take the bull's eye," says the man.

Hardrada is greatly amused. He readies himself to throw.

Men wagering on the king must give huge odds to those willing to take the man's side in the contest.

Hardrada throws. The axe narrowly skims past the bull's head to imbed in the tree. A miss. The men wager afresh. Hardrada steadies himself, throws his second axe. It embeds in the bull's skull a few inches from an eye. He throws his third axe. It lands closer yet.

Men with small fortunes wagered on the king cheer excitedly.

Hardrada, quite satisfied with his throw, looks to the man. The man nods, impressed.

Halfdan taunts Svend, "You are about to learn a lesson, and lose a day's work, boy."

Svend smolders at Halfdan's taunts but remains silent.

The man takes his place to throw. He considers the three axes -- their weight, balance, keenness of edge -- then hands one of the axes to Hardrada.

"You will take only two?" Hardrada would know.

"There are only two eyes," replies the man.

Hardrada scoffs at the audacity. He shrugs, stands clear.

Without further delay, the man takes an axe in each hand, steps forward and throws both axes. Each axe clips an eye from the bull's head!

Before anyone can react, he draws Skullseeker from his back, hurls the battle-axe with both hands. Skullseeker splits the bull's head nearly directly down the center to fall nigh in two pieces from the tree.

Silence falls over the camp.

Hardrada and the warriors gape.

The silence is broken as Svend addresses Halfdan, "Would you care to wager tomorrow's earnings as well?"

The warriors burst into astonished praise. They crowd around the man to slap him on the back and congratulate him in his skill.

Halfdan drifts from the gathering, cursing his lack of good fortune.

The king looks to Svend, affecting sternness. "You might have warned me of his skills," says Hardrada.

"He is known as the woodcutter, " replies Svend, "how much more warning did you need?" Svend suddenly remembers himself, adds, "...Sire."

The king takes Svend by the shoulder, gives him a good shaking to show he was only feigning anger.

Hardrada removes a gold torque from his wrist, presses

it into the man's hand. "This shall not be the last of the wealth your skills earn you."

Hardrada fills his horn again from the keg of mead, then wanders off to another fire to recite his new tale of the burgeoning legend they call Rigsen.

* * *

The evening and the celebration wear on. Svend sits beside the man upwind of the fire with the crew of Eystein's ship surrounding them. Recounts of the axe throwing contest have finally been exhausted. Now grandiose tales of life and battles are retold with the benefit of retrospect, and the mead of poetry.

Ull is in the midst of a story of grand adventures had in a distant land; "...Though their skin is brown as a hazelnut, and their stature that of a half-grown child, they have all the other attributes of a grown woman. And they are easily seduced, their men being soft and childlike themselves. They nearly battle one another to be with a man like myself."

"What he is not telling," says Tarbin, "is half those battling to be with him were their men."

"Well," shrugs Ull, "if one can not tell, what difference does it truly make?"

"Now my wife...," begins Tarbin, continuing the flow of discussion with a tale of his own.

"Which one?" interrupts Tyrulf.

"My wife in Norway is the one I speak of now," says Tarbin, offended not in the least by the gibe. "Later I may tell you of my Dane wife or my Ireland wife, or many of my other wives in lands whose names I do not remember. But now, hold your tongue and listen and I will tell you of a woman who bore to me five fine sons and two daughters, each of them straight-limbed and strong. She gives birth so easily now she can put the bread in the coals to bake, release the child from her belly, and retrieve the bread before it is burned."

Halfdan, finding none more receptive to his prattling at the other fires, staggers his way back to the fire of Eystein's chosen crew. He searches out a mead keg to dip his cup, a cup already filled and drained too often this night. Halfdan stands glowering in the unsure light at the outer reaches of the leaping fire.

"I once had a wife," says Tyrulf, "Alfhild, I believe her name was. But I sailed south to the lands of the Greeks and when I returned she had gone."

"How long was your journey?" asks Svend.

"Not more than two years," says Tyrulf. "I do not understand the caprice of women."

"Capricious or not," says Ull, "I would wager she was off and running before the sail of your ship was out of sight."

Tyrulf dismisses the slight with a wave of his one good hand.

Ull turns his attention to the man, "And you, Rigsen, tell us of your home. Do you have sons, a wife?"

The man looks into his mead cup and remains silent.

Svend speaks in his stead, "My mother's sister is his wife."

"No doubt a fine woman," says Ull. "Come, loosen that stone that serves as your tongue and tell us of her."

Halfdan, into his cups far past reason, and still stinging from his losses to Svend in the axe throwing contest earlier in the night, speaks then, "I believe the only wife this one knows is the boy he calls nephew sitting beside him. That is why he keeps the fuzzy-cheeked lad so close at all times."

Svend bolts to his feet, yanks his hand axe from his belt, brandishes it in his tight fist.

"Halfdan," calls Tyrulf, "silence yourself and take your cup to another fire. No one here cares for your vile slander."

"I have spoken not a word to you, Tyrulf. You have no cause to begin a feud with me," barks Halfdan.

Men of other fires congregate to the brewing fight, irresistible, the lure of violence.

"Well, my drunken friend," says Tarbin, "we all remember the feud you began with this very man in Trondheim before we sailed, and how you crawled on your belly to be free of it."

"I crawl from no man," slurs Halfdan, "and my quarrel is not with this bastard offspring of Ymir, but with the weak-kneed Svend who stands facing me, axe in hand. It is my right to defend myself against such a threat."

"The boy is no threat to you," says Ull. "Go away Halfdan. And in future times resist mixing ale and mead in your belly... if you are to have a future."

"I will fight him," shouts Svend. "I do not fear this man. I have seen him on the battlefield. He only attacks those already half-dead or lacking weapons. I am as much a man as he."

"You have all heard him," roars Halfdan gesturing broadly to encompass all who have gathered, "he slanders me, and he wishes to fight. It is my right to have justice, and no man's right to interfere."

The man, who sits coiled and ready to slay, had not known Forni was there at his shoulder, but the Ancient One now whispers in his ear, "Does your trothful wife not deserve to be told of as much as any man of saga? As much as yourself?"

Svend angles himself in his stance, ready to spring across the fire.

Halfdan's face is contorted in a hateful snarl as he clears his sword from its scabbard.

"My wife," speaks the man in a voice that carries, "Sassa is her name. When I first laid eyes upon her I was certain my grandfather had returned from Valhöll to make good on his promise to kill me, for it was clear the Valkyrie had come in the night and had taken me to an audience with Freyja herself."

The overwhelmed wonder in his voice, and the oddity of such a string of words from the man, startles silence into the listeners. Thoughts of violence and all else, for the moment, are forgotten.

"Gold loses its luster when compared to her hair which she oft wears unbound and free-flowing, draping far past her waist. When she sits on her bench at our table it gathers on the pelts covering the floor. The nine maidens of the sea rage in jealousy at the color and brightness of her eyes. Her lips are full and red and when they part in smile, the sun dims in the sky. Her skin... as white and pure as fresh-drawn milk, and there is a small blue vein running here," the man gestures absently to his own face, "across her temple. A crease here above her nose when she is angry, and here at the corner of her eyes when she laughs. And when she is angry, the earth shudders and your soul is rent. But when she laughs, your heart swells and flutters as a birds. And she laughs often and freely. It is the sound of summer rain on still water. Sassa. She finds delight in newborn spring kids, and in goslings breaking free of their shells, and with our fine, fine daughters, Kari and Nanna: Nanna, impatient and brash as a sudden summer storm. Kari, silent and brooding as the winter itself." The man pauses with newfound revelation. "They are their father's daughters," he says, "and Sassa... Sassa loves them for it."

The man pauses for a long moment which leaves the listeners wondering if he has finished his telling.

"Her carriage," the man finally continues, "would make queens and ladies of the highest birth, bow at her coming. And no man nor god can force his eyes away in her presence. Sassa is my wife."

The listeners are awed at the telling, nod with appreciative smiles, raise cups to drink in honor of Sassa.

Forni calls to Halfdan, "Halfdan, raise your cup and drink to the lady Sassa, and let this feud be done."

Svend still stands ready to fight.

Halfdan's sword is held naked in his hand, but energy for the fight has been lost, stolen by love. Sneering at the gathering, Halfdan upturns his cup to spill on the ground. He tosses the cup itself into the fire and is gone from sight.

"Would you have me to cast runes to tell how this feud will end?" asks Forni.

"I already know how it ends," says the man.

* * *

Svend stews in his anger late into the night. When his restless stirring wakes the man, Svend turns on his uncle and hisses, "You treat me as if I am a child still. I have killed men the same as you and warrant equal respect."

The man props himself up to listen to Svend's grievance.

"You chase away Halfdan as if I were a lamb to be protected from a wolf. But I have become a wolf also and am not in need of your protection!" Svend hastily gathers his bow and sleeping blanket, tromps away to another fire.

The man has naught for reply and is at a loss as to the remedy for Svend's anger, so he moves to a spot where he can be in view of Svend at the nearby fire and lies in watch the night through until the sun is pursued above the horizon and the camp stirs awake.

* * *

The huscarls of King Harold Godwinson's army discuss tactics for the coming battle as they adjust themselves uncomfortably in their saddles. Too many hours on horseback for soldiers who prefer to fight on foot.

King Harold and Gyrth ride at the head of the seven divisions of professional soldiers they have mustered to now. Nearly ten thousand conscripted soldiers of the fyrd trail behind as they travel at a steady clip northward along the Roman road.

The day is not yet gone when a forward scout races his exhausted mount to meet them.

"York has fallen without a fight, Sire!" blurted from the

scout as he reins up hard before the king and his commanders. The column is called to a halt.

"Hardrada is not delayed at York with a siege?" asks an earl of the southern lands.

"There are nary any left to defend the city," says the scout, "yet the enemy has not entered the walls."

"You are certain Hardrada does not occupy the city," demands the king.

"Yes, Sire. Your brother Tostig leads them away to Stamford Bridge to receive hostages and gafol."

"And this you saw with your own eyes," confirms Gyrth.

"I did not ride before I witnessed their army turn from York and I questioned the city's leaders as to the reason."

"Well done," says Gyrth. He dismisses the scout to rest himself and his mount. Leads the king aside for counsel.

"My plan was to come upon them as they lay siege to the city," says King Godwinson, lament heavy in his voice and manner. "Now they will regroup on a field of their choosing."

"Perhaps," ventures Gyrth, "then again, perhaps Tostig has not turned as far traitor as we imagined."

The king's curiosity is piqued by Gyrth's pondering.

"If Hardrada's army had settled inside the walls of York, dislodging him would have been nigh impossible. It would at very least cost us half the army and the entirety of your remaining treasury."

"You believe Tostig has deliberately chosen a more favorable field of battle for us?"

"It would stand to reason he might expect to receive a higher standing from you, his brother, than the king of Norway."

"But the reason he assaults me now," says Harold, "is I refused to reinstate him after his exile by the thegns of Yorkshire. Why should he not expect similar treatment from me now?"

"I do not wish to disparage our family name," says Gyrth.

"What could be more disparaging than a brother turned usurper?"

Gyrth speaks freely, "It has long been suspected Tostig fought so poorly against the Scots in their invasion because he was a friend to King Malcolm. I believe his loyalties to friends and kin run deeper than his ambitions. Hardrada is Tostig's ally, but you are his blood."

The king worries the thought over in his mind. "I would that it is true. Tostig has always been of peculiar mind. One never knows on which side he may fall in a quarrel."

"Yet if it is so, or if he straddles the stream, it would explain his turning Hardrada away from York."

The king is frustrated by the myriad possibilities of Tostig's inclinations. He turns dark of mind and countenance. "There are many things that might explain it, and I shall ask Tostig when I see him next." The king shakes off the angry thought and returns his mind to matters more pressing. "I do not know Stamford Bridge well," he says.

"I will find one who does," says Gyrth as he takes leave of the king to query the local fyrd of that shire.

Gyrth finds one named Rowan for his untamed mane the color of a wind-blown brand. Rowan claims to have fished the banks of the river Derwent at Stamford Bridge as a child. Captain and soldier go to the king in the waning hours of the day to give counsel of the battleground.

"There is a single bridge, Sire, wide and strong. As many as four or five men could travel abreast. It spans the river Derwent from west to east," says Rowan as he draws a sand-map in the earth at the king's feet. "The river itself is deep and fast moving. There is a great expanse of fields on both banks."

"Does the ground lay flat or does it slope?" asks the king.

"It slopes well enough toward the river from the west, and lies more gently on the east," says Rowan.

Gyrth and Harold Godwinson study the crude map and information imparted by Rowan.

"If they camp on the west bank in line with our approach," says Harold, "their backs will be to the river. Their retreat would be hampered by an attempt to cross the bridge."

"King Hardrada is a warrior of uncounted battles," says Gyrth, "I would count on him making camp on the east bank. A narrow crossing to his fore and his ships to his rear, as you would in his place."

"But his ships are still at Riccall, are they not?"

"By every word we have received."

"Then we might march to his fleet, attack in his absence, then face Hardrada himself."

Gyrth considers the plan. "The bulk of his army resides with his fleet, it would likely not be the easier path to victory. In addition, I would be inclined to give Hardrada an option to flee. A man with no opportunity for retreat fights twice as fiercely."

"True enough," says the king, "yet I would be done with this threat once and for all. I have no desire to drive them away only to have them return in the spring, or the spring following."

"Then let us meet them head on," says Gyrth, "our numbers are greater. With our army between theirs and the city, their supplies will dwindle quickly. Even if we are fought to a stand-still, we can surely outlast them."

"We haven't the time to starve them out of the country. The Normans threaten to make the channel crossing on the change of the wind. What we do must be done swiftly and decisively."

"Spoken like a king," says Gyrth with pride. "Night has nearly overtaken us. Let us have a meal and sleep. As soon as it is light enough to make the highway from the moors, we will march and put more miles behind us than any army has before."

"I would gain a mile tonight," says King Godwinson, "or even a half if that is all that is possible. Every foot gained now is one less for the following days."

At the king's command, the army is rallied and urged on

into the dusk on the road to Stamford Bridge.

* * *

Each afternoon now Sassa makes the trek to Trondheim to gaze out onto the fjord, searching the horizon for a sail. She returns home each night after nightfall with a basket of fruit or nuts or fish.

The home stores grow fat with honey, corn and wheat. The secret bin beneath the bed fills with coin. In the yard, three new goats and several geese graze: stock taken in trade for firewood. Fodder enough for the longest of winters fills the loft.

With the small share of treasure issued to her from the returned ship, Sassa has purchased a sturdy new wood-splitting axe for her husband, and colored glass bead necklaces for the girls. A finger ring for Tora. On her return from the village this night, Sassa carried a basket full of small green apples which she slices thin for drying.

Tora watches her sister from near the fire where she works a bit of the great boar's hide for new boots for Kari and Nanna. "We have food enough for three winters without pause," says Tora, "or do you prepare so soon for the feast of Yule?"

"When my husband and Svend return they will be hungry. You know their appetite as well as I."

"Together they eat as Thor and Loki," agrees Tora, "but if they do not return you will have the best fed goats in all of Norway."

Sassa's breath catches. She stops her cutting of apples, glares at her sister.

Tora is stunned by her own thoughtless words.

"They will return," says Sassa, urgent and sure.

"Of course," says Tora with haste, "I only meant if their return is not until after the winter. But of course they will return."

Kari and Nanna stare silently at their aunt from where they play quietly in the fresh straw of the stall. Their wide eyes and despairing expressions worry Sassa. She bids them come to her. The girls obediently go to their mother. Sassa sits on a stool at the table, holds her girls by the hands as she speaks in earnest, "You have no need to worry about your father. He is the strongest of men and knows well how to care for himself."

"I do not worry," says Kari.

Sassa is surprised by the calm confidence of her eldest child's words.

"I miss him terribly," continues Kari, "but do not worry because father told me a secret before he went away."

"A secret," whispers Sassa, her voice nearly taken from her.

"Yes. He told me how to summon him when we truly, truly need him."

"What did he tell you?" urges Sassa, trying her best to keep desperation from her voice.

"Father said it was a secret and I could only tell you when you most desperately need to hear."

"Then tell me now," says Sassa, her eyes welling against her will, "please, Kari."

The child speaks with conviction beyond her years, "Father told me if we were ever scared or lonely, we only need tell our favorite story of him and it would be as if he were here with us."

Sassa presses tears from her eyes, wipes them away with the sleeve of her dress. A sad smile overtakes her features. "Tell me. Tell me your favorite story of your father."

Kari sits with her legs crossed on the furs covering the floor at her mother's feet. Nanna sits also to listen. Tora clenches the boar hide and remains silent.

Kari begins, "Once when I was little and you were home with Nanna, father took me into the village. My feet never touched the ground all the way there. He rode me on his shoulders and I pretended I was flying far above the world in Freyja's falcon coat.

"When we got to the village there were lots of people and many vendors selling goods from their shops. One was selling bits of beehive with the honey still in it. Father stopped and gave the man coin and the man broke off a piece of the comb and gave it to me. It was warm and sweet. Rich honey dripped from it.

"Father held me by the hand and we went on our way, but there were so many people and so many things to look at. Something caught my eye, I don't remember what it was, but I didn't take care enough of my honeycomb and it fell to the ground and was covered with dirt.

"I felt so ashamed. I was very sad and I told father I wanted to wash it off, that maybe it was still okay, but he said the honey would wash away with the water. I wished to cry but dared not because it was my own fault that I had dropped it and I knew it was a great treasure and had cost a lot.

"But father took my hand and led me back to the man with the honey. He paid and I was given another piece of the comb, this one even larger and more filled with honey than the last. And it was the finest honey I have ever tasted."

Sassa coughs a bit of laughter despite her broken heart. She smiles through her tears as she looks in wonder at her daughter.

"I have a story also!" says Nanna excitedly, not wanting to be left out. "Once a man with a horse and a cart came to get firewood and I told the man I wanted to ride on his horse but he said I could not and father gave the man extra wood and the man let me ride on the horse for a long ways."

Sassa and Tora can not restrain their joyful laughter at the story and the telling.

"Now you, mother," says Kari. "Father said you should tell a story also if you wished he were here."

Sassa composes herself, wipes her cheeks dry and smiles

upon her daughters. They look back to their mother with keen anticipation.

"Once, long ago, before your father and I were blessed with two beautiful daughters, and I was merely a girl myself, my own father gave to us as a wedding gift, a young goat. It was not a fine animal, nor strong, but a sickly nanny that gave no milk and hobbled around the yard. It had come into this world weak and lame. My father would have added it to the stew-pot the day it was born, but I stole it away and suckled the tiny kid with my own fingers dipped in a bowl of her mother's milk, so it lived and it grew.

"When your father and I were wed, my father gave us the goat so we might have meat through our first winter.

"When the winter grew cold and there was not enough food for us, nor fodder for the animals, your father took up his knife to slaughter my goat.

"I was not as brave as you, Kari," Sassa tells her daughter, "I cried and cried at my special goat having to be slaughtered.

"With tears still in my eyes, your father put away his knife, bundled himself in furs and went out into the terrible winter cold. He was gone most of the day, but he returned with a bushel of old barley stalks, wilted and soaked through. He would not tell me where he found the fodder, we had no coin for such things in those days, but I suspect he traveled to the farm far up the glen where grains are grown, and dug through the snow in the fields to find it.

"In any case, he was so very cold when he returned that it took half the night huddled at the fire before he stopped shaking and his color returned.

"He dried the barley and fed my little nanny with his own hands.

"It was a long winter. When we became very hungry your father would go out into the storm and climb into the mountains and dig through the snow with his hands, into the caves where the adders spend the winter. He killed basket-fulls for the stew-pot."

"You ate snakes?" exclaims Nanna.

"I ate many and was glad to have them," says Sassa. "And when there were no snakes and no bread and our stomachs were knotted with hunger, we shared the dried grain with the animals. But never once, no matter how much his stomach growled and complained, did your father pick up his knife and approach my little goat again."

"What happened to her?" Kari would know, "your nanny goat?"

Sassa smiles broadly and allows her tears to flow unchecked. "She is in the yard yet. You play with her and her kids daily."

The tale excites the young girls greatly. They look to Tora next. "Aunt Tora, tell us a story about father also," plead the girls.

Tora smiles at the children and at her sister, comes to them to take a seat beside Sassa.

"Your father is the greatest man I have ever known," says Tora, "for he made a promise that, kept or not, relieved the agony of my broken heart. And if that were all he had ever done, I would speak his name until my death with love and reverence. But more so, he gives love to my baby sister and my beautiful nieces, and that makes him great also."

When Kari and Nanna are put to bed, and Sassa and Tora clean the night's bowls in the washing tub, Tora says to Sassa, "I seem to remember more of your goat tale than you tell. I remember father did not heed your pleas and would have made stew of that newborn kid if you had not stolen her in the night and run off into the woods. We searched a day and a night for you and thought the wolves had taken both you and that scrawny creature you loved so much."

Sassa grins in memory. "And that part of the tale shall remain between sisters," she says, "for I would not have my own daughters acting so foolishly."

❋ ❋ ❋

The sun burns white in a pale sky unencumbered by the faintest of clouds. Norsemen seek shade beneath the raining boughs of the willow trees that grow lush on the banks of the river Derwent. Small birds and flying insects sing and drone in a constant din, joining the rush of the river and trilling of frogs.

The man sits leaning with his back against a tall alder to watch Svend hunt the reeds on the edge of the river with his bow for fish and fat, croaking bull-frogs.

The contingent of a hundred of Hardrada's fighting men remain posted on the west side of the river as foreguards to warn of Saxon troops, but none are expected and the men lounge lazily beneath their makeshift shelters out of the hateful sun.

Forni approaches the man where he lolls idly picking at the lush grass in the dappled shade. The old man sits, his long spear leaning on his shoulder.

"Is it as you dreamed it would be?" queries Forni.

"War?" answers the man, "It is not. We hurry to a place then wait. Then hurry to the next place to wait some more. We take a city only to give it back. We plunder townships without warriors and strip the dead of their wealth."

"That is war," says Forni. "What did you imagine, the enemy would be waiting for you, lined up endlessly to be cut down by your axe?"

"Yes," says the man flatly. He shares an ironic smile with the Ancient One.

The man's brow furrows with question as he plucks at the grass. "I do not understand one thing. Many of those fighting drew back and did not engage fully as if..." the man studies his words carefully before speaking them, "as if they were unsure of their own intentions."

Forni pulls his hat from his head, wipes the sweat from his brow with a stained sleeve. "The coward believes he will live forever if he holds back in the battle. But in old age he shall have no peace though spears have spared his limbs."

"Why would a coward go to war at all?" the man wonders.

"The desire to war is innate in man. Even the coward," says Forni, "he can not help himself. He is drawn mindlessly like a moth to a torch. In the young it is stronger even than love or family."

Both men look to Svend where he stalks frogs through the reeds at the edge of the river.

"That can not be disputed," says the man with regret.

"How would you have war, if you were its creator?"

The man considers the question before he replies, "To fight with men of like mind and skill and desire until you are killed... or kill them all."

"You have described the daily work of the einherjar on the fields of Valhöll," says Forni as he tiredly shoves himself to his feet, "and not all men are destined for that, the greatest of fates." As Forni shoulders his spear and moves away, he calls back to the man, "Though you, son of Rig, I believe will see it for yourself one day... if Freyja does not steal you away first."

❋ ❋ ❋

King Harold Godwinson rides at the head of his army as it is hurried north along the ancient Roman highway.

Gyrth has dismounted to travel on foot with the fyrd as they are gathered at each shire they pass. The conscripted foot-soldiers struggle to keep pace with the mounted huscarls and nobles. The daunting rate of travel forces the reluctant recruits to move at a half-trot for hours on end. Gyrth trots alongside them, urging them on with encouraging banter and inspiring compliments.

The commoners of the army are roused by a member of the royal house, the king's brother and captain no less, who travels with them. He bears the same load of arms and armor and goods, breathes the same dust kicked up by the horses of three-thousand mounted nobles and huscarls, and takes rest only when the whole of them do. This is a nobleman to be admired and followed.

More of the fyrd are gathered along the way, the farmer/soldiers having been called to arms by scouts who ride ahead, sounding the call to battle as they go. The mass of the fyrd carry crudely forged spears. What little armor they possess is ill fitting and poorly maintained. Not all carry shields, but those who do grumble at being forced to march with such an encumbrance. Veterans who have warred before confide to their fellows that their shield shall soon become their best friend. In the heat of the battle they will wish they had two to hide behind, one on each arm.

The pace of the army is relentless so by midday the Saxons are stretched many miles along the road.

The men on foot stumble and shuffle along, their heads lolling on their scrawny necks, their eyes only on the road before them. Each step threatens to be their last. Even Gyrth has ceased his words of encouragement and trudges on, helping to their feet men who have fallen by the roadside.

Distressed by the condition of the fyrd, Gyrth regains his horse and rides to the lead of the column to speak with the king, "King Harold!" calls Gyrth, "a word please."

The king reins his horse aside. Gyrth draws to a halt facing him. King Godwinson's horse is lathered beneath the saddle, and the king himself shows through his slumped posture and lined face how taxing the day has been.

"Harold, we have gained good ground, but I fear the men on foot will be of little use if we encounter the enemy before they can be gathered and rested," says Gyrth.

The king stands in his stirrups to gain better vantage of the trailing army. "I do not see the end of the column."

"And will not without a goodly ride in the opposite direction," says Gyrth. "These are not professional soldiers. They have no training or tolerance for the march."

"Then they must gain tolerance for we lack the time for

stragglers," says the king.

"We can hurry them at the point of a spear or the end of a lash, and they may make the field alongside you," says Gyrth, "but they will be half-dead and unable to fight."

The king sneers in frustration, "Then put spear and lash to them and bring them half-dead and we will hope to restore them before we engage Hardrada."

"And if we encounter the enemy before they can be rested?"

"Then they will be used to dull Norse axes," says King Godwinson, his frustration rising, "for it seems they serve little other use. Press them on!" The king spurs his mount away to regain his place at the head of the army.

Vexed, but without recourse, Gyrth dismounts, hands the reins to a retainer and heads back on foot toward the rear of the column.

* * *

It is several hours after dark has fallen, long after the king and huscarls have made camp, that the final man of the fyrd can be brought up, fed and put to rest.

Gyrth moves among the army ensuring the men, exhausted as they may be, eat what they can before sleep. The men sit slumped in silence around the camp's fires without the energy for banter. Many sleep where they sit, cold stew and stale bread forgotten in their limp hands.

Orm and his men have rested and eaten and look none the worse for wear. Orm carries a skin of wine, drinks from it often as he kicks awake sleeping soldiers to berate them for their weakness.

Gyrth imagines Orm has taken rest and refreshment in every village they passed where he harangued the citizens to take the road to war. But the lieutenant, by whatever means, has done his job. The Saxon army has amassed to more than five times the three-thousand huscarls of their standing force. Fifteen-thousand swords and spears will face the enemy two days hence: one day on the march, one day to recover and to form.

The plan is sound, Gyrth knows. But he also knows no plan of battle, no matter how sound, survives the first clash of arms.

❊ ❊ ❊

The man shares in the meal of frogs and fish Svend has collected with arrows tethered by a long leash to his bow. The bounty is plentiful. Ull, Tyrulf and Tarbin join the two for a reprieve from yet another meal of English beef.

"Svend, you prove yourself quite useful on the field of battle, and in camp," says Ull,

"Tomorrow you must show me your secret for taking such a fine bounty from these English rivers."

Svend beams with the praise, then his brow wrinkles. "Tomorrow? How long will we be camped here?"

"The king has granted the people of York three days to gather the hostages and goods promised," explains Tyrulf.

"Then what shall we do?" Svend would know.

Tyrulf sucks clean the bone of the hind leg of a boiled frog, speaks around the meat, "Then on to the next English city, then the next, gathering English thralls and wealth until their king has none left for himself."

❊ ❊ ❊

Late into the night as the Northmen sleep, the man roams away from the camp, his mind troubled, his body restless. He has never in his memory spent so long idle. Back home, even in the winter months, hands must remain busy; the fire must be kept, the roof mended, the livestock tended and the stalls mucked. Stores of food and fodder must continually be re-assessed and meals adjusted accordingly.

Here, at war, with the weather fine if overly warm, he lies otiose. Not even wood to be cut, as the camp's cooks take on the duty.

He longs to be home. He imagines the long cool evenings holding Sassa in his arms as they watch the last of the sun flare its brilliance as it retreats into the ocean for the night.

Save for his promise to return Svend safely to his mother, his reasons for coming all this way have become obscure and faded. To gain a name? That was given before they set sail. Son of Rig: a name and lineage of which to be proud. To win Freyja's attention for a place at her table in Sessrúmnir? How could the goddess' attention be had by slaughtering frightened men as they plead for mercy? Thus far he has done little more to distinguish himself than any other man.

The thoughts trouble him greatly as he makes his way to the bridge spanning the river Derwent. The man stands mid-way across the bridge, looks to the north and east, to home. He knows he will never return to this England, not for all the land and riches promised. Never leave Sassa and his girls again, not to war nor raid nor for any amount of wealth or glory. Not until death. The purpose and promise of war -- to grant him heroes rights and a honored seat in the halls of Asgard -- seems unattainable here. War is of no benefit to him.

But battle! Battle: One man against one. One against many. There lies glory! A man might find himself worthy to sit with Sassa in Freyja's hall if his enemy were great enough. If he faced strife so overwhelming as to tax himself beyond even his own knowledge of his capacity. That is the making of a hero! But where to find that sort of man, and how to make them an enemy? The man does not know the answer to his questions and wishes Forni were there to answer for him. In a quick change of mind, the man scoffs at his senseless wish. Forni would only answer in riddle, as is his want. And to this -- the man's midnight wanderings -- Forni has already spoken:

'The fool lies awake at night to worry. A weary man when morning comes, he finds all as bad as before.'

The man smiles at his folly. He looks down at the blackness of the flowing river through the slats of the bridge, set nearly wide enough to drop a hand-axe through. He grips the handrail which runs waist-high the entire span of the bridge on both sides, gives it a shake. It creaks and trembles in his grasp. Such workmanship would not last a single winter in Norway, he thinks.

He looks from east to west. The low fires of the main and foreguard camps dance and glow in the night, but there is no movement.

The man sighs, vexed,, raises his voice to the stars which cloud the sky in milky silver bands, "Allfather, how may I gain a seat at your table?"

No sound comes to him but the song of insects and frogs and the rush of the river beneath his feet.

He gathers himself and once again raises his voice, considering his words with greater care this time, "Allfather, I would not put to you a question, but a request. I have never asked the Aesir for a thing, not in my life. Not when my grandfather hung dead in the ash. Not when my wife went cold and hungry in winter. Not when I was blessed with daughters instead of sons, for I would have it no other way. But I will ask now, and pray I have earned your favor. Odin, and the Aesir all, send me an enemy that will grant me a place in the great halls of Asgard."

* * *

The road is taken in the false dawn, the Saxon army picking their way along the highway in the graying morn.

Gyrth has had little rest between putting the last soldier to sleep and rousing them again, too few hours later. A morning meal of stale bread and dried meat on the march to sustain them until mid-day.

The army has covered far more ground in the previous three days than Gyrth would have thought possible. They now stand less than a day's hard march from Stamford Bridge.

The farmers and tradesmen of the fyrd, though worn from the distance and speed traveled, seem in better spirits this day with the end of the journey in sight, as though they have forgotten the end of the journey means the beginning of the fight. Much repeated banter amongst themselves have assured the fyrd, the army they will face is only a small fraction of the number they themselves possess. Further, Norse invaders have often been known to accept treasure in lieu of blood. It is an uplifting thought to a common man that negotiations for peace, not war, lie at the end of this trying march. The men of the fyrd speak confidently of this outcome. Some are so encouraged by their own rhetoric they venture to boast how in truth they long to do battle with the Norwegians.

The cock-crowing banter dwindles as the day wears on. With the slow-moving sun broiling men in their armor, weapons and shields chafing backs and shoulders raw, the army trudges onward. Boasts of prowess in battle become grumbles of discontent; the day is too hot, the food too little, rest, much needed. Will the war be long? With harvest coming, will farms go unattended? Will the king be willing to reimburse them for their losses? The last muttered beneath the breath as not to raise the attention or ire of huscarls who prod them along.

Of course the huscarls are eager to war. They ride fine horses while the common soldier walks. They receive pay while a farmer's crops grow overripe in the field, and a tradesman's shop goes without patrons. Huscarls receive fresh bread, meat, buttermilk from stock wagons, while the men of the fyrd have only what they can carry.

Gyrth hears all, but dismisses the grousing as an army's due. It is always so, and always has been. It amuses the captain to envision the legendary Greeks and Romans of old, their soldiers no doubt complaining of the same matters on the march.

Stories of quibbling grievance never told in the history of those great nations. Winners write the histories, and history has little tolerance for fighting men bellyaching of tired feet and sore backs.

Toward the end of the day, the column slows and compresses. Gyrth calls for his horse, rides to meet with the king.

In the township of Tadcaster on the border of Yorkshire, King Godwinson has called a halt to the march.

By the time Gyrth reaches the head of the army, the king's tent has been erected with Harold taking his rest inside.

Gyrth is granted admittance to the king's tent. The captain enters and is alarmed to find his brother reclining on his cot, his leg propped on pillows and his features contorted in a painful grimace.

"Harold, what ails you?" queries Gyrth.

"My leg," says the king, "an ache I can not bear another mile this day. We are nearly upon York. The meeting place at Stamford Bridge is just beyond that. I will take a rest before we proceed." Harold winces as he adjusts himself on his bed.

Too many hours in the saddle for one so unaccustomed, thinks Gyrth. A leg will lose feeling, then ache terribly. He has seen it many times before and his mind is relieved as to the health of his brother. "Have scouts been sent on to York?" asks Gyrth.

"Aye," says Harold, "and beyond to gain a full accounting of Hardrada's force. I only now wait on word to form the plan of battle. Leave me now. Wake me when the scouts return."

Gyrth takes his leave. He stands overlooking the Saxon camp. Fifteen thousand fighting men, three-thousand of which, the fearsome Dane huscarls, have battled many times before. Irony in the fact these most formidable of professional warriors are hardly removed from the Norwegians they will face on the field. They still carry the mannerisms of the Danish raiders from which they were spawned, fight with axes over swords, wear their hair and beards in the fashion of the Northlands, and though baptized Christian, each and every one are

245

still known to murmur curses in the names of the old gods. Man for man they are as fine a fighting troop as the world has seen, Gyrth knows, and he is proud to command them.

Gyrth moves among the professional warriors now. He is greeted at each fire with hearty welcomes and the gruff manner of men who face death as their living. Each man maintains his weapons at hand; his great two-handed Dane axe, a sword and long knife at his belt. Tall, heavy shields of English fashion, the king's Fighting Man crest emblazoned on each, lean ready at arms reach.

"How do you fare after such a march?" asks Gyrth to a band of huscarls.

A huge warrior with a nose flattened broad years ago by a shield strike answers for them all, "March? I believed us to be on a leisurely stroll to view the countryside."

"And where are these fearsome Norwegians we were promised at the outset?" is chimed by another, his forked beard dripping with crimson wine plundered from a local village.

"They await your smiling face even now, only a short ride past York," says Gyrth.

"If they haven't sailed for home already," another grumbles as he remains intent upon carving his name in the haft of his long axe.

"It is Hardrada we face," says Gyrth, "I would not count on him sailing until he has either gained what he has come for, or carries my spear in his belly."

The men raise cups to their captain's bold speech and usher him on his way with a bawdy song not learned in a Christian land.

Gyrth is welcomed much the same at fire after fire. Squad upon squad of huscarls affecting nonchalance, yet with the underlying coiled tension of a pack of hounds to be released upon a bear.

The day falls to night before the first scout returns from his reconnoiter of the Norwegian camp. Gyrth ushers the scout to the king's tent for his report.

"I could find little sign of an army at Stamford Bridge," says the scout, "only a contingent force of no more than a thousand men camped on the east bank of the river, and a foreguard of five score to the west. I then rode on to Riccall. The main portion of their army is camped at their ships which string beyond sight along the river's bank."

"Could their main army be gathering even now to meet the smaller force at Stamford Bridge?" asks the king.

"The army at the ships seemed content in camp and were not by any indication I could see preparing a march," replies the scout.

"Did you see Hardrada?" queries Gyrth.

"Or Tostig," adds the king.

"Both at Stamford Bridge," says the scout, "or who I supposed was Hardrada, as the man stands nearly seven feet and is nigh as broad at the shoulder as he is tall."

"That would be Hardrada," says Gyrth.

"And your brother Tostig, Sire. I know him well from his days in Northumbria."

"And you are sure of their numbers," states Gyrth, "no more than a thousand with Hardrada."

"As well as I might be."

The king studies the numbers, then addresses Gyrth, "What are your thoughts on the division of their force? Will they be sailing upriver to the next town? Have we miscalculated?"

"I do not believe it is so," answers Gyrth, "They are to receive hostages at Stamford Bridge and expect no resistance. That is likely the reason for the small number."

"And have they posted sentries along the road?" asks the king of the scout.

"None further than half a mile in any direction from either camp."

The king stands from his bench to rub his leg as if willing it to life. "I would ride on Hardrada and Tostig before reinforcements can be brought up from Riccall."

"Agreed," says Gyrth, "but if we march tonight we may stumble upon their scouts without knowing, and by first light they will have brought up the main force of their army."

"They are expecting a contingent from York to bring the hostages and Danegeld on the morrow," says the king, "if we approach at the expected time, we may engage them before they can sound the alarm to the remainder of their army."

"Without proper sentries they will have little warning," agrees Gyrth, "and the forest surrounding the meadows where they camp is dense enough to hide the true size of our force."

"Then on the coming day," says King Godwinson, "we drive this scourge from our land."

❊ ❊ ❊

The night fires light the meadows to a dancing, flickering parody of day. Thick aroma of roasting beef drifts for miles. The contingent of Norwegians set to receive hostages and treasure at Stamford Bridge on the following day, break open the remaining kegs of mead and ale to celebrate the coming march on London and the mounting of King Hardrada upon the throne. Hardrada himself roams the camp to rouse warriors with glorious tales of the crushing battles and heaping treasure hoards to come.

"Men!" bellows the king, his voice rising above the din of drunken warriors and roaring fires, "On the morrow we receive merely the first of the vast treasure this land will offer up to us. This country is truly like a wanton Frank whore, her treasure ready and willing to be taken. For did the lady that is Yorkshire not spread her legs wide for us on our approach?"

The men roar in agreement and laughter, the king's skill with words, a pleasure to them all.

"We took her fighting men as easily as if it were her virginity!" shouts the king.

The listeners are roused to an even greater fervor.

Hardrada must wait to be heard above the resounding din, "And now in return for our kindness for not ravaging her further, she willingly offers us more treasure. Two-hundred cattle, one-hundred sheep, a thousand pounds of silver and half a thousand pounds of gold!"

The army shouts its excitement at the prospect.

The king holds his hands up for silence. "And let us not forget... a hundred of their highest born lads and ladies!"

The men laugh and disparage as to the worth of high-born English.

The king smiles at the embellishments to his speech. "Yet this wealth is not bound for my own coffers, but for yours! Every man who fights under my banner will share in the spoils of this land equally and fairly. When we finish with England we will be an army of kings, all!"

The Norsemen are whipped into a frenzy by the king's words.

Hardrada has to shout at the top of his voice to be heard even by those nearest to him, "Kings vassal to me, of course!"

Laughter and skol from the men within hearing range, and the king's words repeated to ripple through those gathered to delight the very last of them.

The man stands removed from the others, entertained by Hardrada's speech, raised by the jubilant mood of the army, yet with his mind dwelling on other matters.

Perhaps this business of warring is not as inane as he had come to imagine. Possibly there was some use to it after all: Poor rulers deposed. New rulers instated to lend their wisdom to a land and to history. Stale blood of the high-born infused with fresh lines of conquering peoples. Stagnant cultures overtaken by the daring, outgoing, adventurous. Timid gods usurped by the bold. Bloodlines of the brave, the strong and the clever perpetuated over the cowardly, weak and stupid. How else but war to affect the required change? War as fire: direful, yet essential for rebirth and renewal.

Perhaps.... Then again, perhaps all just thoughts born of a charismatic ruler's rousing speech.

The man scoffs at himself, for his thoughts now travel much as he imagines Forni's do, if Forni's thoughts can indeed be reckoned.

But within war, battle! A feeling like none other the man has experienced nor heard tell of. Nothing more vibrant or soul-lifting. Nothing to give a more dizzying joy of life! Truly man is born to fight!

The previous clash of arms at Fulford comes to the man clearly now. Not with the reeling adrenaline-fueled ecstasy it had been in the moment, but given the crystal clear vantage of retrospect. He sees each thrust, slice, parry of his opponents and of his own. Further he sees the movement of the battle in whole: The Saxons had chosen the field to have a swamp to their flank and a river to guard their fore. It had played to their advantage at the outset when they forced Tostig's Fleming and Scot mercenaries back, using the marsh as a barrier to press against. Then the same obstacle had been their undoing as Hardrada's troops pivoted agilely and trapped the Saxons between the river and swamp. Without room to maneuver the Saxons were crushed and annihilated.

The man sees himself within the fray with clarity, setting upon his enemy with Skullseeker without thought as to where each strike would fall. Shields as much a target as necks and limbs. Now, with calm lucidity, he sees many clean killing opportunities on each soldier who faced him. A shield held high to protect the head left legs exposed. A sword overthrust revealed half the torso. A canted shield, and the neck became unprotected.

The man frees Skullseeker, closes his eyes and slowly directs the weapon to the targets displayed in his mind. He performs a dance with his soothseen opponents. Skullseeker travels in tight arcs. The haft is thrust as a bludgeon, used to block, parry, turn away swords and spears. Two hands on the haft for power and speed. One hand now as the free hand seizes a spear, pulls a shield from its protective position. The motion of his axe in battle so different than the repetitive strokes required to split wood, yet the same: one must know where to cut to cause a tree to fall in the proper direction. How to follow the grain of the wood to split cleanly and avoid knots that would bind a blade. Not so different after all, the man knows. Skills to be learned, to be perfected, to become known for.

His dance carries the man deep into the night until each and every man killed on the battlefield at Fulford has been killed again, and yet again... each successive time with greater skill and efficiency.

When he has cleared the battlefield of his mind, the man opens his eyes to find Forni squatting, his back against a tree, barely discernible from the shadows. The sire of kings stands, moves away to be lost in the dark, and the man feels his unvoiced approval.

❊ ❊ ❊

The cocky banter of the fyrd is no more as the troops raised by levy don their armor and prepare for battle. Conscripted soldiers empty their stomachs of the recently eaten meal. Many quake terribly, their quivering hands unable to fasten buckles or tie up trousers. Many more grow pale and sickly at the prospect of the day to come. They look eagerly to the huscarls, whom in the previous days they disparaged as being privileged. Now their thoughts turn to the guidance and comfort these professional men of violence will bring.

The huscarls methodically prepare, each with their own ritual and superstitions. Some pray. Others curse, loud, brash and incessant. Most remain wrapped in their own thoughts, maintain their own counsel. All steely-eyed and stone faced as is their manner facing mortal combat.

Gyrth consults with the king and his advisors as to the most recent scout reports that naught has changed over the night -- that Hardrada still stands with only a fraction of his army at Stamford Bridge -- then takes his leave to make his own preparations.

Nothing new in this day, Gyrth tells himself as he notes the familiar tightness in his stomach and shallowness of breath that proceeds each battle, no matter how many engaged in. A terse smile creases his lips. This life, these feelings, freely chosen. A thing to be reveled in. On these days of fear, excitement, anxiety... he questions his rightness of mind and is never unhappy with the answer.

Armored and weapons to hand, the Saxon army stands ready.

* * *

Stamford Bridge, England. 25 September, 1066

T he man slept little yet has found new energy in the night's revelations. Upon waking to the sound of fires being rekindled and the smell of porridge boiling, the man takes Skullseeker to a quiet spot at the edge of the meadow to continue his drills, his enemies resurrected anew in his mind only to be killed, and killed again.

Halfdan gathers with others of like mind to mock the man's antics, though they watch from afar and keep their voices low.

The day wears on, the man becomes satisfied with his skills, holsters Skullseeker and goes in search of a meal.

At the fire he finds an empty porridge pot and naught but bones of the roast beef from the night before. None of the other fires have any more to offer, so he takes up a spear and heads to cross the bridge to hunt the herd of cattle which graze there.

Svend hurries after his uncle, calls to him, "Uncle, you went on the hunt already. Allow me to collect a beef today."

The man looks down on his nephew passively until Svend feels compelled to say more.

"When last we spoke my words were harsh and without thought," says Svend, "You are my kin and are sworn to protect me. I am ashamed that I seemed ungrateful to you for that."

"Yet you are a man and a warrior," says the man, "and I have no cause to treat you otherwise."

"You are my uncle and you act only as an uncle should," maintains Svend.

The man is gratified, smiles down on the lad and hands over the spear. Svend eagerly takes the weapon, hurries across the bridge.

The man sets about rekindling a fire to prepare hot coals for Svend's kill when his eyes are taken to the sky. Forni's ravens croak madly as they circle to alight on a tall elm above their master's head. Forni is already standing by the time the birds come to rest. He takes up his spear, looks from beneath his broad-brimmed hat to the west.

The man follows Forni's gaze. Glints of light in the forest beyond the river, like sun sparkling on flowing water. He draws Skullseeker, runs for the bridge even before he fully understands that the glinting light is not sun on water, but sun on steel! He crosses the bridge at a run searching for Svend, finds him not far, crouched over a downed beef dressing it for the fire.

Svend looks up at the approach of his uncle, smiles. "You are in time. I will need help returning the meat to camp."

Svend's smile falls as he looks to where the man looks. They see the first of the riders -- King Harold Godwinson's Men-at-Arms banner fluttering above -- as the Saxon army charges from the tree line into the meadow. The Fighting Man standard leads the billowing Dragon of Wessex banner and is followed by three-thousand mounted huscarls.

Svend snatches up his spear to face the charging army, but the man clenches his arm in such a grip as to cause it to numb, runs him toward the bridge.

The small Norwegian contingent of a hundred men on the west side of the river begin to stir and shout. They take up arms and form a shield wall with the few shields they possess, but they seem a wall of sand against the coming tide in the face of the Saxon army which charges upon them in numbers beyond counting.

Dane huscarls are loath to fight on horseback and would dismount to do battle, but the number of enemy they face is inconsequential. They bear their mounts down upon the assembled Norwegians, ride through them without pause. The war steeds need little assistance from their riders as the murderous wave of thousand-pound creatures churn the hundred defenders beneath their striking hooves at a dead run.

In normal times the fyrd would be sent forth first to draw out an enemy's attack, allowing the huscarls to assess strength and tactics so they might counter more effectively. But such caution and tactics are an affront to the huscarls facing a foreguard of a mere one-hundred of the enemy. The Danes, full of battle fury and unwilling to relinquish the slaughter to the fyrd, continue their charge on horseback to the bridge.

When the man and Svend reach the bridge it is crowded with warriors who in their haste to engage the Saxons, crossed to the west field. But the slaughter of their countrymen was apace and absolute, and they now heed the calls of their commanders to retreat to the east bank.

The man shoves Svend onto the bridge and the lad is carried along with the press of warriors flooding to rejoin their main body.

Skullseeker in hand, the man remains at the western foot of the bridge until the last of his countrymen dashes past to the east. He would turn and follow, but the first wave of enemy horsemen are already upon him. He understands he and his fellows would be run down before they reached the far side. The man steels himself to his fate, backs onto the bridge to narrow his enemies approach, readies himself against the wave of charging horses and riders.

The lead huscarl stands in his stirrups, his sword raised to strike, when the man suddenly steps forward directly in the path of the horse, drives the head of Skullseeker forward like a battering ram into the beasts neck. The mount screams, rears, topples backward, spilling its brave rider to the ground. The rider is pinned beneath a thousand pounds of frantically writhing horseflesh. The man is himself hurled backward by the impact, scrambles quickly to his feet on the downslope of the bridge. The following horse is so close upon the first that as it skids to a halt its forelegs catch against the fallen animal and it tumbles headlong over the other in a stiff cartwheel which sends its rider soaring past the man onto the bridge to land with crushing impact. The man leaps clear of the panicked horse as it scrambles to regain its feet, skittering on the unsure footing of the bridge planks before bolting back the direction it came, riderless, its wild eyes flashing white in terror and confusion.

A huscarl reins around the riderless horse, bears down upon the man, but his mount shies away from the floundering animal at the foot of the bridge which screams and thrashes its four legs in helpless panic. The rider is forced to clutch his mount with both hands to prevent being thrown, and can not bring his weapon to bear.

War-horses pile upon one another, rear up on their hind legs, bolt sideways in their madness to retreat from the crazed berserker who stands at the foot of the bridge.

The man swings his battle-axe, cleaves through the nearest rider's leg into the ribs of his mount. The rider is thrown, his severed leg dangling by a thread of flesh. His mount screeches in agony, mortally wounded, barrels into the press of horses behind in an attempt to escape.

The trailing horses are thrown into hysterical disarray. It is all the riders can do to remain mounted. Many warriors are thrown from their steeds, trampled beneath the churning hooves of the stampede.

Huscarls leap from their panicked horses, release them to flee. They form up in ranks to assault the man on the bridge.

The rider thrown onto the bridge gains his wits and his feet, rushes the man from behind with his great axe raised. But the man is quicker, thrusts the haft of Skullseeker rearward. It catches the huscarl in the chest, causing him to drop his own axe and fall to his knees, his breath hammered from him. With a back-handed swing of Skullseeker, the man cuts cleanly through the warrior's neck. The Dane's head topples onto the deck of the bridge, rolls to a stop against the rail.

The hundreds of Dane huscarls that have already dismounted their unmanageable warhorses have regrouped, shields secured across their backs, great axes gripped in both hands. They take more caution in their next advance on the bridge.

The fallen horse creates a deadly barrier to the entrance of the bridge, thrashing its sharp hooves in its futile attempts to regain its feet. The horse's rider curses the animal profanely as he remains trapped, his leg crushed beneath the fallen creature.

The manner in which the dying horse lies forms a narrow funnel onto the bridge. No more than two warriors at a time, taking care, might pass the deadly hooves unscathed.

The man stands brandishing Skullseeker just beyond the flailing beast to study the advance of the huscarls.

The professional soldiers understand the obstacle as well. A huge Dane with beaded beard and hair bound in silver wire calls to the Saxon army in general, "A spear!" he shouts above the thunderous roar of the vast army which now piles upon itself as they flood the broad meadow, "Lend me a spear!"

A member of the fyrd, a goodly distance behind the huscarls, misunderstands the Dane's request and casts his long spear at the giant berserker who stands baring the entrance to the bridge. The distance is long, the cast weak. The spear falls short. The man has ample time to step aside, allow the spear to imbed in the planks at his feet.

Without pause, he switches Skullseeker to his off-hand, pulls the spear from the planks with his throwing hand, cross-steps to build momentum and hurls the spear back to its owner.

The Saxon who threw the spear is able to duck low behind his shield so that the streaking spear clears his head. But the press of men is so dense behind him, the spear finds a resting place in the belly of another soldier. The speared man buckles around the shaft, slumps to the ground to die in dumb shock.

Furious, the Dane shouts his demand again, "A spear to

my hand, fools! Give me a spear to kill this infernal creature!"

A spear is brought up. The Dane snatches the weapon, turns it on the floundering horse at the entrance to the bridge, drives it into the creature's chest. The animal's lungs are pierced. The horse snorts a spray of frothy blood through its flaring nostrils, then lies still. Its huffing breathing grows shallow, its dark eyes grow glassy and dim.

The Dane withdraws the spear, trains it on the man who vexes their army with his refusal to die or be moved. He grips the spear in an underhand manner suitable for a powerful thrust and advances past the dead animal onto the bridge. To his flank and rear, huscarls advance in tight formation hidden behind long shields held just below their eyes.

The man can hear the Dane warrior's deep, heavy breathing as he advances with the steady confidence of one who has killed many, and lives still.

With no encumbrances behind the giant of a man who holds the bridge, and with an entire army encroaching, the Dane knows the man, no matter how fierce, will choose to retreat. When the giant is pressed past the crest of the bridge and his fellow huscarls are thick behind him on the downward slope, he will have gained the advantage he needs to assure an easy kill. With this plan, the Dane steadily inches forward behind the point of the long spear.

Suddenly, without warning, the man stops his retreat, lunges forward to grip the haft of the spear and yank the warrior toward him. The Dane, taken by surprise, does not release the spear, but instinctively clinches it tightly as if to resist it being taken from him. He stumbles forward to be met by Skullseeker as the glistering blade cleaves cleanly through the mail shirt on his shoulder to lodge in the ribs of his chest. The Dane issues a grunt of surprise and pain as he drops dead at the man's feet.

The man yanks Skullseeker free, but the huscarl who follows is quick to attack, slashes with his great axe from behind his shield. His action proves too hasty, his reach around his shield limits his swing -- a great axe not an effective weapon when borne with a shield and a single hand -- so that the blade strikes his enemy low on his arm, but does not bite deeply.

Blood from the shallow wound slings in an arc across English shields as the man swings Skullseeker with both hands in a powerful stroke which batters down the defense of the shield-bearing Dane. The warrior bawls in pain as his shield-arm is twisted at an impossible angle, the bones broken in twain with the impact. The back-hand recovery swing of Skullseeker crushes the warrior's helmet, and the skull within. The huscarl drops dead as if he lacked a bone-cage to support his weight.

Another huscarl discards his shield to swing his great axe in an overhead arc, but the warrior lacks the resolve to step far enough forward with the swing. The long-hafted axe misses its intended target by a narrow measure, strikes harmlessly the planks of the bridge.

The man rushes upon the huscarl. The unnerved soul, so assailed, avoids death by abandoning his weapon and hurling himself headlong into his fellows who cluster at the foot of the bridge.

Standing tall with Skullseeker held high above his head, the man roars his blood-mad battle cry.

The Dane huscarls at the foot of the bridge, brave warriors all, are compelled to stay their advance. They press backward into those who crowd forward in the following ranks.

Norwegians on the east bank have gathered what shields they possess to form a shield wall at the eastern foot of the bridge. They watch as the man battles the enemy, and fully expect him to fall at any moment. None have illusions that the thousands of Danes and Saxons who will pour over the bridge in the moments following the man's death, will fail to crush their anemic defenses and overwhelm them in a flood of steel and hate.

But the man does not fall.

BRENT JORDAN

When his countrymen are witness to the deaths of so many of the enemy -- the entire Saxon army brought to a stand-still -- and the defender of the bridge raises his battle cry to the Aesir, Hardrada's troops raise their voices also. They howl at the top of their lungs in bold salute to the hero and his valor. The Norwegians sound on their shields the din of war: clang swords and axes against iron bosses in such a racket that the fyrd in the rear of the Saxon army are chilled to their marrow.

Without understanding or vantage to the battle, the Saxons believe it must be their own army that is in the dire position, for what other event could raise their enemies' spirits so?

Dane huscarls, proud warriors that they are, will not be outdone. They pound upon their own shields with great axes and howl battle cries to add to the thunderous clamor.

The man, deafened by the tumultuous uproar, advances toward the enemy, spear taken from the Dane in one fist, Skull-seeker in the other. Blood-sprayed and gore covered, he appears as the god Tyr in the time before he sacrificed his hand to the wolf.

The whole of the army of England, Danes and Saxons alike, shrinks away from the giant as he approaches with long strides. Soldiers climb over the carcasses of horse and fallen comrades alike in their hasty retreat.

When the man reaches the narrow place between the dead horse and the railing of the bridge, he halts to look down upon the agony-filled face of the Dane pinned beneath the carcass. The downed huscarl hisses in anguish through shattered teeth. He looks up to the man, his eyes wet and glassy with fear and pain. The man drives the spear through the chest of the Dane, ending his misery in this life and sending him to whatever gods will have him.

Withdrawing to the crest of the bridge, the man stands to gaze over the whole of the English army from his vantage point.

The man: husband, father, uncle, woodcutter… no more: Son of Rig!

Rigsen has found his name and his rightful place in this world. A name and place prescribed by the Norns and ordained by the Aesir, and therefore may not be contested.

❊ ❊ ❊

The English soldiery blankets every foot of the plain, and still they pour from the forest like disturbed ants from a hive.

Is there no end to these Saxons? Rigsen wonders, and is elated by the thought. An endless number of enemies. Surely heroes amongst them. Iron sharpens iron. Heroes give rise to heroes.

Dane huscarls in the fore of King Godwinson's host cease their frantic attempt to cross the bridge and busy themselves forming up into organized squads. They are harangued by commanders who shout the order, Rally on me, so an accounting of the battle thus far might be taken.

Rigsen can clearly see confusion ripple through the Saxon ranks, from those a mere spear-throw from him, all the way to the forest where soldiers are just now receiving the perplexing news that they have been delayed in engaging in battle with the Norwegians.

Hearsay flies even faster than the truth through the bewildered multitude. Those at the rear hear ever burgeoning stories that the bridge has been felled. That the king has called a halt to the advance to bargain in Danegeld with the enemy. That the river has been secured by some strange heathen magic that prevents it from being crossed…. These, and many other repeated speculations. To compound the confusion, nearly all the Saxons have vantage of the bridge for the rise of the ground away from the river. They know by their own eyes that the bridge still stands, yet their own eyes can not explain why it has not been taken. Further they can plainly see only a small contingent of Norwegians formed up on the far side, a number that by all rights should be overwhelmed by the huscarls at this very moment. Yet the enemy stands unmolested, jeering and tossing insults in the face of their foes. This puzzling fact only causes the canards to fly faster through the English ranks.

Svend has gathered his bow and quiver and makes lunging attempts to reach the bridge to stand with his uncle. He is held back by Ull and Tarbin, each with an arm of the struggling lad. The men call reason to him.

"Your uncle can not be aided boy," says Tarbin. "His fate is sealed. Leave him to it."

"But we can fight with him," argues Svend as he renews his struggles to break free of the men who secure him. Tarbin and Ull are hard put to maintain their grip on Svend, he struggles so.

Ull pleads to Svend, "If you wish to die alongside your kin, so be it. But if you wish to avenge him ten times over, stand with us and prepare to loose your arrows upon the Saxon cur who take his life."

"He yet lives!" protests Svend. He raises his voice to his uncle, "Uncle! Come to us!"

But Rigsen makes no move to quit the bridge, and there is doubt he can be heard over the clamorous jeering of Hardrada's force.

"Why will he not come?"

"If he turns his back to the English, they will charge. Every foot he gives, they will take up," explains Tarbin. "He will be cut down before he reaches this side of the bridge. I do not know your uncle well, but he seems a man who would be loath to die with his back to the enemy."

Svend's determination to reach his uncle wanes as his mind spins in turmoil.

"Will you stand with us to avenge your kin?" Ull would have Svend's answer.

Svend ceases his struggles, stands free of the grasp of Ull

and Tarbin. "I will," pledges Svend, "and I will kill Saxons in numbers that will be sung of for all time."

* * *

A huscarl commander known as Peder, glares in frustration at the man on the bridge as he paces before his formed squad of Danes. The commander is of middle age, a multitude of battles, and has never been so vexed in his life. In place of a great axe, he carries a naked broadsword of Norse make in his white-knuckled grasp.

One man to turn back the charge of an army! The thought irks Peder into a fury. The enormity of this outrage will not stand. He himself will free the bridge of this Norwegian and cross to engage the enemy before he is put to answer to the captain and king. "Archers!" cries Peder.

From the midst of the great grouping of soldiers, men with bows rally to the front line.

The Norwegians who maintain the shield wall across the river hear the call and witness the scramble of bowmen.

Tyrulf commanding the van, rallies the shield-bearers, "On me!" he calls as he rushes for the bridge, his own shield lashed to his injured arm. The shield-bearing warriors follow at a run.

Peder points with his sword to the man on the bridge. "Feather that insolent fool, and let us be on with this war."

Rigsen stands the bridge unwavering as the Saxon archers draw and loose.

Tyrulf's is the first shield to cover Rigsen. Many more follow, overlap one another to take a bevy of quivering arrows in the thick ash wood.

The Norwegians curse the Saxons for their cowardice. Accusations of argr and veslingr and vamr are hurled, followed by spittle and scornful gestures of disdain and insult.

Svend, enraged, looses an arrow across the river to

imbed in a Saxon shield.

Hundreds of Saxon arrows are returned across the divide. Norwegians scramble for cover from the rain of iron-tipped missiles. After the final arrow has fallen, Tarbin, Ull and Svend push themselves to their feet, check their bodies for shafts. Svend looks sheepishly to the men.

"Please do not do that again," says Tarbin as he brushes dirt and grass from himself.

King Hardrada, puzzled at the delay in battle, comes from his position at the center of his force to inquire of the bizarre twist the day has taken.

"The man called Rigsen has taken the bridge and refuses to yield," says an excited Norwegian upon the king's query.

"Rigsen," the king repeats.

"The man has killed a half-score Saxons already and threatens to kill the remainder if they do not quit the field," tells the warrior.

Despite the grim situation, King Hardrada chuckles and grins at the audacity of a single man thinking to hold back an army. He continues to the bridge surrounded by his eager berserk bodyguard.

* * *

Gyrth forces his mount through the throng of soldiers crowding the bridge. Saxon archers continue to drive shafts into Norwegian shields upon the bridge to no avail.

"Save your arrows," commands Gyrth, "before enough feathers are given for Hardrada's army to fly away upon." Gyrth looks down upon Peder who stands at his horse's shoulder. "Who gave the order to pause the attack?"

"Behind those shields, a giant of an axeman has commanded the bridge and refuses to give way," says Peder.

"A half-score shields against your entire squad?"

"Not the shields nor the men who bear them, but a single berserker. Large as two men combined, and with an axe that could not be wielded by a mortal man."

Gyrth's bewilderment overcomes his anger and frustration. "A single man... or a lone god by your measure, holds the bridge?"

"The others with shields only came forward when I called for archers. Until then, the giant stood the bridge alone."

"So with your decision, you turned a single man into a dozen."

Peder drops his eyes, curses himself under his breath, then looks back up to his captain. "I will remove them now," he states flatly as he turns to his squad. "Forward!"

A thirty-man squad of Dane huscarls begin their advance.

"Hold," commands Gyrth. The huscarls quickly come to. "Surprise has been lost. Pull back, form up with shields and hold your position. I shall return with word from the king on how we will proceed." Gyrth reins his horse around and presses back through the army to consult with his brother.

❊ ❊ ❊

King Hardrada mounts the bridge in the lead of his berserk bodyguard to approach the grouping of shield-bearers.

Rigsen sits at rest in the center of the bridge. Skull-seeker, dripping Saxon blood, lies across his lap. Tyrulf stands protectively above as if shielding him from the sun. The Norwegians on the bridge free their shields of English arrows, but with a wary eye to the Saxon army which works to retreat from the bridge a good distance.

"Tyrulf, surely it was you who secured this bridge in my name," says King Hardrada as he approaches.

"Nay," replies Tyrulf, "it is Rigsen who denies passage."

Rigsen stands to face the king.

Hardrada looks to Rigsen, then past to the killed Saxons who yet litter the western foot of the bridge. His smiling eyes return to Rigsen. "You thought to start the war without me?"

"Forgive my impudence," says Rigsen.

Hardrada bursts into joyful laughter. The king is joined in his mirth by the bold warriors on the bridge.

"You are forgiven," says Hardrada, and there is another round of laughter.

Tostig approaches with his bodyguard of Flems, but not past the eastern foot of the bridge. He calls to the king, "King Hardrada, this delay may work in our favor. We should fall back to the ships and join with our main force. My brother will hesitate to attack in such a situation and we will have the advantage of retreat to the sea if need be."

"I am of other mind," says Hardrada. "Let us go forth and query what it is your brother will offer us to spare him."

"But Sire," simpers Tostig, "please consider their force is many times our own. If we were to gather at the ships..."

"I do not care to fight for the same ground twice," says Hardrada. "We have come this far, let us not give back that which we have taken without contestation."

"At least let us send runners with the command to bring your army forward to us, here," pleads Tostig.

"So be it," says Hardrada, "for I will never hear the end of it if I deny Eystein a hand in the decisive battle."

Tostig turns to a Fleming retainer to issue the command. The Flem sets out at a run on the road to Riccall to summon Hardrada's army.

"Now," says King Hardrada, "let us begin the word-war."

❈ ❈ ❈

King Godwinson is beside himself with news of the events. His extraordinary forced-march and perfectly timed assault, halted by some incomprehensible nonsense of a giant on a bridge.

Thwarted by a child's fairy tale. He limps on his painful leg across the small rise at the edge of the forest from where he had hoped to direct the battle. Now the battle is not fought and he is at a loss to understand why. He curses his aching leg, his ill fortune, the day, the heat, and his brothers, both foe and ally.

Gyrth waits for Harold's initial outburst at the news to dwindle before he speaks again, "Hardrada has no doubt sent word for the remainder of his army to be brought up, but we may still hold the advantage if we can take the eastern field before they arrive."

"Why has the field not already been taken?" Harold would know. A question repeated many times since the news.

"Again, I can not answer to that," says Gyrth. "However, I have formed up the battle squads with the huscarls in the fore, and on your command the bridge will be taken and..."

"That was my initial command! My only command! Yet Hardrada still holds the bridge. There is not another crossing, not for half a day's march."

"What would you have me do?" Gyrth would know, his frustration growing with his brother's rants which do nothing to further the conversation.

"We will negotiate. Discover what Hardrada and Tostig will have to leave us unmolested."

"Harold," entreats Gyrth, forcing the tone of reason into his voice, "at your insistence we have traveled further in fewer days than any army should be able. We have brought an army to field, ready and eager to fight. We hold the superior position and superior force of numbers by more than ten men to one... Fifteen. If we falter now and negotiate a truce, we will appear weak. We will never be free of this, nor any other scourge that plagues our land."

"Our land? We? Our army? You use these terms as if we were peers. I am king, Gyrth, not you. This is my land and my army and if I appear weak it is because my chosen captain, my war-learned brother, has failed me."

Gyrth is crushed by shame heaped upon him by his older brother, his king, and offers no reply.

"Gather a guard and the nobles," says Harold. "You will ride to face Hardrada and Tostig. And you will discover a way to win this day, be it by force or bribe. And if you fail, it will be you who is remembered for it."

❋ ❋ ❋

Rigsen remains alone at the apex of the bridge as King Hardrada, Tostig and a score of their personal guard take to the western meadow to meet with nearly thirty Dane huscarls and Saxon nobles lead by Gyrth Godwinson.

The King of England, Harold Godwinson, stripped of his kingly garb, and dressed and disguised as a retainer beneath a shadowing cowl, rides hidden deep within their ranks.

From his elevated vantage point on the bridge, Rigsen watches the opposing groups come together and is once again gratified war is not his chosen trade. Bandying words fore and back in the hopes of achieving treasure and peace is a foul calling. Skill with sharp words is a poor substitute for skill with sharp steel.

Svend joins his uncle on the bridge to stand at his shoulder. Both men look on as nobles meet to parley on the battlefield.

"I tried to come to your side," says Svend, "but I was held back and could not break free. They said you would fall too soon for me to be of aid. But I knew you would not fall."

"I can fall the same as any man," says Rigsen.

"Nay. You have already stood longer than any other man could have. I believe you to truly be the son of the god Heimdall. And if your grandfather watches this day from Valhöll, he could not but agree and be proud. The men already speak your name with the reverence of a hero of legend."

Rigsen looks down on his nephew with a grin. "I see you have taken the path of Bragi, as well as Ullr. And who is to say who spawned us? Only our own mothers would know for certain."

"Aye, you speak true," says Svend, curbing his manner to suit the listener.

The kinsmen fall silent to share more than their words.

❊ ❊ ❊

Gyrth followed by a troop of thirty mounted Saxon nobles and huscarls on foot, reins in his horse as he comes to face King Hardrada.

A Dane huscarl addresses Hardrada in the language of the Norwegians, "Will you speak in the Saxon language or that of Norway?"

"I speak the Saxon language as well as any man," says Hardrada, "and the oafish language of the Danes as well."

The Dane translator bristles but holds his tongue.

Gyrth, satisfied he needs no interpreter, addresses King Hardrada, "Hail King Hardrada of Norway. You have entered into our land bringing war without cause nor right. We would now have you take your leave in peace."

"I am sure you would," says Hardrada, "but who is it who addresses me with what I already know?"

"I am Gyrth Godwinson, brother to the king, Earl of East Anglia, captain of the king's army. I speak for the king."

"Has the king fallen mute? Can he not speak for himself? And the two of you," mocks Hardrada as he gestures back to Tostig, "must have much to discuss."

"I have naught to say to my traitor brother," says Gyrth, but his eyes hold Tostig's for a moment in worry. If Harold is discovered....

Tostig stands quartered behind Hardrada, eyes his brother Harold hidden deep within the ranks. Tostig looks to the English king with quick glances, not yet of mind to reveal his true identity. This he proves with tightly closed lips.

Harold, peeking from beneath his cowl, returns his brother's looks with caution and with silent prayers that Tostig will maintain his secret.

"What does your king have to offer in exchange for peace?" Hardrada would know.

Gyrth adjusts himself in his saddle, sits erect. "He offers the lives of your army, your ships, and the plunder already stolen from his people."

"These are things I already have," says Hardrada feigning boredom. "I have come for the crown, will he offer that?"

"King Hardrada," says Gyrth, struggling with his patience, "you are a man of many battles. A man of legend even beyond your own country. I should not need to remind you your army is vastly outnumbered in a land greatly unknown to you, and could be easily flanked and..."

"Easily...?" scoffs Hardrada with a grandiose gesture, "Easy is not a word you will use when speaking of my army... captain Gyrth Godwinson."

"This is not the time nor the place for couching speech, and I shall not insult you with sweet words," says Gyrth no longer muting the anger in his voice. "Withdraw from this field or be forced from it."

Hardrada smiles at Gyrth, barely needing to incline his head to match the mounted Saxon's eyes. "Tell your king to make himself known in the coming battle and I shall seek him out on the field. Then we shall have this conversation again, king to king." Being his final words, Hardrada turns his back to his enemy and strides toward the bridge.

Hardrada's bodyguard backs away brandishing weapons, baring teeth, growling like the half-bears they are rumored to be.

Tostig lingers with his guard of half-dozen Flems. When Hardrada has gone beyond range of hearing, Tostig sheepishly approaches his brother, Harold.

"Tostig," says Harold, "I knew your venom ran deep, but to return with King Hardrada, I thought beyond even you."

"You left me little choice."

"Your choices were many. You could have acted with more prudence in the earlship I had granted you. You could have remained in Scotland until our anger with one another had faded. You could have begged my forgiveness."

"Beg your forgiveness! I am your brother. We share a mother and father. I am brother to earls and a king. Why should I beg of anyone?"

"You are my brother, and now you are servant to another king," reminds Harold.

"I am a peer, an ally," insists Tostig. "And Hardrada, though not my brother, nor kin to my people, has never required my begging to remain so."

Harold sighs, slumps in his saddle. "Tostig, we are of blood, still. I would have our transgressions against one another dismissed and embrace you once more. Abandon this war and come into my fold and I shall restore you as earl of the northern shires."

Tostig is shaken by the offer. "You would grant me so much?"

"I would."

Tostig mulls the thought, breathlessly looks up to Harold. "What of King Hardrada? What shall we offer him to return to his own land?"

King Godwinson spits in his response, "I will grant him six feet of English soil. Possibly seven feet, as he is taller than most."

"But Harold, surely he could be given something. A token to save face by. He is a proud man, but a reasonable man."

"I care nothing of his pride nor his reason. The offer I have made is a final one. How say you, Tostig?"

Tostig studies the matter for a moment with a heavy heart and deep lament. He looks to his brother, the sorrow in his eyes as telling as his words, "I shall not be remembered as the man who lured a king to this country only to betray him."

King Harold nods once in understanding, sharply reins his horse about and spurs back to his army.

Gyrth looks sadly upon Tostig. "Tostig, you shall die this day for nothing more than misplaced honor. Loyal to a king who battles our own kin."

"Honor, misplaced or not, is all I have left," says Tostig.

Gyrth studies his wayward brother for another moment, then follows his king at a gallop.

From his position at the western foot of the bridge, King Hardrada bears witness to the exchange between Tostig and the cowled Saxon. When Tostig approaches, Hardrada is brimming with question, "To whom did you speak at such length?"

Tostig is saddened and defeated. "In truth, it was my brother Harold, the king, with whom I spoke."

King Hardrada is incensed. "The coward hides his identity, and you saw fit to keep it from me also. If I knew that man was the king, I would have killed him on the spot."

"Yes, that is why I kept silent. How can a man assist in the murder of his own brother and be called a man?" Tostig fills his chest with quivering breath. "If one brother is to die today, I would have it be me who falls under the sword."

Hardrada softens, looks across the field to the retreating English king. "Well spoken," says Hardrada, then speaks with a grin, "Your brother stands well enough in his stirrups... for such a puny man."

❊ ❊ ❊

Rigsen has watched the exchange. He understands the outcome.

"Svend, you know more of war now than I. Go find us a place on the field where your bow and my axe can serve us best," bids Rigsen of his nephew.

Svend, excited at being charged with such a duty, does as told and hurries from the bridge.

King Hardrada and his men make their way back across the bridge. "Rigsen, I would have you fight in my own guard. Take your rightful place with the berserk," commands Hardrada as he continues past.

"A great honor," says Rigsen, "but I would refuse it."

Hardrada is frozen in mid-step, turns to give Rigsen a harsh look.

"In its stead I would have a favor," says Rigsen.

"You refuse my command and ask a favor," scoffs Hardrada, his interest piqued by the audacity.

"You have daughters here," says Rigsen.

"Aye, they remain safe in Orkney with their mother until my return."

"Safe," says Rigsen as if the word is foreign to his tongue. "I also have daughters, and a thousand men or ten thousand guarding them would not seem safe enough this day. Is Orkney so far removed from the reach of your enemies? And as for them, what assurance of your return have they?"

"Not so far," admits Hardrada, "and no man can guarantee his return from war. What are you making of all this?"

"My request is that you sail your daughters to true safety, to their home in Norway under the watch of a man from Jarl Eystein's guard by the name of Svend Caldersen."

"This man Svend is kin to you?"

"Yes, and I swore an oath that this request will fulfill."

King Hardrada considers Rigsen's adjure, then shakes his head no. "I can not spare a man. I will need every hand on the field today."

"I have not finished," says Rigsen. "In return for your granting this request, I swear to hold this bridge." Rigsen extends Skullseeker in one hand so the head taps the north rail, then arcs it overhead while switching hands so the head of the great axe taps the south rail. Hardrada's eyes follow the gleaming weapon in its path. "Not a single Saxon shall cross until your ship has sailed to collect your daughters and carry them safely home," concludes Rigsen as he returns Skullseeker to his chest, consecrating his oath.

King Hardrada roars happily at the boldness of the statement, "Son of Rig you are indeed! I would need nothing more than a hundred men such as you, if a hundred were ever born, and I would make the entirety of this great world my own. This is a hero!" The king places a firm hand on Rigsen's shoulder. "I believe your ambition exceeds your grasp. But for your daring, I grant your favor..., if leaving you alone to face the whole of the Saxon army is indeed a favor. I shall have my ship sail to collect my daughters the moment your Svend Caldersen is aboard." The king cocks his head, confides with Rigsen, "This kin to you, will he go willingly?"

"He will not. Svend has the heart and soul of a warrior and will not willingly leave my side nor quit the battlefield," admits Rigsen.

"As I would have suspected. No kin to you could ever be named a coward. But not to worry. Your Svend will indeed quit the field, and willingly for an even greater duty, or my skills of cajolery are not half as great as I believe them to be." The king smiles broadly in prideful pleasure. "This is my word, Rigsen, and so it shall be." The king calls to his troops, "Bring this man all he desires and spare him nothing!" Hardrada's exuberance flows through all within hearing, "What shall you have, Son of Rig? Shields, spears, swords...."

Rigsen studies the offer carefully. "Have you any mead?"

The king hoots his pleasure, "Bring a keg of mead... two! Shields, and a cart to carry it all. And this I decree now. Each man of my army shall give a gift of silver or gold from his own horde so that when this man reaches the afterlife he can look down and know his family, his daughters, and theirs, and theirs for all time after, shall want for nothing!" Then King Hardrada turns to the east to call out, "Svend Caldersen, find me the warrior who is called Svend Caldersen."

The name is repeated through the Norwegian camp by

every man. When Svend hears his name so oft repeated, he is stunned in bewilderment.

Svend hurries to the bridge. He looks to his uncle then to the king in question.

"Svend Caldersen," says King Hardrada, "you have caught my eye. I have watched you in battle. I have been witness to your heroics and have chosen you for a heroic task."

Svend is breathless that the king speaks to him in such a manner.

The king takes an arm ring from his own wrist, places it on Svend. "By this sacred ring you are bound to me in my service, and I am bound in gratitude to you who wear it. You shall be responsible for my loving daughters safe return to my kingdom in Norway. It shall be you, Svend Caldersen, who ensures no harm befalls them on the journey."

Svend's eyes water in stunned pride. He looks to his uncle.

"I am proud of you, Svend," says Rigsen. "Now be on your way and perform your duty with honor."

"What of you uncle? Are you not coming with me?"

"This honor is yours and yours alone. I have my own obligation and my own fate to see to its end."

"But what shall I tell aunt Sassa?"

"Tell her just that," says Rigsen.

Svend stands quivering in indecision. Rigsen pulls Svend near so he can whisper, and none but his nephew may hear. Svend listens intently, closes his eyes, tears are pressed from them. When Rigsen has finished, Svend looks to him, nods stoically. He strides from the bridge as a man, and sets out on the road to Riccall.

Halfdan has heard repeated the happenings on the bridge and his heart grows sick with envy. The boy to be free of the battle, and Rigsen to be given a piece of gold or silver from every warrior's hoard. Nine-thousand men in Hardrada's army. The man will be as rich as the king himself. And what good will such a hoard do him? Wonders Halfdan with spite.

Rigsen is set to stand the bridge alone against the army of the Saxons. He will be overrun and dead in an instant, and all that treasure will be wasted on a wife and children he will never see again. Halfdan's vile animus envelops him in whole and causes him to make his way to the bridge to face Rigsen.

A handcart with two kegs of mead, a half-score shields and many spears and axes is wheeled onto the bridge.

"Place the cart and the shields on the downslope to the western side, so the bridge is narrowed and will provide shelter from arrows and cast spears," commands Hardrada.

The berserk of the king's bodyguard deftly set about the task. The handcart is wedged in place with spears thrust into the wide-spaced slats of the bridge. Shields are bound to the upright spears forming an overlapping wall before and above the cart.

Rigsen watches all this from the apex of the structure when Halfdan approaches him from behind. Rigsen turns to face Halfdan without expression.

"So I am finally rid of you," smirks Halfdan in a low voice so the king and the others do not hear. "Your arrogance has done you in. You will be slaughtered here today, and that beautiful wife you speak so highly of, and her brats, will be left alone. But they will be wealthy. They will be made very rich from coin of every man of this army. And this," sneers Halfdan as he takes a heavy gold torque from his own neck, "of the very finest gold shall be added to their treasure. I give it freely, knowing I will have it back when I go to visit that fine, fine wife of yours, and make her, and her treasure, my own."

Without word or prelude, Rigsen grasps the back of Halfdan's head with one powerful hand, and with all his might, drives his tormentor's face down onto the wood rail of the bridge. Halfdan's skull splinters with a resounding clash of bone on wood. He collapses dead at Rigsen's feet, the contents of his ruined skull spilling onto the bridge.

The king spins at the sound, and all -- Norwegian, Saxon and Dane alike -- watch as Rigsen takes up Halfdan by collar and belt, heaves him over the rail of the bridge into the river Derwent.

Halfdan's body is taken under by the current, and all that remains of the foul creature is his blood, gore and broken teeth, along with his gold torque, on the bridge.

The onlookers from both armies watch astonished as Rigsen kicks that which remains of Halfdan from the bridge into the river below.

The Saxons who stand watch from the western meadow are more shocked and astounded at the happenings than even the Norwegians. Englishmen murmur disturbed words through their ranks;

"The giant has murdered one of his own!"

"The warrior's skull was crushed in a single hand!"

"That is not a man who stands the bridge, but a creature from Hell and should not be tested."

These and many more stories of wonder and dread spread like wind-blown fire through the fifteen-thousand of the Saxon army. Even Gyrth who looks on from his mount is staggered by the event. His mind can take no measure of it.

King Hardrada knows little of the feud between Rigsen and Halfdan, but seizes the opportunity with his agile mind and gilded tongue. He strides to the western foot of the bridge to address the Saxon army with a stentorian announcement; "You have seen what this man does to one of his own. Now come and witness what shall be made of you!" With that, and a grin on his lips, King Hardrada, followed by his guard, marches across to join his kindred in the east meadow.

Rigsen is left to stand the bridge alone.

❖ ❖ ❖

"What is to be made of this?" asks Harold of Gyrth when he has heard the story in full. "Is it trickery of some sort?"

"I do not know," admits Gyrth, "but I do not believe

trickery plays a part. These sons of heathens have their own peculiar sense of honor and tradition, and it would befuddle the mind to think on it too long. The day is nearly half gone. Let us not wonder on the ways of the Northmen any longer, let us engage and erase their ways and mysteries from our land."

"I still hold the hope Hardrada may balk when faced with the full might of our force," states Harold. "Assemble the men by regiment for their Godly blessing, and allow their army to bear witness to our strength. They may turn tail yet."

Gyrth keeps his teeth together and takes his leave to perform the king's bidding.

It seems to Gyrth that Orm is least at hand when needed, and constantly underfoot when he is least desired. Gyrth has not the patience at the moment for his lieutenant, and the wretch clings to him like his own shadow.

"So the kings could not reach an understanding," says Orm.

"They reached an understanding," says Gyrth without ceasing his preparations for battle, "they understand they are to war."

"And Hardrada lacking a proper army to face us? Fortune indeed smiles on us this day."

"Have you prepared?" asks Gyrth, hoping to be rid of his lieutenant.

"What preparations would you have me make? I stand ready to do your bidding."

"Have you reported to the commander of your squad? Have you readied armor and weapons? Are you prepared to fight?"

"Fight?" Orm feigns shock and dismay at his commander's loss of forbearance. "But m'lord, surely my talents can serve in ways other than taking the line with those meant to be fodder for Norse axes."

Gyrth leaves his preparations, turns on his lieutenant. The heat of the day and the tension of the coming battle has sapped the tact from him. He speaks straightforward, "Orm, your only talents lie in sneak-thievery and cruelty that a righteous man could not tolerate. But now is not the time for those talents nor irking me with your pandering. This is the time for war. Now is the time for men to face one another in combat and live or die as their worth dictates. So be gone with you. Good fortune in battle."

Orm, resentful of his captain's biting words, slinks away with silent curses and hateful prayers that Gyrth does not survive the day.

The Saxon ranks are formed up by squads, each under their own commander. The huscarls take the vanguard, with the fyrd in wavering rows behind. The English stretch across the western meadow in such numbers nary a blade of grass is visible between men. Tall spears glint in the sun's rays and colorful shields appear deceptively festive.

The Dane huscarls stand shoulder to shoulder, several columns deep, facing the enemy detachment which lies an easy bow-shot across the river. Yet no shafts are sent in either direction. Every arrow is saved now for a sure kill.

King Godwinson's prelate, Bishop Rice, followed by a bevy of monks carrying buckets sloshing with holy water, travels before the ranks of the three-thousand assembled huscarls, blessing them with flung Adam's-ale and chants in Latin. The Christian Danes take to their knees and bow their heads to accept the benediction.

The thousand Norwegians seem a paltry group facing fifteen times their number, yet they mill on the eastern bank and shout vile insults across the river. Bawdy laughter and outrageous boasts of how the Saxons will fare in battle can be heard far into the ranks of the English army.

The heathen among the Norwegians shout loud speculation as to the worth of a blessing from a god who has never taken up a sword.

King Hardrada -- though claiming Christianity when purposes could be served -- allows the sacrilegious slight by affecting to hear nothing of it.

Rigsen stands alone and waiting at the apex of the bridge in the center of it all. A noise from behind causes Rigsen to turn. Forni kneels on the bridge using a small carving knife to score runes in the planks. He watches Forni for a moment, then questions the sage with gently mocking irony, "Runes of protection should be placed to my front, should they not?"

"You have no need of protection runes. Your fate is fixed," says Forni. "What I score is a reminder." Forni looks up to Rigsen to give his counsel, "There will be many times in the fray when you will think of stepping backward off this bridge. It is natural and common even among heroes. This is your answer to why you will not."

"What does it say?"

Forni slices his thumb with the tip of his spear which lies ever at hand. Blood wells. He stains the runes crimson as he speaks the words, "Cattle die, kindred die, every man is mortal, but I know one thing that never dies; the glory of the great dead."

"Forni, to me!" shouts Hardrada.

Blood soaks into the runes as Forni rises, takes up his spear, goes to the king.

"Harald Sigurdsson. Mighty King Hardrada," bids Forni, "what would you have?"

"War!" announces the king.

The men surrounding Hardrada watch in enraptured anticipation as Forni strolls to the bank of the river, gazes across.

The Dane huscarls, impressive in their ranks -- armor gleaming, weapons at hand -- kneel to receive the blessing of their Christ god bestowed by Bishop Rice.

The bishop is draped in robes of deep hued purple bordered in gold. A tall pointed hat rides his hairless head. Gold rings adorn his fingers, and he bears around his neck a crucifix of solid gold nigh the size of a forging hammer. Bishop Rice chants rote words of the Latin language as he travels slowly down the ranks.

Suddenly the warriors receiving his blessing recoil in

wide-eyed shock and scramble away from the clergyman.

The bishop turns to see for himself what has caused the exclamations from the Danes. Forni's spear streaks into the clergyman's chest, piercing through the back side of the prelate, hardly slowing until the wide tip is buried deep in the soft earth of the meadow. Dead as a landed fish, the bishop remains standing in an improbable backward lean supported by Forni's spear like an effigy posted in a grain field to harry crows: his arms flung outward, his head thrown back lolling on a lax neck, his face cast blindly to the heavens.

Forni, quite pleased with the result, ambles back through Hardrada's warriors where only now men are regaining their wits and voice. They exclaim to all the gods who names they know, that Forni's arm is the greatest they have seen.

Dane huscarls overcome their shock, scream threats across the river: ironic and superfluous in that they are already committed to engage in murderous battle with those they threaten.

An outraged huscarl commander comes forward to extract the spear from the bishop with the intent of sending it back to its owner. Yet when the commander reaches for the spear, his hand suddenly recoils as if he had gripped white-hot iron from a smith's forge. Others crowd around to gape at the spear-shaft emblazoned with magical runes. The words seidr and Odin ripple through the Dane huscarls and beyond to the fyrd on whispered breath.

King Godwinson and Gyrth sit their horses for vantage in the center of the assembled army. Both bore witness with their own eyes to the death of their most holy bishop.

"Do we still wait on Hardrada to become overwhelmed by our might, and flee?" asks Gyrth. He does not await a response to his sarcasm as he spurs his mount forward.

Gyrth reaches the fore-line of the army, dismounts, enlists a retainer to secure his horse to the rear. He addresses the huscarl commander by the name of Cadman who has taken the van, "The enemy forms their shield wall too far from the foot of the bridge," says Gyrth, studying the formation across the river, "it will prove to be their failing. When you reach the far bank form a half-circle in tight formation, shields overlapping to give shelter to those who follow until enough have crossed to assist your advance.

"Aye," says Cadman. The commander is a large Dane of advanced age, but as strong and with more battle experience than any other. "They have narrowed the bridge so only three pressed upon one another may pass at a time. I suspect their archers will attempt to take advantage of our tight grouping."

"Likely," admits Gyrth, "but our own archers will keep theirs at bay."

Cadman nods. "We will go in a wedge, one shield to lead, and one at each shoulder, several ranks deep. This will provide enough shelter from arrows and cast spears until that rubbish they have piled on the bridge can be cleared."

"Well planned," says Gyrth. "God be with you."

Before Gyrth can turn, Cadman queries him, "Commander... why have they left one of their own on the bridge? Surely they know the time for forward scouts is past."

"I do not believe him to be a scout," says Gyrth, "though with the arch of the bridge and his towering height, he can no doubt see London from his vantage point."

Cadman and Gyrth share a taut chuckle at the notion.

"Then to what purpose?" wonders Cadman aloud. He is a third-generation professional soldier who understands little logic other than that which applies to combat. A lone man serves no purpose in battle, and the Dane is oddly troubled by the notion.

"You may ask him when you meet," says Gyrth as he turns to give command to the following fyrd, "Stay close on the heels of the huscarls. And be swift. I have a desire to see for myself the land on the other side of this infernal river."

A half-hearted cheer goes up from the conscripted soldiers as they ready themselves for the charge.

Cadman faces his squad of eager huscarls to bellow his command, "Shields to the fore!"

His courageous troops swing their long shields from their backs to be held at the ready.

"Forward in wedge, on me!" Cadman commands as he raises his own shield to eye-level and boldly leads his men onto the bridge.

His men-at-arms follow, nearly stepping on one another's feet they are formed so tightly as they press forward to battle.

"Form up!" roars Hardrada as he sees the enemy force advance upon the bridge.

The few Norwegians with shields gather tightly, each shield overlapping the next to form a formidable wall of heavy plank wood, braced by sturdy arms. Hardrada himself crowds in behind the shield wall with the remainder of his company filling in behind.

Jeers and insults no longer fly as every breath is reserved now for the fight.

An eerie hush overcomes the battlefield. The excited croaking of Forni's ravens, even more pronounced for the silence. Each man's own breathing and thundering heartbeat, the only sound in his ears.

Rigsen's heart throbs as well. His head swims with dizzying euphoria he has never before felt. A high-pitched buzz in his ears as if summer cicada have taken up lodging inside. He inhales deeply. The smell of fresh sweat on top of rank staleness assails him from the mass of humanity which approaches. The sharp odor of charged anxiousness caries on the dry, hot air. Rigsen exhales long and slow. His heart calms. The incessant tone in his ears fades so he can now hear the shuffling boots of the enemy's steady advance.

He studies their shield formation, unknown to him but clearly designed to press past the barricade, and himself, without pause. Only helms and fierce eyes show above the brightly painted shields. Heavy leather boots below. Determined warriors crouched behind. The glint of hidden swords, spears and great axes ready to be brought to bear.

Rigsen holds Skullseeker in both hands at waist level in the narrow passage between barricade and bridge rail. His massive frame leaves little room on either side. But then it is not the enemy's plan to travel around him.

Cadman shuffles forward in the lead of the huscarl formation. His advance hitches as he closes within a spear's length of the man on the bridge. Why does this giant simply stand with no more concern in his bearing than one waiting on his supper? Could it be this is a heathen sacrifice to appease pagan gods? Or worse to imagine, is his calm brought on by a thing only he knows? Cadman forces the puzzlement from his thoughts. The fight is on the far side of the bridge, not with this lone berserk who appears to possess more nerve than sense. Do not concern yourself with this guardian or sacrifice, whatever his purpose may be, Cadman tells himself, it is not a matter to be worried over. Press on, kill the fool, and secure passage for the army to follow.

Rigsen sees the flicker of doubt in the Dane leader's eyes. It is what he had waited for.

* * *

With the enemy's shield formation now but two paces away, Rigsen strides forward and with his following step raises his boot to put it to the lead shield with all his might and weight behind.

None could have expected the move and Cadman is battered backward, stumbling into the huscarls who follow, leaving a gap in the shield formation. The flanking warriors now suddenly find themselves in the lead, taken with shock, and with their left and right shoulders exposed.

Rigsen swings Skullseeker, hacking through those exposed body parts as if into the trunks of saplings. Efficient, well-practiced, turning two strokes into one flowing, continuous strike.

The cleaved Danes howl in shock and agony. They fall away to add their lifeblood to the bridge already stained.

Cadman regains his feet and wits, discards his shield, charges the man, his own great axe raised to strike. But in his fury and haste the seasoned commander launches himself directly into the iron wolf which caps the head of Skullseeker as Rigsen thrusts the weapon forward like a spear. Cadman is caught in mid-face by the axe-head. The nose-piece of his helm is crushed inward through his ruined countenance. He folds to his knees.

The men behind attempt to catch him from falling, but in their reactions, the soldiers leave themselves exposed. Rigsen levels an overhead swing at the nearest which severs through helm and skull alike.

A gallant huscarl leaps free of the crush surrounding his fallen commander, aims a sideways swipe of his great axe at Rigsen's unprotected legs. Rigsen drops the long haft of Skullseeker to the deck. The Dane's weapon slams Skullseeker's sturdy ash haft into Rigsen's leg with crushing power, but does not find purchase in flesh.

Rigsen, hobbled by the crushing blow, lurches back to the narrow path between barricade and bridge rail as the axe-wielding huscarl aims another strike, this time at Rigsen's bare chest. The toe of the Dane's bit slices through Rigsen's flesh, but not deep enough. Rigsen returns a swing of Skullseeker which splits the huscarl from collarbone to sternum.

The bodies of the slain narrow the bridge further yet, and Dane blood makes footing unsure on the hardwood planks of the sloping bridge. Dauntless huscarls drag the carcass' of their fellows from their path and valiantly reengage the berserker.

Rigsen uses every part of Skullseeker, from toe to nob, to parry, strike, shield. He uses every inch of his extensive reach to strike his weapon home where Dane blades fall short.

Yet another huscarl falls with a leg shattered by the poll of Skullseeker. Another's ribs are collapsed by Rigsen's powerful kick. Still another pours out his life's-blood onto the bridge when the beard of Skullseeker is hooked behind his neck and he is wrenched forward to be impaled onto Rigsen's long knife, drawn for that singular purpose.

Dane huscarls are butchered and maimed beyond recognition, yet their intrepid fellows continue the fight.

When the fray becomes too compressed for Skullseeker's effective use, Rigsen draws his hand axe, reaches over shields held high to hacks at necks, arms, shoulders... whatever can be reached.

Rigsen is forced back past the cart and shields which form his barricade and he finds himself in the clear once again with space to wield the long-hafted Skullseeker. And wield it he does, in expansive sweeps with power no stout Dane can resist!

Huscarl shields are splintered to kindling, the arms holding them are numbed to the shoulder by the mighty impacts. Yet still they press, making headway onto the bridge.

Each backward step is matched by a forward step of the enemy until Rigsen finds himself treading on the runes Forni has scored on the deck of the bridge.

The glory of the great dead. To die retreating, or to die advancing. They are not the same. Only one holds glory.

Emboldened by the Ancient One's runes, and his sole remaining cause and purpose in this life, Rigsen howls his battle cry at the top of his voice as he renews his drive against the enemy. Wielding Skullseeker in one hand, his hand axe in the other, Rigsen furiously slashes and hacks to the left and right in his onward fight. The huscarls are driven back beneath the berserker assault.

Wounded, bloodied, battered, overwhelmed... the final Dane to make the narrow passage on the bridge turns from Rigsen to hasten his escape. The thought proves to be his last as Rigsen's hand axe is hurled at the soldier's unprotected back, severs his spine to drop him in mid-flight.

Gasping for breath, covered in their own blood and the blood of their fellows, the thwarted huscarls gather at the foot of the bridge many paces out of striking distance of the Dane-slayer who stands tall and heaving before them. With their commander and his lieutenants killed or maimed in the skirmish, as brave and competent as the soldiers of the huscarls are, they mill confounded and mystified at what has befallen them.

The Norwegians are exhilarated, drunk with delight at the spectacle they have witnessed. King Hardrada himself raises his sword high overhead, roars mindlessly. The exuberance of the king's voice causes all in his troop to raise their voices also until the combined howling of a thousand blood-mad Norsemen puts to shame Fenrisúlf and all his kin.

❊ ❊ ❊

King Godwinson, furious that his sure victory has been brought to a stand-still by a single enemy warrior, forces his horse through the ranks until he finds Gyrth conferring with his huscarl commanders a short distance from the bridge.

"I have ordered the army to engage Hardrada's forces. Why has it not been done?" demands the king.

"It appears the man on the bridge has yet to receive that order," says Gyrth.

"I do not understand."

]"Nor do I," admits Gyrth.

King Godwinson fumes for a moment longer. The mad howls of the invaders assail him like Satan-spawn singing joyously at their release from the pits of Hell.

"Bring up the archers," commands the king, his voice cracking with emotion borne of angst.

"Harold, we can not...," but Gyrth's protest is cut short as the king's voice is raised to its limit.

"Archers!"

Rigsen watches passively as the Saxon army clears a path for a half-hundred archers. The bowmen take their places behind the shields of huscarls removed twenty ranks deep from the front line. On King Godwinson's command, the archers draw and loose a great flight of arrows to rain upon the bridge.

Rigsen steps behind the barricade of heavy overlapping shields, kneels, the muscles in his back and neck corded tight in anticipation of a flurry of sharp-tipped shafts piercing through him. The thumping of arrows on hardwood is resounding. It brings to Rigsen's mind, a time long ago when he was caught in a terrible hail-storm and was forced to take refuge beneath a wood-roofed out-building until it passed. He remembers hailstones as large as a child's fist splintering the plank roof of the shack, bringing down the ruined shelter on top of his head. He remembers how foolish he had felt when he realized he would likely be killed, not in a great battle by fine warriors, but by overly ambitious rain falling from the sky. All this passes through Rigsen's mind in the instant it takes the great flock of arrows to fall.

In the aftermath, there is silence from both armies as all wait to see if the defender of the bridge yet lives.

Rigsen tentatively checks his body for shafts. Finding none, he stands from behind the barricade.

A mighty cheer rises from the elated Norwegians.

Astounded curses are issued from Saxons. Another flight of arrows hisses from sturdy English bows. In the following moments, hundreds of arrows strike the bridge and barricade until there is nary room for another. Still the Saxon bowmen loose as fast as they can nock.

As arrows rain upon him, Rigsen sits with his back propped against the cart to examine the bit of Skullseeker. He understands now why his grandfather used the butt end to slay. The finely honed bit is dulled, shows wear: a multitude of nicks from mail, bone and helmets. He draws his hone, runs the stone over the blade with a firm hand, caressing the steel with a satisfying rasp that soothes in counterpoint to the constant thump of arrows above and around him.

Hardrada's warriors, in most indecorous terms, dare the Saxons to cease casting arrows and fight like true men. But the bowmen would no doubt refuse to heed even if they understood the language.

Finally, the archers cease their fire. Both armies await the result of the barrage.

King Godwinson shouts a new command, "The man has been downed or is afraid to reveal himself beyond the rampart. Advance now and finish him!"

But before the first of the huscarls can set foot on the bridge, Rigsen again stands clear of the barricade to face them. He drapes Skullseeker across his shoulders, as a man enjoying a sunny summer day.

Joyful, wondrous laughter bursts from Hardrada's army.

"Hold!" commands Gyrth in opposition to the king's demand. The foremost troops remain in place.

Gyrth turns to his brother. "How are men expected to cross the bridge when the shafts of a thousand arrows stand like a tangle of bramble against them?" King Godwinson stews in silence as Gyrth continues, his cold tone an inherent part of his battle demeanor, "Let us retrieve our dead and clear the bridge of what arrows we can to make our next assault less encumbered."

"Every moment delayed brings the main force of Hardrada's army closer," reminds the king.

"True," admits Gyrth, "but our progress thus far has been naught, so I feel the time it takes to clear a path across the bridge will be of little consequence."

King Godwinson dismounts, leans close to Gyrth as to be heard by only his brother, "What manner of creature do we face here?"

Gyrth cringes at the king's query. Fighting men are bound to superstition by their nature. If they were to hear their king express doubt, their confidence might well be put asunder.

"It is only a man," assures Gyrth. "As fierce and resilient as he has proven to be, he bleeds. Any creature who bleeds, can surely die. This man will die soon enough." Gyrth places a steadying hand on his brother's shoulder. "Maintain your resolve and we shall win this war."

The king looks none too sure, his voice trembles, "No hero of legend ever told of could have withstood what this devil has. I fear the powers of Satan have been brought against us."

"Harold!" Gyrth hisses to stem the flow of panic from his brother, "Quiet yourself. I shall go myself to make certain that this is no demon who faces us. And if it is a demon, I shall divine that also. Now, gather your wits and hold your nerve until my return."

* * *

Gyrth takes his leave of the king, makes his way to the foot of the bridge to hail man or devil; whatever manner of creature would be so bold as to dare stop an army in its tracks.

The arched structure is burdened with so many arrows it has taken on the appearance of a great hunch-backed dragon with feathered scales.

As the captain approaches, he is taken with the spectacular physical preeminence of the man who faces him. As an earl and brother to the king, he has traveled and seen much. He has been to Rome and Greece and has gazed with his own eyes upon the statues carved by the masters who have created the most magnificent of manly images. But never, not in all his travels nor in his dreams of heroes and legends, has he seen the match of the man who faces him now.

Gyrth does his best to keep the wonder from his voice as he addresses the man in a clumsy attempt at the Norwegian language, "I would have words."

"Speak in your own language," says Rigsen in the language of the Saxons, "I can not bear my own tongue butchered so."

Gyrth is taken by surprise. "You speak our language."

Rigsen eyes the Saxon. "You come alone so I know you do not come to fight. What do you want?"

Gyrth bristles at the slight but maintains the demeanor of a professional soldier. "Come closer that we might talk."

Rigsen plucks an arrow from a shield, tosses it over the rail into the river below.

Gyrth grins. "There will be no more arrows cast now for fear of striking me."

"And how am I to be certain they do not sacrifice you to have at me?"

Without knowing how to assure the man of his own importance, and unwilling to declare himself captain of the army entire to this warrior, Gyrth simply shakes his head.

Rigsen was only taunting in any case. He was witness to Gyrth meeting with King Hardrada, and knows the Saxon holds high position. Moreover, the Norns have decided his fate long ago. If by arrow now, or some other means later is of trifling concern.

Rigsen comes down the bridge swaying Skullseeker, brushing across the planks in low arcs as if reaping grain. English arrows are scattered to left and right, clearing a path as he treads toward Gyrth at the foot of the bridge.

The army of England, only paces to his rear, gives Gyrth little comfort. He takes an involuntary step in retreat as the giant approaches, yet the man does not continue past the last plank of the bridge as if bound to it by some unearthly tether.

A wide swath free of arrows has been cleared on the bridge by Rigsen's efforts. He cradles Skullseeker in his folded arms, looks down upon the Saxon.

Gyrth stands but a spear's length from the man, and despite himself is again overwhelmed by the inhuman size of the behemoth: Shoulders as broad as a man of the fyrd is tall. Tall as a grown man mounted on a sturdy horse. Densely muscled as an oxen born to the plow. And the axe, the finest Gyrth has ever seen, its intricate designs unflawed by the countless lives it has no doubt claimed.

Gyrth steadies his resolve and his voice, "If you swear to leave them unmolested, I will send unarmed men to gather our dead."

"I am no king," says Rigsen, "I make no truce or treaty with foes. What do I care of your dead? They do not offend me."

"You speak as if I had wronged you, when it is you who has come to my land for murder and plunder."

"If you send one who can wield a sword I will kill him. Then you will need send two to carry him, then four...."

"It is a matter of honor and tradition that an army be allowed to take their dead from the battlefield."

"Honor," scoffs Rigsen, "what do you Saxons know of honor? I stand alone on this bridge with axe and knife to do battle. You cast a thousand shafts at me from behind a thousand shields. Is that English honor?"

"It is not," concedes Gyrth, "and was done against my advice."

"Then what use are your promises to me if your advice is not heeded by your own army?"

"Give me my dead," demands Gyrth, his voice taking an edge, "and I will grant you time to eat, to drink, to rest. Then we will battle again for that is plainly what you desire."

Rigsen turns his back on the Saxon, strides up the bridge. "Take your dead," he calls over his shoulder, "but it will do you little good, for I shall only make more."

* * *

Hot air is forced into lungs worked past their capacity as

Svend runs south to Riccall and the Norwegian fleet. The heat of the day threatens to fell him as much as the effort, yet he drives onward, his uncle's words to be relayed to his aunt Sassa echoing dully in his ears. He runs ever the harder for he knows the words, but not how to speak them. The physical exhaustion he imposes upon himself prevents him dwelling on the matter.

Svend has covered more than half the distance when he comes upon Eystein Orri hurrying the bulk of Hardrada's army north on the same road.

Eystein hails Svend when he is within shouting range, "Svend, is the king overrun?!"

"I run not from battle but on an errand for the king."

"How stands the battle boy!" barks Eystein, showing his great concern.

"On my leaving it had not yet begun, but for my uncle."

Eystein is frustrated without a clear answer to his query, but knows haranguing the lad will do little good. He forces a water flask into Svend's hands. The boy drinks deeply.

"Your uncle...," prompts Eystein.

"He stands the bridge and can not be forced from it. No Saxon can pass though they crash against him like waves on the rock cliffs. I am sworn to escort the kings daughters back to Norway." Svend holds his arm aloft to show proof. "This is the king's ring, and the words I have spoken, his also."

Eystein does not know what to make of Svend's story -- what of it is true and what a young warrior's fancy -- yet by the king's ring he must take the lad at his word.

"Guard well the daughters of the king, for the one called Maria is my betrothed," says Eystein.

"I swear it. But now please hurry your march, for my uncle is under terrible siege and would be renewed in his efforts to find you with him."

"Speed to you also son," says Eystein, then turns to the army. "Onward before no Saxons remain for us to kill!"

The men of the Hardrada's army muster a rousing cheer

though they are verily cooked in their woolen tunics and mail. They press onward.

Svend runs past the vast column of warriors as they regain the pace of their rapid march. He pities the men wearing helms and iron shirts that compound the sun's heat. Great rivers of perspiration run from reddened faces, saturated braids and beards. At the end of the battle train, stout men labor under the yolks of carts filled with armor, shields and weapons of every sort to bring to the nearly naked warriors camped at Stamford Bridge.

By the time Svend has passed the last of the army he can smell the marshes bordering the river and runs all the harder to force away his desire to turn and make his way back to his kindred. The thought of turning his back on the field of battle, he finds hateful. Aboard a ship on the open ocean, land no longer in sight, seems the only sure way to prevent his going against his sworn oath and returning to fight alongside his countrymen.

❊ ❊ ❊

Orm watches Gyrth face the man on the bridge and return unscathed. He curses his ill fortune. The giant has killed or mortally wounded every man sent his way, yet allows Gyrth to come and go without challenge.

If his captain were killed, he could easily slip away unnoticed. But in Orm's skulking mind he knows if he were to abandon his post now it would be his cursed misfortune that Gyrth would call upon him for one task or another in the final moments and his desertion would end in his hanging, likely from the very same bridge he seeks to avoid.

Orm's is the squad that will be sent against the berserker if the next squad of huscarls called upon fails to move the man, and Orm has no intention of crossing blades with the axe-wielding giant.

294

Perhaps a dozen men dead, a score more wounded, half those not to see the morrow. Better than an entire squad of huscarls defeated. Orm rattles through the calculations as he sits in the grass amongst the fyrd, poking in the dirt with the tip of his knife, surrounded by fools who could not think past the tips of their spears.

Thirty men to a squad, a hundred squads of huscarls, and his curse to be among the first. Not a curse, Orm grudgingly admits to himself, for he used his own tongue, skilled in guileful rhetoric to achieve this exact position in the army: far enough back in the ranks to be sheltered from the initial clash of arms; far enough forward to breathe clean air not yet kicked up by a thousand shuffling boots, or four times as many hooves on the march.

Sixty men at most stand between himself and the berserker. The number would once have seemed impossibly large to overcome. But Orm has witnessed for himself the lay of the battle against the hero who holds the bridge, and sixty, nor six-hundred seem a sure number now.

Orm's concern is gnawing, but he is relieved by what little he has learned from the Lord's Bible. He mutters the words now in a grumbling whisper, as if a prayer to be recited for comfort in trying times, "Now the serpent was more crafty than any beast of the field which the Lord God had made." And the verse indeed gives Orm comfort, for it assures him even a man who could not be overcome by force of arms, could be had by treachery... if one were crafty enough. Orm is fully aware that he would be labeled a coward for the leanings of his mind. Yet within the dark folds of that disgraceful mind, it is not cowardice but prudence that forms his schemes: A sage soldier knows when it is wise to flee the battlefield. It is that prudence that has kept him alive when thousands of his fellow soldiers have been killed over the years for their misplaced notions of honor and bravery.

It is the way of a coward to make a virtue of his cowardice.

Plans of how to escape this battle are hatched, abandoned and hatched again in Orm's aberrant mind. If not escape, how to gain such an advantage that the outcome will in no way be in question.

* * *

The mead keg proves full and untapped as Rigsen jostles it on the cart. He stoves the lid with his hand axe, lifts the keg the size of a huddled child above his head and pours the honey mead to quench his parched throat. The host of words exchanged with the enemy's captain as much thirsty work to him as battle itself. As much mead spills down his chest as makes his gullet, but enough is had that he is refreshed and restored with the god's nectar.

He lowers the keg to the cart, overlooks the Dane huscarls and the fyrd beyond in their disorganized ranks. Their army has retreated a good distance from the bridge and have begun to mill and roam. Their once uniform ranks degenerating to a wreck of frustrated huscarls intermingled with curious men of the fyrd who have made their way forward for better vantage of the happenings on the bridge.

Rigsen feels already the mead working its magic to ease the infernal heat of the day, elevate his mind and gladden his heart. His yearning to again swing Skullseeker is bolstered.

With the loud grumbling of his stomach, he comes to the realization he might have asked the king for meat and bread as well as mead. In truth, Rigsen had not expected to live so long as to need to worry about his next meal. But it seems the Norns have their own ideas for him this day, and he finds himself lamenting his lack of foresight.

He understands the enemy facing him are weakened by his appearance as an invincible creature. His countrymen are bolstered by his enduring strength. He dares not call for food, lest it break the spell of both.

Squires yet too young to wield weapons are sent by the Saxons to reclaim their dead. The lads are not but a year or two younger than Svend, notes Rigsen, but appear younger still for their nervous, flighty motions and furtive looks his direction from down-cast eyes. Some weep uncontrollably in terror of being forced into such labor, less due to the grizzly nature of their work, and more in dread of their nearness to the slayer of so many of their finest soldiers. The larger boys team to drag full corpses. Smaller lads gather bits of bodies and viscera to fill woven bags with the stuff, all while keeping an eye on the man as if they expect him to descend upon them like a boy-devouring giant of the sort they were told of in their beds in the darkest of night.

Rigsen ignores the squires, tilts the mead keg again, drinks long and heartily. He sets it down, wrings the dripping nectar from his chin.

A lad with the scant beginnings of a beard, tall and bold of nature, has taken to the foot of the bridge as if on a dare. He looks openly at Rigsen, though his legs remain coiled, ready to carry him away at the slightest lean of the giant in his direction.

Rigsen belches, steps forward, and the bold one recoils as quickly as a frightened rabbit. But Rigsen only stoops to gather up a few severed fingers that lie near to him on the bridge. He favors the brave lad with a menacing grin, tosses the fingers his way.

The lad allows the disjointed bits of Dane to fall to the dirt without reaching for them. He continues to stare in wide-eyed wonder.

"Are you a god?" asks the stripling with the unflinching sincerity of youth.

Rigsen studies the boy: larger than the others, but half-starved and draped in filthy unmended clothing. Likely in his final year as a squire before he takes up arms as a soldier to earn his living, or hasten his death.

"It is what is said of you in the ranks, that you are a god

of the pagans... or a devil."

"What say you?" Rigsen offers.

The boy studies Rigsen with arduous thought. "You appear as a man, but no human man could stand so tall, nor kill so many, so I believe you to be a god... though I am told there is only one, and I do not think you are Him."

The man chuckles in spite of his earnest attempt to remain stoic. "There are many gods. I am son to the one named Heimdall."

"Heimdall," says the lad, struggling with the pronunciation.

"He is the watchman of Asgard," explains Rigsen, "and when he travels across Midgard he is called Rig. He spawned the races of man."

"So it is true, you are the son of a god!"

"As are all men..."

"Then I too...!"

"...except for the English," amends Rigsen.

The bold lad is crestfallen for a moment, then restored as the Son of Rig grins down upon him without malice.

The lad's face grows dark with mortal concern. "Are you to kill us all?"

Rigsen ponders the question while pulling on his beard, allowing his eyes to wander skyward in the manner of a sage elderman. He considers the boy where he stands waiting for the answer in earnest. "I might be inclined to spare one who brought me a loaf of bread and a bit of meat."

The boy bucks up and reels away, then as quickly returns to gather up the severed fingers. He dashes away to be lost in the disorganized ranks of the Saxon army.

Rigsen has barely returned to the wagon to sit and rest his legs when the boy returns at a run, secrets a sack from beneath his ragged shirt, lays it at the foot of the bridge, then turns and is gone.

Rigsen retrieves the sack to find the lad has brought a half a loaf of stale bread that crumbles when broken, and a knot of salted meat gone green at the edges. He returns with his bounty to the apex of the bridge, sits with his long legs stretched before him to make a meal of the scraps. He tips the mead keg frequently and is more accurate in meeting his lips now that the keg has been diminished by a goodly amount of its weight.

He looks to the east bank to Hardrada's army where the warriors have taken up more casual positions. There is little to eat as the Saxons had surprised them in their coming, so most the Norwegians simply lie in the tall grass, their doffed shirts propped on fallen branches to offer shade from the blazing sun.

A stirring on the west bank takes Rigsen's attention.

An immense barrel-chested Dane thrashes to free his arms from his countrymen who seek to restrain his advance on the bridge.

"Leave me to him!" bellows the enraged Dane who has been given the boastful warrior's name of Njal, for he stands an imposing figure even among the well grown men of his kinsfolk.

"No fool is so sturdy that my axe will not cleave him in two with a single strike!"

The Norwegians on the east bank have been roused by the commotion across the river. They gather on the bank to watch.

"I have had all I can stomach of this Norwegian swine who sits and taunts us from his bridge, eating and drinking without care!" says Njal, then turns his hateful gaze upon King Hardrada who has come to the fore of his men gathered on the far bank, and who appears thoroughly amused by the outburst. "I have faced his like before," boasts Njal. "Many of us have as we stood against King Hardrada in his ceaseless attacks on our home of Danmǫrk. Yet does Hardrada stand as king of the Danes? No! Each time he came, we sent him scurrying back to Norway like a whipped cur."

Hardrada remains entertained and unperturbed by the

insults.

"And I will send him scurrying home now," claims Njal. He turns his scowl on Rigsen. "But not before I have his champion's head for my drinking goblet!"

Huscarls struggle to restrain Njal as he renews his efforts to take to the bridge. It is no small feat as the Dane mercenary is a huge fellow who stands less than half a foot shy of the height of the man he challenges.

Orm, grasping at an opportunity for advantage, steps forward to stir the pot, "Let him go against the man on the bridge. Njal is known to all here. He has fought and prevailed in more battles than any two of us combined. Let him prove this walking Norwegian oak is no match for Dane axes!"

The huscarls stand unsure. Their commanders have been called to the rear to confer with Gyrth and the king, and there are none remaining among them to temper their inclinations.

Orm knows as disciplined as the huscarls are, they are also easily set to cause. It will take very little more to embolden action. He uses his well-honed skills to incite them further, "Ten pen says Njal kills this two-legged ox within the count of ten!"

Bawdy jeers go up from the surrounding huscarls. The men release Njal and stand clear of the seething Dane.

The Norwegians have heard the challenge from where they gather on the east bank, and King Hardrada raises his own voice to be heard, "Ten pen and a thousand more says no Saxon sets foot on this bank this day."

Norwegians raise their purses to the Danes in taunting wager.

Njal, once released, stands without moving for a moment, his breath gathered in great drafts into his heaving chest. He glares at his enemy from beneath a sweat-matted shock of red hair. All eyes and expectations upon him now. His nerve gathered, his resolve steeled, Njal brandishes his great axe and strides onto the bridge.

Orm surreptitiously takes a spear for himself, moves to the side away from the grouping of Danes.

Rigsen remains seated without alarm though the huge Dane advances upon the bridge, less than nine paces away, before he halts to issue his challenge.

"Stand and face me and call your name so I might warn Hell of your coming," commands Njal.

Rigsen uses the haft of Skullseeker as a staff to wearily stand as if this new challenge is but a tiresome bother. When he has come to full height upon the crest of the bridge, and Njal cranes his neck to look up to him, Rigsen speaks, "I am Son of Rig. Kin to the mighty Heimdall. When you reach Valhöll you may tell them Rigsen sent you with his blessing. And tell them to prepare a feast for I shall be along shortly."

"A heathen!" shouts Njal, turning to his fellows to scoff with exaggerated bravado. And his turning is his undoing.

Rigsen closes upon the massive Dane with a burst of long strides that carry him down the sloping bridge in less time than the blink of a bird.

Njal spins to face the rush of his enemy, raises his great axe, but Rigsen has already approached within the reach of the long-hafted weapon. With a grip on the shoulder of Skullseeker's haft, Rigsen slices the finely honed bit along Njal's exposed neck before the Dane can fully understand he has been killed.

✻ ✻ ✻

Rigsen's charge carries him crashing into the Dane. Njal is hurled into his fellows by the headlong rush. His weapon falls to the ground as he clasps his hands to the long rent in his neck to attempt to stop the gushing of blood. But the blood will not be stanched. The Dane called Njal falls to his butt, his legs sprawled before him like a child playing in the grass, an expression of disbelief on his face white with shock. He remains sitting like that to die in the field at Stamford Bridge.

The startling end to the fight nearly causes Orm to fail in his plan, but he recovers quickly. From a dozen paces removed to the periphery, Orm launches his spear at the unprotected side of the otherwise occupied Rigsen.

It is a fine cast, strong and straight. Rigsen does not see its flight as he stands looking down on the dying Dane at his feet, so when the spear lodges deeply with a great rattling impact in the rail-post at his flank, he is taken wholly by surprise.

Orm curses, incredulous at his sour luck. Thwarted by a half-foot width of rail-post. The giant remains unscathed!

All eyes follow Orm as he slithers away to be hidden amongst the ranks of the English army.

Gyrth, alerted by the sudden elated uproar and bellowing laughter of the Norwegians from the east bank, storms forward through the ranks of huscarls to find his man Njal dead, and the huscarls staring dumbly down upon his corpse.

Rigsen stands tall, his gaze set to Gyrth, his grin one of pure pleasure.

Rigsen's look, and familiarity with the pride of the Danes, removes the need for questions. Gyrth knows immediately what transpired here.

"Is this sport for you?" shouts Gyrth, incensed, "Your king and country at stake and you take time to game? If you would make sport of this war, then here is your game." He yanks a gold crucifix on a thick chain from around his neck, its value that of a years pay to the highest rank of huscarl. "Gold! This and more to the first man to the east bank!"

The shamed warriors of the huscarl quickly secure shields across their backs, take up their great axes, and hurriedly advance upon the bridge in such numbers and in such a rush, that they struggle amongst themselves to be the first to gain footing.

Again Gyrth raises his voice, urging the maddened warriors forward, "Fight! Fight and earn your fortune! Earn your fame!"

The mad rush onto the bridge is in such haste, Danes pressed so tightly against one another, that Rigsen finds it simple work to slaughter the first number of them to come within range of Skullseeker. He is free to swing his weapon in powerful arcs while the huscarls are constricted within their own ranks, their axe-arms encumbered and forced to their sides. Magnificent Dane warriors are culled like sheep pressed too tightly in a slaughter chute.

With wolf-like fervor Rigsen cleaves Skullseeker through flesh, sinew and bone. Crushes helms and skulls alike. Drives sturdy chain mail into terrible wounds that show clearly bone and entrails of those who had expected protection from the finely woven iron rings.

Glorious cheers of the Norwegians drown out the battle cries of the English army, entire. The man's given name is called. Chants of Rigsen echo over the battlefield to carry through the Nine Realms.

Rigsen himself is only dimly aware it is his title, his name, that is raised by the thousand blood-mad warriors. Yet aware he is. The knowledge sends him into a berserker frenzy of such violence that even Bragi himself would blush at the telling.

Dane huscarls fall riven and crushed, yet still they come, whether by their own volition, or forced onward by the press of warriors to their rear is not known. Ineffective with their long-hafted axes, Danes untether shields from their backs for protection. Yet scant protection shields prove to be as Rigsen drives Skullseeker cleanly through the seasoned planks with little more effort than the birch wood logs he split as his trade in his home in Trondheim.

A thrust spear finds Rigsen's thigh. A sword creases his forearm. An axe opens a rent across his shin to the bone. Shields are battered against his elbows, knees, shoulders. His own ichor is spilled to intermingle with the tide of blood from the multitude of his enemies.

Gyrth screams commands at the top of his voice. Yet if

they are heard above the battle cries of the raging huscarls, they remain unheeded as the Dane axemen press onto the bridge.

Hardrada's warriors slam weapons against shields in an ever-rising din; chant, cheer, howl wolflike in their glorious madness. They raise such a tumult the soldiers of the English fyrd, far to the rear of their vast army, soil themselves with released bladders as they scramble forward believing the battle has begun at last.

Hardrada's shield bearers group tightly at the eastern foot of the bridge, prepare for the inevitable rush of Saxons to flood across the span.

Yet Rigsen gives no ground.

Dane huscarls are further hindered in their attack as their legs are entangled with their dead and dying fellows lying in writhing heaps upon the bridge. Those too wounded to stand are trampled by soldiers just entering the fray. Blood flows thick and sanguine on the planks beneath their feet until the original color of the wood is no longer seen, stained dark, shimmering crimson.

Even the swift-moving river below the bridge runs rich with color as waves of blood flow freely between the planks to be carried away in long, swirling ribbons of red.

The fifteen thousand of the Saxon army takes on the appearance of being drawn through an immense funnel, spanning the entire western plain at the furthest point, then drawing to a mere half-dozen across at the bridge.

Tostig, huddled with his Fleming mercenaries to the rear of Hardrada's Norwegians, has taken stock of the grim situation and knows outnumbered fifteen men to one, this small portion of Hardrada's army will not fare well once the bridge falls to the Saxons. And surely the bridge can not remain in their control much longer. The single man who holds back the army, giant of a hero that he may be, should have fallen hours ago. It is only by some unknown miracle, of what manner Tostig can not guess, that has kept the man alive to this point. Tostig presses his way through the mass of Norwegians to their king.

"King Hardrada!" screeches Tostig above the roar of battle cries, "Let us retreat and join up with your main force so that when we face Harold's army we might make a fight of it."

"One man makes a fight of it now!" bellows Hardrada gleefully as he gestures to Rigsen battling in the center of the bridge against the mass of determined soldiers. "If one man can defeat a hundred, then one-thousand can defeat..." Hardrada throws up his hands in ecstatic wonder. "I know not the number, but far more than your brother can stand to lose!"

"Sire, it is not reasonable to believe that man can stand more than a few moments longer assaulted as he is. If we take those moments to retreat..."

Hardrada points with his sword to the far bank, his face flush with emotion, his voice thunderous with the strength of an aroused king, "It is not reasonable to believe a man could have stood even a single moment in the face of that army. But stand he does, and I see no end to it.

"When the story of my deeds is sung, it shall not tell of my turning my back and leaving this war for the crown of England to a lone hero. That shall not be my legacy! Whether the man is killed in the next instant, or stands the bridge for all time, I shall not retreat."

Tostig does not argue further with the king, as Hardrada's blood is up and is as likely to turn his sword on a dissenting ally, as foe. He resigns himself to the fact his lot has been cast. For worse or better, he will remain at the Norwegian king's side.

* * *

Rigsen's chest heaves with deep breaths that fail to meet his needs. His shoulders flame with exertion. His back knots and coils painfully with the endless strokes of Skullseeker. The euphoria of mead and battle wears thin. Wounds make their presence known on legs, arms and chest where he is cut and battered. His mind wanders from the soldiers within reach, to the sea of the enemy which stretch to the wood line at the far edge of the great meadow, and beyond. Rigsen's boot catches on a misaligned plank. He catches himself with a half step backward. The Dane huscarls secure that half step for their own. Rigsen is forced to regain effective striking range with another reward step. Each axe strike, though still delivered with bone-crushing force, now fail to split shields. The accuracy of those strike wanes. The fine bit of Skullseeker dulls. Rigsen's attack is reduced to great clubbing blows and his shoulder put violently to shields to slow the ever forward progress of the enemy.

The Dane warriors, still impeded by their tightly packed numbers, remain ineffective in their attacks on their lone enemy. Short chopping axe-strokes, and sword thrusts above shields held high are the best they can manage for the press of their company.

Piled at the feet of the battling warriors are the mortally wounded, the dead. Friends and compatriots with broken bones, severed limbs, horrible rents in their bodies which drain their life-force in great gushes. Screams of horror and shuttering moans of agony wear at the nerve of their fellows. In even the most iron-willed, thoughts of revenge lean to thoughts of survival.

Rigsen retreats to the narrows of the barricade... beyond.

The advancing huscarls pull and chop frantically at the cart and the spear-mounted shields that protect their adversary.

Gasping desperately for air, and with withering grunts of exhaustion forced from his constricted throat with each strike of his weapon, Rigsen fights with the desperation of knowing; when the barricade falls, he falls also.

The haft of a spear holding Norse shields splinters with

a resounding snap. The shields it bears are scattered into the press of axe-Danes.

Rigsen levels a strike over the resulting gap in the barricade. A Dane who pulls at the shields is killed. Skullseeker's blade still fine enough.

The following warriors choose to grip their own shields rather than the shields of the barricade, and for the moment the cart remains.

Orm, hidden well back in the midst of the milling fyrd, has taken stock of the battle and knows their enemy flags. He rushes forward to Gyrth, hissing in his excitement, "The berserker tires. Now is the time!"

"We all tire," growls a mortally wounded huscarl through shattered teeth clenched in agony. The bloodied warrior returns from the lead of the attack on Rigsen, makes his way from the bridge holding what remains of his severed axe-arm clenched tightly to his chest to keep it from being left behind. "If you still have energy to give battle advice, then you should take to the bridge to give it." The Dane would say more, but immense suffering stanches his voice. He staggers away to find a suitable place to die.

King Godwinson presses his way to Gyrth also, but with concern and advice counter to Orm's. The king is mortified by the litter of dead and dying soldiers of his army which are dragged in great numbers from the bridge.

"What foils us here?" demands the king.

"To attack with so many in such close quarters is ineffective. Weapons can not be brought to bear without striking a fellow soldier," explains Gyrth.

"Then draw them back and attack with fewer, two or three per wave."

"Two and three have proven to be not enough against the man who holds the bridge."

"Three huscarls, not enough?"

Gyrth, of no mind to answer rhetorical questions, sets his jaw in silence.

"Then draw them back all together and we will make a more effective plan to gain the far bank," says the king.

"Sire," blurts Orm, "the man who holds the bridge can not go on forever. He will soon falter."

King Godwinson gapes at the carnage that surrounds them. "Soon! How many more men to be slaughtered in that time? A score slain already."

"Closer to two score," amends Gyrth, "and many times that number who will not see another day."

"To withdraw now only gives the man reprieve," mewls Orm.

"It is we who need reprieve," says King Godwinson. "Sound the withdraw."

A sounding blast from the command horns carried by the king's attendants send the attacking Dane huscarls scrambling in retreat from the bridge.

※ ※ ※

Rigsen shutters with fatigue as he watches the retreat of his enemy. Skullseeker supports him as he leans his weight against the haft like an aged man with a walking staff. The sturdy bridge beneath him seems to sway slightly. He can not see clearly through eyes stinging with sweat and blood. A heavy knot forms in his stomach in the aftermath of the fight.

King Hardrada, hearing the horns and witnessing the retreat of the enemy, approaches. "Rigsen, you have sent their army running yet again!" the king shouts. Then with a bolstering gesture to his warriors, "Is it your scheme to leave no Saxons for our blades?"

Rigsen suddenly spins to face Hardrada who has just made the foot of the bridge. "Stand clear!" Rigsen commands, brandishing Skullseeker. "This bridge belongs to me. It is mine and mine alone. You, King Hardrada, promised a share of England for all those who fought with you. This whit I claim for my own. Henceforth this bridge shall not be spoken of without my deed being spoken of also."

King Hardrada accedes to Rigsen's brash manner and declaration. He stays his advance and nods his assent without alarm or offense. The king has a clear understanding of the battle-madness that has overtaken the hero. He backs from the bridge.

Rigsen's ire slowly wanes. He slumps, sits heavily with his back to the railing. His head lolls on his corded neck. Sweat streams from his bare torso to soak his woolen trousers through. He allows his eyes to close, his mind to dim. He remains with the full heat of the sun scorching his shoulders until some time later, opening his eyes, he finds Forni seated on the edge of the cart barricade looking down upon him. Forni bears a pair of water-skins, bloated to bursting.

"Am I welcome on your bridge?" asks Forni.

Rigsen takes an offered skin, upends it into his open mouth, over his face, his head, to pour down his chest and back. He only stops for breath, then drinks the skin dry. Though tepid, and tasting of grass and reeds, the water restores and revives.

"You are welcome," says Rigsen.

It is only then Rigsen notes Forni's rune-covered spear has been returned to the Ancient One's hand. How it was restored, Rigsen knows not. He is far too weary of body and mind to query or wonder long.

Forni reveals a curved drinking horn from beneath his cloak: a magnificent vessel, carved and embellished with gold rim and fittings. He dips the bikarr into the open mead keg. He must reach far down to gather the nectar. He raises the brimming horn in salute to Rigsen.

"Only Odin may live on mead alone," says Forni, then drinks.

Rigsen looks wryly to the old sage. "Do I yet live?"

"You do."

"Why?"

"Not even I know the minds of the Norns," says Forni, "but this I do know: Your triumph this day has gained the attention of the Aesir and the Valkyrie and of every being of the Nine Realms. What you have done will be spoken of by men for a thousand years, and ten-thousand beyond that. A heroic feat to be remembered past even the remembering of the gods themselves, perhaps." Forni stands, presses his drinking horn into Rigsen's hands as a gift before leaving the bridge.

Rigsen watches the Ancient One disappear into the ranks of the Norwegians, then empties the horn, the libation all the sweeter for the gift it was born in. He lies down the horn, takes up his hone and sets to work on the blade of Skull-seeker.

✳ ✳ ✳

King Godwinson confers with his brother Gyrth and the great number of nobles who have lent their personal guard and fighting men to the war. They crowd around a hastily drawn map of the river Derwent, surrounding fields and known roads.

"There is a second bridge, here," states an earl pointing to a spot on the map, "no more than nine miles downstream."

"Nine miles march to the bridge, and nine back," says Gyrth, "and the fyrd already worn from the march of the previous days."

"If we travel to the further bridge," says King Godwinson, "there is a chance the remainder of Hardrada's army will arrive in our absence and we will be caught unaware."

"York would be left exposed in our absence," complains an earl of that city. "I fear King Hardrada will be less kind with his second visit there."

"Then we can not leave," states Gyrth, "and we can not stay. We must advance."

"Inform me to how that is done," says the king, "and I

shall make it so."

The nobles ponder the map and dilemma in silence.

"No man would choose death over life," muses King Godwinson. "If the man were to be offered his life..."

"And wealth," interjects an earl.

"Yes, and wealth," agrees the king, "he might yet come from the bridge willingly."

"Rare would be a man who fights with such valor as we have witnessed simply for life and wealth," grumbles Gyrth.

"What else is there?" queries another noble.

Gyrth considers the nobleman with unveiled contempt, then shakes his head knowing even a day-long explanation would serve the nobleman naught.

"I will go to the man with your offer," says Gyrth, "for what good it will do." He looks to his brother, the king. "What shall be the limit of that offer?"

"Let there be no limit," says King Godwinson.

"And if he asks for the crown of England?"

"Then offer it, and it will be a short rein, the time it takes him to enter our camp."

The gathered nobles smile, nod and concur with the king's plan.

"No," states Gyrth flatly, "I shall make no offer that is untrue or done in cunning."

"But we are at war!" blurts an earl of the southlands.

"Then go and make the offer yourself!" barks Gyrth.

The earl drops his eyes from the captain's wrathful gaze.

"Even in war there must be honor. Honor of unbroken oaths."

The king and nobles are shamed, for they know this to be true in legend, yet seldom in practice.

"Then shy of my crown, I will stand by whatever you deem fit," says the king, humbled by his brother's righteousness.

The nobles grumble and stir, but speak no more.

Gyrth bows his head with acceptance of the terms.

"There is no need for worry of giving up the crown. If the man will come to this side for a kingdom, he will come for less. One who will betray for a pound of silver will betray for half. But I caution you all, there may be no price that lures that man from the bridge, for I fear it is only on his death that he relinquishes," warns Gyrth.

"Go then," says King Godwinson, "and discover if it is to be wealth and life for the man, or death."

❊ ❊ ❊

Fine gray dust floats on the still, heated air, trailing long behind the Norwegian army as they march at a trot toward the field at Stamford Bridge where their king and kin lie under attack. Eystein leads the column of fully armored and armed Norsemen. He frets in his mind that though they come with all haste, they shall arrive too late.

The blazing heat of the day has taken its toll on warriors more accustomed to fighting with ice coating their clothes than in this land that lies far too close to Muspelheim. The exhausted men drink from their water flasks often. The water is as quickly shed through their skin to soak their jerkins and trousers which further chafe and burden them in their march. Still the army does not falter nor slow. Not a single word of complaint is heard, only grumbling of the brutality they will inflict upon the next Saxon they encounter.

Eystein can now smell on the still air the extinguished fires of the camp at Stamford Bridge. He rallies the army on, "Just ahead men. Past the next bend and you shall have all the Saxons you desire!"

The men waste no breath on reply, but increase their gait to a full run.

The army suddenly comes over a small rise to the plain east of the river Derwent where King Hardrada and his thousand are camped.

Eystein's first thoughts are spun with confusion. The armies do not battle. They maintain a loose formations, lounging in the trampled grass of the meadows. Many of Hardrada's troop stand in greeting when they see the approach of Eystein and their fellows.

King Hardrada weaves his way from the midst of the gathered warriors, makes his way to receive his captain.

"Eystein!" bellows the king in jovial welcome, "You appear positively harried. Why the rush? You could have taken a long rest and a meal and still the Saxons would remain impotent on the far bank."

"What has happened here? Have you been offered a treaty or concession?"

"That has happened," says Hardrada, gesturing to Rigsen seated at the apex of the bridge.

"So the lad Svend told no tales. Rigsen stands the bridge, and alone!"

"It is true. And he is quite animate about the matter as well. I thought to spell him myself but he would not hear of it," the king chuckles, "I thought him to attack me for one more man to kill."

"He has killed many?"

"An entire squad of thirty or more, to my reckoning," says Hardrada, "yet by the limbs that lie on the west bank, and the color of the river which runs red with Saxon blood, my reckoning could be many times too small."

Eystein gapes at the wonder of it all. "So many Saxons without aid?"

"Unless the Valkyrie fight unseen by his side," says Hardrada. "But rest yourself now, and tell me how it comes to be, and where on this earth you were able to discover such a warrior as this Rigsen."

❋ ❋ ❋

There is an agitated stirring and murmuring from the ranks of the Saxons as they witness the bulk of Hardrada's army enter the field. Even after their losses at Fulford, nigh seven-thousand hulking Norwegians and sinewy Scots bearing shields and glinting with mail and naked blades -- many times the number they had faced only moments before -- now await them on the east bank. Victory that had once seemed daunting, now appears unattainable.

King Harold Godwinson and the high-born nobles that surround him, struggle within their own hearts not to show their angst to their soldiers who look to them for strength. Yet their own strength seems to have fled in the face of such dismay.

Gyrth shows nothing, not fear nor anxiety nor hope as he makes his way to the bridge. He halts short of the foot, bids the troops of Dane huscarls to give room. He ushers them back away from the bridge more than a spear's throw, then turns to face Rigsen.

Rigsen stands, stretches his limbs. The full measure of him leaves his enemy awestruck once again. With the number of fine warriors killed by his hand, he appears more impressive still.

"I have come to talk," calls Gyrth.

Rigsen stops in his stretching, yawns deeply. He pulls the second keg of mead from the cart, places it at the peak of the bridge, sits upon it. The open mead keg rests at his feet. He eschews Forni's drinking horn, lifts the keg to his lips to drink.

Gyrth allows the man to drink his fill and lower the keg before he speaks, "King Harold Godwinson would know your mind as to your price to come down off this bridge."

"The king," muses Rigsen. He puts hone to Skullseeker's bit with the unnerving rasp of stone on steel. "You speak for the king?"

"As his brother and commander of his army, I do."

"Does your king never speak for himself?"

"That question is put to me oft this day," muses Gyrth.

314

"A king must not put himself in unnecessary peril."

"Yet he would put you, his own brother in peril."

"Is it your intent to kill me?" says Gyrth in ironic half-jest.

"Yes. But not until you have spoken your piece."

Gyrth has been among the Danes of the huscarls -- descendants of heathen raiders and warriors themselves -- long enough to understand this Northman speaks in simple earnest, without boast.

"How does it come that you speak our language?" Gyrth would know.

Rigsen closely examines the bit of Skullseeker as he speaks, still many nicks which need his attention, "As a small child, a priest of your land came to the homes of Trondheim to inform the people your Christ god had been taken by our king, the kings of the Danes and Sverige, and therefore must be taken by us as well. The priest said we were to forsake the old gods and bow to the new. My grandfather took the priest, collared him and kept him as his thrall in our home for many years."

"Did your king or your earls not see fit to free the priest from this slavery, they themselves being Christian?"

"Kings and jarls held little sway over my grandfather. Christian kings even less.

"When my grandfather was away on the raids I would have the priest speak only in your language, as I could not bear the sound of my own language coming from his ceaselessly mewling lips, and I learned."

"So he became your teacher, and possibly even your friend in those years," ventures Gyrth.

Rigsen's attention remains on Skullseeker, but a small grin turns his lips. "One day in the years after my grandfather had entered Valhöll, this 'teacher and friend' offended me. So I put my hands to his throat and sent him to meet the god he blathered endlessly of."

Gyrth is shaken by the openness of the confession.

"What did the priest do to anger you?"

"He struck my hound."

"Your hound?!"

"She was a fine hound."

"And what was your age then?"

"I was nearly twelve years," says Rigsen. Then with an impatient look to Gyrth, "Are you to sing my saga?"

"I am not."

"Then speaking of myself wearies me. State what you have come to state."

Gyrth prudently maintains the diplomacy of his mission, "I do not wish to try your patience. I only seek to understand you better so I do not offend with my offer."

"My understanding of the English language remains incomplete. This word, 'offer,' is it akin to bribe?" Rigsen tilts the mead keg to his lips to cover his smirk.

Gyrth takes in a deep steadying breath in the stead of a response to the gibe. "Wine?" queries Gyrth.

"Mead."

Gyrth maintains his silence as Rigsen deliberates, then rolls the nearly empty keg down the sloping bridge. Gyrth stops the keg with a boot, uprights it, peers inside. A cup or two of golden liquid remains.

Rigsen stands from the full mead keg which serves as his stool, cleaves the top with his hand axe, hefts the keg to drink.

Gyrth imagines following suit with the keg at his feet, then thinks better of it. He calls to his army in general, "Bring me a cup!"

As if awaiting the command, the bold lad who questioned Rigsen earlier that day, and has never ventured far from the bridge, dashes forward bearing a hammered copper drinking vessel. The boy stands looking up in reverence at what he has come to know as the demigod on the bridge, until Gyrth shoos him away. Gyrth dips the cup in what remains of the mead, raises it to Rigsen.

"To honor and understanding among enemies. Cheers."

Rigsen retrieves Forni's drinking horn from the deck of the bridge, fills it from his own keg. "Skol."

Both men drink.

* * *

Tostig stands guarded amongst his Fleming soldiers to watch the exchange between Gyrth and Rigsen. From afar he is unable to hear of what they speak and is disconcerted. Tostig seeks out King Hardrada and Eystein to voice his concern.

"My brother Gyrth is a skilled politician. He no doubt makes your man a grand offer to surrender the bridge," says Tostig.

"He may speak until he is quit of wind," says Eystein, "yet he will not move that man with words. I myself have tried and failed."

"It is not words, but wealth and land that Gyrth offers."

"That I have tried also."

"Not in the vast amounts my brother will offer."

"Let it be so," says Hardrada with an offhanded wave, "it is a trifling matter. It is neither shameful nor blasphemous to admit I feel a kinship with Rigsen, and know he seeks a greater reward than wealth, no matter how vast. That man seeks a seat at Odin's table, and that is a position that can not be gained with any amount of worldly wealth."

Tostig fumes in frustration at his knowledge being so summarily dismissed. His kinship to a king has limited his circumspection of speech. "You speak of the heathen as your own kin," hisses Tostig, forgetting himself in his fear. "This is why all of your men should have been baptized in the Christ."

"It is true," says Hardrada without taking offense to Tostig's lack of prudence, "I have sold my own soul to the Christ for a kingdom. But I do not force my folly upon those who yet love the old gods. In truth, I envy that heathen man who stands the bridge. I wish in my heart that the Aesir were bearing witness to my deeds this day."

"It is blasphemous to speak so," says Tostig, "England will never bow to a pagan ruler. Even if you are to take the throne..."

"Tostig. Be silent," warns Eystein with a bludgeoning voice. He has heard enough. His patience with the estranged brother of the English king wears thin to fraying. "Go see to your Fleming mercenaries. Their reluctant tails lagged behind in the march from the ships. They should just now be making the field."

Tostig looks to King Hardrada for support, but none is forthcoming and Eystein will not be overridden. Tostig scurries away as ordered.

Eystein and Hardrada remain to watch Rigsen in conference with Gyrth.

"Did you speak true of the old gods?" asks Eystein of his king and friend.

Hardrada considers the question a moment before answering, "There are times when my scald's tongue flows without prudence."

"And occasion when my own mind flows in the same direction," admits Eystein with a grin.

The king looks upon his favorite captain and son-in-law to be with a sad smile. "I fear both of us are set in our afterlife. Odin is a jealous and vengeful god not prone to forgiveness."

"And neither of us are ones to beg," adds Eystein.

The men stand side by side contemplating the truth of their destiny with disquieted hearts.

* * *

"It seems we have lost the urgency of engaging Hardrada," says King Godwinson with great lament as he and his nobles look upon the gathered strength of the opposing army.

"Yet if your brother succeeds in coaxing the man from

the bridge we still outnumber Hardrada by a goodly number," says a nobleman in way of bolstering his own courage.

"Take that as no consolation," replies the king. "If Gyrth succeeds or fails, the battle will be fought with swords, not numbers."

* * *

Rigsen fills the horn a second time, drains it and feels the lightness it brings flow through his chest, limbs and mind. As it will do, the mead of poetry loosens the man's tongue, and Rigsen waxes on of his grandfather; "A great berserker he was, descended from a line of great berserker. And this his axe, called Skullseeker. I thought to give it a new name," muses Rigsen, turning the haft in his hands so the head catches the sun in its brilliance, "what think you of Saxons Bane?"

"You have been blessed in battle to now," warns Gyrth, "but is it wise to taunt your enemy so? After all, I have not seen even one of your fellows take to the bridge to fight at your side. It seems you have been abandoned."

"The privilege is mine alone, requested from and granted by King Hardrada himself."

"Have you no love of life? Why would you issue such a request?"

"How else to get to Asgard?" shrugs Rigsen.

"The one true God does not require such a sacrifice to gain Heaven, only that you are penitent for your sins."

Rigsen swills the drops of mead remaining in the horn into his mouth, dips it again in the golden liquid. "One true god," he ponders aloud, "then who is it this one true god speaks of when he asks that no other gods be worshipped before him? And what is his son, the Christ, if not a god? And if indeed a god, then there are two."

Gyrth is loath to be mocked, nor will he have his God mocked by a simple heathen who only survives to speak such piffle by dumb chance or some evil sorcery which the Lord, Christ Jesus, would soon overcome. "I will not be scorned in my faith. You have already revealed that you have spent time with a man of my God in your youth. You have the answers to your questions and have clearly already thought on the matters you disdainfully ridicule."

"Yes, I have thought on these matters. But I wonder, have you?" says Rigsen.

"You are well enough versed in our God, I grant you," says Gyrth, "well enough to know you must embrace Him or be damned."

"I know him well enough to know I want no part of him. Not his embrace nor his heaven." A bit of mead sloshes over the rim of the horn as Rigsen raises it to Gyrth in question, "Tell me, when you die, how will you fill your days and nights in this, your one god's heaven?"

"I shall walk with my Lord and savior Christ Jesus."

"Walk...!" scoffs Rigsen with a contemptuous roar. "In Asgard, every morn I shall battle until I am killed. Every evening I will be resurrected in a great hall to feast and drink mead and have tales of the battle sung by silver-tongued scalds. And when the sun sets on each glorious day, I shall love my woman through the night. When I wake, I shall do it again, and again, until Ragnarök."

Frustrated that the conversation has gone astray, but giving to the temperament of men of the North, Gyrth is unwilling to risk ending the negotiations with an abrupt or harsh return to the matter at hand. To take a different tact might prove more fruitful.

"That may be fine for you, to battle, feast and love, but what of your family? Have you no wife and children who await your return?"

The swagger quickly fades from Rigsen's bearing. His gaze falls from his enemy. His thoughts drift to disquieted memory.

Gyrth notes the change in the man's demeanor, presses,

"Tell me, do you have sons? A wife? Tell me of your home."

Rigsen sways in grief, his eyes downcast, unfocused. His strength gone as surely as if his life's-blood had been spilled upon the bridge. "Sassa," he mutters.

Gyrth hears.

Rigsen knows Sassa awaits. He knows she promises Kari and Nanna their father will soon return. With his pride he turns her promises to lies. He sees the tears she tries desperately to hide from their daughters. The sorrow in her look. The grief upon her beautiful features he sees as clearly now as if she stood before him. Grief he promised he would never cause her, and that promise turned to lie also.

Gyrth continues to press, "Come off the bridge. In reward I swear I will send an armada to your home to bring your wife and children to you. You will be granted an earldom as vast and rich as my own. Your wife, Sassa, you say is her name? She and your family entire will live and prosper alongside you for all your days. Do you not wish her by your side to live and grow old with?"

"I wish it with all my heart," says Rigsen.

"Then come from the bridge and make it so."

Rigsen wavers, his heart willing his feet to step forward, to carry him from this accursed bridge, yet they do not move. A simple thing to abandon this fight that he has no true stake in, and live long and peacefully with Sassa at his side. To watch Kari and Nanna grow to women, to marry, to bear children of their own. A few steps is all that lies between him and this beautiful dream. Yet still that first step is not taken.

"Another moment with Sassa is worth more than a thousand years in heaven. But I can not come down," says Rigsen.

"You can," implores Gyrth. "Come and live to hold your love again."

Rigsen simply shakes his head no. "I have made her a promise."

"To die in the service of a king in a land not your own?

That is no promise. And what is a promise to a woman in any case but empty words? Women have no understanding of these things. I assure you, she would much rather have a life with you now, over an eternity later."

"She will…"

Gyrth waits until he believes the man has nothing more to say, but before he can speak…

"…Forgive me," Rigsen says. He stands straighter to look into the eyes of his enemy with resolve born of confidence of knowing his love's heart.

In that moment Gyrth knows he is lost in his cause, yet desperately clings to purpose. "You need not choose one over the other. You may have life now, and an eternity later. That is the promise of the Lord God."

Rigsen can no longer be swayed. He is once again confident in his goal, and the manner in which to achieve it. His strength and swagger return. He scoffs with biting mirth, "Walk in your heaven hand in hand with your Christ like a lost child. I, nor Sassa have use for him. But for your kind offer I shall make you an offer in return. Take your sword in hand and come to me, and I will grant you an opportunity to sit and drink with Odin in his great hall."

Gyrth, a man of war over politics will take no more. He hurls down his cup, lays a hand on the hilt of his sheathed sword. "If your only purpose is to anger me, then you have succeeded. If it is your desire to put an end to these negotiations, then you shall have that as well." Gyrth stands his tallest to glare up at the man on the bridge. "Give me your answer now! What will you take to stand down from this bridge?"

"Bring me men worth fighting," demands Rigsen.

"Men worth fighting? The men you have fought and slain are among the greatest warriors the world has ever known!"

"Then bring me more."

* * *

"He will not relinquish the bridge," Gyrth announces tersely to the king and nobles.

"Then drive him from it with whatever means you possess," says the king.

* * *

Cursed. After watching Gyrth Godwinson fail to move the man from the bridge, Orm knows for certain now that he is cursed by an ungrateful king, captain, God, fates, and the very bitch of a mother that brought him screaming in protest into this world. For he plainly knew the answer before the question was posed: The bridge need be taken by force of arms if it is to be taken at all, and that duty falls to Orm's own squad of huscarls next.

While Gyrth confers with his commanders as to the best way to proceed, Orm goes searching for a solution that will not include risking his own life against the axe of the berserker madman who denies a fortune in land and gold, whose only need and desire is to slaughter more Saxons. Orm would not be one of those Saxons, not if his wits were near as cunning as he knows them to be.

A kernel of a plan has been fermenting in Orm's scheme-fertile mind as he watched his fellows -- warriors far more mighty than himself -- slaughtered on the bridge. Now he drifts away from the fighting men of his squad to grow and nurture that plan. Better to face hanging for desertion than be cleaved asunder by a berserker axe, thinks Orm. He would need a pawn. One of the fyrd would be best. Not overly bright, but ambitious... or courageous. Courageous would be better, Orm knows, for the courageous could be had for less coin.

Orm goes in search of Crompton, the bent and twisted farmer's son he discovered in a village while searching for smiths. The lad had given up the village blacksmith for nothing more than a few words of praise and a meal. Orm well knows this is a lad with anger festering in his breast over his lot in life; that of a farmer, destined to have the fruits of his labors stripped from him without compensation by taxes and levies each time a king goes to war. To be on the other side of that -- to be a soldier of the king's army who does the stripping -- is Crompton's aspiration.

The malcontent is not difficult for Orm to find. He is a fellow others avoid for his incessant grumbling and disparaging of all around him. Lacking a spear or any suitable armament, Crompton has been relegated to the rear of the army to care for the livestock. Orm takes the disgruntled youth aside to feed his anger and resentment with words meant to rile and incite.

"I have been sent on an important errand by King Harold Godwinson," confides Orm. Crompton's eyes go wide and he licks his lips against the dryness that has suddenly taken his throat. Orm looks over his shoulders and lowers his voice as if not to be overheard by others less worthy, "I seek a man who would become a hero. A hero who would sit at banquet with the mighty huscarl and earls of the kingdom... the king himself."

"As a soldier of the king's guard?" croaks Crompton excitedly.

"Aye, of the king's own guard," assures Orm, and his words are like honey to the ears of the daft lad. "Why should it be that only foreign Danes hold the position when sturdy lads of England stand ready to fight? Look to me for your proof. I am an Englishman like you. Not high born and without physical prowess, yet I now stand as a top lieutenant in the king's guard, special counsel to the captain of the army... to the king himself."

"How did you gain such position?"

"In the same way you shall. With an act that will win this war for us."

Crompton becomes frightened, he wets his dry lips again with a darting tongue. An act to win the war means dan-

324

ger. "What must I do?" manages Crompton on his second attempt at the words.

Orm recognizes fear in the lad and soothes it with sweet lies, "It is not an act of courage, but of cunning that I need. Any fool may possess courage. What is needed is the cunning to allow those fools to charge headlong to their doom while you find a better way, a safer more sure way to achieve victory for king and country. I have looked into your eyes, and therefore your soul and heart. You possess such cunning," forswears Orm.

"I do!" agrees Crompton. "Please, allow me to prove myself in this task!"

Orm continues to feed the lad lies sweetened with false oaths he knows will sway, and it is not long before he has Crompton convinced his lot will turn for the better. All his long-held fantasies of the elevated life of a professional soldier will come true with a single act. Crompton listens and believes. After all, this Orm is a high ranking lieutenant in the king's army and would not claim such a thing if it were not so.

❋ ❋ ❋

Rigsen has stanched his wounds the best he can. The strength in his shoulders and back has returned with the brief respite. He is eager once again to clash with the enemy and be on with the fight. The discussion with the enemy captain has emboldened his heart and made his purpose clear: A day of hewing Saxons. Rest and a meal. The ruckus chants of acclaim of his countrymen; the cries of lamentation of his enemy. Then begin the slaughter again the following day. If Sassa were at hand, and it were a bit cooler of weather, this would well-nigh be Valhöll on earth, thinks Rigsen. The thought causes him to smile, then laugh. His laughter turns hearty and long with his head tilted to the soft blue depths of Ymir's skull.

Warriors on both sides of the river watch Rigsen in wonder. Madman to some, hero to others, but to all, a singular marvel of a man.

Rigsen, his mirth drained, his eyes afire, brandishes Skullseeker in both hands. He stands splayed-legged in the center of the bridge to voice his challenge to the army which faces him; "'Cattle die, kindred die, every man is mortal, but the good name never dies of one who has done well.'" Rigsen raises his voice higher yet and his words carry over the army of England, "Come, give immortality to my name!"

Inspired Norwegians rise to their feet, clash arms against shields in a rousing din, but save their voices. Rigsen's the final words required by any and all.

Dane huscarls put axe to shield to sound their own challenge in return, adding to the thunderous cacophony.

Even the fyrd is caught up in the fervor of the coming battle and press forward.

Battle cries and war chants are taken up by both armies. Vast flocks of carrion birds, disturbed from their roost in the forest bordering the expansive meadows, take flight with a thundering burst of wings and excited calls to announce the beginning of the battle.

Yet one raven does not take wing: The raven of Harald Hardrada's Landwaster banner lies flaccid, unstirred.

In answer to Rigsen's challenge, the next so-assigned squad of Dane huscarls take to the bridge, each man's heart impassioned at the prospect of being the one to kill the hero of the Norwegians.

Gyrth would bid the bold soldiers return, for he and his commanders have yet to form a plan different than the one which has failed them to this point. But no single voice would be heard over the roar of battle-mad armies, and no Dane warrior so incensed would heed his command. Instead, Gyrth orders archers to stand ready, and spearmen of the fyrd to take position behind the huscarls who will lead the army across the bridge once the obstruction and berserker have been cleared, for he knows there will be no rest and no retreat until they have succeeded, or perished to a man in the effort.

The squad of twenty-nine Dane huscarls approach Rigsen, not in an impetuous rush, but with practiced efficiency of professional battle-savvy soldiers. They transfer their long shields from their backs to wedge the tips into the wide openings between planks of the bridge. Their shields form a picket line of heavy wood, half a man tall. The soldiers brandish their great axes in both hands to cut and feint at Rigsen from behind their wall of shields. Rigsen is forced to remain beyond the reach of the long-hafted axes. The Danes take up their shields, secure them in the next opening between bridge slats, a plank further up the bridge. Thus the huscarls proceed, shoulder to shoulder, five men abreast, innumerable deep, encroaching a plank at a time up the west slope of the bridge.

Rigsen recognizes the new strategy as an effective one. He will be driven off the bridge, one plank at a time.

Unschooled in warfare but for what he has learned in the past few days, Rigsen can think of no solution other than the one he takes. He feints forward to draw out the long arching strikes of the Danes, then darts in behind their swing to cleave Skullseeker downward into the center man's mail-clad shoulder. The warrior's pain-filled cry serves as his final words in this life as Rigsen leaps back in time to avoid the counter strikes of the huscarls on either side.

The fallen Dane is grabbed immediately by the men in the following rank, passed back until the dead man is no longer a burden to those who fight in the front line.

Rigsen admires the efficiency of these professional soldiers when put to a task. But there is little time for thoughts other than the fight, as a ferocious Dane steps forward of the shield wall to attack in a rapid succession of tight arcs which bring not only the blade of his great axe, but the haft to bear as well.

Rigsen is hard pressed to defend such an attack. He only survives by forcing the axe-wielder to defend a frantic series of downward strokes of Skullseeker until the haft of the Dane's axe is splintered. The bold warrior's skull is crushed within its helm with the following strike.

Shields are advanced another plank. Rigsen realizes with maddening certainty he will be forced from the bridge, foot by foot, if he can not find a method to cease their steady advance.

The heat of battle does not lend itself to deep thought, and Rigsen does not waste time attempting such. He rears back a step then lunges forward to leap the waist-high shields, landing him in the midst of the fierce warriors who face him.

The Danes could not have predicted such a tactic and are caught astounded as the berserker is suddenly amongst them.

Astonishment turns to panicked realization that their own axes can not be brought effectively to bear in such close quarters for their overly long hafts.

Skullseeker, no longer shafted than a wood-splitting axe, is free to swing. The blade bites through mail, flesh, sinew and bone. One enemy after another is attacked in a frantic, bloodying rush that leaves huscarls dead and wounded, tangled, thrashing in agony amongst their fellows.

Tyrulf bellows in incoherent glee from the eastern foot of the bridge, and need be held in check by a bevy of Norse warriors to keep him from joining Rigsen in the fray.

"He kills in uncounted numbers!" shouts Tyrulf.

"The numbers are counted," says Forni from his position at Tyrulf's side. "Counted and commemorated."

"Release me to bloody my sword!" demands Tyrulf.

"We all wish to wet our blades," growls Tarbin. "I will go with you!"

Eystein himself is caught up in the fervor and shouts above the din as he forces his way to the fore of the men anxious to fight at Rigsen's side, "Form up behind me, and let us have at them!"

"Halt!" commands King Hardrada. "The bridge is Rigsen's alone. Let his saga tell that he needed no man to come to his aid. Let no man diminish his glory on this day!"

On that demand the warriors of the great Norwegian army of King Hardrada honor the Son of Rig with their restraint, and stay from the bridge.

* * *

Orm carries one side of a shallow trough, Crompton the other, toward the river. A long spear stolen from an unwary soldier lies in the crib. The two make their way through the anxious ranks of the fyrd on the edge of the Saxon army to the bank a half-mile upriver that is heavily grown with hanging willows, reeds and tall grasses. Out of sight from any man of either army, Orm and Crompton struggle the trough into the water.

Crompton eyes the makeshift craft with trepidation. "Will it float?"

"If it holds water in, it will hold water out," says Orm, "long enough in any case."

Crompton quakes with his nerves, simpers through chattering teeth, "I shall be seen."

"Stay low inside, cling to the overgrown bank and you will not be seen. In with you now."

The terror-stricken lad climbs into the floating trough. It rides low in the water, seeps from the seams, but remains afloat.

Orm quickly hacks thin branches from a willow, tosses them on top of Crompton where he lies in the bottom of the crib. Barely seen beneath the green leafy bows, the boy looks up to Orm with frightened eyes glazed with tears.

Orm hands him the spear. "Do just as I said and you are in no danger. If you do not do it...." Orm allows Crompton to imagine the worst.

"I will do it, I swear."

"Good lad. You shall be the hero of this war."

And with that, Orm shoves the trough from the bank to

drift on the slow current of the shallows, downstream to the bridge.

❁ ❁ ❁

Rigsen batters the Dane huscarls into retreat. Only those killed, or nearly so, remain. The others give way with desperate, arching swings of their great axes to keep Rigsen at bay.

Gyrth needlessly calls to his soldiers to fight on. Needlessly, for each warrior who dares face the Son of Rig and his axe Skullseeker is a hero in his own right, and fights as such.

Yet the hero they face has no peer. Deep cuts, terrible rents cover Rigsen's body by the score. Vital blood flows from arms, chest, legs. His nose has been shattered by a buttstroke of a Dane axe. His eyes swell and blacken. Blood sprays from swollen, split lips with each heaving breath and battle cry. Yet the euphoria of the fight claims the proud warrior in whole, his heart and limbs are filled with untiring vigor.

Flagging and wounded opponents rotate out of the fray to be replaced by those fresh and eager to fight. Each new man to face Rigsen does so with furious energy born of the confidence he shall be the one to bring the hero down. Yet each warrior's dream of victory and glory is shattered along with his bones in the face of the terrible giant.

Better than an entire squad of thirty and half again as many professional soldiers of the Saxon army have been killed, yet nearly three-thousand Dane huscarls remain. Beyond them, a countless number of peasant soldiers of the fyrd, each awaiting their chance to prove themselves against the man on the bridge.

Rigsen remains strangely undaunted by the impossible numbers of his foe. Strangely, even to himself. The vastness of the enemy, their impossible numbers mean nothing to him. Nor does their skill, their determination, nor the terrible weapons they wield with such practiced mastery. His mind tarries on nothing but the fight at hand. His entire being enveloped in the lust of the kill, given wholly and purely to the sake of the fight.

For the effort of the Saxons, the bridge remains free of the vanquished, but the west meadow fills. The sweltering air is rent with the agonized cries of the mortally wounded which number many times that of those already killed.

* * *

Crompton stealthily eases the trough along the overhung bank beneath the willows and tangle of reeds and grasses, using the butt end of the long spear to guide him along. Ahead he sees the bridge and the melee to take it. His heart strains against his chest and he fears it can be heard even above the battle. He can hardly breathe, and swallow not at all for the constriction in his throat. His teeth chatter ceaselessly behind quivering lips. Yet the current carries the caitiff lad relentlessly on his path.

* * *

Rigsen needs no rest now. Skullseeker, light and flowing in his hands as if made of nothing more than silk and fine goose down rather than forged iron and seasoned wood. The blade cuts without effort. The butt crushes bone as easily as grain beneath the stone of a pestle. Even his ruined nose and smashed fingers, the bleeding rents in his flesh, seem a trifle, of no more concern than a tiny splinter of wood.

A tall Dane leaps within the arc of Skullseeker with the thought of stabbing at Rigsen's ribs with his seax, but the thrust is stayed as Rigsen clinches the man's throat with a grip trained and strengthened by a lifetime of gripping broad, heavy logs for splitting. The Dane's instincts override his will and he drops his blade to grip the strangling claw surrounding his neck. Before the Dane can free himself, he hears as much as feels the collapse of the pipe within his throat. His breath is taken from him as he drops to his back coughing frothy blood from his lips.

Rigsen finds himself fighting with his hand axe in his off-hand until the head is buried through mail into ribs, and the dying man's violent convulsions tear the weapon from him. With both hands on Skullseeker's haft, Rigsen clears a great swath about him as he advances down the western slope of the bridge. Brave Danes can do nothing but fall away before him.

The Norwegians are in awe -- the Saxons doubly so -- of what they bear witness to. No man or god of legend has ever fought as this man on the bridge.

And the Son of Rig knows he has succeeded.

EPILOGUE

Valhalla

A frightened lad set to purpose by vile lies from the lips of a dishonorable wretch, drifts unseen beneath the bridge, a sharp tipped spear in hand. He thrusts blindly up through the wide space between planks.

Rigsen feels the spearhead pierce deeply, high into the innermost of his thigh, and understands he has been killed. Lifeblood flows from him in a torrent, his mighty strength drifts from him as quietly as a passing breeze. Suddenly tired, without will to continue the fight, he reaches Skullseeker over the bridge rail, releases the haft. The hero's weapon falls to the river below and is forever lost. His eyes glazing, Rigsen sinks to his knees, draws his long knife, but has no desire to wield it as the world around him grows dim and quiet. The pounding of his enemy's boots charging onto the bridge, the final sound of this world to his ears.

* * *

The restless nanny kicks over the milk bucket. Spilled milk covers the soiled straw, then slowly sinks leaving a white residue to mark its passing. Sassa stares at the spilled milk as if an omen to be read. She does not right the bucket.

She looks to where Kari and Nana play on the wood pile, barely diminished though families come daily to fill carts to brimming for their winter fires and forges.

Sassa stands from the milking stool, enters the house, her fair features heavy in troubled thought. She takes her rune-staves from their keeping place, sits at the table, but does not cast the runes. She remains, holding the bag forgotten in her hands, staring down upon the scarred supper table, and is surprised to find tears falling onto the planks.

Sassa misses her man so. She can find no relief for her sorrow so she does the only thing she knows to allay the aching in her chest. She calls to her girls and they come to her. She bids them, tell her a story of their father.

A queer request, the girls think, telling nighttime stories in the day. But they eagerly launch into their oft-told tales which grow more fond and grand with each recital.

Sassa listens. Her pain eases and she finds a smile.

And forevermore the man's kindred, and those who would be so, recall his deeds and name; by whatever name they know him.

＊ ＊ ＊

The man sinks to his knees. The bridge rumbles with the press of Saxon soldiers who stab at him with spears, rend him with axes and swords. But they are even now too late. Too late by far.

The Son of Rig looks down from high above, cradled weightlessly in the arms of a shining Valkyrie. He knows no pain nor fear nor anger, only a profound sense of satisfaction, and blissful peace within that.

From far above he watches the battle unfold.

He sees King Hardrada fall with an arrow to the throat.

Tostig, with a sudden impulse of valor, takes up the Landwaster.

Eystein rallies the Norwegians to nearly retake the field, then he too falls, defending the body of his king. Then Tostig. Heaped around them the berserk and the stout-hearted men of Eystein's crew.

Battle turns to rout as the Saxons overwhelm the Norwegians. Those who can, flee for the ships with the Saxon army on their heels.

But one remains.

Forni in his flowing cloak and broad-brimmed hat stalks the battlefield, his ravens circling above. He now and again touches a man sprawled in death with the blade of Gungnir. That man rises, gathers to him his shield and arms.

This is all clearly seen by Rigsen, carried in the arms of the Valkyrie.

Brynhildr, the Valkyrie's name, ferries Rigsen away from the battlefield, higher into the light, as if into the sun itself, until he is blinded by its radiance.

The light slowly fades and Rigsen can see clearly again. A great forest of birch on the edge of a sun-drenched field of gilded barley.

The shining Valkyrie Brynhildr lays him gently to earth, and is gone.

It is not hot here, nor is it cold; forever in that perfect moment summer and winter share equally in the day.

Across the field barring the way to a magnificent bridge that sparkles as a rainbow in the gentle sun, stands a giant of a god: Skin as white as the finest snow, a smile that shines as gold. A majestic steed stands at his side, its mane and tail of the brightest flax. It paws at the ground and snorts boldly at Rigsen's approach.

"Son of Rig has come!" announces the god, "And I am proud to share the name. Come, regale me with the saga of your life, though I know it well. I have watched you throughout your time on Midgard, and am filled with joy that the finest of my sons has joined me."

"I must go to wait on Sassa," says Rigsen.

"But she is already here," announces the god.

Rigsen is startled by the news.

The god raises a hand to calm him. "A moment here is many lifetimes in Midgard. Sassa has lived a long and happy life. She lived to play games and share many season festivals with her grandchildren, and their children. And every night tales of her husband, Kari and Nanna's father, were told about the table. Generations of your kin tell your saga even now. Sassa awaits you in Freyja's hall," assures the god.

Rigsen presses with urgency toward the bridge.

"There is no need to hurry," says the god, "she is unaware even a moment has passed."

"Sire, allow me to pass over your bridge and I will tell you all you wish to hear another time, and I will not spare words. But bar me another moment from my way, and you will fall."

The god smiles his golden smile. "It is as I had hoped! You are truly my son. Go without delay then and see for yourself, that which I have told you is true."

The god steps aside. Rigsen passes onto the shimmering path.

The resplendent bridge reflects the sparkling river which runs beneath in a rainbow of color. The way is steep and long. Rigsen ascends the bridge into the mists.

At the far side of the bridge awaits Rigsen's she-hound, coiled with excitement at his approach. Rigsen dares not believe, yet there is no denying it is she. The two greet one another with profound love. Rigsen remains on his knees embracing his first love until the hound becomes as excited as he to continue on their way. The hound bounds happily through an endless field of lush grasses bathed in sun flaring gild-red in its final burst before its setting. Rigsen follows, the joy of his heart lifting him to heights he has never known.

Soon the songs and laughter of einherjar at feast can be heard.

Far across the field stands the greatest of halls, spears

for rafters, golden shields for a roof. Five hundred forty doors does Rigsen count on his way, each door large enough to allow eight-hundred warriors to pass through, shoulder to shoulder.

The god of many names -- Forni, only one -- stands with Gungnir before the great hall. He favors Rigsen with a familiar nod and a look of satisfaction from his single eye. Huginn and Muninn sound a croaking welcome from above.

The songs and laughter from inside the great hall are joyous, the smells of the feast, enticing, but Rigsen does not tarry on his way.

The boisterous songs soon fade as the sun's final light dims to dark. Yet the songs are replaced by sounds even more joyous. A more splendid light from yet another hall in the distance glows in the night. This hall every bit as large as the first, yet even more magnificent: gilded from rafter to foundation and emitting a glimmer which transforms the gloom of night to the brilliance of dawn.

Before the dwelling awaits a woman with locks even brighter than the gold of the hall. Rigsen can not see her face from the distance, but he knows her. He knows her stance and her smell and her touch. He knows her breath, her smile, her voice and her love. He knows her name.

And at last he knows his own.

This saga has been related by Bragi, attested to by the Aesir, and ordained by Odin and therefore may not be contested.

Printed in Great Britain
by Amazon